SURPRISE, TEXAS

A novel by Andy Wilkinson
or a fictional history,
or an historical fiction —
you choose which —
punctuated so as to
encourage and assist you
in reading it aloud,
as recounted by
Thom Ed Jones

ZENCHILADA
PRESS

PUBLISHING IN THE PRESENT MOMENT
WWW.ZENCHILADAPRESS.COM

ABOUT OUR NAME, AND OUR MISSION

We were taking a class from master watercolorist Paul Milosevich. We'd been listening and taking notes for some time before we suddenly realized we were already versed in everything he was teaching, and – what's more – we'd learned it all from him. Whereupon we made an impulsive and plaintive entreaty for instruction on how we might learn to do what we already knew how to do. "Ah," Paul smiled, "that's the Zen of the whole enchilada."

Our mission is to bring story to you and you to story, all in the present moment. That is both the Zen and the enchilada.

Styled by Hartsfield Design, Lubbock.

Library of Congress Number 2018900212

ISBN-13: 978-0-9997561-1-9

for Max Evans,
the truest Surprise of all

Surprise! Texas Roster

Handy Jones, Founder — 1909

The Eliots — 1939
Shad and Rose Edna
Xavier Kelton "Kelly" — b. 1940
Ruth Etta — b. 1946

The Merrimans — 1939
Bob and Sue
Bobbie Sue — b. 1940

The Joneses — 1939
Gene D. and Mary Ellen
Cerridwen Mae "Kerrie Mae" — b. 1940
Thomas Edward "Thom Ed" — b. 1942

Maya Gandhi — During WWII

a blind boy William Roberts "Billy Bob" — b. 1941 ?

Taliesen Jones "Tally" — b. 1959
Kerrie Mae Jones, Mother

Starlight Merriman "Star" — b. 1969
Bobbie Sue Merriman, Mother

The User's Guide to Surprise:
A Note on Sources, a Post-Note on Punctuation, and a Brief on Beginnings

What you will shortly be reading, and, I hope, longly reading, is a curious amalgam. It's a piece of creative nonfiction. Or historical fiction. Or history. Or fiction. Or, as I have come to be most fond of saying, it's factual fiction. It's a report of things I know, either because I was there and did these things, or because I closely questioned those who were there and who did these things, or because—myself falling short in being or in being able to question—I inferred these things from all that I know about them and about these people and about this place.

What you will shortly be reading, and, I hope, roundly reading, is not a square book. Rather, it is an accounting of the lives of particular people and the life of a particular place during a particular time. As with people and places and times, it does not proceed in a march-line but rather scurries in arcs and curves and zig-zags, yet as with all living things will come to a circular whole.

What you will shortly be reading, and, I hope, also loudly reading, is also curiously amalgamated. Aloud, for the natural home of language is in the air—that is, outside of the person—rather than in the mind—that is, inside of the person—language being firstly and most fully a thing spoken so as the mouth and the tongue can taste what words mean when they are born *out of* the self, and so as the ear can feel what words mean when they are received from the other *into* the self.

Words are sound. Punctuation—not itself being audible—ought to be instruction in how to speak those words, a written musical score for the oral symphony of language. Yet—as any grade-school student knows—its symbols and characters and spacings have been largely subjected to the tyranny of grammar, put mainly into the service of the makers of rules and the promulgators of form. In the following pages I will do my best to restore the primacy of the spoken word, by using the long dash to liberate phrases from the prison of parentheses, by employing only lightly the cudgel of the colon and its cousin, the semi-colon, and by importing from the Spaniards the inverted marks that let the speaker know precisely when to modulate the voice in either exclamation or interrogation. I hope this helps us see eye-to-eye and hear mouth-to-ear. If we do, you will note that I have an honest look and a sincere gaze and a well-modulated voice.

1.

LET ME INTRODUCE ME

Call me Thom Ed. My Christian name—what's on my official papers and licenses and union cards and such—is Thomas Edward. Proud of their Welsh heritage, the cultural and historical as much as the genetic, my parents named me for the poets Thomas, Edward from the War to End All Wars and Dylan from the Bar to End All Bars. Had I been born in Wales, or maybe anywhere other than Texas, there would have been the possibility of being called Thomas, or Tommy growing into Tom, or of Edward with Eddie maturing to Ed. But I was born into the Tribe of the Two Name People, so it was Tom Ed from the beginning.

I put the *h* back in myself after I learned that Tom had come from Thomas. Second grade, maybe. I knew it was silent, that *h*, but I put it back just out of pure intuition. And, well, maybe a touch of contrariness. Much later, as a student of language and alphabet—the both of which allow us storytellers to become writers—sometime around the time I first slogged my way through Graves's *The White Goddess*, I came to appreciate that in every language in which it appears *h* is a quarrelsome letter, an horrendous letter, serving to divide those who pronounce it one way from those who pronounce it the other, splitting those who use it from those who keep it quiet, almost always cleaving the haves from the have-nots and separating those who think language a thing to be used from those who think language a thing to be owned. Succinctly put, it is a letter perfectly suited to my people. And so I continue to hew to my *h*, not so much as a badge to present to the world but rather as a reminder to myself of my past, and of the past of my people, the Two Names and the Nick Names and all the Proper Names before them.

Of those names, the surnames are Jones, all my tribe, up all branches of the tree. Leek-waving Joneses as far back as anyone can determine. The limbs later to bear my father were early immigrants to America, dropping first on its shores in the 1600s and soon working their way west to Pennsylvania, then on to Tennessee after the Civil War and at its conclusion thence quickly to Texas. By the late 1800s they'd set down in Stonewall County in the town of New Brandenburg on the west side of the Double Mountain Fork of the Brazos River.

Mother's Joneses didn't come to the United States until later, going straight to Kansas as soon as it was opened for settlement in 1854. Throughout its history, Clan Jones has been just as unlikely to start a fight as it has been unlikely to run from one. That made Bleeding Kansas a most difficult spot for the Joneses, and so as to be able to live in peace, or at least to be able to fight only in their own battles, my mother's people also took to Texas—I would say at the end of the Civil War, except that the Civil War has yet to end in the parts of Kansas where the Joneses had taken roost—her migrant Joneses coming to rest in Haskell County in the hamlet of Rule on the other side of the Double Mountain Fork, less than a dozen miles northeast from the settlements of my father's Joneses.

During the War to End All Wars, the war that produced such great poetry and such wretched history, the Texicans of German descent who'd founded New Brandenburg changed the town's name to Old Glory, thinking to assuage worries about their loyalty. My father's clan of left-leaning populist Joneses took no position on the issue, never themselves having had questions about their neighbors' fealty to America. The Joneses were patriots, perhaps to a fault, fully believing that America was the home of not only the brave, but also the free. They took both traits seriously and were especially fond of anyone brave enough to act free, men like Eugene V. Debs, the labor organizer and perennial Socialist candidate for President, who was known to slip in and out of their community from time to time, a place where he was comfortable among friends and sympathizers, and, some thought, lovers.

In 1914 my grandmother—of the Old Glory Joneses—had become pregnant without so much as a nod toward either church or state, a condition that at the time was no more than an eyebrow-lifter, especially given how often such events occurred in that epoch when admitting to the use of prophylactics was a greater shame than the pregnancy out of wedlock what surely came without their employment. But tongues went to work when she refused to identify the father and then began wagging in high gear when she made clear her intent to keep the merry-begot child and raise it on her own. When my dad was born early in the next year, she named him Eugene Debs Jones, calling him Gene D. That sealed the deal as far as the common wisdom was concerned, and to this day the old-timers in that area refer to my dad as Little Gene, a twinkle in their eye.

My mother's bunch—the Rule Joneses—were farmers and so when it came to movements were given more to the populists than to the socialists or to the labor unions. When she was born in 1918, my mother was named Mary Ellen in honor of Mary 'Yellin' Ellen' Lease, the deep-voiced, powerful orator who, it was said, hurled sentences as Jove hurled thunderbolts. Mother's people had surely seen Mary Yellin' Lease, who, as had my mother's Joneses, made her first march in Kansas before bringing her talents to Texas on her way to fame in New York.

Three years apart in age and further separated by a river and a county line, my mother and dad didn't meet until college. They both wound up at McMurry, a Methodist school of higher education in Abilene, Texas. Brand-spanking new, founded in 1920 as a two-year college, by 1925 it was offering its first four-year degree and actively seeking out the notable student scholars in the region, amongst whom numbered Gene D. Jones and, a few years after, Mary Ellen Jones. In turn, Mother and Dad knew about the stellar faculty that the Wesleyeans had assembled—among them Curry Holden in history and Julia Eugenia Luke in English, as well as a host of teachers in music and the arts—and they knew that the college boasted not only a newspaper, *The War Whoop*, and a yearbook, *The Totem*, but also a literary annual, *The Galleon*. The two became sweethearts whilst writing and editing for the three publications, married after Dad's graduation, and then as soon as Mother earned her sheepskin moved to Canyon in the Panhandle so as to earn their teaching certificates at West Texas State Normal College.

It was the era of the Great Depression and, worse, the Dust Bowl. Teaching jobs were hard to come by, and harder to hold. The newly-married and newly-certified Joneses would no sooner take posts in one of the area towns before the town would run out of money. They'd load up their stuff, find another pair of jobs, move, and start over again. Eventually, they put down roots in Surprise.

2.

A SHORT HISTORY OF SURPRISE

¡Joy the fever! —Handy Jones

The Double-Joneses weren't looking for Surprise, or any surprise, for that matter. What with the dust and depression of the Dirty Thirties added to their own misadventures with the various school districts who hired them fully knowing that their coffers were empty and then fired them when the ruse could no longer be maintained, my parents were looking for anything other than another surprise. But amidst the whirlwind of disappointments, the kaleidoscope of misdirections, my folks saw an interesting newspaper-ad thumb-tacked to the bulletin board in the Post Office in Becton, the last town where they'd tried to snag a couple of jobs. It read, simply, *School Needs Help! Cable Handy Jones, Surprise, Texas! Joy the fever!*

The blatant lack of bullschickle in the plea was appealing, given the shoveling and groveling they'd had to do already. And ¿what did *Joy the fever!* mean? And ¿who was Handy Jones? ¿A kinsman, another Welshman cast out into the desert diaspora? ¿Superintendent Jones? ¿Mayor Jones? ¿Professor Jones?

Well, no. And yes. And, really, ¿what did it matter? They cabled, but didn't wait for a cable in return. It took them little more than a day to get there. Partly that was because they went through Lubbock and stopped to see some friends, and partly that was because they also stopped at Jim Perkins's cafe in Lamesa for a chicken-fried steak, seeing as how Jim's joint was the very birthplace of the national food of Texas. And partly it was because there were no road signs to direct them to Surprise. Which, philosophically, should have been expected.

Upon their arrival, Handy Jones was there to greet them as if not only were they expected but also as if he knew when they'd show up. An elderly, tall, grizzled Army cavalry veteran, he was rocked back in a chair on the veranda of the only building in town—an old school house that still bore the name Salt Lake Schools—playing an unknown but comforting tune on an ancient fiddle. When Mom and Dad drove up, Handy put down the saw box, stuck out a very large hand, and called them by name. Handy could see that the Joneses had come to stay, even though the Joneses didn't yet know it.

He asked them about their story. They told it. They asked him about his. He told most of it, watering-down some as he wasn't a boastful man and kept a few details to himself, the kind of stuff that might be taken as bragging. Most important, the Joneses noted he was perhaps the happiest man they'd ever met.

When asked about the balance of the advertisement, the curious admonition that concluded it, Handy Jones grew happier still as he explained it was his philosophy of living and, by implication, the way that life was lived in Surprise. ¡Enjoy the moment! he said. ¡Live in the present! Someone passing through many years before had heard his proclamation and had given him a phrase, a French phrase, one that they promised perfectly described both Handy and Surprise. They wrote it down for him, as Handy's many talents and achievements lacked only that of reducing the world to written words. After relating the little story, he produced for my folks a well-worn, hand-written note on which was scriven, in a distinctly old-world European hand, *Joie de vivre, Handy! Joie de vivre!* As Handy couldn't interpret the written word in his own language, much less that of the Gauls, a local cowpuncher who'd spent time in France during the War to End All Wars admitted to be able to read the Language of Love and so translated the French phrase, more or less correctly, as *Joy the fever!* Handy was happy with that, as were my parental Joneses.

Hearing this last bit, there was nothing to do, thought Gene D. and Mary Ellen, than to unload there and then, enlisting therewith in the here and now of Surprise. In doing so, they became one of the Foundling Surprises, along with two other families, the Eliots and the Merrimans, who had moved in shortly before. As we Jones and Eliot and Merriman children were growing up in Surprise, my educator parents presented to us the Short History of Surprise as if it came straight from the Story of the First Beginning. And I present it to you, too, forthwith.

Handy Jones had been born a slave-child in the Piney Woods of Texas in the closing days of the Civil War. A musician most familiar with the violin but strong enough to march with the tuba, he had enlisted in the United States Army in the latter capacity, first seeing duty with the 10th Cavalry at Fort Davis but also serving in the Spanish-American War, including participating in the Battle of San Juan Hill. In Remington's famous painting, look for the glint of rifle fire off the polished brass of a hélicon; somewhat hidden behind its bell is Handy Jones. Retiring after a quarter-century of service, Jones relocated to far West Texas, where the vastness of its open plains and big skies were daily physical reminders of his freedom from the servitude of his forebears. He settled in 1907 in the new town of Salt Lake, situated near a large saline playa of the same name in Andrews County.

Much to his dismay, the town's founders decided to rename the nascent city for General William R. 'Pecos Bill' Shafter, who purported to have discovered the lake during the Llano Estacado Expedition of 1875. Private Jones had developed an early dislike for General Shafter owing to commander Shafter's mistreatment of Lt. Henry O. Flipper at Fort Davis, the lieutenant being a West Point graduate whose principal failings were his intelligence, his hard-work, and his black skin. Private Jones's dislike later grew to disgust at what he saw as Shafter's cowardice and sloth in the Spanish-American conflict.

Consequently, Jones would have none of living in a town dubbed Shafter Lake. He removed himself a full day's ride west-south-west, some twenty-odd miles, struck his claim for a new township, immediately after which he hurried to Odessa for the nearest telegraph station so as to be able to cable the authorities in order to register a name for the village. He originally planned to call it Flipperton, in honor of the 10th Cavalry's only black officer, but thought the name unwieldy. He then opted for Parker, in tribute to the lieutenant who commanded the Gatling gun detachment that protected the troops as they assaulted San Juan Heights, but quickly learned that there already existed a Parker, Texas. His next choice was Nolan, after the valiant lieutenant who had once befriended Flipper, but that name, too, was already in use. Somewhat in frustration, he ordered the telegraph operator to tell the authorities *just surprise me*. But the operator, having little familiarity with African-American speech patterns, only understood Jones to say *Surprise*. Unsurprisingly, that name was available, and by the time the paperwork arrived, it was too late to correct the mistake. Though it took some time, Jones later came to like, even love, the odd name.

Had Jones been as patient as he was Handy he'd not have found it necessary to go into the town-building business at all, for Shafter Lake had been on the map scarcely three years before neighboring Andrews was named county seat in the election of 1910, a contest fraught with skulduggery and intimations of fraud. In little more time than it takes to cast a ballot, all 500 souls that made up the totality of the census of Shafter Lake left the town they had so recently named for the corpulent general, most of them relocating to the victorious hamlet. Had he stayed, as its sole occupant Handy Jones could have renamed it as he saw fit.

But it was just as well. For a song, he bought the only serviceable structure in Shafter Lake, a three-story school building, moving it over the shinnery and greasewood to his new town. Most urban planners consider it to be one of the Lone Star State's earliest known instances of repurposing. Handy was in no way nostalgic for the plantation life of his youth, but he missed mightily the big, cool verandas common to the black clay architecture of Houston County. So as soon as the school house had been set and leveled, smack-yas-yas-yas in the middle of Surprise, he built a large, well-shaded porch all around the first floor. A man of simple needs, he made his quarters in the top-most space of the building, a small attic graced by a windowed cupola from which he could see horizon in all the four directions. When he tired of playing his fiddle on the veranda, he could sit in his land-locked lighthouse and cast tunes however far the wind was blowing that evening. Handy Jones never married, was never known to have had children, and, once Surprise had been born, never took hand in its governance. Neither was he ever known to be without a fiddle or a smile or a kind word, a formula that led to a long and pleasant life.

As a town, Surprise was a come-and-go party. It had little enterprise of its own. Since it was not incorporated and the county seat sat in Andrews, there were no offices representing public officials, never even so much as the shingle of a precinct constable. Early on in their quest for support from the county, the Surprises—which is what the locals came to call themselves—the Surprises learned that their town site was in what was originally called Santa Fe County, a huge piece of West Texas real estate that also encompassed all of present-day New Mexico east of the Rio Grande. One or two hardy Surprises attempted to operate as officials of the former county, but were swatted back like so many troublesome flies. At least for a time there was a school, until the county consolidated all public education districts in the 1930s, severing even that small vestigial connection to the larger world of Federal, state, and local government. What Surprise schooling took place thereafter was of the guerrilla variety, home-schooling before the concept existed, but with admirable results as the teaching staff consisted solely of Joneses.

Whatever was there, little or big, was all home-grown. From the time that automobiles and other motorized conveyances troubled the landscape, Surprise had a Ser-Sta-Gro, the predecessor of today's convenience store, the generic name having been shortened from service-station-grocery. If Surprise had ever had streets, the Ser-Sta-Gro could be said to be located catty-corner south-east from the old school house. It was situated in a small, sturdy building constructed of caliche rock, topped with a tin roof that extended over its pair of glass-cyl-inder gasoline pumps. The caliche rocks being of various sizes and shapes lent an organic feel to the little station, a nice counterpoint to its metal shed personality. It had no in-ground storage vessels but rather a couple of large, rusted tanks squatting just above the ground behind the building, one to hold diesel oil and the other to hold low-test gasoline. Inside there was a coin-operated soft-drink box, the kind with a chinese-puzzle-maze-metal-slot holding the bottles vertically by the neck, the cooling done strictly by ice. Past it were a few shelves intended to hold a small selection of grocery items. Toward the back wall were a few Maytag wringer-washers, as no dwelling in the neighborhood was equipped with such a convenience, not to mention the neighborhood itself was far removed from other neighborhoods sporting washaterias and laundromats.

There was one other permanent structure that graced the Surprise skyline, a water tower, the kind that looked like the Tin Man's hat atop a round tank stuck on spindly legs. As the water taps never numbered more than a few dozen, the tower didn't tower at all, towering in fact over nothing. In the main, it was nondescript, other than a faded ! painted on the sides where, in most other settle-ments, the town's name would appear. Its most notable feature was that it had been dry and empty for dozens of years, the Ogallala wells that supplied it having gone dry in the 1950s with the unfortunate, simultaneous advent of drought and irrigation, the wells replaced with rain-catchment roofs and—all too often— water carried in from somewhere else.

The dwellings were all portable. Not that there wasn't a silk-stocking row for those Surprises who were more well-off, and not that there wasn't a poor side of town for those that weren't. Actually, not a poor side *per se*, as every-thing was subject to rearrangement, the whole residential aspect of the town being fitted-out with wheels, but rather there was a poor kind of housing and a fine kind of housing. The Surprises of means lived in Airstream trailers, some in older models and some in newer, but all of quality and all in fine repair. The older Airstreams were, in fact, the more valuable, some having become highly-sought-after collectibles. The ordinary Surprises—if one can envision an ordinary Surprise—and the poorer Surprises—again, if one can envision a poor Surprise—lived for the most part in surplused oil field mobile homes or in worn-out canned-ham camper trailers, the latter being those cheap seasonal vehicles employed by the tin-can tourists. Sadly, social stratification was a fact even in Surprise, though it is fair to say that the strata were of only the slightest differentiation, one that might easily escape the eye of the newcomer or the casual observer.

Along with the Ser-Sta-Gro, one of the first and most enduring businesses was the drive-out movie, which had longevity but no address. Run by the Merriman family—as opposed to a walk-in or a drive-in, the kind of theatre set-ups found only in towns and cities of some substance—the drive-out was more of a hit-and-run operation, consisting simply of a screen carried far out into the countryside, illuminated from a projector fired by a gasoline generator. An announcement was made of the movie to be shown, the approximate coordinates of that night's location, and a ticket-price. Everyone knew the show couldn't begin before dusk, and in the flat, level country the moveable site was easily found. One of the favorites was the Gene Autry series *The Phantom Empire* and its full-feature companion, *Radio Ranch*.

Community meetings were held in the second floor auditorium of the school house on the few-and-far-between occasions when such were needed. An *ad hoc* village council would form from time-to-time as problems cropped-up or as opportunities presented themselves—and, often, the problems and the opportunities were the same, which was, the locals said, no surprise. These come-and-go meetings were fine examples of anarchistic self-governance, mixtures of coffee-shop bull-session and city council deliberation with a lot of chamber of commerce boosterism thrown in for good measure. There was, perhaps, a little more of the latter, Bob Merriman dubbing these occasional conventions the Chamber-Pot of Commercialism.

Bob's off-handed humor was prescient, maybe even profound. If ever such were to be studied by learned universities, it's certain that meetings would be uncovered for what they really are: drags on the economy, obstacles to progress, and the obstructionist bastions of the backwards, the stupid, and the lazy. Not that such study will ever happen, because no organization of whatever ilk could hope to begin studies of meetings without first meeting about it. Suffice it to say that meetings cause problems, they never solve them. All this was known to the stalwarts of Surprise, who were always happy to meet one another but never, ever happy to hold a meeting.

The Chamber-Pot of Commercialism was no exception. All that was good and wholesome and unique about Surprise was owed to its home-grown anarchists. What little trouble came to Surprise—other, of course, than the trouble regularly meted-out by Mother Nature—came by way of newcomers seeking to make their new place as screwed-up as the place they'd just left, and most often had left because the old place had gotten too screwed-up. A case in point is the saga of the exclamation point. The Great Depression hit everyone in America pretty hard. But it was the drought of the Dirty Thirties that most hurt rural folks in the part of the nation that came to be called the Dust Bowl and whose nether-most region included Surprise. Having the right attitude, thought the Surprises, would be crucial to survive between the rock and the hard place in which they found themselves. So without convening a council or petitioning the citizenry or any other formal act, a couple of renegade Surprises took it upon themselves to change the town's name simply by adding an exclamation point, making Surprise, Texas into Surprise! Texas. Under cover of dark, they changed what few signs there were, then painted an exclamation point on the water tower. The new punctuation added vim and vigor, they thought, and stressed the underlying philosophical premise of Surprise as a community which was to be wholly-focused on the present. And what, they reasoned, was more immediate, more present, than an exclamation point. The period belongs to the past, the question mark to the future, and commas and semi-colons and colons are nothing more than troublesome interruptions, what meetings would be if meetings were marks of punctuation.

No one seemed to mind, and, if truth be told, not many even noticed. But when the oil boom cranked up after the Second World War, Surprise gained a few new names on the census roles, folks who were from ordinary places and who found it odd to be living in a town with a name that included punctuation of any kind, nevertheless an exclamation point. A town council was convened, one in which the punctuationistas who'd made the change some twenty years before failed to speak up—which is to be expected from anarchists—the upshot being the offending marks were removed wherever they could be found. Though that's many years ago, beneath its otherwise tranquil surface Surprise remains split into two camps, those in favor of the exclamation point and ¡those against!

More important to the civil conduct of the community, there was always a cafe of sorts on the first floor of the Old School House. Operated on the honor basis, a coffee pot was kept going twenty-four-seven with the understanding that if you poured a cup you left a dime in the change can and that if you poured the last cup you made a fresh pot. For those requiring more than coffee there was an ice box with a limited array of comestibles next to a butane-fueled range that served as the forerunner of the microwave, the kitchenette being governed under the same rules as the coffee pot.

Most Surprises cobbled-together their economic lives by working some in the oil patch, day-working on nearby ranches, teaching school, or running various mail-order businesses. For while Surprise was in the middle of all the petroleum exploration in the region, it was *exactly* in the middle, meaning it was surrounded by distant oil plays but had none of its own. Lacking pump jacks and tank farms leant it a pure, if impoverished, air. People lived in Surprise but worked pretty much elsewhere. It was a suburban without an urban, a bedroom community cut loose from the rest of the house.

And as the jobs came and went, so did the Surprises. No one built permanent dwellings, as no one really had any sense of permanence. There was the Ser-Sta-Gro and the empty water tank and the school house building with its large and spacious four-sided veranda and its quirky community coffee house, but all around it was a constantly-changing array of mobile homes, trailer houses, and portable buildings. There was one hotel, The Shifting Sands Mobile Motel, fashioned out of surplus oil-patch portable buildings and old trailer houses, the kind of trailer homes with the little-bitty spaceship windows, an enterprise started by the Eliots, who, from time-to-time and purely for enjoyment, would host what they called *sand dune ballets* in which people were invited to hook their pickups or feed trucks or large automobiles to the trailer-house-motel-cabins and move them around whilst music blared from a loudspeaker, dropping the rental rooms wherever they were when the music stopped, a sort of grand version of musical chairs. The favorite songs for the ballets were *Minnie's Yoo-Hoo*—when Bob Merriman was available to screen the 1930 Mickey Mouseville Jazzband rendition of the tune—and Henry Hall's 1932 cut of *The Teddy Bears' Picnic*. The quirky custom was the most amusing when the rooms were occupied.

One small, indeed, very small mark of permanence was the Shafter Lake Skipping Stone Museum. During the course of the two years in which the towns coexisted a brief rivalry developed. In lieu of any organized sports into which civic pride could be channeled—there not being enough able-bodied youth in either town to mount a complete team in anything other than doubles tennis, which itself was out of the question given the abundance of high minds and dearth of net, court, or rackets—Handy Jones suggested a stone-skipping contest be held on the shore of Shafter Lake. The water was so salty, he reasoned, the stones might not even sink, making it easier to determine the winning skips. And it was indeed salty, but not so much as to hold even the lightest skipper once its forward inertia had been spent, so the winning skips sank quickly into the slimy muck just beneath the lake's briny surface, leading to vehement arguments over who should carry home the various ribbons and as to which community had prevailed overall.

Nevertheless, two decades after the demise of the town of Shafter Lake, the drought of the 1930s dried up the lake to the point that Handy was able to walk out on the salty crust of the mud-cracked lake bed and retrieve the once-sunken skipping stones. As they weren't marked or painted so as to identify from which jurisdiction they'd originated, Handy was free to interpret which was whose, and, not surprisingly, the ones furthest out into the lake were deemed to have been skipped by the Surprise team. Handy returned them to Surprise, where a small space was cleared out on a shelf in the Ser-Sta-Gro and the stones artfully arranged upon it. Legend captions were carefully hand-lettered on recipe cards and a tiny velvet rope fashioned from pipe cleaners, mounted on popsicle sticks, then strung around the stones to separate them from the electricians' section whose rolls of of black tape and the single box of assorted fuses took up the balance of the shelf. And while several attempts were made to have the museum recognized by the various associations around the state and nation, all to no avail, a professionally-painted sign was nevertheless ordered from a shop in Odessa and hung on the veranda outside the door of the Ser-Sta-Gro, reading, in rather ornate script, 'Shafter Lake Skipping Stone Museum Inside—Gallery Guide One Quarter Dollar'. The honor system was, of course, used for purchases of the gallery guides.

Surprise did have a couple of semi-permanent features, things that in other communities would serve to etch their very permanent place in the affairs of history. Graveyards, for instance. Many's the case in the American West where all that survives of a town is its bone-orchard. But Surprise had none. Not that people didn't die in Surprise. Far from it. Life was always exacting on the Alkali Prairies and not everyone measured up to its challenges. Yet the dead Surprises most often belonged to families elsewhere, to distant tribes and clans, and most often the quick brought the dead back to their own ilk. As a result, the few whose remains were destined to remain in Surprise were scattered here and there. Not like it sounds—the graves were simply not organized into a community of their own. In Surprise, the dead remained as they had been in life, as individuals. The proprietors of the Shifting Sands Mobile Motel had set aside one particularly well-worn trailer to serve as a portable mausoleum, an idea ahead of its time, almost like a drive-thru funeral parlor. And there were a few Surprises who, when the end was nigh, chose simply to walk as far out into the mesquite as their condition would permit, settle down with a good book or a bottle of hootch or a big fatty, let Nature take her course, and endorse the coyotes as their undertakers and memorial designers.

Though it sounds paradoxical to use *most* as a modifier to *semi-permanent*— the most semi-permanent feature of Surprise is its location. While it's true that the Old School House and the water tank and the Ser-Sta-Gro are each well-rooted, everything else about the village is subject to relocation. There is no Main Street, no Broadway, no First Avenue, only a maze of well-worn cow meanders. No stop lights, street lights, or street signs. In fact, no state road markers point the way to Surprise, none that note its town limits, as all those were stolen so regularly the highway department soon gave up the task of corralling Surprise. And, anyways, no proper roads ever went there—they only drew within scruffling distance. Just finding Surprise was itself a surprise.

Though there was a stop sign. Only one. Actually, it was no stop sign at all, or else it was two stop signs with the effect of four, a four-way stop in a place with no roads or streets. Whether it was legally empowered to stop anything moving along any of the four cardinal directions is an issue that has yet to be decided in a court of law. No one is quite sure whether it represented either an anarchist's solution to a perceived problem, or a prank, or even a piece of art. What it was was two honest-to-God-government-issue stop signs, stolen at sometime from some real municipality somewhere, each of which had been bent evenly in the middle to a ninety-degree fold, top to bottom, then fastened to a single pole, one on one side and the other on the other. The pole was set in concrete poured into the drive-wheel of an old Hudson, the wheel having been laid on its side so that the two-sign-four-way-stop could be hefted about and moved from trouble-spot to trouble-spot as the vagaries of traffic flow and accident occurrence dictated. As a finishing touch !s had been added, making the contraption into a Stop! sign. It was apt to be found any place, but seemed to have no governing effect on whatever traffic might or might not be moving at the time. Which was just as well.

3.

BURNT NORTON

ὁδὸς ἄνω κάτω μία καὶ ὡυτή *(The way upward and the way downward are the same.) —Heraclitus*

Handy Jones provided my parents with a teacherage, a 1936 Airstream Silver Cloud that had been abandoned by the most recent couple to hold the faculty positions in Surprise. In exchange, my parents promised to teach Handy to read. The Airstream was almost new, if a bit musty, and outfitted with several items that the last occupants had neglected to pack in their haste to get back to— as they put it—civilization. There were a few canned goods that remained good, some stale crackers that wound up as chicken feed, linens that only needed a good washing, and a few books. One was a collection of T. S. Eliot's latest poems. Dad started Handy's reading lessons with that, *Burnt Norton* quickly becoming Handy's favorite. And as Handy was no handier with English than he was with the Greek epigraphs of which Eliot was so fond, Handy soon became proficient in the language of the ancients. ¡Joy the fever!

There is no direct way, no one way to Surprise. Even Handy Jones had been looking to start a different town, only to wind up by surprise in Surprise. So it's no surprise that the Foundling Families got there in the same way. And, as it might have been phrased by King James, it is meet and right that they did so. Or as we Surprises would say, it was just as well.

The Merrimans lit first, shortly ahead of the Eliots. Robert 'Bob' Merriman was born in 1919 near Wichita Falls into the middle line-up of an oil field worker's brood. His daddy had gotten started in Spindle Top at the turn of the century before leaving the Gulf Coast for the Red River when the Electra Fields started popping in 1911. The next big play was the Yates, near Fort Stockton, in 1926, and soon as he could Bob's daddy hauled the whole litter with him to the Trans-Pecos.

Young Bob loved the entrepreneurial foundation of the oil bidness. He loved the rambler-gambler, roll-the-dice optimists like his daddy. Mostly, he loved the free-enterprise theory behind it all. Yet what he liked in theory he didn't much like in practice. On the whole, the men he worked with weren't optimists. They were unreliable and crude, difficult to deal with when they were broke and impossible when they were flush. The work itself was dirty, nasty, and dangerous. And not feeling much camaraderie with the rough-necks he'd been around all his life, Bob found it lonely on a rig, especially at night, so lonely that he developed a fine rapport with the Trans-Pecos coyote packs, trading his howls back and forth with theirs in what must have been one of mankind's original social networking systems. To make matters worse, for a young man who had an itch in his jeans for more than money, it was too many hours a week, too many hours of the day, fifty-two-times-twenty-four-seven.

When the circus came to Fort Stockton in the summer of 1938, young Bob had to do a lot of finagling to talk his daddy into giving him a night off. Not much entertainment came the way of Fort Stockton. Not that *this* circus was much entertainment. It was only a small, family-owned-and-operated troupe that set up its one, smallish tent near Comanche Springs, ironic since the show was called 'The Sioux City Sioux's Super Revue'. The irony was dampened some by there not being a Native American of any tribe in the outfit as the whole kit-and-kaboodle was owned by an Iowa farm family, the MacSwains, who'd sold out when land skyrocketed after Armistice Day and straight-way invested their kitty in the run-down show. The Iowans looked uncomfortable in their faux-Sioux get-ups, by heritage less suited to deerskin than to tartan, less to loin cloth than to kilt, and with their big, raw hands better fitted for hoes and bagpipes than for lances and bows.

All but one little Indian of their traveling tribe, that is. Their main attraction had come to be sixteen-year-old Susan Suzanne MacSwain, whose Scots-Iowan heritage had bestowed upon her a natural empathy for animals and whose physical attributes made her a must-see at the big top—long braids, tight-fitted garments made of skimpy skins that were mostly fringe, and lots and lots of leg above her beaded moccasins. Plus a big top all her own. They billed her as 'Sue-Sue Sioux, The Savage Princess Who Tamed the Savage Wolves of the Savanna'.

Sue-Sue, as she'd been called since babyhood, loved the animals. But already she'd grown to hate show biz. Not that she wasn't good at what she did. Far from it. She was leagues ahead of the horse-whisperers who'd be holding clinics and posing for photos in the next century, not because she was the first to whisper to animals or even better at whispering. Fact is, her voice was incongruously shrill and loud and a little cutesy, more varsity pep squad than Zen animal trainer. No, she didn't whisper at all. Instead she used a natural, unexplainable gift of mental telepathy, a gift that couldn't be switched on-and-off as could a whisper, a gift that couldn't be talked about in words. She understood the animals and they understood her, more on an intellectual than an emotional level. Cool as cucumbers in the ring, they were all of them able to work together as one being, all without giving up their individual identities. They were compadres, coequals, not split into the tamer and the tamed.

As a child prodigy, she hadn't minded the spotlight and the attention, didn't really even notice. She thought the applause and the cheers and the hoots and the hollers were sparked by her working so well in concert with the animals. That had to be the case, she felt sure, as the critters themselves certainly weren't much to see, even for the country rubes in the audiences in the little towns they played. For the Sioux City Sioux's Super Revue's was a meager menagerie. The shabby little show didn't have any tigers or lions or leopards. It had no seals or bears. There was one very old elephant cow, too tired for tricks, useful only for the short parade from her wagon to the tent after which she was staked to the side of the arena like a backdrop. Sue-Sue did at least have a pair of horses on which she could do all the expected routines. But the beasts of whom she was most proud, and who were always saved for the night's finale, were her dozen or so Savage Wolves.

Her costume had come into focus, too, but not by design. Management could never manage enough extra cash for new skins. As little Sue-Sue grew larger, the fringed deerskin outfit stubbornly stayed the same size, so that every season there was more of Sue-Sue to be seen. And more applause and cheers and hoots and hollers. And afore long, cat-calls. By the time the Sioux City Sioux's Super Revue had raised its tent poles that night in Fort Stockton, she'd attracted a foul, regular following that showed up in each and every town, their sole interest being to raise their own tent poles as they howled along during the wolf act in hopes of causing a costume malfunction.

Sue-Sue's parents, as truly naive as stereotypical Iowa farm folk are portrayed, even these simple souls had begun to be disturbed by their little girl's increasingly edgy popularity. But ticket sales were climbing through the tent top. Maybe they'd be able to afford a big cat, or a high-wire act, or even a real clown. Maybe even, if there was something left, a new costume. It was something to think about, but it was thinking they would put off until the off-season.

If the parents MacSwain were able to stifle their concerns, that was not the case with the animals. Where once their extra-sensory communications with Sue-Sue were all business, now they were jumbled up with compassion, with warning. The animals knew things they hadn't yet told Sue-Sue, things about the hopelessness of cages, about the shame of servitude, about the slow death that comes from being owned, about how being desired only for the corporeal body can leave the heart incapable of desire.

Looking back on that night in Fort Stockton, Mrs. Merriman, as I knew Sue-Sue, would often say, equally often with a sigh, that the wordless messages being delivered by her animals had reached a crescendo, one she felt but didn't yet understand. A human crescendo was building too, ticket sales setting a new record, sparked almost wholly by the hooligan contingent that had lined up in droves for the one-show-only performance. As the night's bill unfolded, each successive espial of the Savage Princess elicited a larger and louder and coarser and cruder ruckus from the stands until, by the beginning of the Savage Wolf act, the grubby tent belonging to the Sioux City Sioux's Super Revue was a-tremble, heaving and pulsing with testosterone and lust.

It was too much for the wolves. Ignoring the mentally-shouted pleas of their mistress, for the first time ever they burst from the ring, snarling and howling, fangs bared, foam flecking their muzzles, as if shot from the human canon the MacSwain's could never afford, leaping in a beautiful arc smack dab into the worst of the gunsels. Panic swept the rickety bleachers. Moms and pops gathered up their chicks and hustled them toward the rows of parked wagons and cars and trucks, curiously ignored by the wolves, people would remark years later.

As the crazed canines plunged into the mass of clod-hopper-clad lechers, one young man stood calmly to the side. It was Bob Merriman. All those lonesome nights on the rigs conversing with the coyotes had given him an understanding of his own. All this night he'd watched the guffawing and pantomiming of the street-corner boys, all this night he'd listened as they'd hurled insults in four-letter promises at the striking young Princess. All this night he'd felt growing inside him the same revulsion that convulsed the wolves, the same disgust that snapped their mental leashes and was about to explode into raw, primal hatred.

Instinctively, Bob dropped to his knees, threw his head back and began to howl. The wolves stopped dead in their pursuit of the stampeding-doofus-Don-Juans, turned back toward Bob, cocked their ears, then deliberately, in ones and twos, gathered around the young oilman. In moments they were howling together as a pack, all of them, Bob and the wolves, a howl that sent shivers up the retreating backs of the boorish bullies, a howl that filled the big top, and a howl that soon included the cheerleader voice of the erst-while Savage Princess.

When the howling finally stopped, Bob took Sue-Sue by the hand, led her out of the empty tent to his truck, then drove far, far out into the greasewood flats along the Pecos River. After introducing her to the coyotes with a few yips and yaps, they spent the night in a long, magnificent conversation without speaking a single word, for it is so that the meeting of kindred spirits is never an affair of language. At daybreak they drove the short haul into New Mexico and were married at mid-morning by the Magistrate Judge of Jal.

Bob telephoned his daddy from Tucson, summarized as best he could a thing that he himself didn't yet understand, then asked if the senior Merriman knew of any work in California. And Daddy did. Bob and Sue Merriman—one of the first things she did after the brief wedding ritual was unload one of the Sues—the two Merrimans were soon in Los Angeles, Bob working in the new Wilmington Field.

They were soon pregnant, too. And just as soon tired of the city and the oil works. They missed the big, wide open space of their first night together. They missed conversing with the coyotes. Besides, Bob and Sue were born entre-preneurs, not born employees. From a bankrupt wildcatter Bob bought a hard-ly-used 1938 Airstream Clipper, which for Sue was a huge improvement over the Sioux City Sioux's Super Revue gypsy wagon in which she'd grown up. The two-and-a-half of them loaded up in the shiny house-on-wheels and headed back to the Trans-Pecos prairies.

Along the way, they concocted an enterprise. There were almost no movie theaters in West Texas, and no drive-ins at all. ¿Why not? they thought, ¿go into the drive-out movie business? Buy a projector and a portable generator, build a collapsible screen, and show films out with the coyotes. Almost no overhead. No need to buy land. Only open up when the weather was right and the moon was new. They began acquiring equipment along the way. Once they struck Jal on the return trek they began to search in earnest for a place with the darkest nights. It's not surprising they found that place in Surprise. By early fall of 1939 they were the happy neighbors of Handy Jones, the profitable proprietors of the Flatland Drive-Out Theatre, and about to be the proud parents of baby Bobbie Sue.

The Eliots' story is the same as the Merrimans', only different. Which could be said about all of us, *¿n'est-ce pas?* The difference is this: for the Merrimans, living begat drama, but for the Eliots, drama begat living. Shadrach 'Shad' Eliot was born in Crane, Texas in 1918 to a saddle-leather-faced clan of day-work ranch folk, sired by a hellion cowboy but raised by a God-fearing cattle woman. He cracked out working for his granddad and uncles, but his first job drawing wages was punching Herefords on the McElroy Ranch for Joe Bob Kelton. Shad admired, even revered the legendary foreman. But never liked him. Occasioned by his upbringing, Shad talked mostly in parables, a habit which permitted him to tip-toe around a curse closely enough to make his point but at enough distance to avoid his own eternal damnation. One parable he repeated often was that to break even in this country a man had to be tough, but to come out on top in this country a man had to be mean, and Joe Bob Kelton—Shad would always insert a long, dramatic pause *right here*—Joe Bob Kelton always come out on top.

Besides his penchant for parables, Shad was a reciter. He was good at memorization, good at delivery, and had a quirky taste for poetry. For his fifteenth birthday he'd been given *The Complete Poems of Robert Service*, and for his sixteenth a first-edition of Badger Clark's *Sun and Saddle Leather*. A couple of years later, on his own he bought the 1920 Knopf edition of *Poems by T. S. Eliot*, mainly because they shared the same last name. But after he read the first two lines of the opening stanza of *Gerontion*, the first poem in the book—*Here I am, an old man in a dry month, / Being read to by a boy, waiting for rain.*—well then, Shad began to memorize every piece in the Eliot collection. Tom Eliot, Shad thought, might really be kin. As would anyone who understood waiting for rain.

Rose Edna Flores, her middle name bestowed in honor of the poet Millay, was born on Halloween of 1918 in Dallas. Her father was a Spanish diplomat of means, her New York mother a graduate of Smith College and a follower of the Free Love Movement. Stuck in what the Flores family saw as a rustic frontier outpost, they nevertheless sought a proper education for their Rose and enrolled her in Hockaday, the best girls' school that the city on the Trinity had to offer.

Rose Edna, however, was a head-strong, unconventional young woman who loved the freedom of expression offered by the arts and hated the confinements of the classroom. She was expelled enough times from Hockaday that even her father's dossier and her mother's connection to Smith weren't sufficient to regain her matriculation. Not in the least abashed, she took her exclusion from higher education as opportunity and, drawing on her good looks and youthful talent, became a dancer and singer, plying her trade in the jazz clubs of Deep Ellum, where she soon built a large and loyal local following.

Some time before, Flores padre, a Catholic, and Flores madre, a Universalist, had taken a hasty poll of their acquaintances and discovered more 'wets' amongst the Methodists than any other Protestant sect. There was, of course, no need to even put the question to the Catholics. So as to be able to give Rose Edna at least a nominally religious upbringing, the family's compromise was to move its letter of membership to one of John Wesley's congregations.

Besides their hogging of the middle of the dogmatic road, the Methodists were also responsible for the Chautauqua Movement and were religious about keeping the traveling events moving along the byways of America's hinterlands. For the convenience of the sinners and mis-directed, a large Chautauqua show operated by a modernist outfit called the Circuit Riders was held in Deep Ellum in the opening days of 1938. At the evening's conclusion, a few laymen and at least one District Superintendent snuck away for a little jazz, and, if correspondents were truthful, a little hootch. They fell into both, along with a little kootch to go with the hootch, when they caught Rose Edna's act at the Mystery Club.

In the dark and smoky depths of that sultry saloon, it was Rose Edna's custom to make extra tips by autographing the shirt tails of well-heeled fans, which that night included, amongst the Methodist laity in the audience, the manager of the Chautauqua. Next day, she was on the bill and on the road with the Circuit Riders. They worked their way across Texas, first down through the Hill Country and then westward-ho. By mid-spring they'd planted their tent in Crane, ready to give the locals some lecture, some revival, and a little jiggle dance, all in one night: The Word, Hallelujah, and ¡Amen!

It's important at this juncture in the story to point out that Chautauqua Lake in New York—where the movement was founded and from whence it got its name—is a place wholly different than the Castle Mountains in Texas, those scabby little hills that flank the eastern approach to Crane and over-lay that ancient trail with a coarse blanket of mesquite scrub and bear grass and cactus and what may be the highest density of rattlesnakes per square yard as can be found anywhere on earth. Not to mention the winds that scour the alkali flats of the Trans-Pecos every spring.

The tent went up easy that afternoon, the first lectures got underway as planned. A breeze stirred, a good thing as it was already hot in the desert reaches of West Texas. A crowd was slowly gathering, town folk mostly, but a few cowpunchers sauntering in with the intent of making sport of the city-slickers. Shad was the one and only cowpoke who'd come to hear the talks, drawn by a poetry recitation listed on the advance flyer. The reading had no sooner gotten underway—some stilted Longfellow piece, long and dry and drawn-out—when a blast of wind, hurricane in strength but dirt in composition, roared up from the Pecos River Valley and lifted the canvas top several dozen feet into the sky where it hung there, the ropes not yet having given up, flapping in the gale like Uncle John's BVDs hung out to dry. The townspeople were used to this sort of miscreance on their Mother Nature's part, especially this season of the year, and had already grabbed their picnic baskets and blankets at the first whisper of the galloping gale. But not so the Chautauquans. One young girl, a pretty thing, stood stock still in the vortex of gravel and dust, too dazed to be frightened. Shad jumped to action, knowing what goes up at one moment must come down soon thereafter. Holding his Stetson with his left hand he looped his right arm around her waist and carried her upwind out from under the now-tenuous bulbous structure.

And just in time. The wind dropped nearly as quickly as it'd come up, the remains of the tent draping itself in a shroud over the remaining performers. The pretty girl must have still been a little shocked over the excitement of it all, because when Shad introduced himself she looked incredulously at him for a moment before telling the young cowboy that he didn't look not one bit like the poet. Shad was a slow talker but a quick thinker. He didn't write 'em, he offered, but he could damn sure recite 'em, and a lot better than the Longfellows who were holding court before the wind hit. Prove it, she said. So Shad jumped up on a bench, took off his hat, fanned his fanny with it as if he were coming out of the chute on a bare-back bronc, hollered out a robust ¡Yee, Haw! and then lit into *The Love Song of J. Alfred Prufrock,* delivering the whole thing right out of his own marble jar.

Rose Edna was struck dumb, her eyes grown both moist and fiery. The two looked a long time at one another, so long that those around them began to grow uncomfortable, before Shad broke the silence by quoting from the middle of the poem—the hardest place to pick up a line, we might point out—*Do I dare / Disturb the universe? / In a minute there is time / For decisions and revisions which a minute will reverse.* He let the last words hang in the still-swirling dust for as long as had the ill-fated canvas, then he picked her up off the ground and kissed her.

They met Shad's mother that night, then rode horseback to Odessa the next day to catch the train back to Dallas, where they met the Floreses. They married there, then came back to Odessa to collect Shad's riggings and gear before searching out a likely place for a ranch. At the depot they ran into Joe Bob Kelton. He asked what they were doing. They told him. I can give you some suggestions, the gruff old man offered. Surprise us, Rose Edna said, gaily. Joe Bob never smiled, but nodded, then took a scrap of paper from his pocket and, with a dull bullet pencil, scratched out a map to the town founded by Handy Jones.

4.

THE SIX SURPRISES

We were the Five Surprises. Before us, no one had ever come to Surprise on purpose. Even Handy Jones, the First Surprise, came to what he thought was somewhere else and was surprised when it became Surprise. We didn't come here on purpose either. We began here. It's most certain that there were some others before us that were conceived in Surprise, but as far as anyone knows, we were the first to be born in Surprise.

An unsurprising and niggling little detail is that the Five Surprises are really not five but six, the Big Three Surprises and Los Dos Surprises and, coming along a bit later, the Odd Surprise. The Big Three all hatched out in 1940. Bobbie Sue Merriman, on Valentine's Day, is the Senior Surprise. My sister Kerrie Mae came on May Day, and Kelly rounded out the first bunch on the last and final day of August. Los Dos Surprises were myself, your humble reporter, born on the first of July, 1942—why my mother couldn't wait a few days, I'll never know—and the tail-gunner, Ruth Etta Eliot, born on the Summer Solstice, 1944.

As I've earlier implied, the Merrimans are doers, the Joneses are thinkers, and the Eliots are dramatists. Bob and Sue Merriman produced Bobbie Sue. Strait-forward job of naming. The lefty-Welsh-poet-teacher Joneses named my sister Ceridwen Mai—Ceridwen for the white goddess of poetry and Mai for the month of May—though were practical enough to call her Kerrie Mae in a nod to the hard *C* of Ceridwen as well as in celebration of both her affiliation with the Tribe of the Two Name People and the day on which she entered the tipi. Me, they named for Welsh poets.

It's said the Eliots conducted loud, raging discussions over how and what to name their brood, discussions that would have been debates had the volume been turned down. But the naming arguments would have been only particular versions of the ritualized shouting matches that both Eliots enjoyed immensely, routines that always followed the same course and, thankfully, always ended in effective compromises. Growing up, we Five Surprises tried never to miss one. The pattern was this. Except when shouting, Shad was the strong, silent type. He'd state his position, then fold up behind the latest copy of *The Livestock Weekly*, reading slowly as Rose Edna's plaints grew louder and louder, page by page, more plaintive and more passionate, until, his silence worn down, he'd stand up as tall as the polished aluminum ceiling of their Airstream would permit, slam the paper onto the fold-out dining table, shout ¡Daddurnit! and stomp out of the trailer. That was the cue for Rose Edna, who'd grown up in circumstances that permitted hired-help, to throw her head back, fling the dorsal side of her right forearm over her forehead, her hand open and limp and helpless, while at the same time finding with the other hand a firm grasp on the Formica table top before exclaiming in the most pitiful of voices ¡I'm just a nigrah in my own how-us! as she collapsed to the floor in a slow and stately, swan-like sinking motion. It was a joy to watch, a bit of domestic drama that had been refined and perfected over generations. Even if none of the Five Surprises had the slightest hint of what a nigrah was—and would have been aghast had we known. On cue, as if carefully choreographed and tirelessly rehearsed, Shad would appear in the door way, step carefully and gently over the crumpled form of his beloved, then settle himself again behind the bunker of *The Livestock Weekly* as Rose Edna arose and dusted herself off. Then, calmly and deliberately, they would hammer out the details of their latest treaty.

In the Great Naming Discussion, the agreement was that each parent would have complete freedom to pick one of each child's two surnames, the choice of first name and middle name alternating with each successive kiddo. Bear in mind that I said the Eliots were dramatic people, not simple people. Being the gallant cowboy, Shad let Rose Edna take the first first-name, and so their first-born was first-named Xavier, for her favorite band leader, and middle-named Kelton, for Shad's ranch foreman idol. One thing that likely propelled the boy into grease-paint and onto the boards was the complete and total inability of anyone to come up with a Two Name version of Xavier Kelton, clearly forcing him into a life of make-believe and impersonation as he could never muster more than Kelly, which was nothing other than a one-name-nick-name. For their daughter, having first dibs Shad picked Ruth in honor of The Babe, with the missus opting for Etta, a real triple-whammy that paid simultaneous homage to three other Ettas—Kitt and James, the singers, and Kett, the cartoon cutie—resulting in

Ruth Etta Eliot, like Bobbie Sue Merriman, filled with meaning and satisfying the Two Name People custom from the git-go.

The Odd Surprise was an indeterminate year or so younger than Ruth Etta and didn't get to Surprise 'til time to start school. A skinny blind kid named William Roberts, his scuffle-folk family called him Blind Billy Bob, a moniker that our parents all abhorred and so we called him, at first, Three-B and then just Threeb after he'd become one of the gang. More later about the Robertses, the only sorry Surprises.

Let me clear up something right now. Unless it's purely horrific, childhood is always looked back upon as idyllic, the more idyllic the later in adulthood its memory is invoked. That's because children are things built for the future but living wholly in the present, both of which bring the spirit as close to perfection as is possible on this side of the veil. Even so, I'll still tell you—without reservation—that childhood spent in Surprise was in no way horrific and in every way idyllic.

The basic reason is that we did not live like the Ordinaries. You know, the ordinary people who live in ordinary places and do ordinary things in ordinary ways. At the outset, our circumstances weren't ordinary. They were pecuniary. We had none of the subterranean deposits that enriched and despoiled the places around us. That was our good fortune, in the main because our place wouldn't support very many people, and there are not many things wrong with the world that having fewer people wouldn't either ease or flat-out fix. Not to mention that none of the Surprises were rich, either, meaning that they were never predisposed—as are all rich folk, and let me repeat, all rich folk—to confuse the luck of having money with some intrinsic and innate quality or achievement of their own, like hard work or good looks or smarts. Being rich is a fact of fate, like being hit on the head by a meteorite, the difference being that you'll be remembered fondly if you leave this earthly plane by means of being whacked by a rock from Outer Space. And no one remembers the rich with fondness.

Besides which, our place was and is too tough for the Ordinaries. They give up quickly here. Then they move back where they came from and talk bad about us. Which is just as well. It cuts down on the future in-migrations of Ordinaries. We, ourselves, didn't understand how much sand we'd packed into our own gullets except on the few and infrequent occasions in which we had dealings with the Ordinaries. Like when we went to town—which wasn't often—where we really stood out. Really stood out. We talked differently. We were all great readers and our parents provided us with great reading materials, the classics as well as contemporary cutting-edge philosophy and literary criticism. Some mighty fine comic books, too. So we weren't afraid to use metaphors in our speech, or employ humor, or perfect our demonstrative language. And the older generation of Surprises cursed oddly, saying things like *gaddurnit* and *foockle* instead of the *g_d_* and *f_* words, not only adding levity to any situation in which cussing would have escalated the anger and the tension but also completely perplexing the Ordinaries when one of us urchins would suggest that they foockle themselves. It may be that we dressed a little oddly, too, as until the summer that Bobbie Sue and my sis discovered tie-front-crop-tops and tap pants, by our appearance the Ordinaries took the lot of us to be Mennonites. And the couple of semesters that we tried enrollment in the public schools the Ordinaries treated us like exchange students from a country that they couldn't identify but were sure they'd seen featured in *National Geographic*.

Nor was the place of our place ordinary, either. We had none of the postcard bull-feathers that Chambers of Commerce and State Tourism Agencies are prone to pointing out as beauty. Our soil is dirt, not soil, the distinction being that things grow in soil but dirt is only dust in larger volumes, a substance that just makes you dusty and, well, *dirty*. Our trees aren't trees, but shrubs. Sometimes big shrubs, but shrubs nonetheless. And with thorns. And without shade. And with a thirst that kills the green grass that might have the audacity to try to grow all around all around all around all around. It's too hot in the summer. It's too cold in the winter. Spring and fall are merely artifacts of the calendar. The wind blows to one degree or another always, day or night, stormy or clear. There is no time during the year that the clothing for any one season can be put away as it's impossible to predict when summer garments may be needed in the winter or when coats may be needed in the summer. It doesn't rain much, and it doesn't rain often, and the whole year's precipitation is apt to come all at one time. That said, we have three-hundred-and-sixty degrees of horizon and one-hundred-and-eighty-degrees of sky that allow us to see a change in the weather coming two days away and give us the sublime chance to see the geese as they are taking off from Canada headed south and allow us to get dizzy watching the stars whirling in the heavens and allow us to grow horny peeking at the moon flirting with the sun and allow us to be knocked stupid by the meteors and the Marfa Lights and then allow us to be ready to believe surely and certainly that all the angels that fly to and from the firmaments soar above Surprise.

And if all the above ain't enough, we had our idol Handy Jones, who was the very personification of an idyll. And we had the mystery of Maya Gandhi. And we had the routine idols of our idyllic parents. It wasn't 'Father Knows Best' or 'Leave It to Beaver' or 'Petticoat Junction'. But it wasn't 'The Twilight Zone', either. Or 'Doctor Phil'.

I've given you the where-for and the what-how about Handy, but not about Gandhi. Maya Gandhi, that is. She showed up in the 1940s during the war, not so early that we Five Surprises don't remember her arrival and not so late that we Five Surprises were surprised to see her show up. She came pulling her tipi on a travois behind an old knock-headed gelding whose only distinguishing mark was a big red dot in the middle of his forehead. She called him Punto Rojo, and so did we. He may have rivaled a bristlecone pine in longevity, as he was old when he got here and so far as I know there are no reports of his death. He couldn't see well, and he read minds better than he could hear. Yes, he read minds. And not mentally-delivered orders. He responded best to requests, and better yet to requests couched in a flattering manner.

There was also all about her, always, a cloud of puppies, small yipping and yapping little curs that were perpetually underfoot. No old dogs, just puppies. None ever had names, none ever would. Atop Punto Rojo she packed along a tabla drum imported from the Sub-Continent of India but with Mayan and Comanche symbols tattooed on its head. She wore a pancho of many colors, almost as large as her tipi, and above it a sombrero the size of the largest of the sovereign states of New England. In the winter she added a serape as bright as a summer rainbow, as much for show as for warmth.

Maya Gandhi, who was always called by the two names together, never Maya and never Miss Gandhi, was of indeterminate age and origin. She herself proclaimed her ethnicity to be Indian-Indian, and I suspect that's as accurate as any demographer could make it. Her father had been an anthropologist from the Malabar Coast of Keralam but educated in Delhi and who'd traveled to Mexico to study Los Indios, where he met her mother, a Yaqui. She was a vagabond but not a vagrant, nomadic but not no-account, peripatetic but not without place. Though we never knew exactly where she made her camps —and never felt compelled to investigate—in practice she was never more than a brief Punto Rojo ramble from Surprise.

Maya Gandhi rarely spoke, but, like Handy Jones, smiled as brightly as the sun, and as often. She supported herself by selling stuffed fry breads, popular far and wide, filled with a tender, delicious meat of unspecifiable origin, seasoned in a way that defied categorization. She had a couple of panniers made from hand-woven bear-grass she would fill with the hot and aromatic super-tacos, then load onto Punto Rojo before leading him out the few miles to the highway. Her customers were highway patrolmen, Border Patrol agents, truckers, oil field workers, smugglers, traveling salesmen, cowpunchers, and riffraff of all kinds, all of whom went well out of their way to find her spot on any given day. Wherever she set up shop, the area around her became a neutral zone where otherwise arch-enemies collected in peace to eat or pickup for take-away what she advertised as 'Traditional Indian-Indian Hot Dogs'. Every now and again newcomers would point out what I've just pointed out to you, that there were no old dogs in her entourage, just nameless puppies. But Maya Gandhi's customers hushed them. No one wanted to know the specifics, the possibilities. Which may have lead the stuffed-fry-bread aficionados to call their favorite fast food 'hush puppies'.

Maya Gandhi also carried on a discreet trade in peyote buttons. She didn't see that part of her business as business, but rather as community service, the provision not of entertainment but of enlightenment. She'd secret them somewhere on Punto Rojo's riggings, for the sensitive equine was able by both training and talent to detect the vibes of a narc or a small-time government satrap, at which sensing he'd first roll his eyes one way then prick his ears the other, the ears singling out the potential threat, then make quite a show—raring up, pawing the air and snorting and whinnying—before bolting off into the scrub brush thicket. When the vibe was especially offensive to the valiant steed he'd ensure that his escape route was right over the top of the intruding governmental regulator. Now and again the terrified functionary would pull a pistol from his pants, planning to eviscerate the escaping equine, but the shotgun that Maya Gandhi kept under her technicolor poncho always proved to be a potent problem-solver. During these slight kerfuffles the regulars rarely, if ever, looked up from happily munching their hush puppy lunches.

Back to the routine idylls of our folks, the Foundling Families. You've already gotten a little taste of the Eliots, so let's keep on keepin'-on, as Shad would put it. A man of few, but colorful, words, he never lost his interest in poetry. He kept on cowboying, leasing a spot of pasture here and there, turning it back at the first interference from the parcel's windshield-manager overseer, only to have to repeat the process on another sorry scrap of dirt with another sorry bunch of townies. It's an irony of the universe that them what has the knowledge rarely ever has the money, and them what has the money almost never have any other asset. He'd have been a hell of a ranch manager. But as it was, he pieced together a living by day-working, trading horses, buying and selling tack and bits and spurs, and doing an occasional poetry recitation at chuck-wagon suppers thrown by the *nouveau riche* oil barons down in Midland.

When she could, Rose Edna taught private voice and dance lessons in town. When she couldn't, she sang and danced while she did the trailer-work and gardening and such. When the weather was favorable, she preferred to do as much of her chores in as few of her clothes as possible. It was a carry-over from her days in Deep Ellum. Very often even in the nude, and especially when sun-bathing in the Adirondack lounge chair Shad had built for her from discarded shipping pallets. Living in a trailer house enforces a certain intimacy, a certain tolerance of togetherness that alters one's notion of privacy, so no one in Surprise was either surprised or offended by Rose Edna *au naturel*. Not to mention that she had a beautiful voice, danced with verve and grace, and just plain looked good naked. Even the other women said so. And, indeed, her carefree and joyful inhabitation of her own body set an example for the other Surprises, so that the little proto-village had more the insouciant air of an exotic resort spa than the hard-scrabble grit of an oilfield hamlet.

But then it was the case that each Surprise rose to become an example for all the other Surprises. Bob Merriman, to take the next case, set the standard for busy. And—second only to Handy Jones—for happy. Bob's incessant work and indefatigable merriment rubbed off, first and foremost, on his small family. Indeed, there were never people more appropriately named than the Merrimans. Sue was happy in the way of the Zen masters, being, as she was, always in the present moment, and busy in their way as well, having early in her circus days mastered the art of doing-not-doing, though her Iowegian forebears would have blanched at the categorization. She never lost her touch with or her empathy for the animal kingdom and so brought in much needed cash to the Merriman trailer-house-hold by taking on the gentling of the most difficult horses from a vast region around Surprise. Their daughter Bobbie Sue did not fall far from either tree, and was from the start the ringleader, motivator, and Den Mother for we Five Surprises.

The Flatlands Drive-Out Movie Theatre business kept all three Merrimans busy enough. The generator was a mechanic's nightmare, or dream, depending on how much the mechanic enjoyed working with baling wire and duct tape. The projectors were always in imminent danger of blowing a bulb or busting a belt. The screen, too, rarely escaped a showing without some disfigurement caused by wind gusts or birds or the overexcitement of the rowdies when the night's feature featured a film rated near the end of the alphabet. Then there was the concession trailer to keep stocked, especially with the home-vintage wine for which Bob became famous, a potion so powerful that some described it as hallucinogenic and was ever certain to draw an eager audience, even when the night's film was a yawner. He called it *Sinfandel,* and kept the ingredients on the hush-hush.

Acquiring the more prosaic portions of the concession trailer stocks led to another family business, the Merriman Minibus Food Coop, the dash between Co and Op in Co-Op having been inadvertently omitted, an oversight which quickly caused the little VW eleven-window Splittie bus to become known to all, far and wide, as the Coop. Bob, and, later, Bobbie Sue, would take orders from the Surprises before flying the Coop to one of the larger regional municipalities like Lubbock or even Amarillo or Abilene where they'd load up supplies to refill the larders of the Surprise families and the shelves of the Ser-Sta-Gro. Bobbie Sue soon became a first-rate gatherer-upper, a skill not to be dismissed, and, along the way, developed a sixth sense for the mechanical maintenance and repairs often demanded by the boxy, underpowered VolksWagon, a prescient phalanx of abilities that she would put to good use later on during The Summer of Love.

The merchant-minded Merrimans also instigated what became a Surprise staple, and—so far as is known—the only such emporium in existence, thence or since. Though in some ways it should have been expected as an enterprise that would have come about on its own in our mini-mobile-metropolis, that place where the extraordinary is pretty ordinary and the ordinary is pretty extraordinary. Specifically, it was the ordinary mystery of disappearing sox. Never mind that neither the Ser-Sta-Gro's honor-system washateria ever numbered more than three Maytag electric wringer-tubs nor that the village's stable population census ever numbered more than a small multiple of said appliance roster, still, on wash-days there always appeared a few extra socks—anklets, crew-sox, Bobby-sox, work-socks, athletic-socks, dress-socks, garter-socks, sox of all sizes and shapes and descriptions—sox whose mates had gone missing in the short traverse betwixt laundry-basket-to-tub-to-wringer-to-clothes-line. At first, the odd remainders were simply socked-away in storage, awaiting the occasional sock-exchange in which locals would meet over coffee to sort through the stack of orphans with the intent of creating matches. Which always produced fine fellowship and healthy gossip but never, ever produced a true pairing-up of lost toe-keepers. Which eventually led to a lonely-hose heap of unwieldy dimensions. Bob Merriman—always quick to see opportunity in the inopportune— took things in hand by simply recasting the problem as a potential revenue source: the free inventory for a new mail-order business, The One-Sock-Shop. The clever clearinghouse was advertised in *Coronet*—as *Pageant* refused paid marketing—along with hand-drawn posters in regional laundromats. Send us your extra sox and a small fee for shipping and handling—read the announcements—and we'll send you back a free pair. With no carrying-costs and a marvelous mark-up it wasn't long before sox became important stock-in-trade enhancements to the Surprise GNP.

My own progenitors, the double-tree full of Joneses, were the perfect compliment to the other two Foundling Families. My folks were smart, maybe even brilliant, as well as well-read and thoughtful, but completely hapless in the practical world. Dad knew the history of the automobile, the metallurgy and physics and chemistry that made the horseless carriages wheel down the road, but was perfectly unable to change a spark plug or an oil filter. Mom had read the entirety of The Great Books but couldn't find her grocery list. So in exchange for the practical works and assistances of the Merrimans and the Eliots, the Joneses became the scholars and school-teachers of Surprise. They subscribed to the best journals and magazines, titles like *Poetry, The Prairie Schooner*, and *The Partisan Review,* and one or two subversive rags like *The Daily Worker.* They bought interesting books. They shared them all, with adults and children alike, holding regular weekly salons that served both as classroom for the wee ones and discussion group for the big ones.

It also fell to Gene and Mary Ellen to serve as the Surprise Sunday School teachers and clergy. The Merrimans were too blasted busy for church meetings and rituals. The Eliots were still waiting for the evangelists of the Free Love Movement to make it this far west. And Handy Jones and Maya Gandhi lived in spiritual worlds light-years from the present realm of existence. So my peeps drew enough from the writings of Eugene V. Debs to cobble together a thing that was part prayer, part praise, part affirmation, and part incitement, a document that was read or recited at meals and funerals and often before the MovieTone News at the Flatlands Drive-Out Theatre shows, a stirring piece that Handy Jones came to call 'The Surprise Pledge of Unallegiance'. I reproduce it for you *in toto*.

I pledge allegiance to the disunited state of humankind, and to all those oppressed by the republics of church and state and Mammon. I pledge my own life to the belief that all living things are good, and that I am no better than the worst of them and no worse than the best. I pledge my confidence that one bright morning the light will prevail over the darkness, the right over the wrong, the good over the evil, the industrious over the slothful, and to that glorious day I pledge my heart and head and hands to the work of freeing the slave, of feeding the hungry, to hearing the silent, to loving the unloved. Amen.

I have given short-shrift to the Robertses. Though any shrift I give them will be shrift too much. They were, to my knowledge, the only Surprises of poor quality. They arrived about the time that we Five Surprises would have been starting public school, had there been a public school in Surprise. No one ever knew exactly how they found their way to the City of Curiosity, or why, other than a vague story that the couple had been bumming-about with various low-rent traveling street fair shows as clowns in a flesh-and-blood Punch and Judy act—dismissed from each and every one when it became obvious that the punching wasn't show-bidness—and had blown in on a foul wind looking for a gig. They rattled into our town in a pieced-together pickup of dubious origin, lacking title, tags, or any functioning safety equipment. Lashed on behind was an old oilfield portable work shack, little more than a tin shed on rickety running gear and four bald tires, never meant to be lived in, the one door secured by a hasp on the outside.

The Roberts *père* and *mère* were themselves of mixed heritage, one or two dollops of oilfield trash with some carny and cedar-cutter thrown in. Unable to have children of their own, or perhaps too ignorant to do so, they turned instead to adoption. When their unabilities extended to their having failed to satisfy the slightest requirements of any agency, they wound up with an infant that no one else wanted, a blind boy they christened William but called Blind Billy Bob, the red-neck-nick-name at pointed and pained opposition to his thick blair hair and south-of-the-border soft-brown skin. By the time their rig gave up in Surprise, Blind Billy Bob was four or five years old.

The crime 'no visible means of support' was enacted to deal with cases like the Robertses. They existed, but no one knew how. Maybe they ran on pure-dee venom. The old man wore over-hauls and a sleeveless undershirt, chewed some kind of concoction he called terbacky, and spoke in a language comprised almost exclusively of epithets and curses. The old woman had the appearance of a tarp thrown over a pile of gin trash, and uttered only grunts and slobbers. Neither ever laughed, except in derision, and nothing but a discouraging word was ever heard coming from their home on the range.

Blind Billy Bob was the only good thing about them. Not just good. He was a marvel. He behaved as if he had eyes, relying on his ears and nose and fingers to fill in the gaps his sightless sockets had left. He was also modest. When anyone praised his heightened senses, he shrugged it off—*I cain't hear no better'n any a you, I jist lissen better. I ain't got better smellin' or tetch, I jist pay better attention.* But no matter. Along with his extraordinary faculties he was sweet of temperament and as bright as the light bulb he couldn't see.

His owners—we refused to acknowledge them as parents—cussed him constantly, calling him a little-pepper-bellied-short-sighted-sumbitch and other things not printable on these pages. Our parents didn't like it in the least, and even the sunny Handy Jones gave the Robertses the juju eye. One slow morning when a fog had rolled across the scrub brush the night before and the Surprise Anarchists' Club had lingered a little longer than usual in the Old School House cafe, sipping the last of their coffees and enjoying the slow start to the day, Maya Gandhi showed up carrying little Blind Billy Bob, deposited him on the veranda, propped him up, and came inside to get a wet rag. Though he made not a sound, not a whimper, it was easy to see that his eyes, long blind, were now recently black.

Even idyllic people have their limits. No one said a thing. No one needed to. Maya Gandhi and Handy took over the first-aid triage while the others headed over to the Roberts's shack. Someone twisted the hasp closed, someone else snapped a padlock in it, and yet another hitched the clap-trap contraption to a pickup. They pulled the barely-rolling scrap heap far, far, far out into the greasewood desert, a cloud of dust following along, punctuated by the curses spewing from the trailer shed. Somewhere in New Mexico they unhitched the mess, tossed the padlock key into a cholla cactus, then headed back to make more coffee. If the Robertses got out, they didn't come back, for they were not to be seen in Surprise again.

When the members of the Surprise Anarchists' Club returned, a brief election was held. By acclamation the boy was voted into full Surprise citizenship, and, with the lighting of a few candles and using the Debs liturgy, rechristened Three-B. Handy Jones set about fashioning him a room in the Old School House and, later that day, the Odd Surprise went for the first time to a school other than the school of hard knocks.

5.

A SONG OF SURPRISE

We played lots of music in Surprise. And not because there was nothing else to do. There was always plenty else to do. We put off just about anything and everything else we could get away with so's we could play music. Because who would want to live in a world where music was only played when there was nothing else to do. I wouldn't. And we didn't.

Long before Chatwin trekked about Down Under, discovering what he might just as well have found in his own home country—an ancient thing still alive and well in the Saturday sing-a-longs held by the descendants of the Brigantes, weekly raising their stout tankards and their strong voices in the pubs scattered along the River Don—long before the term *songline* entered our consciousness, Handy Jones had discovered the Song of Surprise.

The melody came to him while he was leveling the Old School House after he'd drug it cross-country from Shafter Lake and plopped it down into what would soon be Surprise. He hummed it over and over to himself while he worked, scared lest he lose it. Over and over. Over and over. Soon as the last wedge was driven, the last stone in place—just as the sun was dropping into the far reaches of New Mexico, its western arc lighting up the bare mesquite as if they were the incandescent bones of lightbulbs, all at the same time and with the same light as it was flicking flecks of neon on the greasewood and the cedars—as soon as he could, Handy Jones pulled out his fiddle and played the Song of Surprise again and again, until his fingers knew it as well as his heart knew it.

From that day forward, Handy played the song every day, often in the morning from down on the veranda but most usually of an evening, perched up high in his cupola of the four directions. Without the song, he feared that Surprise would melt into the mists of myth and memory. So he taught it to us, each and every one. Though he needn't have. We heard it in the womb and every day thereafter.

It was in our genes, our spatial DNA, the spiral helical horizon that is made of the ties that bind.

I would like to describe the Song of Surprise to you, but I can't. For it's no easier than telling someone how your mother's voice sounds, how your father smiles, what the morning smells like, or what the geese are saying when they pass overhead in the night of winter. All I can truly say is that there's nothing special about it, except that it's ours.

For instrumentation, Surprise was equipped a bubble shy of the basics. We had Handy Jones and his fiddle. We had voices, the first instrument of humankind. We had Maya Gandhi's drum. Plus one time the Denver Bongos Six-Man Black Light Football Squad left behind a set of their eponymous skins after having 45ed the Frankel City Five Plus One Irregulars. And in the Old School House was an ancient piano, scuffed and scratched and dented and damaged, the few ivories that still clung to its keys so yellowed and cracked it looked less like a piano and more like a large oaken Cheshire Cat in which the smile had disappeared and only the fur had remained, all-in-all a piano that could no longer even be counted upon for rickety renditions of Bible-camp classics like 'Chopsticks' or 'Heart and Soul'.

When the first flight of the Five Surprises began to reach the age in which fond parents recognize in their offspring the entire array of human talents, the Foundling Families began to cast about for something suitable upon which to build the kiddos' musical chops. But there weren't many practical choices. Guitars were too expensive and took up too much space in an Airstream. Violins were the right size, but came with a steep learning curve, one that could test the tolerance of even the most doting dad or nascent stage-mom. And most other instruments, horns and woodwinds and such, belong in much larger ensembles than could ever be formed in Surprise.

Luckily, my folks, the Double-Joneses, though farm-raised were college-educated, and in the ivied halls along the grassy quads of old McMurry had been thoroughly exposed to the charms of the ukulele. Cute little things, ukuleles were cheap, easily learned, and took up hardly any territory in a college dorm room or a student pension. Or an Airstream. Each Jones had brought their own ukulele with them to Surprise. Bob Merriman was fond of the little music machines as well, having heard ukulele master George Formby playing 'When I'm Cleaning Windows' in the USO club at Midland Army Air Field. The popular Lancashire entertainer had evidently come this side of the pond in a secret reverse-lend-lease deal to bolster American morale during the Second War to End All Wars, using the indisputable logic that hardly anything makes a fighting man happier than the hula-hula rhythms of the ukulele. Rose Edna, of course, didn't get much uke exposure in Deep Ellum but became plenty familiar with them on the Chautauqua road. And amongst the Foundling Families' collections of 78s—right there along with Jimmie Rodgers and Benny Goodman and the Carter Family— were platters cut by all the ukulele greats, the afore-mentioned Formby as well as Cliff 'Ukulele Ike' Edwards and Wendell Hall, the latter better known as 'The Red-Headed Music Maker'.

Kerrie Mae, my sis, picked it up first, learning on our mom's Harmony soprano model, with Bobbie Sue right behind her on a Martin tenor borrowed from my dad. The Father Merriman, who regularly traveled far and wide, soon began picking up used ukes—what he called 'useduleles'—and bringing them back for approval. In short order Bobbie Sue had an array of different styles, including a resonator model that gave her playing the edginess of Sister Rosetta Tharpe and, of course, a banjo-ukulele of the kind Bob fondly recalled from Formby's Permian Basin performance. Kelly instantly saw that the primary value of the tiny devices was to serve as a prop for his varied performance shenanigans, so, correspondingly, he learned only what he needed in order to get by, meaning a few chords here and there but played with a lot of visual pizzazz. Me, I was all thumbling and bumbling, but worked hard enough to not be left out.

The radio was no surprise to Surprises. Graced with a renewable and predictable supply of wind on the Scrub-Brush Prairie, we put it to good use with wind chargers, mostly the reliable Zenith, though, predictably, Bob Merriman built his own with no more than a truck generator and blades he hand-carved from mesquite posts. The towers holding up the chargers did double duty as antennae, so when the Aurora Borealis was shimmering somewhere up above the Oklahoma Panhandle, pushing the electromagnetic sphere to the south, we could reliably pull in KOMA from OKC. Likewise a good hurricane would send us the signals of WWL fastened onto the damp winds from New Orleans and which sometimes cut a wide enough swath to drag along WSM from Nashville. The border radio stations, on the other hand, were so strong that if you had one or two tooth-fillings you needed neither radio nor battery to listen to any and all broadcasts from the X-call-letter crowd. XERA, 'The Sunshine Station Between the Nations', was the local favorite. We were, in short, cosmopolitan consumers of radio air-play.

Plus, we Five Surprises got almost as much music from the movies, for, thanks to the Merrimans, Surprise was at all times a movie theatre just waiting to happen. Bowing to the obvious, Threeb, the Odd Surprise, shouldn't have been as thoroughly invested in film as the rest of us. Yet he was there for every showing, owing to Bob Merriman.

Here's how it came about. The Original Bobster needed a delivery person, seeing as how Bobbie Sue was already pretty busy with the concession sales side of the business and his esposa Sue was often out on location performing her mental telepathy transformations on difficult horses. So Bob Merriman figured he ought to teach Threeb to drive, calculating that the Odd Surprise would be a dependable delivery boy—what with the fewer distractions that his condition occasioned—and could be counted upon to get the concessions out to the drive-out in plenty of time for the show. That would allow the Senior Merriman more time for his role as Winemaster of Sinfandel Sellers. So Bob set about resurrecting an old work truck that some Passing Surprise had abandoned on his way to a less-demanding environment, an ugly machine which in color could best be categorized as dented and in gears rated no higher than granny, seeing as how the rig's transfer box had failed to transfer. Next, he welded up a set of thirty-foot-long curb feelers and attached them all around the vehicle's perimeter, then replaced the truck-bed with a modern version of the old cattle-trail chuck box. With its strange slow-moving profile and pulsating palps it was straight-way dubbed the Creepy-Crawly and was, without question, the perfect laboratory for Threeb's experiments in driving. In no time, and with no major damage and without a single life lost—unless you want to be niggling enough to count the one or two of Maya Gandhi's nameless fur-balls that turned up shy of a taco—Threeb was motivating about with abandon, and was a fixture at every movie-showing as he soon became Bob's favorite concession stand pilot.

The Odd Surprise added much more than his delivery skills to the Flatlands Drive-Out Theatre experience. He soon began offering advice on which films to screen, and of those screened which to offer on repeat nights and which to bring back later for encore runs, for, it so turned out, he had both excellent taste and cultured refinement. Odd, you might say, given his occluded oculars. Thing was, he selected and evaluated the various Hollywood offerings with his ears.

Short the one physical sense from the git-go, he'd long made up for the loss by sharpening the remaining four and by adding a sixth, or maybe even a seventh or eighth. Threeb disdained complimentary amazement over his listening skills, never wavering from his routine response—I don't hear or touch or taste or smell any better than any of you, I just pay better attention—though now he also spoke with refinement, having paid some of that attention to the lingo and patter of the better-educated Surprises.

From the nuances in the delivery of their lines he could infer the facial expressions of the actors, especially their eyes, the latter an exceedingly ironic skill. He could deduce body movements merely from the actors' pauses and their hesitations and their silences. Adding in the sound-effects and the score, he could not only summarize the plot but offer-up a startlingly-accurate prediction of what was up next.

And ¡the music, the songs! Why, he could have been a disc-jockey. And should have been. He knew who cut what and when and where, the release dates and whether or not the recorded song preceded its use in the film and he knew if the radio version was different than the soundtrack version, and which was better. And remembered it all.

At the same time, he wasn't just a walking catalog, not just an inventory. It was his assessment for the music as art that was unequaled, his outlook shaped and his skills and knowledge sharpened—without question, I'd say—by having shared a roof with Handy Jones, imbibing as he did the full measure of the Song of Surprise almost each and every waking moment, so that his exposure was not just to the thing itself but to the very ethos from whence it sprung, the cosmological constant of life-imitating-art, a concept as fundamental to the *weltanschauung* of Handy Jones as was the speed of light to that of Al Einstein. Come to think of it, had Handy been a shade or two lighter and worn a tweed coat, he might have been mistaken for the somewhat-better-known Prophet of Physics.

So it came to pass that Threeb took the Song of Surprise the next and logical step. Surprise had been sung into existence, for sure, but the Song could do more than just keep it alive. Much more. The songline was life-imitating-art. The movie music was art-imitating-life. Threeb's brilliant insight was to put them together, life-imitating-art-imitating-life. With the Song, he realized, we could also change Surprise. And if we could change Surprise, we could change the world. Without knowing it, the Odd Surprise had become the first Beat, the first Hippie, the first New-Ager.

6.

BY THE WAY, ¿HOW ARE THINGS IN YOUR TOWN?

The melodies and beats of music, the flow and meter of poetry—these permeated daily life in Surprise. That's because it was so close to the melodies and beats and flows and meters of the natural world. In turn, Surprise was so near to the natural world because it was known from the beginning that the hamlet's existence was both ephemeral and the better for its ephemerality, seeing as how it's a place built on wheels by people on the move, sung into existence by an outcast who discovered the Song of Surprise and forever dependent upon its singing for its continued existence. That, coupled with Threeb's E-equals-M-C-square-ish discovery of the life-imitates-art-imitates-life equation, meant that ordinary life in Surprise was extraordinarily musical.

And somewhat expected. The Ukuladies, for one. Music came naturally to both Bobbie Sue and my sis Kerrie Mae. They began playing the ukulele as kids, little more than tykes, really. Bobbie Sue, being her mother's daughter, was born to the spotlight, and, being her father's daughter, was saturated with get-up-and-go. Kerrie Mae, both the eldest child and the only daughter of baccalaureated teachers, brought a studied air to the ensemble's mien and a Welsh poet's musicological ear to the selection of their material. Tall and lithe, Kerrie Mae was the maypole around which Bobbie Sue danced the be-bop boogie. Kelly and I were merely accessories after the fact. I wasn't much of a picker, more square than hipster, only interested in being part of the band because I had a bad case of the hots for Bobbie Sue, as if not every one else did, either, and as if she'd notice a young annoyance like me even if I was the only boy in the burg, or in the band. For the same reasons I was always stuck in right field in softball, I was saddled with the bongos in The Ukuladies. Kelly was sweet on my sister and, besides, was more genetically drawn to the footlights than was the moth to the flame, so, he too joined-in with the self-appointed role of comic-relief-chief, often in grass-skirt-and-coconut-shell-bra drag. His little sister Ruth Etta, despite her youth, could not be kept away from live music. Cute as a Kewpie Doll, she could dance before she could walk, sing before she could talk, and had her daddy's photographic memory for lyrics, instantly becoming proof of W. C. Fields's admonition regarding sharing the stage with children. Rounding out the combo was Threeb, sound-man from the start, roadie and pilot soon thereafter, guru much later.

When in town, the Ukuladies both practiced and performed in the second-floor auditorium of the Old School House, none of the Airstreams being commodious enough for such an assembly of musicians and their instruments. The ever-resourceful Bob Merriman found and procured for the band a very clean, hardly-used Fender Dual Pro Twin amplifier and an RCA 44A ribbon microphone, then built a tall stand that could hold the bi-directional mic chin-high in the center of the group. The homemade PA filled the auditorium to full, but the stand also broke-down for travel, making it possible for the Ukuladies to book gigs in the small towns 'round about. Though there wasn't much diameter in 'round-about as, unless Bob had time to transport them in the Coop, the only bandwagon conveyance to be had was the Creepy-Crawly, seeing as how it was the sole and single vehicle approved for operation by their driver/roadie/sound-man. With a highway speed of between five and ten miles-per-hour, depending upon the direction and amount of wind and road grade, the Creepy-Crawly was both a curse and a blessing. A curse for the obvious: it took a long time to get to the gig. A blessing for the not-so-obvious: once at the city-limits of the destination town, it took a long time to get to the venue. Perhaps the first set of wheels to define low-and-slow, the Creepy-Crawly cut quite a figure, surrounded by the vibrating and undulating curb-feelers, a young-brown-Ray-Charles-look-a-like behind the steering wheel, The Ukuladies standing up in the back, playing and singing, sort of like the winning float in a one-float parade. It moved so slowly and so stately that it gave the curious local Ordinaries a fine chance to walk alongside and behind it, forming a natural procession that wound around through the town and up to the stage, a built-in-SRO crowd, everyone arriving just in time for the evening's entertainment. ¡Synchronicity!

There were a few Accidentals of the First Order that added to the musical fabric of Surprise by bringing both warp and woof with them. Our favorites, by acclamation, were the Denver Bongos. In the 1930s, a lonesome Nebraskan developed six-man football in order to allow the smallest of towns to join their larger neighbors in giving up their fall Fridays and building healthy-or-not-so-healthy animosities with their nearest opponents. The pared-down game spread quickly to Texas, which held its first half-yas-yas-yassed contest between Sylvester and Dowell in the whole-yas-yas-yassed stadium in Rotan. With all players being eligible receivers, what the new version of the old slug-fest contest lacked in the number of bodies slamming into one another on the field it more than made up for in the speed of play and the primacy of offense. Scoreboards were soon getting such a workout that the Texas leagues added a mercy rule: if at any time after the half one team led by 45 points, the game was called. The new rule added to the lexicon; the team that won in such manner was said to have 'forty-fived' their opponents.

Not surprisingly, Surprise had only a history of near-misses with six-man football. Might could have fielded a team in the late 1920s when the Yates oil play was peaking, but, ¿wouldn't you know? six-man rules were a decade away. And when the speedy pigskin pastime had made it that far south and west, the Yates had played down and its associated pool of young fellows had dwindled and dried up, much like the salt lake at Shafter. The Surprises, being such a resourceful bunch, set about writing new rules for an even smaller and faster game—more sandlot than gridiron—with just two men to a side and the goal line in the middle of the field, which saved money on marking chalk and conveniently allowed the overall dimensions of the field to vary based upon the space available. It was a dandy sport, save only a lack of opponents, for it turned out that the only other communities as small as Surprise were ghost-towns, and none of them were very sports-minded. Satisfactorily, though, the enterprising Surprises' hard work paid off when Pablo Johnson stopped by on his way back to Santa Monica, saw one of the proto-intra-city-two-on-two football games in Surprise, then took the rules back with him to form the world's first beach volleyball league.

The Second War to End All Wars had put a drag on professional sports, really on all sports, leaving a huge hunger ready to be satisfied when the boys began coming back from the fronts. Seeing an opportunity, an entrepreneurial cavy of businessmen in the Mile-High City moved quickly to form the Denver Bongos, a cracker-jack six-man football exhibition team, modeled after the Harlem Globetrotters. The plan was to travel from town to town taking on local six-man squads or even full-fledged regular-roster teams—'Six of One, Almost a Dozen of the Other' was their motto—after which they'd take the gate and the merchandise sales. Not only was the football fast and furious, each game was an event. The evenings started with a Black-Tights-and-Beret Bongo Beauty Queen contest pitting the local lovelies against one another, the winner earning the privilege of leading the team out onto the field that night while wearing her black tights and beating out a jungle tattoo on a custom, all-black pair of bongo drums. Speaking of black, the team colors were black on black, a hipster look back when hipsters were beatniks, though it made individual players hard to identify for fans and sportscasters, not that it really mattered as each jersey bore the number 45 in tribute to how often the Bongos won their games on the mercy rule. Nor did the speedy high-country gridiron-grinders wear helmets, just black berets. Along the way, their fans had developed a modern, restrained, hip-nick habit of snapping their fingers and chanting *cool, man, cool* instead of the more traditional, Neanderthal custom of clapping and yelling such boorish, bourgeois blather as *rah, rah, rah, sis-boom-bah.* Though, when the action got particularly hot, an occasional fan could be heard to shout *¡I dig it! ¡I dig it!* That, and the Bongos' penchant for playing only in venues capable of illuminating the gridiron with black-light, narrowed their prospects for commercial success and eventually left them little more than a football footnote.

But they were still grooving and perhaps in their prime when the sexy-sixsters came to the prickly-pear prairies 'round about Surprise. Not to play any team that we Five Surprises could field, no, they simply needed neutral ground for lodging. It was a constant problem for the black-clad bongo-beaters, seeing as how not only did they always forty-five the locals but they also almost always made off with one or more of the beauty queen contestants. A man wearing a black beret and black turtleneck and shiny steel cleats is hard for a country girl to resist. So they made it a team rule not to quarter in a town where'd they'd out-scored their opponents, if you get my drift.

Luckily, one of their advance men had stumbled into Surprise by misdirection but was rewarded for his surprise by uncovering the Shifting Sands Mobile Motel. For there were other folks, the intrepid sorts, who came to Surprise on purpose, came to visit one of the Surprises-In-Residence, or perhaps had business here. *Bid-ness.* Weren't anywhere to stay, though, if the visits were overnight, as none of the Surprises' nests were big enough for guest accommodations, and no one had yet built a hotel on wheels.

Until the Eliots. Shad was always in need of employment, as day-working was always seasonal and mostly unpredictable and as the bit-and-spur-and-tack trade was spotty at best. Prowling the region a-horseback, however, he had the best and first view of abandoned trailers, those quarters left behind by the fizzling of the various oilfield booms and boomlets. He'd mark 'em with a piece of bandana, then bring back Bob Merriman to help him haul the swag back to the home territory. Rose Edna would crank up the Victrola, slap on a 78 of The Four Lads singing 'Istanbul', peel off her threads, and set to cleaning the new rental space. Once a little trailer-house-decorator spit-and-polish was applied by Ruth Etta, the old Kozy Coach or Streamlite or Vagabond was ready for service in the Shifting Sands Mobile Motel.

After concluding a week of forty-fiving in the little burgs around the Alkali Desert—Frankel City, Patricia, Notrees, Goldsmith, all on the Texas side; Nadine, Monument, and Jal 'cross the New Mexican border—and after developing a first-rate fondness for Maya Gandhi's hush puppies, chased after with Bob Merriman's Sinfandel, the Denver Bongos cleared out of the Shifting Sands Mobile Motel, leaving behind only fond memories, one black bean-bag chair, and a couple pairs of bongo drums, the latter soon part of the percussion line of the Ukuladies. Oh, and a not-insubstantial bevy of beauties in the far-flung towns around Surprise who never, ever again uttered the word 'daddy-o' without a far-away, dreamy look, punctuated with a slow, faint finger-snap.

The Shifting Sands Ballets—which I described earlier—involved lots of music. But there was nothing naturally logical about them. Artificially logical, yes. But not natural. They grew out of necessity. Though long removed from their Old-Glory-Rule neighborhood, my Double-Jones parents retained close ties to the home-ground. Soon after the adrenaline stirred by Dubya-Dubya-Dos had spent itself, word came to my folks that a new, dark stain of demagoguery had swept as far west as the old populist hang-outs on the Brazos and were oozing our way. Hectored by the elected hangers-on in our nation's capitol—who'd themselves contributed little or nothing to the war effort save waving the flag—J. Emperor Hoover and his Fee-Bees—what local sheriffs and flat-feet called the boss and the operatives of the FBI—these conspiracy mongers were building their dossiers on homosexuals and disloyal Americans so as to be ready to jail 'em all the moment that the next war broke out. As subscribers to *The Daily Worker* my Jones clan would be the first in their cross-hairs.

The heart of the problem was the feeding frenzy going on in Washington betwixt the Senate—led by Joe McCarthy and his henchman, Herman 'Little Joe From Idaho' Welker—and the House Un-American Activities Commission—cheered on by Thomas and Hart, a couple of joiks from Joisey. Plain and simple, there just weren't enough queers and commies to go around, which drove up the market on subversives and sent the Fee-Bees out to the far reaches of the nation's hinterlands in search of prey. Gene D. and Mary Ellen read the news, talked to their home-peeps, knew what was going on, and felt like the Surprises ought to be informed. They were prepared to emigrate if Handy Jones and the other Foundling Families deemed it best.

A council commenced on the veranda, but was soon counted serious enough to move upstairs into the auditorium. The problem was laid-out and the consequences made clear, my Double-Joneses concluding the briefing with their gallant offer to take their Silver Cloud on the road. A long silence ensued. The normally-reticent Shad was first to stand and speak. He recited the whole of Yeats's 'Easter, 1916'. On the last line, the final repetition of *A terrible beauty is born,* Rose Edna chimed-in with Sister Rosetta Tharpe's 'Strange Things Happening Every Day', sung at first *a cappella,* but quickly joined by the ukuleles of Kerrie Mae and Bobbie Sue. After Handy Jones and Maya Gandhi ended the community musical response with a fiddle-and-tabla duet on The Song of Surprise, it was Bob Merriman's turn to weigh-in—Listen up, he said. Here's the plan. An it don't involve no road trips. Least ways, not ourn. I ain't got no truck with runnin'.—to which Handy Jones nodded in agreement, his constant smile this time touched with a glint of steel.

Bob asked that Sue write up a renter's notice for the trailer-cabins of the Shifting Sands Mobile Motel, which my mom volunteered to type-up on mimeo so that a copy could be posted in each trailer. The notice gave check-in and check-out times, maximum rates, and, in all capital letters, warned the occupants that it was a long-standing local custom to stage, time and again, a Shifting Sands Mobile Motel Ballet, which, the warning continued, was harmless but came at unpredictable times. Along with the renter's notice postings, my dad was instructed to provide each trailer with a copy of the Bible, the Bill of Rights, a well-thumbed edition of *The Daily Worker,* and the Debs-inspired Pledge of

Unallegiance—That one'll guzzle their gizzards, said Bob. Finally, the Merry-Meister borrowed an extra Victrola from the Eliots.

Kelly and Threeb and I were given our assignments along with the Large Surprises, a thing that we did not take lightly but surely did take with pride. There were rehearsals, debriefings, and slight realignments of duties and responsibilities. And just in time. Punto Rojo's ears began twitching moments after our last tune-up on the ballet, and, seemingly on cue, a fleet of government-gray Nash-Ramblers rumbled into Surprise. They stopped first at the Ser-Sta-Gro, made inquiries, were sent to the Shifting Sands Mobile Motel where they booked a number of trailers for the night, after which they went to the Old School House for a cup of coffee where they asked whether or not there was a local cafe and, when they expressed surprise at realizing they were at that moment situated in the only bean joint in town, came up short after Handy Jones offered to hunt down a couple of armadillos to roast for their supper. Tastes jist like possum on the half-shell, offered Handy. The Fee-Bees declined—politely, I might add—then bought up all the soda crackers and canned beans and Spam that the Ser-Sta-Gro carried in its inventory—indeed, several cans of which had been there from the inception of the Ser-Sta-Gro a few decades back, well-exceeding any best-if-sold-by package labeling—before the Federales repaired to their trailer-cabins.

We waited for a good half-hour after the last lamp in the last aluminum cocoon went dark before quietly hooking each trailer to a pickup or automobile or horse. When all the connections were secure, Bob Merriman cranked up a Victrola with Blind Boy Fuller's 'Step It Up and Go', cuing us by shooting off a flare just as he dropped the needle in the groove. We fired up our machines and wagon teams, took the hand-brakes off our wheels, and began pulling the trailers around the mesquite thickets in a beautiful, well-choreographed, elegant ballet. All that was missing were toe-shoes and tutus. Lights went on in the cabins and doors were flung open, only to be hastily snapped back shut as the prickly pear and cholla scraped along the metal sides of the rolling rooms. We couldn't hear what the mid-pay-grade government grays were saying, but we read lips well enough to know that they hadn't read their rental notices or, if read, hadn't fully comprehended our local custom.

When Blind Boy Fuller had finished, Bob-the-Merry had the second Victrola cranked and ready with The Weavers' 'Tzena, Tzena, Tzena'. And while it was playing he cued-up Kokomo Arnold's 'The Twelves' on the first player, and, once that one was underway, flipped The Weavers platter to be ready for the final number in the last movement of the ballet, 'Goodnight, Irene'. We kept the tin-cans moving until Irene was tucked away, then dropped the trailers wherever they happened to be on the sound of the final note. The dust hadn't quite settled when the dazed and disoriented detectives de-camped from their bobbled and bangled boudoirs. As they staggered out into the thorny thicket they were waved over to a big bonfire above which Handy Jones and Maya Gandhi were roasting small animals. As a set of bongos could be heard playing in the darkness just beyond the glow of the fire, the Surprises all left their posts to form a big welcoming circle, softly singing the chorus to 'Goodnight, Irene' over and over. In a perfect complement, all the local coyotes were a-howl, as we'd been sure to pick that night's ballet songs from a list of the wily canines' very favorites.

There was much head-scratching by the discombobulated bureaucrats, though, all-in-all, they took it right well, even to the point of seemingly being genuinely touched when Maya Gandhi offered each G-man a Surprise memento that consisted of small lap robes, little quilts oddly fashioned from rectangular, multi-colored patches of fur. 'Lap Puppies', she called them, beaming. One or two, it was said later, wound up in the National Museum of Crime and Punishment, prominently featured in the J. Emperor Hoover Cross-Dressing Disguise Display.

The Fee-Bees got up earlier the next morning than any of us Surprises had anticipated. They were gone long before sun-up, but left their cabins tidy, the beds well-made with the linens tight enough to bounce a quarter off the top chiffon. There was a helpful note stuck with a piece of chewing-gum to the door of the head-man's hang-out that gave instructions on how to submit a proper invoice for payment for lodging. While she was cleaning up the next afternoon, Rose Edna found a yellow-pad that had been carelessly left behind on the honcho's bed stand. My father Jones applied the obliquely-held pencil-lead soft-stroking technique to the pad, revealing the indentations left by the note written on the now-long-gone sheet above it. I'll summarize—tell Big Suck this tip didn't pan-out. Crazies here. Pass on info about them to National Geo's Native Peoples Exploitation Team—then, sadly, he'd ended—how the [foockle] long till I get my gold watch????

Years later, I managed, through the force of the Freedom of Information Act and the good offices of a pal in the NSA, to obtain a copy of the after-action report filed on this, the very first Shifting Sands Ballet. Other than translating 'Big Suck' to 'Director Hoover', it read pretty much the same as the yellow-pad missive cleverly illuminated by my dad so many years ago.

The Shifting Sands Mobile Motel Ballets were repeated from time-to-time, never with so much preparation or with so much riding on the outcome as had encumbered the first performance. Still, there were occasions. Sometimes it was out of boredom. Sometimes it was to give the what-for to the why-nots, the I-wish-you-wouldn'ts, the guests who were never so welcome as when they left. Not long after J. Emperor Hoover's hench-squad took their powder, we held a second Shifting Sands Ballet as a tribute, though it was more a dirge than a ballet.

It was danced in honor of Venable Jones of Idella, one of my dad's or mother's second or third cousins, once or twice-removed. We actually never knew exactly which or how far. Cousin Jones had been a life-long bachelor—a thing that made him peculiar—a cotton-farmer of the one-row school—a thing that made him pitiful—and a Yellow-Dog-Democrat and conscientious objector, a man who never so much as owned a flyswatter, let alone knew how to operate one—all things that made him suspect. He was odd, there was no doubting that, but a God-fearing man who gave to the Presbyterians in spite of their modernist leanings. The Fee-Bees, in their awful sweep through the Brazos River upland cotton country, had come upon an old stack of Facts for Farmers newspapers in Cousin's outhouse. It was a leftist rag, all right, but one that had been saved and conserved for a practical purpose, given the evidence. In retrospect, a good legal-eagle defense-man would have asked the government goons if there were any pages missing after their visit to the one-holer.

Bodily movements and political movements are more closely connected than we think, and on that philosophy, and on the simple need of the hunter not to come home with an empty game-bag, the Fee-Bees arrested their meadowlark and hauled him off to Dallas as a Communist sympathizer. The judge never blinked, turning Venable Jones free at first wink of the indictment, but the damage had been done. Cousin Venable had been set adrift from home and hearth, from friend and family, and from belief in either the All-Mighty or the All-American. When the bailiff went to set him loose, Cousin Vee was found hanging by his shoelaces from the window bars of his cell, a note sticking out of the center chest pocket of his over-hauls.

For the kick-off, instead of the up-tempo stuff, Bob M. substituted Peetie Wheatstraw's 1941 cut of 'Give Me Flowers While I'm Living', filled-in the middle ground with a bootleg Sacred Harp shaped-note recording of 'Ye Objects of Sense and Enjoyments of Time', then closed with The Carter Family's 1927 recording of 'Will the Circle Be Unbroken?' At the end, Shad Eliot read Cousin Venable's hand-written suicide note aloud, giving it the intonation of a prayer: *Innocence is no antidote for loneliness.*

By the way, ¿how are things in your town?

7.

PARADISE LEFT

The world was all before them, where to choose — John Milton, "Paradise Lost"

It was the Summer of '58, and the First Flight of the Five Surprises was fledging. Hatched together, they were adorable babies, cute chicks, and beautiful teenagers, though they looked nothing alike. And though they behaved nothing alike, either, they were together so often that from the git-go they were treated as a single, three-headed child, even by their parents. Los Dos Surprises, Ruth Etta and me, we were always hangers-on, despite never being excluded by the Big Three from whatever was happening in Surprise. Threeb, the Odd Surprise, living as he did in a different astral plane, was the Universal Constant, a part of everything and everyone, but also apart from both.

Like the goddess Ceridwen for whom she was named, Kerrie Mae was the intellectual, the reader, the mother of the poet but not the poet herself, calm and analytical, the bed-rock center of the trio. Like Muriel Rukeyser, whom she adored, my sis grew to be tall and broad-shouldered with an elegant profile and with legs—as others have told me—longer than a preacher's public prayer. She seldom spoke, communicating volumes with a slight lift of an eyebrow or with the hint of a smile or a frown. Or by doing, her first choice in saying what needed to be said.

She was also brilliant. I say this as her little brother, forever doomed to the expectation to be as smart as my older sister and forever doomed to fall short. Though none of the Five Surprises endured regular stints at any of the public school systems owned and operated by the Ordinaries, the Double-Joneses saw to it we were ensconced in class when any of the standardized tests were offered, and we took them all. And we all did well. Save for Kerrie Mae, who did better than well, acing them every one. Long before she was ready to fly the coop, she'd been offered full-ride scholarships to several of the best universities in the Continental U. S. of A.

One would expect, and one's expectations would be correct, that Bobbie Sue was the perfect complement to Kerrie Mae. If a yardstick were to be employed, it could be shown that the-girl-next-door Miss Merriman was a full head shorter than Miss Jones. A seamstress's tape would have returned fewer inches in her waist, more alphabet in her bosom, and more swing in her hips. But, truth is, her physical measurements were merely abstractions because she filled up a space, any space, the moment she entered. Fashioned of pure energy, she was never at rest, though had she held still for even the slightest instant it would be clearly seen that she was strikingly beautiful, a Greek goddess plucked from a beach-blanket-bingo movie.

Bobbie Sue was the Queen of Expressions, her most common being 'Golly'—said almost under the breath—then 'Golly-gosh'—with a bit more emphasis—and 'Golly-gosh-golly'—saved for the most astounding of situations. When she really hated someone, she'd smile like a televangelist's wife and utter, somewhere between and purr and a croon, 'Well, bless their heart'—the length of the spaces between the words telling just how mad she was, the longer the space, the more venom. She was never known to brood or whine or complain, neither was she ever known to wax nostalgic or nurse a hurt. Always facing forward, the past meant nothing to her, nothing at all. I, of course, was desperately in love with Bobbie Sue, and never more so than when she discovered Levi shorts.

It was natural then, with Kerrie Mae the guardian of all that was and Bobbie Sue the spark of all that would be, that Kelly was the one that is. Without intent or even recognition and certainly without understanding, he lived perfectly in the moment. It was the fuel of his humor. Though I should point out that one can be most humorous when one doesn't consider the consequences of humor, and as Kelly's vocabulary was mostly physical, it had no correspondent for consequence. When not mugging for camera or audience, he was a handsome lad, having the dark and sultry features of a Spanish Grandee—courtesy of his mother's royalty—coupled with the laconic ruggedness of a B-movie western hero—courtesy of his dad's cow-puncher tribe.

Kelly had an instinct for the spotlight, not for where it was but for where it was about to be, an instinct that for accuracy and ruthlessness could only be compared to the shark's instinct for blood. He had his father's perfect memory for lines and his mother's perfect sense of drama. He was, in long and in short, the perfect thespian. And he was my best bud, my pal, my hero, and my constant responsibility.

Ruth Etta was exactly like her older brother, only reversed, flip-flopped. She was just as funny, but always the butt of her own jokes. Just as dramatic, but always the target of her own drama. In conclusive proof that there was, indeed, a God, she also inherited her mother's penchant for nakedness, and the body that went with it. By the Summer of 1958, though she was only fourteen, she was already equipped for the main stage.

As for me, well, I was tall like Kerrie Mae, and, like her, a reader. But where she read to learn about the world, I read to learn how to write about it. She wanted to know, I wanted to know how to show other people what to know and how to know it. Some like to eat, some like to cook; I'm a cook. I always thought myself to be gangly when I was around Kelly, and frumpy when I was around Bobbie Sue. Nevertheless, in photographs I wasn't unhandsome.

To complete the Five Surprises Plus One, Threeb was growing up, too. We were all plagued by acne, he was plagued by visions. We had wet dreams and left embarrassing spots on garments and bed-sheets, he had hallucinations and—on the darkest of nights—could be seen to have an aura like a full-body halo. If he'd ridden into Jerusalem on a mule, he'd have been taken for a blind Jesus. To which Kelly would have surely shouted out, ¡Jesus! Heal Thyself. And been sorely surprised and a little offended when the crowd turned the rocks on him.

The world was on the cusp in 1958. *The Daily Worker* sent forth its last edition on the Ides of January, its blue-collar song picked up, not by the good-night-David-and-good-night-Chet mainstream choir, but instead shaken-rattled-and-rolled by a new music flooding the radio waves. The Hula Hoop set about training the first generation of go-go dancers. ¿So what if the Dodgers left Brooklyn? They went to L. A. ¿Wasn't everybody doing it? *Gigi* was on the screen, Elvis was in the Army, the Everlys and Buddy Holly and The Killer were on the radio, Ike was on the golf course. The enemy of the revolution is nostalgia. ¡Long live The King!

It was the spring of springing-out, the summer of so-longs. Kerrie Mae, after mulling about it over the whole of the winter, had decided to study biochemistry at the University of California at Berkeley. Kelly and I never did understand what biochemistry was. And still don't. Bobbie Sue may not have, either, but, bound and determined to remain as close to her pal as possible, accepted a sand volleyball scholarship at Santa Monica College so as at least to be on the same side of the continent as Kerrie Mae. Because Kelly hadn't even yet considered where he might climb the higher rungs of education, the two girls—perhaps in exasperation, perhaps in resignation, but most likely in recognition of the reality of their best boy buddy—the two girls had already laid their plans without requiring his participation in their consultations. Bob Merriman found another VW minibus, this one rigged-out as a camper, which he offered for the trip west. So, come mid-August, it was to be Wagons, ¡Ho! for Bobbie Sue and Kerrie Mae. A road trip into the sunset, drop off Kerrie Mae in the Bay Area, thence Bobbie Sue down to SoCal with the wheels.

Kelly did have plans. He always had plans. He just never knew about them until they were well underway. Last fall, he'd kiped a trip up to Lubbock with a drama class from Odessa Permian or Andrews High or maybe the Notrees Glee Club. While he was in the Hub City he'd seen a production in the then-new Lubbock Little Theatre building, met a couple of young actors there. One, Barry Corbin, was going to Texas Tech in the fall to study drama. ¿Why don't you come, too? he asked Kelly. Having no answer to the contrary, Kelly decided that, once the VW camper bus had faded into New Mexico, he'd hook his thumb north to Lubbock.

In a place as small as Surprise, there weren't other kids to date, so the First Flight of the Five Surprises always did things together. They didn't date in the strict sense of wearing one-another's ring or letter-sweater—as there were neither ring nor letter-sweater in Surprise—and didn't go steady. No, wait, they *did* go steady. The three of them went steady. They were always out together, the Sock-Hop Three Musketeers. But as the world wasn't yet ready for such an arrangement, Bobbie Sue decided early on that Kerrie Mae and Kelly would be sweethearts, and the two of them accepted it as a given, to the point they planned—or perhaps Bobbie Sue planned for them—to go off to their respective colleges and then marry once they'd become diploma-ed.

In mid-August after their high school graduation, the night before the two girls were to leave in the Merriman VW camper-bus for California and Kelly was to hitchhike up to the Llano Estacado, Bobbie Sue organized a going-away party for the three of them. She borrowed her dad's drive-out movie rig, snitched a couple of bottles of his Sinfandel, talked Maya Gandhi out of a couple of peyote buttons, and the three of them went far out onto the prairie to watch their favorite films. Kelly picked 'The Phantom Empire', long a top choice amongst the Surprises, while Kerrie Mae chose a new, intellectual foreign film, 'The Seventh Seal'. Bobbie Sue brought along a surprise feature, an uncensored copy of 'And God Created Woman', one her dad won from a Dallas film distributor in a poker match.

A born facilitator, Bobbie Sue had chosen her movie with a specific intent. She was certain that her two best friends had yet to consummate their romance—indeed, when had they ever been alone for such an endeavor—and she was afraid that, if they didn't, each might fall to someone else once they got to college. She didn't understand why that should bother her at all, but it bothered her mightily. Bobbie Sue figured the combination of the Sinfandel and the Bardot film would be enough to propel the two nascent lovers into action. She planned to save the peyote for herself, which would allow her to withdraw into her own space while her two besties cemented their spiritual bonds in the natural, physical way.

It was a beautiful night. A new moon allowed the clear West Texas sky to vibrate with millions of stars. A light, cool breeze wafted over the intimate drive-out audience, intoxicating them with the perfume of every blossom of every prickly-pear and every desert willow from miles around. The Sinfandel was intoxicating on its own, and Bobbie Sue could see the eyes of her companions become first dreamy and then, when the Bardot feature got rolling, even lustful. But the two beautiful fumblers seemed frozen, filled with desire but unable to make the first move. So Bobbie Sue, ever a woman of action, took charge. She stood up from their picnic blanket and, with the images of the Bardot film playing on her, began a slow, provocative strip-tease. Fully naked, she bent over, pulled Kerrie Mae to her feet, and began to undress her as well. Shocked for the first moment, Kerrie Mae uncharacteristically began to giggle, then laugh. Without prompting or discussion, the two then set upon Kelly, standing him up, unbuttoning and unzipping shirt and Levis and pulling off Jockey shorts and socks until the three of them were dancing naked in the flickering light of the movie projector, their clothes strewn about the scrub-brush.

Bobbie Sue stepped back so as to let Kerrie Mae and Kelly have their way with one another. But the two just stood and stared, each mesmerized by the other's beauty but as stock-still as statues. No idler, Bobbie Sue put her arms around them both, creating a three-way embrace before issuing the command for a kiss, which unintentionally became a three-way kiss, an unintentionally-long kiss. Very long. When they broke, they were startled. Not just Kerrie Mae and Kelly, but Bobbie Sue, too. In that instant, the three understood with a knowledge beyond words that they were lovers, all of them, each of them, together.

The night became beautiful in a different way. Within the musty-musky depths of one another's physical selves—the flurry of shared fingers and tongues all gravitating to the dark triangles around which vibrated and undulated and gyrated the larger, single triangle of Bobbie Sue and Kerrie Mae and Kelly— within that paradise of skin and motion the spiritual universe became infinite with the possibility of perfection in love. Every cell was a stimulus, every cell a receptor. Taste and touch and mind and body and heart and soul all wrapped around one another, a ceaseless climbing-up to the bright and shining window into the center of the Universe. When the first light of dawn awoke them, they looked on the old world in a new way, freed from the boundaries of childhood but without having given up its wonder and its joy. It was love, and they knew it. Coming back to Surprise, they pledged that love, each to each, without ever having said a word.

¡Golly, gosh, golly!

Saturday morning, the two girls set out for California. Somewhere along Route 66, they stopped and got matching tattoos on their left shoulder blades. Kerrie Mae drew out a Venn Diagram of three intersecting circles, which Bobbie Sue modified by making the center space shared by all three circles into the shape of a heart. They never told anyone of the circles, or why they never married, or who was the father of the child that had sprung to life in Kerrie Mae's womb before they'd ever reached the Golden State.

Years later, in New York City, Kelly awoke from a strange, paradoxical dream of both longing and satisfaction. All he could remember was an image. That next morning he sketched it for a tattoo artist who placed it tastefully on the young actor's left shoulder. It was a Venn Diagram of three intersecting circles, the space shared by the three geometric forms in the unmistakable organic shape of a heart.

8.

POSTCARDS HOME

On the same Friday as the going-away party that the First Flight of the Five Surprises threw for themselves, and a mere fifty-two leagues give-or-take to the north-north-east, Saint Buddy Holly was marrying a pretty young Puerto Rican whom the locals in Lubbock feared to be Mexican. The next day, whilst Bobbie Sue and Kerrie Mae were packing up for their California expedition, the newly-weds were winging their way to a honeymoon in Acapulco, after which they chose not to return to the Prejudice Plains but, instead, to relocate to far-away New-York-New-York. A scant few months later—about the same time my parents got the postcard with the casual mention of a baby on its way into the next generation of Surprises—Buddy Holly died in a plane crash, his halo head-gear intact but an eternity of words and notes scattered across the Iowan tundra.

Things went on in Surprise the same as they always had, excepting that nothing was at all the same. Kelly had hitched his way up to the Hub City, managed to enroll for the fall semester at Texas Tech, and, helped along by his almost-Mexican profile, snagged a bus-boy's position at Bruce's Aztec Inn. Like his nest-mates on the Golden Coast, he was too busy to write often, and the cards that he managed to post in the dorm-lobby mail-box were mostly of the hi-mom-and-dad-summer-camp-is-still-fun variety. One note did mention that he'd been picked as the under-study for a non-speaking spear-carrier role at Lubbock Little Theatre.

Sadness had rolled in to Surprise on a mist, not a fog, just a dull depression that took the bright edge off every ordinary thing. Ruth Etta and Threeb and I found ourselves listening mostly to instrumentals, for songs with words always reminded us of our absent companions. 'Beyond the Sea' made Ruth Etta break down in tears, 'There Goes My Baby' had the same effect on me, and for Threeb, who was a step or two ahead of us in musical sophistication, what did him in was

Dinah Washington's 'What a Difference a Day Makes'. Throughout that year, Dave Brubeck may have saved our lives. Certainly saved our dispositions.

Threeb at least had his own music. Ruth Etta and I had only been part of the larger combo of the Ukuladies, neither of us talented enough to set toes to tapping on our own. Handy Jones, perhaps seeing his own twilight better than we saw it, stepped up his work with the Song of Surprise by longer and more intense sessions with the Odd Surprise. Maya Gandhi, too, recognized Threeb's gifts and took him into her tipi for lessons on her Indian-Indian tabla. We were glad for him, but were having trouble finding our own gladness.

The First Flight having flown and the Odd Surprise having grown so intently focused on the philosophy and power of music, Ruth Etta and I found ourselves more and more together, more and more often. She had all her mother's charms, both the physical and the goofy, all wrapped-up in her father's poetic serious-ness. It was an awkward combination, as awkward as that last sentence, but—once unraveled—a melding that revealed untold powers. Early in spring, the mesquites having just signaled the last danger of frost by the sudden uncurling of their bright, light-yellow-green leaves, I happened onto Ruth Etta dancing in a clearing behind the Eliot's Airstream, their Victrola on the ground, 'Blue Rondo A La Turk' spinning on the platter, her body fully aware of all the possibilities of the variations of the song's 9/8 meters. It was mesmerizing. She felt me watching, turned and smiled, dancing now for me as before she'd been dancing only for herself. Never has denim done so much.

By May, then, it was with more than relief when my mother Jones asked Ruth Etta and me to accompany her to Berkeley so as to be present to help with the new baby. We took the Greyhound to Los Angeles where Bobbie Sue was to meet us. As none of our little trio had ever been that far west, we were both big-eyed and bug-eyed the whole roll, taking in the grand vistas and the visual conun-drums of the American West, a landscape that, heretofore, we'd only known from comic books and oater movies. During the long night across the Sonoran Desert both Mother Jones and Ruth Etta managed to catch a few winks, but between the stars and planets swirling around the waning gibbous moon and Ruth Etta's head in my lap, there was no sleeping for me. Once or twice I looked down to catch her awake, looking up at me, some of those same astral lights in her eyes and the soft edges of the moon dusting her lips. She would be fifteen on the second full moon after—the perfect time, I thought, for our first kiss. If I could wait that long. It was probably best that my mother was a light sleeper.

When our ride lurched into the L. A. terminal, we could see the VW camper-bus at the curb, Bobbie Sue standing beside it, waving gaily. What a rush it gave us as just the sight of her confirmed that all was still well in the world, even though the pretty teenager who'd left Surprise a scant nine months before had become a startlingly-beautiful young woman. Curiouser and curiouser, the more I reveled in Bobbie Sue's cover-girl good looks, the more I wanted Ruth Etta, whose hand I had taken while I helped her down the steps of the motor-coach, holding it longer and tighter than was necessary for safety. I could scarcely let go, even when it was time for the group hug, though I was ecstatic that Ruth Etta and I were the last to unclench.

It took a moment or two to retrieve our luggage, then stuff it in the tiny camp-mobile before we lit out for Highway 1 and the Brainy City across the bay from the Paris of the West. Despite the stupendous scenery along the coastal road, or perhaps because of it, the whole trip was a constant gab-fest. Bobbie Sue told us that Kerrie Mae's first year at Berkeley had gone well, all 'A's and the Dean's Honor List twice, and that Bobbie Sue herself had doubled-up on hours and would graduate with her two-year degree at the end of the summer after which the two of them had decided that Bobbie Sue could move north and the three of them would find a nice, big used Airstream to share, maybe even a thirty-foot Liner, make a living playing music together—they'd formed a duet they called the Byamaniacs in tribute to Wally Byam, the inventor of the Airstream and whom they'd just met that winter—maybe also pick up a few odd jobs to help with extra expenses, all the while Bobbie Sue would help with the baby and Kerrie Mae could better focus on school. Really, it was a one-young-woman gab-fest, for if she took a breath between Ventura and San Luis Obispo I couldn't detect it, Bobbie Sue evidently having mastered the continuous breathing practiced by her bag-piping Scots-Irish forbears.

Our only disappointment on the trip so far was that—our knowledge of western geography lacking in the finer details—we'd really looked forward to crossing the Golden Gate, only to find our route carrying us over the longer-but-more-prosaic Bay Bridge instead. Still, by the time we got to Berkeley, the sun was setting and the famous Erector Set monument cut a beautiful silhouette against it. And Kerrie Mae, radiant from the sun on the outside and glowing from the new life growing impatient on the inside, was a monument all her own when we came upon her, standing at the gate of her small student lodging.

We all piled into her tiny address, unloaded our stuff, then went out for Chinese. Ruth Etta and I would rather have ordered Chinese in, for that's what they did in the movies, but acquiesced to the more practical notion of eating in someone else's space, where they'd have to do the dishes and take out the trash on their own. Golly gosh—said Bobbie Sue—you're payin' 'em to do that anyways.

After we'd all read our fortunes and returned to Kerrie Mae's cockroach castle, it was another gab-fest, this one all night long. I was the only representative of my gender present, being son and brother and admirer and hopeful boyfriend, so it bade me to listen more and talk less. Which fit my participant-observer writer's persona, the mien of the geek outsider having always been with me. Even without my contribution, the words ricocheting around the room vibrated the mysterious waters of creation enough so that the baby, either wishing to participate in the conversation or to admonish us all to shut up and allow some sleep-eye, elected to make an entrance into the world early on the morn. It was a fine baby boy, complete with all his fingers and toes and with all his working parts in order, at least as well as could be told in such short sketch. Kerrie Mae named him Taliesin after the Welsh poet-prince, which pleased my mother to no end, but refused to give him a middle name, which pleased my mother not at all, as Mother had suspected, or hoped, that one or more given names might give away the secret of the baby's sire.

He was beautiful, as are all babies in the eyes of those with whom they share genes. Being his uncle, I saw myself in Taliesin, and saw his mother and my own mother and my father, too. But still, I saw him to be his own person, even this early, even in swaddling clothes in his bassinet. It was his eyes, mostly, for in the eyes of the baby we see both the wisdom and the wonder of the world, watching and learning but already knowing. As my fine, new nephew was to soon teach me, babies grow in a very fast arc: cooing and babbling at the beginning, they admire our adult knowledge of the world, soaking up our foggy words, our carefully-modulated noises, processing them in the infinite minds that Providence has wedged into their tiny heads, until, by the age of two or so, they can speak fully and fluently, though in a language incomprehensible to us adults, their one-time mentors, and so they enter a time of impatience and occasional rage, the 'terrible twos' about which you hear so much, a stage that cures itself along about the age of four or five when, now fully conversant in the speech of their tribe, they will thence forward and for the remainder of our lives treat us—their elders—with no better and no more than kind condescension.

When Mother and son were discharged the following day, Bobbie Sue wrenched herself away and drove back to the City of the Angels in order to pack up her few belongings so as to return to the Bay and look for a better, bigger, brighter space for the new, half-nuclear family. Mother and Ruth Etta and I took a motel room a few blocks down the street so as to give Kerrie Mae and the miniature Jones both space and time. I thought mightily about suggesting that Ruth Etta and I hold down the rented cabin in order to allow both Mothers Jones time with the baby, but feared that my motives would be far too transparent.

On the day after the new mother-son combo came home, my own mother Jones undertook to change his diaper. The moment the young poet-prince's male member was uncovered it commenced to spray about the room, provoking my usually staid mother to shriek something on the order of *put a towel on that tiny tally-whacker before it soaks us all,* or at least that's what we remember her shouting. When the gusher was stopped and the laughter following had stopped, the littlest Surprise, christened with the most royal of names, became, from thence forward, known simply as Tally. Which was just as well, since he only had one name, and that one being a name of formal proportions, he would never be able to fully fit in with the Tribe of the Two-Name People, and though a nick-name was not in any way a cure-all, it could, nevertheless, help bridge the chasm.

Writing it down in the Double-Jones family Bible, our mother Jones also realized that Tally had been born on the same day of the month as had his own mother, Kerrie Mae, who'd never have mentioned said fact had it not been discovered otherwise. Things on our arrival had gone at such speed and in such jumble that we'd clean forgotten about the one impending birthday commemoration in our fluster over the about-to-be-birthday. We had, however, brought Kerrie Mae several presents, which she was able to unwrap between diapering and feeding.

By now, Bobbie Sue had returned from SoCal with a lead on a fine, used Airstream Liner, a thirty-footer, one tracked down by her resourceful father Bob, so the crew of us helped to move the new family to better, larger, more Surprising quarters. Ruth Etta and Mother and I stayed a day or two more to help the new crew settle in, making short trips to a nearby five-and-dime on their behalf to help round-out their housing implements and then, on our own behalf, making a bakery run to procure cakes, one large enough for nineteen candles and the other just big enough to write 'Tally' on it in icing.

The trip back home lacked the excitement and the anticipation, the newness and the sense of discovery of the trip out to the coast. ¿How could it be otherwise? the baby was born, we'd reunited with Kerrie Mae and Bobbie Sue, we'd seen the American West unroll into the Pacific. My mother was so worn-out that she slept almost the whole way to Odessa, even though now we were passing in daylight through the landscape that had been hidden by night the week or so before. Her loss, I'd say, for the other side of our round-trip-tickets wasn't a drag, either, as we'd lucked into seats on a Greyhound Scenicruiser—you know, the bus with the upper-level observation deck that's always on the cover of the Rand-McNally, speeding across a Maynard Dixon desert.

Mother preferred the shade of the lower deck, while Ruth Etta and I fairly jumped at the chance to sit up top for the panoramic view of the wide-open spaces. And for the view of one-another's own wide-open eyes. Mostly alone, we talked as we wished, held hands when we could, asking with word and touch and look all the important things that lovers need to know about one another. After we'd ridden far enough into the darkening night to lose the landscape, I made a pillow of my jean jacket in my lap. Ruth Etta smiled, shook her head no, saying, You're the star-gazer—pointing up at the clear glass dome over our heads—you watch tonight. Then she moved the jean-jacket-pillow to her own lap, pulled me down onto it, spending the next couple of hundred miles with her fingers entwined in my hair.

It was red-eye morning when we pulled into the terminal in the Jackrabbit Capital of Texas. Threeb and the Foundling Families were all there, anxious to get us back but mostly interested in our tales of the new mother and child. With great foresight—and let's leave that joke alone—Threeb was the only one to insist that we take photographs, so one of our many preparations had been to learn how to operate the brand-spanking-new Kodak Brownie Starflash that Bob Merriman had located at the brand-spanking-new Gibson's Discount Center in Abilene. We returned with a pile of snap-shots, passing them around before we'd even collected our luggage. In deference to his having been smart enough to suggest the idea, Threeb got first crack at each print, which he slowly and deliberately and lightly rubbed with his fingers, pausing here and there on the photograph, his facial expressions changing as his fingertips moved from face to face on the image, all the while he was humming and half-singing a song we didn't recognize but later learned was an obscure African Methodist Episcopal church hymn passed along to him by Handy Jones, entitled 'Eyes for the Blind'. I, for one, would gladly be the passenger in any vessel piloted or steered by the Odd Surprise, whose name I would also vote to be officially changed to The Continual Surprise.

It was a happy ride back to the co-ordinates of home. Several trips west were discussed and planned before we ever caught the welcoming glimpse of a sun-beam bouncing off a curved aluminum cocoon. There was no mention of who was the father, nor did anyone seem in the least even interested in the question. We had a community supper that evening in the second-floor auditorium of the Old School House. The snap-shots were passed around again and again, and each of us had to take the floor to relate our versions of everything that had happened. Then Handy Jones and Maya Gandhi and Threeb showed-off a few new musical numbers they'd worked up before lighting into The Song Of Surprise to close out the program. There were a couple of smiles when Ruth Etta and I were caught hugging good-night, and I'll swear I heard someone joke that not all the stories of the Famous Trip West had yet been told.

Bobbie Sue's moving north to set-up house with Kerrie Mae and little Tally was not just a decision of the heart, it turned out to be down-right practical. Pooling their time and talents and energy eased the load on everyone. Soon the Surprise Box at the Post Office in Andrews was the busiest it had ever been. Although we'd not been as smart as Threeb had been in suggesting taking the camera to Berkeley in the first place, we'd been smart enough to leave it there, and aforelong we were getting photojournalism updates on a weekly basis.

Postcards, too. Kerrie Mae reported that Tally's favorite song on the radio was Dave 'Baby' Cortez's 'The Happy Organ'. He liked it so much that Bobbie Sue went out and bought a new, plug-in-electrically-powered portable Crosley hi-fi, then brought back to the Airstream Liner an arm-load of 45s that included Dave 'Baby''s jazzed-up Hammond B-3 version of 'Shortnin' Bread' along with several of Tally's other favorites, titles like 'The Purple People Eater' and 'The Battle of New Orleans' and 'Mack the Knife'. When we got a list of the songs that made up the Small Surprise's musical milieu, we hastened to send out several discs that would better shape his young, formative, and impressionable musical mind.

We assumed that, between Bobbie Sue and Kerrie Mae, we'd not need to add to the baby's ukulele repertoire, so we included Brubeck, of course, along with some more jazz, a sampling of the blues greats we'd grown up with, and some new music that Kelly had written about, especially some albums by his new pal Ramblin' Jack Elliott.

Which brings to mind that, while we were galavanting around the American West, Kelly had packed up his thumb and set out for the American East. Some of his Lubbock Little Theatre buddies had made it clear that the real stage work was to be found in New York, going so far as to give him names and addresses that were good for meals and a couch. By instinct, Kelly wound up in the Village, hung out some at Washington Square, and one night at the Gaslight saw two Stetsons on the other side of the room. Up until that moment, Kelly's own battered and dirty silver-belly rancher-roll was the only Western-creased hat he'd seen anywhere since the last ride he'd caught after leaving Texas. He made his way across the club and introduced himself to the hats' owners, who turned out to be a couple of folk singers, Peter La Farge and Ramblin' Jack Elliott. Hi, I'm Kelly one-l-one-t Eliot, the actor—he said. The three had a few drinks. Well, maybe more than a few. Kelly and R. Jack compared last names, R. Jack admiring that Kelly was named for the poet and Kelly admiring that R. Jack had made his last name up by promoting his certificated first name. By the next morning, Eliot and Elliott had struck a pact, Kelly having added another l and another t and R. Jack having been granted a lifetime citizenship to Surprise. And as all of us who know R. Jack know, he's certainly been a Surprise ever since.

Kelly wrote in a follow-up postcard—drawing on his experience with the Ukuladies—that he'd formed a group called The Polka 'Pokes, inspired by having seen the Sgro Brothers' TV appearance on Herb Shriner's 'Two For the Money'. The 'Pokes dressed only in cowboy gear, played only harmonicas—but a full range of the hand-held reeds, including bass, chordal, and chromatic—performing any and all requests, but only in polka time. Being the sole dance band in Greenwich Village, The Polka 'Pokes stayed busy, the basket tips going a long way toward helping Kelly support his acting habit.

Axiom found while translating the DNA of Handy Jones: When you don't know what to do, do what you know.

9.

THE STILL POINT

With Bobbie Sue living and working out west, Pater Bob was running short-handed in all his varied business endeavors, so Ruth Etta and I pitched-in to help-out with the Flatlands Drive-Out Theatre. We got to earn a little money, we got to watch a lot of movies, and—best of all—we got to spend a lot of time together with no questions asked. Being the first Surprise romance made us the centerpiece of what little talk the tiny town could muster-up in lieu of gossip. It wasn't that anyone was mean or spiteful or resentful or judgmental, it's just that they were curious. And maybe hopeful. The first Surprise Baby was 'way out west in California, and, frankly, the consensus was that Ruth Etta and I were the most logical hope for local regeneration.

Little of that registered on us, as you might imagine. We appreciated their interest, up to a point. We just wanted to be wherever the other one was, doing whatever the other one was doing, feeling whatever the other one was feeling. We had no grand plans for our responsibility to the tribe, only the small schemes of young lovers. We were so gooey and syrupy and sweetsey that just being around us could give you a toothache. Not to mention that it was purt-nigh-to-impossible to get real, honest-to-golly-gosh alone-time in a postage-stamp outpost such as ours, for Surprise was small-town raised to *n-the-negative-power.*

If necessity is the mother of invention, passion is the child of opportunity. We managed to sneak a kiss or two when we could. We thought we were being cool about it, but I'm sure that we were espied in the midst of a lip-lock every now and again. Yet the opportunities were so far and few between and their duration so brief that we weren't getting much experience in what we'd heard was called 'making out', a curious phrase that seemed more akin to financial success than to finding true love and as with its cruder cousin, 'scoring', more concerned with achievement than with moving to a higher plane of relationship. Plain and simple, we weren't very good at kissing, the idea of the kiss still being more wonderful than the kiss itself.

Regardless, Ruth Etta and I still had a case of the hots, the temperature of our condition rising with the first stirrings of spring as the natural world commenced its annual business of sprouting and unfurling and blooming, Mother Nature having a fine sense of sex, which we, of course, equated with romance. It was the spring of what was to be a big year, 1960, the artificial world readying itself for the political races of the fall and, in the other major race, Stengel's Yankee royalty already sailing toward a pennant though—unbeknownst to them—also cruising to a bruising upset series loss that would come to the unheralded Pirates. If all that weren't enough, Elvis was just out of the Army, Chevrolet's Corvair was on its way to showrooms across the nation, and Bob Merriman had just scored a big deal on his own.

In the mid-1950s the Superior Oil Company had built a trailer town at Big Lake to house their workers. Not just run-of-the-mill trailers, but Airstream trailers, acres and acres and acres of them. When the oilies began moving away later in the decade, the shiny silver shelters began appearing on the used market and the Master Merriman was there to scope-out and scoop-up the best of the lot. He'd already managed to collect most of the primo units, but one last keeper came along just as he was winding down his Airstream recovery operation, his hired-help already having heave-hoed to the four winds. He needed a driver to pick up the last prize 'Stream, a nice twenty-five foot Cruiser he'd earmarked for the Eliots' Shifting Sands Mobile Motel. Rose Edna didn't have a driver's license, Bob complained, plus Shad was busy day-working and Ruth Etta was a bit young to entrust with traveling alone to Big Lake and thence on to the Tall City to outfit the re-hab with new Firestones.

Opportunity was writ large. I, said I, would be glad to drive. By golly, said Bob, that'll work. Take my truck 'cause it's got air-conditioning and take Ruth Etta with you so you kids can have an afternoon piddling around in town. Pick up the Cruiser in Big Lake, get the tires changed in Midland, enjoy a nice dinner at Luigi's while you wait for the new treads, and don't get any tickets from the Highway Control. And 'member, forecast is windy all day long. Gotta keep both mitts on the wheel. The last said with a smile that told me that Bob was wise to us.

A snap, says I. Ruth Etta, who'd gotten wind of the windfall, was packed and ready by the time I'd gotten the shotgun-seat cleared out on Big Bob's truck. She had a croker sack stuffed with a few things to carry along, which I didn't grouse about, though the amount of stuff in the bag seemed excessive for a down-to-Big-Lake-and-back foray.

There was a heap of hand-holding and much moon-eying on the two-some-thing-hours down to Big Lake, but the seller was ready with the goods and it took us no time to hook up and point ourselves toward the Tall City. We found the tire dealer pretty quick, especially being that we were two hicks from the scrub-brush-sticks—though, in fairness, we had been to California once, had thoroughly dried behind our ears, and had plucked every last hayseed from our hair—then we pounced on the spaghetti at Luigi's, though we had to walk a few blocks downtown to find what was Midland's finest eatery. It had taken a couple of hours to pull the slick-tire 'Stream from Big Lake, wrestling the wind the whole way, and another couple to fit out the new rubber, so, all-in-all, we'd been gone almost the whole day by the time it was time to make time back to Surprise. Ruth Etta suggested that we call ahead with our schedule. My heart sank, as I'd hoped for some time alone sometime on this trip, but, what-the-foockle, life is what it is, so I smiled, a little unconvincingly I imagine, and gave her a pocketful of change for the pay phone.

She was smiling, too, when she hopped up into the cab of the Merriman Transport Truck after the long-distance call, but she was really smiling. Told 'em we were just about to order our supper, she said, and they said to have a nice eye-talian dinner and watch out for deers and drunks on the way back, since it'd be dark 'time we got underway for our Surprise return and, 'sides, there's a full moon tonight and who knows what that'll lead to. She reached over and put her hand on my right thigh. Didn't move it. Just left it there. Do you know how to get out of town? she said. My mouth'd gone dry already, so I just nodded.

I took Telephone Road, the 'way-back-way to the back way. When we'd gotten far enough north that the Twin Cities were little more than a luminescent rim on the southern horizon—a mere line of glitter in the rear-view mirror—Ruth Etta commanded that I find a pull-off. Which I did. The rig was still settling-in to full-stop when she grabbed the croker sack she'd packed for the trip, jumped down from the cab, and gave me explicit instructions to count to one-hundred before I came back to the Cruiser.

I said you can count on me, even though I counted as fast as I could, but, dang it, there's a lot of integers in a hundred. Which was just as well. Soon's I arrived at the centenary number I hustled out of the cab, rushed around almost to the door of the Airstream before I remembered I'd left the keys in the truck and the engine running and the lights on, so I had to retrace my steps and secure the tow vehicle. By the time I got back to the trailer door, Ruth Etta was waiting for me. She'd changed from her five-oh-ones and plaid flannel shirt to a simple, black, strapless dress with a pleated skirt, no shoes or socks, her hair down. Just in time, she said, cranking up a Victrola that must have been part of the contents of the croker sack.

It was the Drifters, singing dance with me, dance with me, dance with me, Ruth Etta holding her arms out to hold me closer, closer and closer while the music played, Ruth Etta swaying with the rhythm, first holding my hips to hers, then with her hands working up my back to my shoulders arriving at my neck at the exact moment Ben E. King crooned the command to put her lips to mine. And she did.

In a blur of moments, moments made of a spate of buttons and zippers and fasteners the like of which I'd never seen before, we were no longer dancers, we were the music itself, we were the melody and the rhythm, we were the beat and the tune. The dance went on all around us. We had become the song for the whole world. We will be lovers when the music ends, promised the real King. And we were.

The Victrola had wound down completely, the needle no longer bouncing against the label, the silence in the Cruiser louder than any alarm clock. ¿May I help you get dressed? I asked, surprising myself, not knowing why I would wish such a strange thing. I want that more than anything in the world, Ruth Etta said, and so I did, and so we did, slowly, carefully, getting one another present-able. It is inexplicable, there are really no words for it, but helping her into her underthings of silk and cotton and wire and then pulling on and buttoning her jeans and snapping the pearl fasteners on her shirt was more intimate, far more intimate, than just having been deep inside her body.

We never stopped touching all the ride back to Surprise. We spoke not a word. We didn't need to. By the time we pulled up beside the Ser-Sta-Gro and shut down the engine, the truck cab was filled with words and ideas and wishes and dreams and hopes and plans and vows and promises. They poured out the moment we opened the doors, a pool of love spreading out from us into our village, welling-up into the night. Handy Jones and Maya Gandhi and Threeb felt it first, emerging from the Old School House and the tipi, then the Foundling Family parents coming out in ones and twos from their trailers until we all stood together in the center of Surprise, our smiles as big and bright as the full April moon overhead.

10.
LETTERS

Our active, vibrant spring strolled into a sultry summer. The Ventures got it going walking, not running, followed right behind by Fats Domino who picked up the baton and would walk it all the way to New Orleans, which maybe was fine as a summer place but wasn't *tout-de-suite*-enough for us, all the while a local boy from Wink was making waves on the airwaves by feeling lonely. Ruth Etta and I had no truck with either walking or slow string arrangements or loneliness, so when Elvis started wailing that it's now or never we were ready for him. By now he meant August, and I was on my way to college. My parents the Double-Joneses had called up their old prof Billy Holden, finagled me a spot in the freshman class, bought me a new suit of clothes and a bus ticket, then the whole of Surprise caravanned over to the Greyhound Transfer Station in Odessa to see me off, politely averting their eyes before I boarded so's Ruth Etta and I could have a good-bye-see-you-on-the-holidays kiss. When I could no longer spy her from the window of the Highway Traveler coach, I took out ballpoint and paper and began my first letter to Ruth Etta.

We Surprises have always been a well-read lot. It's what we did when we weren't working or playing music or eating or, well, whatever else we might be doing when we could be doing it. Not only did we read a lot, what we read was good stuff. To say that we were well-off-the-beaten-path of contemporary culture was an Understatement of the First Order—an award, I might add, that has only rarely ever been bestowed, and never so far as I know in recent times— our medallion-ed understated condition offering up two, very large benefits. The first of which is that we weren't bombarded every moment of every hour of every day with the low-brow, low-class schickle of the shekel-spurred mass-media, or beaten-up by the bombastic blather of the bourgeoisie, or plastered by the pompous palaver of the politicos. The second was that whatever reading matter that mattered was brought to our ranks on purpose by fine folks with fine minds. All the intellectual and philosophical journals and periodicals, the best of the new best-seller lists, all the classics—those are the things that made up our reading material, the textbooks of our school not having been chosen by pompous pointy-headed pip-squeak political appointees. And it's worth noting that true Surprises were always students, always learning, no matter their ages or achievements. Why, the water-closets of our Airstreams were better-outfitted with world-renowned literature than were the best reading-rooms of the best libraries in the country.

Surprisingly, though, we didn't get much experience in writing. Leaving the World of Mammon to the Mammonites, we didn't have much cause for correspondence beyond Surprise. And since we could easily communicate with anyone within Surprise using a voice only slightly louder than a low croon, we didn't need to write much or often to our neighbors and family and friends to get their attention, or to ask a question, or to pass along a bit of information. So Ruth Etta and I resolved to write to each other, often, every day if we could, and to save our letters for the future generations of Surprise. We knew, too, without saying it aloud, that letters were the only arms and lips and fingers that could reach so far and carry so much love.

My first few missals were about college life and goings-on in the Hub City. My dorm room was in Sneed Hall, a venerable lodging situated on the edge of campus along College Avenue. Broadway Drug was across the street with a shiny soda fountain where they served up malts and shakes and a decent hamburger and, if you weren't eating or getting toothpaste or some other such something, there were rows of shelves stocked with things you didn't need but wanted all the more 'cause you didn't need 'em. Dorm food was in no way home-cooking, and if you had a little money and you were tired of drug store 'burgers, the Tower of Pizza was only a couple of blocks away down Main Street and Little Italy about the same the other direction. There was even a Chinese restaurant 'way away past the far south-west corner of campus, too far to walk but someone with wheels was often going there and you could snag a ride.

There were some kids whose folks were well-off and gave them spending change, but most students didn't have any spare money so they worked after school and on weekends. Being of the penurious persuasion, I got a job checking and sacking groceries at the Piggly-Wiggly store at 34th Street and College Avenue, a little over a mile-long-but-certainly-doable walk from Sneed. I actually liked to hoof it, provided the weather was nice, and I always liked the work when I got there. Grocery stores are clean, pleasant places where the work isn't too hard and where you can meet a lot of people. Management depended upon school kids, too, so they understood us pretty well and were especially helpful in scheduling work hours around our classes. They helped out in other ways, too, like giving us first crack at buying the day-old bakery goods and the scratch-and-dent-and-unlabeled canned goods.

Better yet, across College Avenue and down the block across 34th Street from the grocery store were both the Village Movie Theatre and U. V. Blake's Records. On coke-break, I could hike over, slip into Blake's listening booth, and get a drop on the newest tunes. When I expressed interest in the old stuff, too, the blues and race records and hillbilly and such that no one else cared about, the old man that ran the place took a liking to me and would always have something cool set aside for when I came in. First paycheck I bought Ruth Etta a copy of each version of 'The Twist', Chubby Checker's hit and Hank Ballard's older version, so she could compare the two. If I'd give him money for postage, the old man would package the discs properly and put 'em in the mail for me, which was a real help. We got paid every other week, so twice a month a musical surprise arrived in Surprise for Ruth Etta.

School itself was no big shake. Being a child of the Double-Joneses and the little brother of their brilliant daughter, I'd grown up with book-learning. Sue Merriman taught us all about animals and critters and the natural world. Between Handy Jones and Maya Gandhi and Rose Edna Eliot, we got all the social sciences and religion that we deserved, and some we didn't. Bob Merriman and Shad Eliot schooled us in what they called makin'-do and gettin'-by and shade-tree-in', topics the college catalog renamed business and economics and management. Only two of my courses seemed to be built on new topics. One, geology, was pure-dee-fascinating, providing me with names for sights I'd seen on the Great California Expedition and presenting me with reasonable explanations for how things got to be what they are.

The other subject that piqued my interest was mathematics. Cyphering was just another tool to use in Surprise, so I'd never come face-to-face with it as a thing to study. Our tribe were patient trial-and-error people and first-rate estimators. Shad Eliot, for example, was damn-near one-hundred percent fail-safe in counting stock in a pasture, even a pasture measured in sections, even a pasture with brush thick enough and tall enough to hide a horse. Bob Merriman was of the naught-and-carry school who did most of the math he needed in his head, unless the problem called for paper figuring in which case he'd resort to a bullet pencil applied to one of the index cards he carried in the bib pocket of his over-hauls.

Now, here I was in college taking Algebra One and having a swell time of it. In some ways it was self-explanatory, a language with built-in definitions, the equals sign being nothing more than a tiny, symbolic dictionary entry that told you that the stuff that was on one side of it was the same—or as they said in the trade, 'equal to'—the stuff that was on the other side of it. The very best part of Algebra One was that it was, in one sense, one very real sense, all made up, a fiction that produced a reality. Let *n* equal blah, blah, blah—a problem would start out—followed by, if *a* is this and *b* is that, then find *c*. So, there you go: make up a few things, arrange them just-so around the equal sign, and, presto, you've solved for something you didn't know before. And if that wasn't enough to send you, then there were imaginary numbers. ¿How cool is that? numbers that don't exist in the real world so you have to ¡invent them in your head! In the real world, you can have no horses 'cause you never had them, you can have no horses 'cause you once had them and now you don't, but in Algebra World you could have less than no horses, you could have *negative horses*. That'll bend your brain, until you understand that algebra is just literature writ in a language of symbols, its equations and theories really nothing more than poems and short-stories and, probably in Algebra Two, plays and novels, with Calculus One and Two likely delivering screen plays and movie scripts.

Kerrie Mae went to college knowing what she wanted to study. And, by the letters she and Bobbie Sue were sending back from the Golden State, doing very well at it, already about to start graduate school. Now, between the effects of writing letters to Ruth Etta and taking Algebra One, I knew what I wanted to know how to be. A writer. I wanted to be a writer. A fiction writer.

Without luck, I perused the undergraduate catalog for writing courses, so I made an appointment with my English professor, explained as best I could my new-found interest—though I don't think that she ever understood the algebra connection—then sought her advice. ¿Ever thought about being a teacher? she said. My folks are teachers, I replied, among the most admirable people on the planet, I added, but I want to be a writer, I concluded. Well, she said, you can't learn that in school. You can only learn to be a writer by writing, she added, peering at me over her eye-glasses, then making a fuss thumbing through her desk-calendar to see if any other hopeless appointments awaited her. I offered my thanks, then made for the door. I wasn't quite to the hall when she straightened-up in her chair and fairly shouted out, Try the Toreador.

The Daily Toreador, she meant, the student newspaper. Sure. ¿Why hadn't I thought of that? I asked myself as I marched myself straight-way over to the Journalism Building. They didn't have any openings as the semester was already well underway. But do you have a music critic, I inquired. They didn't. But within a half-hour they did. My first column was entitled 'Get Straight On the Twist' in which I laid out the facts about Hank Ballard and his Real-Mc-Coy-version of the undulation-adulation teenage-craze. Letters poured in, most in Chubby's defense. But the editor of The Toreador, a wise-acre upperclassman from Dallas, only cared that they were getting mail in response to my piece. I was in like Flynn. I was now a writer.

In our letters, Ruth Etta and I also shared news about her brother Kelly, who sent us each a card now and then, letting us know about the roles he was getting, mostly soap opera stuff, but also a few speaking parts in other shows. We compared because the facts each time had a curious drift. He asked his sister about their folks, and he'd ask me about some of the pals he'd left behind in Lubbock, so I made inquiries and reported back. I also let him know I was writing. Good, he said, write us a hit play or movie or television series and get me the heck out of the Alphabet Streets. I promised I would. One thing that I didn't share with Ruth Etta was that he always ended his cards to me with an instruction to hurry up and marry Ruth Etta as he was tired of her writing just to tell him about me. I promised I would do that, too.

As soon as it hit the racks, Mister Blake had set aside a copy of the Drifters' 'Save the Last Dance for Me'. I listened to it once, knew it was going to be a big hit, and asked him to send it right away to Ruth Etta, but not before I'd stuck a note in the record shuck that read, I hope you get the drift… love, Thom Ed. I followed with a letter that was the first one not to mention local news and the day-to-day doings of higher education. It was, instead, all about how I felt. How I felt about life, how I felt about coming to understand that my calling was to be a fiction writer, how I felt about her. It was a doozy. I'd even gone so far as to buy some special stationery at Varsity Bookstore, along with a fancy fountain pen with a pump-fill barrel, a gold nib, and a companion bottle of brown ink, a color I thought to be different enough from black or blue or blue-black, but not too precious. I told her what I wanted to do with her and how I wanted to do it. I might have added how often I wanted to do it, too. The letter fairly reeked of passion.

Almost immediately I got a reply from Ruth Etta. It was just a postcard on which she'd written, in all caps, GOLLY-GOSH-GOLLY. That was all I needed. I got out the new one-hundred-percent rag-cotton stationery and my fancy fountain pen and went to work again. I used every adjective I knew, most of them twice, in addition to giving my knowledge of adverbs a good workout. I made myself blush more than once, such that I had to keep the pages shielded with my left hand as I wrote with my right. I delved into detail, leaving the obvious unsaid but not leaving any obscurity sheltered by a single unturned stone. It was so hot that I thought I might not even need a stamp as it might find its way unaided, a self-guided missal.

This time Ruth Etta's reply was instructive. Quit using the fancy new nib and tastefully-chosen ink, she said. Because, she continued, from the start of our correspondence I have developed the habit that with each new letter I take a bath, dry off, then rub the letter over my entire body before going to bed, in order, she explained, to bring myself sweet dreams by osmosis and, she mentioned in complaint, the ink almost always smears, especially the longer and more intensely I rub. And added, blushingly, where I rub. That very day I sold the pen on the cheap to a rich kid on the second floor and with the proceeds bought a box of H-grade drafting pencils. To this day the mere sight of one-H-or-more graphite sends shivers and quakes throughout my whole body. No soft lead for me.

Not many of my fellow students had either time or resources to return home for the short Thanksgiving break, so a few of us from Sneed dressed-up as best we could then car-pooled over to the Furr's Cafeteria in the Family Park Shopping Center at 34th Street and Avenue H. The Muzak alternated holiday pieces with 'The Theme from A Summer Place', over and over and over. There was lots of blue hair, all of it nodding in time with the floridly-arpeggiated piano arrangements. I could hardly wait to get back to campus.

Christmas break was better, though Surprise was so busy I had no opportunity for a Ruth Etta tetta-tetta. Kelly was home, so we heard all about The Big Apple and everyone vowed to get a television set so as to be able to watch him on the soaps, though the size of the rabbit-ear antennae that would be needed to pull a VHF signal into Surprise would have required a major feat of civil engineering. Bobbie Sue and Kerrie Mae had driven all the way back straight-through, alternating turns at the wheel. Tally, the Littlest Surprise, was walking and talking and seemed to have no interest in sleep. He took right away to the rest of the tribe.

Yule Tide in Surprise was the same as living inside a Christmas tree. All around the village the mesquite and shinnery and cedar and cactus were strewn with tinsel, festooned with lights, hung with decorations and glass balls and strings of popcorn—which the deer found festive—and hung with candy-canes—which the rest of the critters received with thanks. Handy Jones dressed as Santa Claus on December 1st of every year and remained in the red-velour-and-white-rabbit-fur until the 12th day after Christmas. Maya Gandhi busied herself baking and broiling and boiling and broasting until, come Christmas Eve, she'd prepared enough food for a feast of fatuous proportions. Threeb, we learned later, had done all the decorating.

The First Flight of the Five Surprises got the first attention, but I, too, was plied with questions about college life, and realized while relating the facts from the flatlands of Lubbock that I had a lot to say about how much I liked working at the Piggly-Wiggly and how I really, really dug hanging out at U. V. Blake's Records and about how being a columnist at the Toreador was honing my new-found writing skills—keeping mum about the Ruth Etta Letters, though she and I traded knowing smiles when the talk turned to word-crafting—and I realized, all of a moment, that I didn't have much to say about classes and studies. It was if the college was merely a backdrop for the rest of my life, a necessary but insufficient condition. Kerrie Mae and Bobbie Sue and Kelly noticed, too, and, in drips and drabs, made it clear that I might want to become a writer by writing. Come to New-York-New-York, Kelly urged, or to Berkeley, said the girls. Only Ruth Etta was silent.

I noticed, too, that when the holiday wound-down and it was time to leave, the First Flight of the Five Surprises were sad to part with family and friends, but eager to get back to their new lives. Not me. I returned with the proverbial albatross about my neck. The only good thing about leaving was being able to write more letters to Ruth Etta.

11.
SURPRISE VISIT

Mathematics, as I had discovered, is a fiction that creates a reality. College, I was soon to find, is a reality that creates a fiction. Though maybe that's overstating it. If you want to be a scientist, like my sister, or an engineer or an architect or an attorney or a professor, college can get you there. It can be useful. And before higher education became an industry, college was a place to broaden your mind, to take time to experiment with different ways of thinking, to be able to explore choices about what to do in this world—your last chance in life, maybe, to be a generalist. Once-upon-a-time, the ivied halls would have welcomed a mind like that of Handy Jones, would have rewarded the entrepreneurial spirit of Bob Merriman and the communal sense of Maya Gandhi, would have exalted in the reflective naturalism of the Double-Joneses or Sue Merriman's mystic naturalism or Shad Eliot's practical naturalism or Rose Edna's naturalist abandonment of convention. And once upon a time the registrars of the ivory towers would have carved-out a space for the un-plumbed mysteries of a blind film critic.

Not in the Go-Go-Sixties. Now it was a place to learn how to conform to a norm, albeit a norm you chose when you selected your major, your minor, your fraternity, your sorority, your sport, your spouse. Which still might be useful, if that's what you wanted, if you knew so early in life something so elusive about yourself as what you wanted, something even more elusive as what might be useful in your life-to-come. But not—I repeat, not—if you wished to choose the life of a writer. The worst thing that could happen to you in college would be that you learned to write there, for you'd come out writing like them.

Telling the Surprises at Christmas break all about my college experience, I'd heard myself describing mostly meringue and very little pie. I guess before then I'd been too busy checking and sacking groceries, too busy listening to the new vinyl in a booth at U. V. Blake's, too busy meeting new folks. And, maybe, I'd been confused by the notion that college was made for Thom Ed, rather than whether or not Thom Ed was made for college.

Fortunately, these prim institutions have evolved with some odd behaviors that are perversely beneficial. Fraternities and sororities and student governments and sports, all these extracurricular activities can give the average scholars— and quite a few of the below-average scholars—a sense of belonging, an arena in which to shine, even a purpose for their post-collegiate worlds. A reason to gut-out those four years. But for the odd ducks, the strangers in a strange land that would populate Heinlein's novel of that very year, colleges come equipped with the ritual of Spring Break. The timing is perfect. Winter is waning, the world is greening, and student and teacher alike have been gritting their collective teeth through three-quarters of the academic year. Mother Nature always knows when to shake things up, when to indulge and when to reward and when to rest and when to invigorate. In the spring, she moves us to action. ¡Clean out that closet! ¡Plow that furrow! ¡Plant those seeds! ¡Take hope once more!

So during Spring Break of 1961 I bought a bus ticket down to Odessa, hitched rides as far north and west as they would take me, then walked from the last, nearest paved road into Surprise. I became a double-Surprise, you might say, as I'd alerted no one about my impending arrival. I was welcomed, nonetheless, and no more so than by my sweetheart, though throughout the burg hung the unspoken question, one which I could flower-up in the language of needing a break from my studies or planning for the future or working for life-goals or making my mark, but which really boiled down to ¿what-in-heckle-are-you-doing-here-when-you-should-be-in-school? My parents the Double-Joneses, having been collegians, were familiar with its arcania and no doubt remembered Spring Breaks of their own. Though they didn't say so, they likely knew that my presence in Surprise likely meant my permanent absence in Lubbock.

The first moment we had alone, I told Ruth Etta how amongst our letters and my work at the Toreador and my study of algebra that now I knew that what I wanted to be was a fiction writer and I was going to California to do it and without stopping or even breathing I asked her to come with me. ¡Come with me! There was a long pause… I am always with you, she said, a kindly smile breaking her lips. No, I mean in California, I clarified. *I* mean *in the universe,* she smiled more than she spoke, *I* mean I am always with you, anywhere and everywhere, *in The Whole Universe.* On a mission and not listening well, *now,* I pleaded *now,* this very moment. Not now, she whispered, not now—I have already come to be with you for ever and for forever. But—it was my turn to whisper—I can't leave you here. But you have to leave, and I can't go with you, she said firmly, her resolve now as thick and radiant as lipstick on her words. Before I could ask why, she answered. One day you can return here to write, she explained slowly and evenly, but you will never become a writer if you don't leave here first, and if I leave, she asked hypothetically, what will ever bring you back. ¿You mean back to Surprise? I wondered. I mean back to *anywhere,* she concluded.

Had you been there, you might have thought that, for a moment, I had begun to cry. You would have been wrong, of course, because I never actually cry, not with boo-hooing and sobbing and bawling and such. None of that is in my nature. Not in the nature of any of the Surprises, so far as I know. But I will concede that my eyes got wet and the wetness ran down my cheeks until I couldn't see or speak before Ruth Etta took my face in her hands and quietly, simply, perfectly kissed my eyes, then kissed the trail that what might have been tears had left, after which, nuzzling my nose with hers, she murmured ¿Have I made you sad? Beautiful, was all I could croak in reply. Speechless, I kissed her in return, then for a long time, a very long time, we could not kiss each other enough. Though we tried as best we knew how.

A week or so later Bob the Benevolent lent Ruth Etta and me the use of his truck for the ride back to Odessa. I'd already made arrangements with my roomie at Sneed to forward my pitifully-small box of belongings to the bus station in Odessa if—by the Monday after Spring Break—he hadn't heard from me otherwise and, sure enough, I was able to collect my goods when I got my ticket. We had several hours before the Scenicruiser was scheduled to depart for points west, so we ate a nice lunch and took in 'Breathless', which had just made it to a movie-house in the Jack Rabbit Capital of Texas. Just before time to board, Ruth Etta—who always knew more than I knew and always knew what I knew before I knew it—asked me what I had meant by *beautiful.* It is my new standard, I said: if ever I can assemble words on paper as beautifully as you speak them into the air, I will know, at that moment, that I have become a *writer.* And I will remember the beauty that made me what I am.

It's a little over a thousand miles from Odessa to LA and a little short of a whole day. In case you're wondering, it's also three two-page letters and ten postcards.

12.

GHOST WRITERS ON THE SLY

Bobbie Sue and Kerrie Mae and Tally all drove down in the VW camper bus from Berkeley to meet me at the Bus Terminal of the Angels. Ever since learning of my relocation plans, Bobbie Sue had been bobbie-suing all over Loss Angle-ese. She'd found me a used-but-livable twenty-two-foot Airstream Flying Cloud, just right for a single man, she said, a rent-to-own TLC-needed unit. Plus she'd been cutting out employment want-ads for writers. Both she and my sis suggested that I try to get on with some Hollywood bunch that did script overhauls.

We had a fine time that day and the next, fitting out the old 'Stream with fitted sheets—the curved one is a real challenge—collecting utensils and other house-keeping odds and ends at the local thrift shops and locating me a slightly-used 1951 Smith-Corona portable, the Silent model, though I never knew silent as compared to what. Not a peep about why-aren't-you-in-school. They both seemed to get it. Or they'd gotten the word from Ruth Etta. Regardless, Tally was amazing. Approaching only his second birthday, he was not only talking but talking in poetry. Fact is, he hadn't yet learned to speak in prose as he'd been the constant companion to either his mom Kerrie Mae or his aunt Bobbie Sue at coffee-house readings or just hanging out with them at City Lights Bookstore. I was mighty sad to see them head back north to the Brainy Bay.

Yet it was meet and right that they should do so. If they'd stayed, I'd never have gotten down to the business of business, which was to find a writing job. As it was, I had several interviews right away, all of them good, there only being a couple of explainable hiccups. One was that I quickly learned to quit mentioning how algebra connected with fiction writing—lots of glazed eyeballs over that—and the second was that growing up in the remotest of remote hinterlands in the remotest region of a remote state had, by dint of force, produced a citizen—that being me—who had almost no visible footprints in the bureaucratic paper-trail that so consumes the evaluative mechanisms of the Western World. Without having left lots of traces, no responsible corporation was willing to hire me.

Except one. Ghost Writers On the Sly was an odd bunch. Their offices were in a warehouse in West L. A. when I went to make my application, but had been moved to Sherman Oaks when I came back for my initial interview a few days after. On my follow-up face-to-face, no more than a week later, they'd moved again, this time to a strip-mall in Burbank. I didn't care. I just needed a job. Which I got, as they seemed appreciative of my lack of traceable background and, I might say without puffing up too much, a bit in awe of it.

They didn't seem to do film scripts, much to my dismay. Still, as I said, I needed a job. My first assignment was writing fortunes. The kind that go in cookies. Fortune cookies. Which turn out to be not a Chinese tradition at all but rather one invented by young David Jung right here in Los Angeles in 1918. Though that's an unimportant trifle. It was my job to write them. Which I did. But if I thought college was boring and pointless, this took the cake. Or rather the cookie. Soon, I couldn't help myself. I began to write, instead, misfortunes, things like 'You should see your cardiologist.' and 'Eat this cookie. Somewhere in China a small child has lost his cookies.' and 'Consider hiring a private eye to follow your loved one.' and 'Someone you dislike very much will soon come into a large sum of money.'

The first Misfortune Cookies went out in a batch to a single, small, mom-and-pop Chinese beanery near the corner of Figueroa and Bartlett. Their business boomed, to their baffled delight. There were lines out the door and around the block. Several rickshaws were added to the delivery squad. They made inquiries—¿was it the new noodles, was it the extra ounce of MSG on every plate, was it the plastic sheeting they'd awkwardly applied to the menus?—and were astonished to learn that it was their fortune cookies that had become all the rage. People from the length and breadth of The City of the Angels were making their way to the edge of China Town for the edgy predictions. Not speaking any Californian, after hiring a translator Mom and Pop were aghast to see what had caused all the fuss. Indignant, they switched fortune cookie suppliers, causing their business to immediately return to mediocre, which, evidently, they preferred. I suggested that the extra fortune slips be used in banitsas, but L. A. didn't have a bunch of Bulgarian ex-pats large enough to make it economically feasible. My next attempt was to insert them into chile rellenos; the market was there, but our laboratory folks could never solve the cheese-adherence issues.

Management at Ghost Writers On the Sly valued my experiments nonetheless, assigned a newbie to take over the Misfortune Cookie Series, and moved me on to greener pastures. My next assignment was to compose the epigrams that churches put up on their marquees. I am sad to say it was even more tiring than writing fortune cookie fortunes, akin to being force-fed sugar icing. ¿Why not resurrect my last triumph, I thought? So I wrote 'I'm saved / You're lost'. No one seemed to mind. Then it was 'God loves me / but He doesn't like you' and, assertively, 'The Bible is proof that God speaks English' then, prophetically, 'You can't buy your way into Heaven / Leave your money with us'. This go-'round there were no complaints. *Au contraire,* I'd created a monster. Management were forced to staff my new division—now formally called The Department of My God Is Better Than Your God—with several additional writers. Soon we'd branched-out into political ads and campaigns, forced to add drafters fluent in all the major languages.

I shone as a star in our dark little corner of the night. I had achieved glory, but not riches. Times were lean. I made money however I could, short of legal or moral transgressions. Though some came close. Like Santa Busking. December of '61 I took a Santa Claus gig at the brand-spanking-new Seibu Department Store at Wilshire and Fairfax, an upscale Japanese dry-goods emporium. I was ridiculed by the other red-suits around L.A. who called me Santa Craws, along with a few things too crude to mention, some of which involved the short chopstick and where I could put it. Since I was forced to rent the suit and beard for the whole season, when I wasn't on duty at Seibu's I'd wander down Wilshire until I found a business that was short a Santy where I'd set up shop on my own, ho-ho-ho-ing as I collected tips for listening to little kids' wish-lists and admonishing them to-be-good-for-goodness-sake. Only a few proprietors sent me packing, and, all-in-all, I don't figure I disappointed many children, while the parents—each and every one—seemed pleased.

In the one-thing-leads-to-another category, whilst returning the Saint Nick suit to the costume shop 'round the corner from my trailer town I chanced to catch—from the corner of my eye—a newly-dry-cleaned clown get-up, bloomers and blouse neatly-pressed, white gloves washed and fluffy, wig and nose in a clear bag safety-pinned to the big collar, the whole lot dangling on a peg near the cash-register just above an enormous pair of brogans. As an added bonus, the costumer offered to throw in free registration for the next week's Clown Around Conference, a symposium of silliness that promised pratfall practice courses, workshops in water-squirting flowers, and other esoteric prankster practica. Fresh from having kiped Kriss Kringle's kisser for some spare change, I was mentally and monetarily motivated for an encore enterprise. Clowning could be the thing, I thought, the memory of the mugs of the smiling kiddoes and the glowing grins of gratitude on their mommies and daddies convincing me—on the spot—to maneuver myself into becoming a maven of merriment. Trouble is, I'd never had experience with the painted Pirandellos, coming as I had from pretty-much clown-free country, a gap in my upbringing that left me unprepared for how quickly the happy faces that had once lined-up for Father Christmas metamorphosed into howls of horror and twisted visages of fear when presented with a real, live jester. Worse, the icing on the cake—or the meringue on the pie—came about at the aforementioned Clown convention. Coming face-paint-to-face-paint with the professional wisecrack-crowd gave me the clown-creepies; their funniness is but the thinnest of veneers over a fundamental frightfulness. Fast as I could I returned the big-button uniform, though I was stuck with several jars of maquillage and two big tubes of lip-stick.

But, lucky for me, the corner-office people at Ghost Writers let me stake-out even more territory to add to my paycheck. I began to write horoscopes, then bumper-stickers. Tasked with these assignments, I realized that I had a strong philosophical streak, occasioned, undoubtedly, by my having grown up in Surprise. Problem was, that same Surprise-raising left me a bit socially-awkward, a little too literal, and far too kind. My best work was an automotive bumper slogan with a peel-off backing that read 'Schickle Happens'. Once I'd translated it from Surprise-slang it could be found on cars and trucks world-wide. And still can.

Despite my success, it wasn't the kind of writing I'd come west to do. I kept up my correspondence with Ruth Etta, traded the occasional postcard with Kelly, and swapped lots of letters with the Bay Area Surprises, including some very nice drawings sent by Tally. I inquired from time-to-time about script re-writing assignments, but the powers-that-be at Ghost Writers politely-but-firmly skirted my requests and, instead, gave me odder and odder duties. One was to be a blessing.

Ghost Writers On the Sly, it turned out, was just a front for Shade Tree Slogans, Ltd., which, in turn, was a front for Shadow Slogans, Inc., which was very likely a front for something else. A couple years back the various company names had mistakenly been included in local telephone listings. My mission, should I choose to accept it, was to form a squadron of loyal and dedicated agents whose job was to fan-out across the Greater Los Angeles Metropolitan Area, locate all the directories in which the names had been printed, and, without annoying the public or tipping off any foreign or domestic government services, redact said names from the phone books.

Since it was a clandestine program, we changed our new subsidiary company's name every few weeks, beginning with Homeline Security, which soon became Phoneland Security, and so on, using nothing that would smack of anything other than Mother-Flag-and-Apple-Pie. I decided to call my operatives the GPS—the Grease Pencil Squad—then dressed them like Mormon missionaries and sent them door-to-door. It was brilliant. Folks were so glad to find out that my minions weren't Saints of the Latter Day that no one ever declined to produce their old telephone directories when asked or complained when the GPS troops used their grease-pencils to black-out the offending entries, thereby returning secrecy to the secret and security to the secured.

Speaking of spooks, my bosses were both ghostly and sly. Indeed, I'd only come face-to-face with a couple of the company men, and that was during my employment interviews. I worked out of my Flying Cloud, dropped off my completed drafts in a large mail box at whatever that week's headquarters address might be, and, whenever there was a new assignment, would receive instructions through the mail in the envelope with my paycheck. Once I even got instructions via cable-gram, and another time I saw a low-flying pigeon in the confines of my trailer park, fluttering around each mail box without landing, in what looked for all the world like an attempt to locate a specific trailer space. I am convinced to this day that the suspiciously-behaving bird was a carrier-pigeon with a message from the staff of Ghost Writers On the Sly.

So it was with great surprise that I saw one of my bosses on television. I didn't have a set myself, never having developed either habit or interest. Being a workaholic and having a girl back home, I didn't get out at all, but had seen a flyer on the wall of the trailer-park-washateria announcing the next meeting for a local Canasta Club, so I joined-up just to have a little social interaction. They were an interesting, if quirky, bunch, but convivial and full of hail-fellow-well-met. One of the guys worked in the movies doing special effects, which I found intriguing as I didn't even know that there were ordinary effects. Another was a C.P.A. with a very large pompadour whose clientele was comprised almost-exclusively of hair-dressers with a sprinkling of performers drawn from the new phenomenon of Elvis impersonators, look-a-likes who'd been taking advantage of The King's absence during his stint in the Army to dress and groom themselves for gyrating and lip-syncing to the old hits whilst opening a supermarket here or a used-car dealership there. A third of our group was a straight-faced taxidermist, one other behaved as if he were on the lam, and a couple more were sellers of insurance or consumer goods or the like. Amongst the last batch was a wholesale appliance rep who always brought the latest, lightest, smartest television set to our games—a real novelty at the time, the TV set, I mean, not the canasta—tuning in baseball, prize fights, or whatever variety show might be airing that night, just to give us a little background ambience.

One game night, whilst one of the fellows was loading both decks of cards into the hand-crank shuffling machine, I happened to glance up at that evening's miniature Zenith or RCA or Phillips during the broadcast of a news story covering the New York City newspaper strike. Despite the tiny, grainy, black-and-white picture with the slowly-rolling horizontal bands, I recognized an unmistakable image. J. Emperor Hoover, speaking to the television reporters, was clearly in a bind. From the clown-pancake-make-up-smirk-smile right down to the manicured pinkies clinching the prepared press-release it was obvious that The Big Fed couldn't decide which he hated more, the strikers or the publishers. Just as clear, standing just behind him and just over his right shoulder, was what at first glance appeared to be one of the afore-mentioned fake Elvises but who— once I went into full-squint—could be clearly identified as the senior of the two Ghost Writers who'd hired me a little over a year before. ¡Golly-gosh! This bore some thought. I became so preoccupied that I failed to realize that I was holding a concealed canasta, much to my partner's consternation.

After the game, I stopped at the payphone on the wall outside the washateria and called my sis. I gave her the goods, especially about the GPS and the Ghost Writer at the Emperor's elbow. We talked. She put Bobbie Sue on the phone and we talked. Tally asked to talk, too, but then just listened when he took the handset—I don't care if he is a toddler, it's awkward talking into dead air, especially adult-baby-talk—then Kerrie Mae got back on the line, said she'd just read a brand-spanking-new book at City Lights, written by George Woodcock on the topic of anarchism. I'm sending you a copy, she said. Read it. You'll know what to do. As she hung up, I could hear Tally in the background saying something about his dipsy-doodle uncle not letting him get a word in edgewise—the tyke speaking in meter and rhyme, of course.

When the book came a couple of days later, I did as I'd been told. Sister was right. The day after, I found another trailer park, this one at Bundy Drive and West Olympic in Santa Monica. Left a note on the corkboard in the washateria looking to hire someone with a pickup truck. Got a tow out the following day. On the next I sent my resignation to the spooks at Ghost Writers.

Then I went on a reading binge. Somewhere, someplace, there are twelve-step programs for people with reading addictions. Hi. I'm Thom Ed. I'm a reader. Polite applause. Nods all around the room. Sympathetic looks. You know our kind. We're never good at sports. We carry a book to the dinner table, especially in cafes. We bury our faces in them on subways and trains and airplanes. We have stacks on the nightstand beside our beds. They're hung on cute little racks by the toilet, scattered on the coffee table, tucked under the Barkalounger, wedged behind the sofa. We have read the Eleventh Commandment and treasure it above all others: Thou shalt not leave a used-book store empty handed. Amen.

Until my binge, I'd had the same dumb idea about anarchists as has Joe Q. Public—maybe the same dumb idea you've got—that anarchists wear masks, speak broken English with funny accents, carry around round bombs with fuses that beg and ache and yearn and cry out for the touch of a match. They eat turnips and rutabagas and beets and drink wodka. Poor twits. Can't even spell the name of their own hootch.

But no. No. I say, again, ¡No! Anarchists, it turns out, are me. Anarchists are Surprise, Texas, a hotbed of anarchy. Because anarchy is the only step—and I repeat, the only step—between chaos and dictatorship. A democracy, a true one—if ever such existed—is a dictatorship of the masses, no more than mob rule with a dash of etiquette. A republic is a dictatorship of the elite, bearing no more than the etiquette of taste and, maybe, discernment. The other dicta-torships are obvious and have no etiquette of any kind other than submission, being nothing more than the brickbats of organization: crown, church, and army. Chaos we know, too. It scares the schickle out of us.

But anarchy is not so easy to know. For anarchists are most concerned with a practical way of living in an otherwise impractical world. They do not attract attention to themselves. Indeed, no one who calls themselves an anarchist is an anarchist, for which reason it is philosophically impossible, fundamentally impossible, practically impossible, for there ever to be a group, a political party, a movement to be anarchistic if they publicly and openly own-up to anarchy.

So Surprise never set out to be a haven for anarchists. It never set out to *be* anything. It just *became,* and it just *is.* It grew from the earth as had the mesquites and prickly-pear and greasewood and cholla in which it is immersed. It is organic. It is naturally anarchistic. I now pronounce it organarchistic. A product of and evidence of organarchy. After a week of this organorgasm of organarchic reading and thinking and concluding, I rested. And was thankful to the God of Abraham for the concept—the concept of rest, I mean.

I had now missed a couple of weeks of Canasta, which was just as well. The fellows told me that a pair of older Mormon Missionaries had been by looking for me. Said I'd won a free LP of the Greatest Rhumba Hits of the Tabernacle Choir and wanted to deliver it personally. It was a good thing that the C.P.A. was LDS himself and recognized the guys as phonies. Figured they were mob collection muscle and wanted to know if I played the ponies over at Santa Anita. Yes, I told him, knowing the truth was worse than that. The Canasta Club seemed relieved when I told 'em I'd taken up bowling. All but Ray, the special effects man, who said to look him up if I ever got out to Hollywood.

I didn't stay but a week or so in Santa Monica before finding yet another trailer space, this time in an ideal location on Victory Boulevard in Burbank, not far from a Ralph's Grocery and pretty close to a Pup-and-Taco. I lodged the Flying Cloud there, swapped my Silent for another portable of the same model—knowing just enough forensics to realize that my previous writings could be easily traced to the old machine through the uniquities that distinguish the type-bars and platens and so forth on each and every individual typewriter—then set to work finding a real writing job. But not before I counted my blessings. Not only had I'd dodged the shiny horns and the steel hooves of the red-eyed herd, but now I had something to write about. ¡Yipee-yi-yaaaaay, yipee-yi-yooooooh!

13.

LONG DISTANCE CALL

It was the year of turning out. I feared that I was boring, but it turns out that I was only frugal. Though, some would argue, what's the difference. Either way, I had enough bottle-caps in my tin-can to carry me through for a while, so I figured I'd try to get proper work instead of just get any work. Right off the bat, I managed to snag a couple of re-writes courtesy of—it turns out—some influence from Bobbie Sue. Because it was writing in which I wasn't personally invested, I was able to be most objective and very logical and, it turns out, I was also good at it, so, it turns out, I started getting more assignments. I didn't mind not getting mentioned in the credits and I also didn't blab around town what I was doing on which script—which, it turns out, also made me popular with directors and producers—though I think they didn't know that I spent no time in the usual Hollywood hangouts, which, it turns out, made it easy for me to be discreet. Lastly, but not hardly leastly, with all that work it turns out that I had to make a few changes in my day-to-day living.

Like a telephone. The deadline for a re-write is always yesterday. No time for the U. S. Mail. No time for a carrier pigeon. The Flying Cloud wasn't fitted-out for tethering to the Bell System—¿isn't the whole idea of an Airstream to be able to pick up and take off at any given moment?—so I had to snake the phone line through a vent under the refrigerator, which made the inside wall of the clothes closet the best place to hang A. Graham's wall-mount rotary dial. It seemed awkward at first, but after a while I came to like having it up and out of the way and out of sight. Once I was able to find an extra-long cord for the handset, I could even sit on the sofa or the side of the bed if I was enjoying or enduring a lengthy telephone call.

You know how one thing always leads to another, sometimes in leaps and bounds and sometimes in bits and pieces. Because I started getting re-write jobs, it meant I had to get a telephone, which meant more re-write jobs and a little more money, which came just in time for the next thing to which I was led, that being a car. I had to get the re-writes over to the studios, after all, and sometimes I had to pick them up. I found a low-mileage one-owner 1957 Nash Rambler station wagon, the Cross Country model, pink and white, clean as a pin though not nearly so sharp, a luggage rack on top and a three-speed stick on the steering column, as fast in any one gear as in any of the others. But—and here was the clincher— it could pull the Flying Cloud if needed. It had no air conditioning—what the heckle, this was California, after all—and no radio. Luckily a few feelers around the trailer park turned up a pre-owned, black-and-gold Sony TR-620 shirt-pocket- size-AM-band-only-model that had six transistors and used them all. It even had a clever wire stand that, in lounge mode, folded back to prop-up the radio on a table or a nightstand or—if you drove slowly and carefully—the dash of a Nash.

It was the right time to go modern. For one thing, the airwaves were exploding with music. The TR-620 wasn't the same as a listening booth at U. V. Blake's, but it let me keep sampling and tasting what was new, even if there was a disc-jockey running the cafeteria line. An active listener, I kept up with who most often spun platters that I liked but who also played tunes that stretched my ears a little. There was The Squeakin' Deacon speakin' on KFOX and Bobby Dale on KFWB and, of course, the same border radio voices that I already knew from back home, including the Howling Rooster and the friendly tones of Paul-your-good-neigh- bor-along-the-way-Kallinger.

For another thing, the Nash Rambler was the very spirit of handy. Not as handy as Handy Jones, not as spiritual as Maya Gandhi's Punto Rojo, but the essence of low-heeled-sensible-shoes if such had been conflated into iron and steel and rubber and plastic and Naugahyde. It was chrome made practical, design made useful, paint for a purpose, cheese-whiz slapped into gee-whiz. It gave me purchase to wheel up the coast to see sister Kerrie Mae and nephew Tally and dear Bobbie Sue. It was a dream for toting groceries from Ralph's or taking laundry to the laundry. Most of all, it made of me a true Californio, as the land of perpetual sunshine was a place never intended for the pedestrian, being instead from time immemorial a country of freeways and highways and byways, an earthly plane sculpted of macadam and concrete, a world a-hum with wheels.

There was one more thing, the last thing, the best thing that modernity conferred: the gift of Ruth Etta's voice. Well, in all fairness, modernity and algebra. Let us start with the math, a three-part problem. I was born into this life in 1942, so by now, 1962, with a birthday looming, I was right-nigh twenty years of age, a mere pup in the big scheme of things—given Biblical promises of three-score-and-ten and actuarial assurances of slightly more than that—but, all the same, it turns out, very likely equipped with my life's entire supply of hormones. A person can ration some things. But other things have biological instructions that do not give a schickle for apportionment of any kind.

Part two of the math problem is the integer *one, uno, un, ichi.* Up until my sashay into the sunset, my procession to the Pacific, my leap into L.A., I'd lived either in an Airstream with my family or in Sneed Hall with my roomie. Now I lived alone. Which means that when the hormones came visiting, I was free to entertain them. I'd been led to believe, or expect—as if there's some difference 'twixt belief and expectation—that release would bring relief. Oh, ¡not so! Give these visitors an inch and they'll take twelve. Well, that's bragging, but you get the long and the short of it. They moved in, camped out, then made their occasional soirees into habitual matins and routine matinees. Once a snake-charming Hindu playing a pungi, I was now nothing more than fantasy-beefcake arm-wrestling a snake. I'd begun to lose concentration; I verged on losing control; I found myself avoiding looking at my palms and—at least once—awoke from a daydream in which I was plotting the theft of an eye-chart to post just above the sofa on the other end of the Flying Cloud.

I needed a solution. And it came. But not by serendipity. By algebra. And through modernity. Two knowns, one unknown. I'd seen that before. The two knowns on one side, the unknown on the other. The solution came when I let the telephone line be the equals sign. At once, I felt like Albert E. in the Swiss patent office: let's see, if I set the speed of hormones to be a constant, then, oh yeah, that'll make Ruth Etta equal to the mass of one lonely boy times the hormonal-miles-per-hour-squared. A long distance call to my beloved, my sweetie, my soul-mate, my desire, would make me no longer alone. ¡A chicken-choker no more!

My funds were not measured in terms of the lemniscate, that lazy-figure-eight, the symbol for infinity. In comparison to my prior monetary status, I was flush. But long-distance telephony was still the province of the wealthy, the top-daddies, the fat-cats, the upper-crust. I knew I'd need to budget my bottle caps. To that end, Ruth Etta and I exchanged postal cards in the service of setting out a schedule for our communiqués. Gas was the new petroleum play in the Permanent Basin, not as many wildcatters as in the past few decades since consolidation was now the current oil-patch watchword, which had a good ring to it for Surprise as a more stable class of transients were coming through to avail themselves of the Shifting Sands Mobile Motel and all the accoutrements of The City at the Center of the Universe Which Was No Place At All. The Ser-Sta-Gro was moving enough merchandise to both keep the comestibles rotated past the best-sold-by-dates and keep the shelving dusted as well; the inventory of odd bits of hosiery were turning over more regularly in the One Sock Shop; Threeb was busier than a huntin' dog with double-feature demand for flicks at the Flatlands Drive-Out Theatre; and Bob Merriman was merrily rehabbing away, restoring and selling more old Airstreams that had been left to decay after the last oil boom a decade before.

In the realm of communication with the larger world outside the grease-wood flats, the first bow to the inevitable, the first nod to necessity, the first arrow of accommodation was the installation of a pay-phone on the veranda of the Old School House. Which, of course, wasn't nearly enough service. When the line of Surprises fidgeting with their dimes began to wrap around the building, several of the Foundling Families installed the twisted-pair-land-line-speaking-receptacles in their own Airstreams—in which, independently of my own experiment, they also discovered the vent below the refrigerator cabinet through which they could run Ma Bell's tether to the outside world. By this time, having attained her womanhood, Ruth Etta had taken domain over her own 'Stream and—once learning of my advance into the scheme of long-distance-calling—installed her very own phone. It wasn't Heaven, but we could hear the Pearly Gates squeaking.

We chose Mondays after lunch, Texas time. By then the few weekend overnighters would have moved out of the Shifting Sands Mobile Motel, the Monday-Friday crowd would not yet have arrived before the close of business that afternoon, and—given the time difference—it would be just after I'd finished laying-out the week of re-writing ahead of me. Back in Surprise, the regulars would be at their regularity, the irregulars would still be abed, and Ruth Etta would have some time to herself. I lived alone in a trailer park, so my world would be my own.

Our calls went something like this. I had to do the dialing. Sunny Southern Cal had been graced with direct-dial-long-distance for a decade, a convenience that wouldn't reach the Oil Patch of West Texas for another couple of years. Were Ruth Etta to initiate the call, she'd have had to do it through the operator and the charges would have been almost double, just shy of seven bucks for a ten-minute talk—that at a time when seven bucks was a week's worth of breakfast at the diner, or a whole tank of gas for the Nash, or a half-dozen pizza-pies, or enough loaves of bread to wear out a toaster.

So I'd dial Ruth Etta's number from my phone. A few clicks, a few faint Telstar noises, and a few moments later an operator came on the line, ¿May I have the number you're calling, plea-yuz? I'd tell her. Thank-kew; more satellite sounds, until ¡at last! the distant ringing of a distant telephone. ¿How?—I've always wondered—could Ma Bell's engineers make a telephone jingling eleven-hundred miles away sound like it was eleven-hundred miles away. Such attention to detail. Besides which that far-away-sounding brrrring-brrrring made the long-distance charges a little easier to bear.

She'd pick up. Shifting Sands Mobile Motel, Ruth Etta speaking—in case of the rare event that it wasn't me on the other end. Hey, Kid—I'd say, jauntily. Hey, back—she'd say, softly. How's things?—me, still jaunty. Ever thing good, 'cept one—now coyly, but firmly, she'd reply. Me, too—my turn to speak softly, slowly. We both knew what the one thing was and ever would be. Eleven-hundred miles. Because there was no need to say it, to belabor it, there would always follow a long silence, a long pause filled with the longing of love, long enough to imagine that I could hear her breath, her heart, hear the meadowlarks in the meadow, hear the wind ambling through the acacia. She always thought, she'd say later, years later, that in those broad, quiet spaces she could hear the Pacific, no matter that I was in inland Burbank.

Then it was chatter, chatter, chatter. Daily stuff, how's-it-what's-it-when'd-it-why's-it-who's-it. Ten minutes of nothing but ordinary things, for we'd learned quickly that the extraordinary only reminded us of that eleven-hundred miles. Second or third call, I think it was, I'd made the mistake of asking her what she was wearing. ¿What do you want me to be wearing? she'd answered. I like you more in less, most in least, the mathematician in me said before I could stop him, and then immediately, before we could stop the non-mathematicians in each of ourselves, we'd plunged into the realm of telephornication. Not that it wasn't good. Oh, no, it was ¡golly-gosh-golly-terrific! But—and not that I was checking my John Cameron Swayze—we could rent a room cheaper than the long-distance charges that followed in the aftermath of the Incident of the Heavy Breathing. And, besides, it was mighty risky for Ruth Etta as the Surprises had a bad habit of being, well, surprising, apt to pop-in to anyone's Airstream both unannounced and without the employment of so much as a door-knock or a halloo-the-camp. In which case there would have been plenty of surprise to go all around Surprise.

From thence forward, we saved the talk of romance and the romance of talk for our letters. It was just as well. We pledged to keep them, told one another where each had secreted the missives between the interior cabin walls and the shiny-art-deco-aero-skins of the respective 'Streams. We began to build an archive, amassing the physical evidence of how-then-becomes-now, the documentation of what it was like then, of what we did then, of how we did it then, of who we were then. It was a way to remember never to forget.

More than that—it's always more than that ¿isn't it?—our conscious evaluation of what should be spoken and what should be written turned out to be the greatest tool for me as a writer. Maybe the greatest tool for me as an artist, maybe the greatest tool for me as a human being. Not by teaching me how to write, not by teaching me how to write better, but by teaching me why to write. We had stumbled upon the difference between the word spoken and the word written, between the language on the page and the language in the air, between the singer and the song.

In our heads grew a Venn diagram, one circle for the written word, another circle for the spoken word, the two almost-but-not-quite-completely overlapping, a diagram in which each are independent and separate and yet in which each are individually and mutually understandable, but in which each could take you to a place the other couldn't, the same as between a poem and a song, part of the difference being that the wisdom of the written word comes from the mind and the wisdom of the spoken word comes from the heart, the written word having been built and assembled, chiseled out of the rock, the spoken word having flowed in a spring out of the side of the same rock, not assembled in any way but born wholly on a current that appears from nowhere over and under and around the rock. And surrounding both circles of the written and the spoken is another, the circle from whence all knowledge comes, un-utterable, unthinkable, unknowable except through its children, the two ways of words. ¡Rave On! said Buddy Holly to A. Einstein, to George Gamow, to Fred Hoyle, ¡Rave On! Ma Bell, ¡Rave On! just as Saint Van Morrison would later sing ¡Rave On! John Donne, ¡Rave On! Though Buddy shouted it first, crooned it first to Ruth Etta and I, who were the first to hear it, to understand it—she the brilliance of the spoken word, me the plodding craft of the word written—for Ruth Etta and I had come upon the Big Bang Theory of the Communication of What Can Be Known. All, it turns out, because we were so far apart in distance and so close in love. ¡Rave On! ¡Rave On! ¡Rave On!

14.

WUBBA, WUBBA, WUBBA

I fear that my constitutional tendency toward frankness, my penchant for openness, my Joe-Friday-just-the-facts-ma'am stoicism, these things may have led you to think me a nerd, a square, a fuddy-duddy. Not a doofus or a dolt or a ding-a-ling, to be sure, as you're already aware, after all, I'm a writer whose short résumé includes having worked for a pseudo-government front operation—the nefarious and shadowy bunch ruthless enough to make after me with goons masquerading as Mormon Missionaries—I'm a writer, I remind you, parenthetically. No, it's that you are only liable to see me as nothing more than a Monkey-Wards guy in a Macy's world, a fellow who drives a Nash and lives in a trailer park and whose only romantic outlet is a teenage girl a thousand miles away in a little hamlet that might only be known to to the outside world through the works of the intrepid explorers of the Mesquite and Shinnery Division of the National Geographic Society.

It's all my fault, for I haven't told you the whole of it. The whole of me, I mean. What I ought to say is that I'm not just a foockle-brain who sits at home writing moon-eyed letters to his sweetheart, saving and scrimping his coppers and nickels for one, single ten-minute telephone call each Monday. No. Not at all. I get out and I do things. I'm not a shaker, but I'm a mover. Even though I'm spoken for— you also know that—so I don't cruise the cocktail joints for chicks. But I read the newest books and the latest magazines. I go out to listen to music, favoring the country-western crowd at The Palomino on Lankershim in North Hollywood or the folkies at The Troubadour on Santa Monica in West Hollywood. I sometimes wish I were smart enough for jazz, but I'm not. Sigh. I go to movies at a variety of indoor air-conditioned theaters. I only make this little addendum to my report to say I am not a geek—the term proffered exactly one decade ago by Heinlein in 'The Year of the Jackpot' in order to describe the nerdy stay-at-homes—I advance to you that no, no, no, I am no Potiphar Breen, I am not the essence of geekness, the gentleman of geek, the geek guru. Though Ruth Etta would make a fine Meade Barstow, I'm not afraid to add.

When I could—meaning when I was up north spending Tally time with Kerrie Mae and Bobbie Sue—I frequented the City Lights. When I couldn't—which was most of the time—I patronized Williams Bookstore on 6th in downtown San Pedro. Not as hip, but a fine, solid establishment of long-standing—founded, I wave a leek in pride, by a Welshman—and now marking over half a century as a purveyor of letters. Inside, the shop smelled of books, though not with the suffocating, musty, heaviness of the antiquarian dealerships. Looking around, it was wall-to-wall and floor-to-ceiling with all sizes and coverings and dimensions of volumes, though not in the helter-skelter, haphazard heaps of the used-paper-back-book buyers. In the experience of the moment, it had an air of playful gravitas, a description for which you will have to derive your own counter-example. It was—in short and long— where gathered the members of our clan, the readers.

Because Bradbury's brilliant and frightening 'Fahrenheit 451' had already become the backdrop for all us bookers, places such as City Lights and Williams had perforce risen to a higher plane, to a sphere beyond the profit-and-loss-customer-service-retail-industry in which they once quartered, having now found their mission expanded to include a spiritual role, one of holy function, of symbolic utility. Bookstores such as these are the watch-fires fighting back the black night of censorship, they are the tenders of the entire Bell Curve of ideas and words and opinions and beliefs and interests, not just the mass-mediocre-middle, but all the entire stretch from one little and unsettling end to the other—*piss-poor-to-piss-rich-and-inbetween-every-son-of-a-bitch* read a bell-curve-shaped tattoo once found on the body of a statistician who had leapt to his pre-actuarial demise after having discovered his wife abed with a non-standard deviation. Bookstores such as these are the places where anyone can peruse what they will without a sideways glance from either purveyor or fellow patron, the places where philosophy and poetry and pornography can populate shelves side-by-side without an eyebrow raised. It will be a sad world if ever the deadening drivers of organization—the governments and the religions and the corporations, I name them as if they are separate and not each a differing facet of the same evil—if ever they grind these word-and-idea-tabernacles under the crush of commercialism. For the independent bookstores are the hidden glens, the sheltered caverns, the box-canyon retreats, the back-water anchorages that offer protection and elbow-room for the Dream Time of The Aboriginals of Independent Thought, they are where the intellect goes to shop, where the dream goes to work, where the anarchist goes to church.

On recommendations from all three of the Northern-Most-Surprises, Bobbie Sue and Kerrie Mae and Young Tally—I'm not fooling, he groked the book on his own—I picked up Heinlein's 'Stranger In a Strange Land'. Like everyone else, I was smitten with it. We Surprises are, I fairly wager, the original Fair Witnesses, such that I considered telephoning the author—now that I was connected to the world at large by means of the twisted pair, replete with direct-dial-long-distance—to learn when, exactly, he'd spent time in the Kingdom of the Permanent Basin and, perhaps, to probe the intimacy of his knowledge of Airstream engineering and his familiarity with the Philosophy of Handy Jones. Instead, I hopped into the Nash and rambled myself straight back to San Pedro to see what else of Heinlein's work I could purchase, in short order walking away with a collection of short stories in a volume entitled 'The Menace from Earth', the 1959 cloth-cover first edition issued by Gnome Press of Hicksville, NY, mine being one of only five thousand.

First in the T-of-C was "The Year of the Jackpot". The principle protagonist, Potiphar Breen, is a statistician in Los Angeles—now, there's a prescription for loneliness, upon which we've already touched—who, as the story opens, is having his exact breakfast in his regular diner, after which, walking outside at his usual time, sees the second protagonist, Meade Barstow, who—very unusually and not at all in the normative range of events—is stripping-off her clothing at the bus-stop. Potiphar comes to the rescue by wrapping his coat about her just as she faints, then carrying her back to his apartment. When she comes to, Potiphar fills her in. She's shocked, has no idea why she was doing such a thing. He knows, he's a statistician. We think that we act independently, he says, but no, we're lemmings, and the same thing has been going on all over L. A., though hushed-up by the news media. This is the year, he says, that the human race is giving the universe the finger—I'm paraphrasing Potiphar, you understand— while it lets its collective hair down and says wubba, wubba, wubba—no longer paraphrasing, as I've no clear idea of what one wubba conveys, much less a triad of wubbas. Somehow, she finds his a satisfactory explanation, so they become lovers and decide to abandon the city and strike out for the Mojave. There are travails en route—a flood, an earthquake, an attempted car-jacking which Meade, surprising herself, thwarts with a gun—you know, the sorts of things that go on in L. A. on a statistically daily basis. On the way, Potiphar and Meade decide to marry themselves to one-another.

After they're out in God's countryside and no longer living in sin, they watch a mushroom cloud rising up in the west as L. A. is consumed in an atomic blast, and, indeed, enough of the world has destroyed itself in the mad practice of M.A.D. that peace almost immediately reigns across the smoldering planet. In the nuclear dénouement, Potiphar catches up on his reading, including a paper in an obscure but never-the-less his personal favorite journal of astrophysics in which an even-more-obscure scientist calculates the exact requirements for the Sun to explode in a nova. His perusal complete, the two newly-weds enjoy the evening together, interrupted only when a large sunspot appears on Sol's face. There's something wrong with the sunset, says Meade. No, says Potiphar, there's something wrong with the sun.

As was Potiphar Breen—¿what drove Heinlein to such odd naming conventions?—I was catching up on my own reading before moving on to the movies, and, just as it had been for old Potty, the current year was a very grim calendar page on the literary-celluloid-current-events front. One exception was a brief cultural respite in June when a new band, The Beach Boys—comprised of several nicely-dressed young men from nearby Hawthorne, most of them of the same, clean-cut family and all of whom seemed completely out of place for either the Palomino or the Troubadour—cut an equally-clean 45 single about their four-speed-dual-quad-posi-traction-409, an automobile that I easily imagined was light-years beyond my Nash-Rambler station-wagon. Though not nearly so handy.

The best theatrical releases of the year were months off. 'Lolita' had come out in June, but I dared not tempt the tenuous balance of my hormonal detente with such a flick. 'Billy Bud', 'The Music Man', 'Mutiny on the Bounty', these would not arrive in theaters until October, to be followed shortly afterwards by 'The Longest Day' and 'The Manchurian Candidate'. The Christmas break would feature 'Lawrence of Arabia'—somebody, please, get me a glass of water—and, to crown the year, 'To Kill a Mockingbird'. ¿And where, in all that, was escapism? Except for the terrific dance numbers in the Robert-Preston-Shirley-Jones romp, of course. There was so much angst on the silver screen in 1962 that the sales of black turtlenecks must have gone through the roof. There hadn't been this much finger-snapping since the farewell tour of the Denver Bongos. I was thinking of finding a Canasta group that was short a dealer.

Giddy-up, giddy-up, as you will—so four days after I turned twenty, the day after the birthday of Our Nation of Mother, Flag, and Apple Pie—American International Pictures released Ray Milland's apocalyptic-noire opus 'Panic in Year Zero!' One of my re-write contacts had given me a ticket so I caught it on opening day—dagnab the angst, and ¡full-speed-ahead! No reviews yet, so no prejudgements on my part. It started off OK—Les Baxter's music is a good way to start anything—with homey shots of the Baldwins, a family of suburban Los Angelenos, up at four AM—despite the film being lit as bright as midday— loading up their new-ish Kenskill trailer house which was already hitched to their 1962 Mercury Monterey four-door hard-top—a sporty set of wheels in snappy contrast to the big aluminum box trailer which, one supposes, would have been an Airstream in a production with a bigger budget, but then, hey, the Baldwins weren't 'Streamers, ¿were they? just the standard-fare-American-fam preparing to head out of town for a fishing vacation up in the hills. By quarter of six they're well out of the city, climbing up mountain switch-back after mountain switch-back. Suddenly, a distant rumble, flashes in the sky behind them. ¿Is that lightning? ¿Can you get something on the radio?—we hear nothing but static—¿Not even CONELRAD? Mary Mitchell asks from the back seat—more static. Only bits and pieces of CONELRAD, we learn. Let's stop and call mother in L. A. says wife Jean Hagen. Conveniently, a couple of switch-backs later and after a fair amount of over-the-limit driving on the wrong side of the white line, the Kenskill crazily careening behind them, they whip into a un-paved scenic-view-turn-out on the other side of the road in the middle of nowheresville that's convenient-ly-equipped with a phone booth. Milland can't get anything but a dim-witted Operator, I'm sorry sir there are no lines open to Los Angeles. As his dime clangs into the coin box everyone gets out of the Merc, looking back toward L. A. just in time to see an enormous mushroom cloud rising up, up, up from the City of the Angels, lightning flashing in its boiling tower. Best visuals of the whole flick. And best choreography. Frankie, who should be listed in the film credits as The Master of the Obvious, says to Milland, We've had it, Dad, haven't we.

It goes on like that for another hour-and-twenty with loads of shots of panicked escapees and wild-driving looters, conveyed in the main by incessant close-ups of rolling tires and hubcaps and bumpers and grills—you'd think the cinematographer thought there was an Oscar category for automotive chrome—interspersed with studio-lot scenes of little towns off the beaten path that look like they were laid-out amidst a squabble between the set designers for 'The Andy Griffith Show' and 'The Twilight Zone'. It's a survival flick with good hair-dos and plenty of smokes, the love-child of 'On the Beach' and 'Swiss Family Robinson'.

Still, it was disturbing. Not the violence. When someone's shot in this pic, there are no bullet holes, no blood, no gore. When there's a fist-fight, all it takes is one punch to end it. There are three rapes, no rape scenes—in fact, the rape of the Baldwin's daughter is merely intimated by the film's second-best choreographic routine as her two goon attackers dance her back-and-forth betwixt them. What's scary is Rick/Frankie. And Harry/Ray. And Doctor Strong. No, I didn't make that up: Powell Strong, MD. Frankie starts out as a gee-dad-airheaded teenager, but moves oh-so-quickly-and-effortlessly from surprised shock at seeing his dad punch-out a nice-enough hardware store proprietor who won't take a check—like in the impending Armageddon a check will clear a bank somewhere in Hell—to being proud of his dad's instant adoption of greater and greater brutality and then even more quickly to enjoying the brutality on his own. They ditch the Kenskill in favor of living in a cave. Cave men. They become cave men. Nothing subtle about that reference. Dad Harry ricochets on the one hand from tough-guy-private-investigator ordering his family around as if they were his operatives in a Dashiell Hammett novel to anguished deliberations on the inhumanity of man to men.

The dialog pings around the script in the same way. Mom: don't try to frighten me, I'm already frightened. Dad: that's a safe way to be. Mom: what do you want to do, ¿write off the rest of the world? Dad: I'll return to civilization when civilization becomes civil again. Dad to Doctor Strong: we won the war. Doctor Strong's repartee: well, ding-ding for us. Then Doctor Strong adds: but be careful out there, our country is still full of thieving, murdering patriots.

Ding-ding for us indeed.

Though the movie wasn't Heinlein's work—a Jay Simms screenplay, the guy who gave us 'The Killer Shrews' and 'The Giant Gila Monster', taken from Ward Moore's story 'Lot's Daughter'—it seemed to me to take up where Heinlein left off. Mushroom cloud at the end of 'Jackpot'; mushroom cloud at the beginning of 'Year Zero'. Potty and Meade looking into the end of things; Harry and Ann and family busily organizing life after the end of things. Potty, the idealistic young Heinlein, the Heinlein of the End Poverty In California Movement of the 1930s; Harry, the world-weary older Heinlein, the Tramp Royale of the 1960s in Conservative Springs, Colorado.

As I pondered the dichotomies, the disconnected connections, I became confused. ¿Is a thing a thing and not some other thing? Or ¿is red ever blue, day ever night? ¿Are rights and wrongs interchangeable, is meanness ever kindness, is nice ever not? ¿Is a thing ever both? ¿All? ¿Is there a motivation for meanness outside of the meanness itself?

Pondering, you might already know, is merely angst in its Sunday-go-to-meeting clothes. And I was all dressed-up. Which was convenient. Because along with all this, the real world was coming to blows. Mother Nature—who is willing to remain in the background of current events only for short stretches of time—asserted her newsworthiness on Columbus Day, whacking The Golden State and the whole West Coast of North American with her newest daughter, Tropical Storm Freda. The headline-scribes at the local rags promptly dubbed poor Freda 'The Big Blow', a moniker not aimed at appeasing either her or her mom, and so, without proper deference paid the two ladies, the younger wreaked her wreckage for almost a week until she withered-away into unseasonably-cool zephyrs somewhere over the plains of Canada.

No sooner had Freda's howl died down to a whimper and the water rolled back to the sea and the Red Cross management returned to their corporate offices, the Roushkies and the Amuricans began squaring-off in the balmy Caribbean, threatening to come to blows of their own over Cuber. It was a hissing contest of the first water—hissing with an 'h' as in pumpernickel, Mother Double-Jones would discretely put it—slavishly covered by network television in a fine reprise of the Gillette Friday Night Fights that had been off the air for a couple of years now. On our side of the ring was Handsome Jack, Boston-bred, steeled in the Pacific in a sinking Patrol Torpedo boat, the silver spoon of this youth now a fierce glint in his affable-but-dangerous smile. On the other side, in the dark trunks, was the Ukrainian Mister Potato Head, Nick the Shoe-Banger, still smarting from having been denied admission to Disneyland on his last visit state-side. Back-and-forth it went, feints and parries, step-drags and pivots, every move played out on television screens in living-rooms all across the nation. The first real swing was Kennedy's prime-time announcement of the blockade, a boob-tube jab-and-grab, soon countered by Khrushev's fake feint U-2 punches, a technique that

Cassius Clay would adopt a dozen years later as the rope-a-dope. While sports casters ringside discussed the various merits of Jack's right-cross and Nikita's left hook, audiences world-wide were well aware of the silos and bomber-bays filled with hay-makers that each contender kept in reserve. When the bell rang to end the week-long round, we were all ready for a station break, which, for our side, came with the Thanksgiving holiday.

None of the Pacific Coast Surprises had time to motor back to Amazement Acres so, instead, we collected in Berkeley for our turkey. There was plenty of catching-up talk during the cooking and carving and consuming. Kerrie Mae was a-bubble over her graduate research, something to do with raising fish in greenhouses in the desert in ponds fed by subterranean aquifers—the fish in the ponds, I mean, and the ponds in the greenhouses—where the fish did in the water what bears do in the woods, their through-put not in the least offensive to the aqua-culture plants floating therein which then, instead, considered the piscine pre-compost nutritious and tasty which then made the flora grow as happy as pigs in, well, schickle, which then made the whole-kit-and-kaboodle a closed system but one wide-open for profitability, just perfect—she beamed—for a place like the Homeland of Handy Jones. We remaining three were enthralled and enheartened, yet enthused that she'd finished her report whilst we were still chopping and boiling and sautéing and stuffing.

Bobbie Sue, too, bedazzled us with a fine summary of her dailies. Kerrie Mae remained on her full-ride scholarship, a full gallop for tuition and fees and books but no more than a dog-trot when it came to the pittance she received for teaching and researching. To make up the difference in pace, Bobbie Sue not only helped out with Tally, thus avoiding the cost of day-care, but also picked up odd jobs here and there. She was on-call at several movie houses to fill-in for under-the-weather projectionists, she helped out with several horse-trainers whose oil-patch colleagues had given her the best of references, and she had grown to be the favorite go-fer-Jill-of-all-trades for the intelligentsia of the City by the Bay.

The latter role began simply enough. Discovering City Lights Bookstore almost the moment they arrived, the three quickly became regulars. The other habitués—whose names I'd drop if it wouldn't make us all sound like name-drop-pers—equally quickly took a fancy to the Three-Part-Family. The two young women were smart and beautiful and had fine sensibilities for literature. That they were not flirty or on-the-make made them insanely attractive. Then there was their little Tally, cute and precious and precocious, learning to speak right before the very eyes of the bookstore familiars and, as I noted some time back, with his first utterances coming in short poems—haiku and sonnets—which soon became long forms—sestinas and rondelets—and eventually epic-length ballads. When it became common knowledge that Tally was but a nickname for Taliesin, the Lights of the City Lights fairly threw themselves at his feet, swearing amongst themselves that the toddler was without question or discussion the reincarnation of the Sixth Century Bard of the Britons.

As if all of the above wasn't enough, Bobbie Sue also possessed the VW split-window bus. Which would have stood out on its own, both for its unusualness and for its usefulness, but was even more striking owing to the paint job that she and Tally had given it. Rather, were giving it, as the Splittie remained forever a work-in-progress. And, yes, she and Tally. He was not only a born wordsmith, but also a born painter. When he had more to say than he had words with which to say it, which was often, without breaking stride he'd pull a Magic Slate out of his tiny over-hauls and commence to draw. The utilitarian box-on-wheels soon sported a large, brightly-colored sun in place of the VW symbol on the nose and around the sides a whole garden of flowers and birds and caterpillars and lady-bugs all woven in-and-out and together with abstract whorls and swirls. Tally would draw them first on the Slate, then Bobbie Sue would translate them into color on the V-Dub. They—the vivacious young woman, the pint-sized poet, and the Magic Slate Bus—were soon seen all over San Fran and the Bay Area, making deliveries and pick-ups and running errands in the most efficacious and peaceful fashion. It would only be a few years until such automotive adornment was commonplace in the Paris of the West.

Though I was pressed ever-so-kindly to discuss the scripts for which I'd been hired as a mop-up man, all I wanted to talk about were the short stories and novels I'd read and the movie I'd seen and the bad weather I'd endured and the nuclear-hair-trigger-diplomacy that had scared the bejeezus out of us all. Kerrie Mae and Bobbie Sue were party to the whole of it, of course, having recommended 'Stranger' to me, which led to 'Jackpot', which I sent them when I sent a copy of 'The Menace from Earth' to Ruth Etta, and all had heeded my suggestion to see 'Zero'. Ruth Etta had been spared Freda, but none of us could escape Cuber. So we could all talk turkey with a common currency.

I feared it was just me. Stuck in Burbank in an aluminum can, one phone call a week to my beloved, writing the rest of the seven days on someone else's scripts, perhaps I was prone to paranoia. Maybe the world wasn't as bad as I thought. Maybe it was just *my* world that was as bad as I thought. Maybe even my world wasn't bad. Maybe, it was just me.

But between mouthfuls of turkey and stuffing and mashed potatoes and hot rolls and giblet gravy and green beans I heard the same fears, the same questions, the same concerns, the same anguish. My table-mates, my kith and kin, my companions across the Universe, they, too, suffered as I suffered. Even Tally, whose Magic Slate drawings had taken on the look of 'Guernica'. We were not only all in it together, whatever *it* is, we were also of the same mind about it.

We hatched a plan. Let's bring Ruth Etta out for Christmas, said Kerrie Mae and Bobbie Sue. Tally also nodded vigorously in the affirmative. You two need time together, they said, with a wink. Tally winked, too, taking us all by surprise. Even in my befuddled state of excitement at the mere idea of our cohabitation, however brief the mention or how vague the living arrangements, I was still flustered and a bit red-faced. Tally's wink became a smile. ¿Who knows how long civilization has got left on its library card? they said. And let's call Kelly, they said further. Tally nodded even more, but still smiling. It's time for the next generation of Surprises to step up. Move forward. Face the world. The Universe. We all raised our drumsticks.

Then—still waving our turkey legs—we called Threeb and invited him, too. He declined, reminding us that he'd already received his Christmas and was busy using it. By gift he meant the used Perkins Brailler I'd found whilst I was switching typewriters during the Ghost Writers On the Sly escapade. I sent that months and months ago, so it hardly counts as a stocking-stuffer, I stuttered. D-d-d-d-don't t-t-t-t-talk l-l-like P-p-p-p-porky, he threebled, with a smile that could be heard over the long-distance c-c-connection. After our unmanly giggling subsided, the Odd Surprise reported that he'd been typing up the Epic of Handy Jones, Complete With His Philosophy and Remarks of Wisdom, Volume I. Handy was still handy, but getting no younger, and there was no sense in letting the keys of the Perkins go idle. I'll be there in spirit, he said. And we hung up the phone.

It's called Thanksgiving for a reason. Daddy, let your mind roll on. Wubba, wubba, wubba.

15.

ROCKIN' AROUND THE CHRISTMAS TREE

I had a pal in the movie biz who'd come up with a good deal on a plane ticket for a Continental flight from Houston to Los Angeles with a stop in Midland. Ruth Etta would board there. Kelly would fly from New York to either L. A. or San Francisco, wherever he could get the best schedule. We wouldn't be home for Christmas, but at least the Outland Surprises would all be together. Kerrie Mae and Bobbie Sue advanced the plan to the Eliots and the Double-Joneses. Not surprisingly, the only objection from the Alkali Ranges was that Tally wasn't coming back to see the grandparents and grand-aunts-and-uncles. Sheesh.

Christmas Day fell on Tuesday, the Winter Solstice fell on the Saturday before. In each Ruth Etta found great significance. I looked into them myself. Tuesday, *Tiw's* Day, *Tiw* the Old English for the proto-Germanic *Tiwas,* the god of war and law, but also from the same stem that gives us the word 'deity'. Saturday, Saturn's Day, Saturn being the sixth planet from the sun, the planet with the beautiful rings, named after the Roman god of agriculture. More to my interest, the moon was waning and would be new the day after Boxing Day. It was the time of year when Orion came into his own. But it was important to Ruth Etta that we be together on the Solstice, so we booked her flight for Saturn's Day arrival.

I was worried about the weather. The whole of December had been gray and cloudy and damp and cold, the papers announcing it a record for Sunny So-Cal. On the nineteenth, the day the Mona Lisa arrived in New York in the cargo hold of the S. S. France—the papers announced, though their announcement rankled with implications that the Frog Nation should pay a little more deference to such a work of art, even if it was merely an Italian painting—on that Tuesday, the sky cleared over The City of the Angels and stayed pristine through the holidays.

Ruth Etta's aeroplane and my Nash-Rambler arrived at LAX as planned. An hour or so to retrieve her luggage and the American Motors Mobile was rolling north along California One. We knew we couldn't make Berkeley that day, so the scheme was to stop at the half-way point, which would be San Luis Obispo. I had learned of an historic inn there—the Milestone Mo-Tel, the first ever motor lodge anywhere in the Known Universe—which, it seemed to me, might be of interest to the proprietress of the Surprise Shifting Sands Mobile Motel. Regardless, it would make a logical resting place for the night.

Ruth Etta was delighted with the idea, but insisted that we make time for a pull-out somewhere along the way, somewhere scenic where we could see and hear the Pacific. ¡I knew the exact spot! Mugu Rock, just past Malibu Canyon. ¿Why? I asked her. You'll see, she answered, coyly. The Nash fairly burned-up the macadam.

An hour-and-change and three-dozen miles later we found the roadside attraction and pulled in. Before I'd managed to cut the engine and set the foot-brake, Ruth Etta had bounced out of the Nash and bounded across the parking lot toward the bounding main. She'd just brought herself up short of the surf when I caught up to her. The afternoon was sunny but cool, a brisk breeze blowing in off the sea, Ruth Etta facing into it, her arms wrapped around herself to hold her sweater. In one hand she held a sheet of paper. The sun— still above us but already headed down into the ocean—made a halo of her hair.

Struck by the scene, I stood, stock-still, stuck between the desire to stand outside and watch her and the desire to step inside and join her. Chivalry came to the rescue. As chivalry should. Ruth Etta was shaking. Without a second thought, I slipped my arms around hers, holding her shoulders to my chest. We stood quietly for a long time, watching the waves while the sunlight and the warmth of our bodies first slowed, then stopped the shivering. I was certain I wanted nothing more. Until Ruth Etta broke the silence. No, let me say that properly. She did not break the silence, she did not break anything at all. Rather, she turned the silence into words, gave voice to a moment that had, up to then, been voiceless.

I want to marry you, she said. I want the same thing, I replied, as much with my arms as with my voice, knowing now the nothing more I wanted only seconds ago—when spoken—was everything. We should marry ourselves, she continued, just as they did in the story. ¿On their way out of Los Angeles, like us?—I said in a question—¿today? ¿this afternoon? ¿this moment? Yes, exactly yes, she answered. Silence. I have a ceremony, she explained, that starts with a poem I've written for us to read, one to the other and together, here, now, on the beach, then—she added—a ceremony that finishes with the exchanging of gifts this evening. ¿Gifts? I felt a slight panic. I had only brought Christmas gifts. Don't worry, she countered, Handy Jones and Maya Gandhi made them for us. ¿They know? I asked. Of course, she laughed softly, they all know.

Everyone in Surprise read the book of short stories you sent, and everyone took it as your proposal—here Ruth Etta began a discourse—We all felt the same way about the world, like you felt, about what was going on in it. About what was happening to it. About how there are things larger than Surprise. Larger than us. The missile crisis, for starters. And maybe for finishers. There is no time for waiting, they all said. If we forego the present for fear of the future, your Father Jones said while your Mother Jones held his hand and smiled at us both, we will have neither present nor future. Then your Mother Jones added, In times like these you should not waste time alone when your time should be spent together—Ruth Etta still had more to report—My Father Eliot said to me, If you wish to marry him, write a poem. To which my Mother Eliot added, And wear something special, then went to digging in a trunk filled with frivolities. Some of which I have on now, Ruth Etta added, blushing. The Merrimans were, well, merry. And, of course—Ruth Etta sighed—Handy and Maya know how the spirit meets the world and how to make permanent places in the world for the spirit, just as Surprise was made, so they made us gifts that will make of each of us a permanent place for the other.

Then let us begin, I said.

She held the sheet of paper out where we could both read it, both facing west, me looking over her shoulder, the perfume of her hair and skin mingling with the salt spray. I'll start, we'll trade verses, she instructed, then we'll read the last verse together.

By light of stars
The moon upon
We bless each, us—
We bless us, one.

The earth and sea
Beneath the sun
They bless each, us—
They bless us, one.

Of all the world
We're chosen from
We bless each, us—
We bless us, one.

The new is born
The old is done
We bless each, us—
We bless us, one.

What once was two
One has become
We bless each, us—
We bless us, one.

Ruth Etta had turned to me as we read the last verse together. When we finished I kissed her forehead. ¿Where do I get such ideas? I should have smeared one on her like Peck did Gardner in 'On the Beach'. Afterwards we held hands as we walked back to the Rambler. It gave me time to think. I opened the tail-gate so we could sit and look out to the Pacific. ¿Are you happy? Ruth Etta asked. More than that—I said—the thought of you makes me happy. Your presence makes me ecstatic. Now you've made me complete.

I'm honest, if not cinematic. Maybe it was the short hike from the beach, or maybe it was perching on the business-end of the Cross Country Rambler Station Wagon, but whichever or whatever, I began to ramble. A Surprise Soliloquy. It rolled out of me in a tide, pulsing in waves. I give it to you as best I remember.

You are both poet and poem, Ruth Etta. I am neither, only a writer and his words. I think in sentences, not lines; in paragraphs, not verses. You and I are here on the Winter Solstice, the deepest time of the year, the time of rest and repose, the time of healing. The equinoxes are the practical days, the balanced days, the one of sowing and the other of reaping. Love is in balance then, too. The solstices are the impractical days, the everything-and-nothing days, the one of passion and the other of reflection. Love in the summer solstice comes from the height of desire, love in the winter solstice from the depth of commitment. The Summer Solstice is the day of romance, the Winter

Solstice the day of marriage. And today it is Saturn's Day, his planet to be seen low in the southwest over the ocean in the gloaming, so that we also marry under his rings.

¿Who else will understand us? We are Surprises, from a place where we govern without government, where we are religious without church, where we are patriots without flag or country, where we are students and teachers without schools, where love and work are ways and not destinations, where our beliefs are what we are and not what we profess, where love is the only thing that triumphs over reason.

Now it was her turn to kiss *me* on the forehead. Let's find a room, she cooed.

Back to the rings. In L. A. we could have checked into any hotel or motel or motor court without benefit of the-outward-and-visible-symbol-of-the-in-ward-and-invisible-grace-of-marriage. But not in the hinterlands. So I'd already planned to acquire a pair, just for the benefit of the desk clerk up ahead, and perforce would have had them for the unexpected ceremony at Mugu Rock except that I didn't know Ruth Etta's finger size and, obviously, didn't want to ask her ahead of time. Instead, I'd gone to the public library and with their collection of regional Yellow Pages scoped-out a jeweler's store in Santa Barbara not far off the main highway. It was the last Saturn's Day before Christmas; I expected that they'd be open late. They were. We picked up a nice, simple set of silver bands. Ruth Etta preferred them to gold. So did my jar of bottle-caps.

After our matrimonial shopping excursion, we found our way back to California One and set our sights again on the half-way point. But events—what actually happens—have a way of changing plans—the things you intend to happen. It soon became clear we wouldn't make San Luis Obispo until very late. Too late for us newlyweds. Rolling into Pismo Beach we came across a brand-new motel, right on the water, the SeaCrest Ocean Front. Ruth Etta and I just got married, I said to the clerk, letting him see my shiny new ring. ¿Jones? he asked, snidely, as I began to fill out the paperwork. Yes, Jones, I riposted, advancing my California Drivers' License across the counter. Very well, he sighed. ¿Do you want the Bridal? No, Ruth Etta interjected, I'll just hold 'im by 'is ears 'til I get used to 'im. The clerk and I were equally shocked, though the bride giggled all the way to the room.

We were quartered on the surf side. Once the luggage was unloaded and toted and stacked, we strolled down to the beach, found a little eatery that offered sautéed abalone, then watched Saturn blink-on over the Pacific as Sol dipped into the glimmering western horizon. Back in the room, Ruth Etta locked the door, twisted the deadbolt, then affixed the chain lock. I reached to kiss her, but she stopped me. Ceremony first, she said, we start by disrobing one another. So we did. She kept the pace, slowing me down if my fumbling became too frantic, helping me along when I became sledgehammered by the beauty unfolding before me. I was both manic and dumbfounded when Mama Eliot's choice of frivolities hove into view, a veritable clothing conundrum that left nothing to the imagination while at the very same time expanded the imagination to the far limits of the Universe of Erotic Ideas.

Once our wearables had found their way to the new motel's multi-colored-trendy-shag-carpeted floor, Ruth Etta continued her instructions. Next we shower together. You wash me, I wash you, she said, evenly. Soap has never been so exquisite, I thought, nor water so intoxicating. Now, you dry me, and I dry you, she continued, arming us each with only a hand-towel. Those won't soak up very much, I offered. Enough, she said, explaining that we needed damp skin as she produced the gift that Maya Gandhi had prepared, a handmade cloth sack filled with Indian Perfume, the Indian-Indian Medicine Woman's own concoction of dried sage and herbs and flowers. You rub this over me, and I rub it over you, Ruth Etta instructed. We did. I was about to die. Just as I commenced my descent into the realms of animal lust, she kissed me primly on the nose, stepped across the suite to dig into her suitcase, and produced the final element of the ceremony, a pair of necklaces fashioned by Handy Jones from polished mescal beans and tiny, hand-rubbed owl bones. We tie these on one another, she said, and wear them always, so that the love we make tonight will forever be blessed with the spirit of the sage by visions as strong as the mescal in the wisdom of the owl. Now, she said, kiss me anywhere and everywhere you've never kissed me before.

¡Joy the fever!

On the drive the next day we made plans of our dreams all the while we dreamed of our plans. The American Motors Cross-Country and California One were made for each other, one the prose and the other the poetry of the highway, one the traveling living-room and the other the picture outside the picture-window. It was the bourgeoisie-on-wheels in a boogie-woogie down the bohemian back-road, a pink-and-white cloud skiffing merrily along the Pacific coast. San Luis Obispo.

Carmel. Santa Cruz. San Francisco. Then over the bridge and into the Enclave of Gray Matter, the Hide-Out of the High IQ, the Capitol of Clever.

As I wrangled the Rambler into a parking space alongside the World's Merriest Mini-bus, Bobbie Sue and Kerrie Mae and Tally fairly burst from their 'Stream in a hail of halloos and howdies, most of the cacophony coming from the Littlest Surprise who, at half-a-year-away from his fourth birthday, had advanced from babbling and prattling to clearly-enunciated but rapidly-delivered and seemingly-unending discourse, a veritable linguistic fire-hydrant. We were still in the midst of our happy-dance hug-fest when Bobbie Sue caught sight of our sparkly-new rings. More excitement, more hugs, a few joyful tears shared amongst the ladies—with Tally and I maintaining our manly reserve in the Department of Lacrimae—then an abrupt silence.

We have some bad news, Kerrie Mae offered. Ruth Etta and I gasped, almost in unison, ¿Handy? ¿Maya Gandhi? ¿one of the folks? No, no, no, interjected the girls, also almost in unison. Nothing like that. It's Kelly, Kerrie Mae continued. He cabled us with the report that he got a last-minute gig, an understudy role on a Broadway show. He said to tell you—she looked straight at me—that he's got great news. It'll be your Christmas present—my sister intoned—in a second cable that you can't open—now with a happy smirk—'til we exchange gifts. Relieved, we all set about unloading the Cross Country Wagon and setting up arrangements for our holiday week.

It was the Surprise tradition to have egg-nog with plenty of nog and a casual repast of finger-foods with come-and-get-it ham and potato salad on Christmas Eve, followed by the singing of Christmas carols, afterwards capping-off the evening with a riot of ribbon and wrapping paper during the shameless orgy of opening presents in the gift exchange. Santa came overnight, leaving the big gifts and filling the stockings. Then it was Christmas dinner of turkey-and-dressing and barbecued-brisket-and-beans—no healthy vegetables allowed—followed by a fat and lazy, satisfied afternoon.

Living in our 'Streams had resulted in a few modifications to American-standard Christmas operating procedures. For starters, we had no fireplaces and no chimneys, a clear problem for Jolly Old Saint Nick. The Surprise solution was to leave a ceremonial door key with a plate of cookies and a glass of milk on the portable front steps, then hang the empty stockings on a festive rope strung across the living area just before donning our kerchiefs and caps and settling our brains for our long winter naps. Then, instead of a Christmas tree—even the small ones being too big for even the spacious thirty-two-footer luxury models—we collected cedar boughs on Christmas Eve's Eve, decorated them with strings of colored popcorn and bits of tinsel before distributing the bright and fragrant treelets around the interior cabin. In the city, Bobbie Sue had no difficulty acquiring an armful of broken branches from a nearby Christmas tree stand run by the Berkeley College-Ghetto Rotarians. In another change sparked by living in the city, the ceremonial front-door key was carefully chosen not to fit any known lock.

We had a wonderful time. We were traditionalists. At least as traditional as Surprises go. Tally told us—several times—that he was glad we didn't believe in a Postmodernist Santa. ¿Where does he get that stuff? we wondered. And then, we wondered as well, ¿what in the heckle is a Postmodernist Santa? There followed some limited discussion about reducing his time at The City Lights Bookstore. Christmas Eve chow was great. The carols were also great, including a new one now very popular on the radio, 'Do You Hear What I Hear?'—written specifically about the Missile Crisis—along with all the white-bread standards and a few African-American numbers like 'Go, Tell It On the Mountain' and some pop-music-numbers like 'Rockin' Around the Christmas Tree' and 'The Little Drummer Boy'—with Tally and I entrusted with the choicest part, the *pah-rumps* and *pum-pum-pums*.

We set out the key and cookies and milk, hung the stockings, and Tally unrolled his pallet and went straight to sleep. Kerrie Mae and Bobbie Sue prepared the Wally Byam Master Suite for us newly-weds after which they repaired to the other bed. The moon was almost new, and overhead, beyond the city lights of the Bay Area and far above the aluminum skin of the Airstream, a star shone brightly as we found our way to sleep.

Santa brought Tally an Etch a Sketch and a brand-new toy imported from Denmark called Legos. In the gift exchange the night before he'd gotten a treasure trove of books. Ruth Etta and I brought him 'The Phantom Tollbooth' while the Double-Joneses sent 'A Child's Christmas in Wales', both the 1952 LP recording by Dylan Thomas himself along with the 1955 print edition of the book. The Merrimans found a pristine copy of 'How the Grinch Stole Christmas'

and the Eliots selected the year's New York Times award-winner, 'The Island of
Fish in the Trees'. Maya Gandhi and Handy Jones each sent mysterious packages
of edibles, which the toddler relished but did not offer to share. Threeb sent a
poem, written in Braille, which Tally apparently could read, laughing aloud as
his chubby little fingers flew over the bumps. One day I would like to know *that*
story. Kelly had sent him a Spud Gun, and should have sent an endowment along
with it to replace the broken lamps and dishes that ensued. Not to mention the
raft of eyeless potatoes that it left behind—sad little stories, each and every one.

The grown-ups gave and got mostly utilitarian gifts, clothing and toiletries and
the like, though, being the bookish bunch we were, there were also many of the year's
new titles given. Kerrie Mae received Kuhn's 'The Structure of Scientific Revolutions', Bobbie Sue got a signed copy of Kesey's 'One Flew Over the Cuckoo's Nest',
Ruth Etta was presented Carson's 'Silent Spring', a copy of Steinbeck's 'Travels With
Charley' was wrapped for mailing to Kelly, and, probably owing to my penchant for
Heinlein and Bradbury, I landed Burgess's 'A Clockwork Orange'. We were almost
finished picking up the bits of ribbon and torn paper so as to make way for setting
the table for dinner when Kerrie Mae jumped up, went to digging in a hiding place in
one of the cupboards, then produced an envelope. Here, she said sheepishly, I almost
forgot Kelly's cablegram. Me, too, I exclaimed. Read it, she said, now more canine
than ovine, We want to know what the big surprise is from the New York Surprise.
Me, too, I answered as I tore off the end, blew into the cream-colored envelope so as
to puff-out the sides, and extracted the single sheet with a flourish.

THOM ED JONES
BERKELEY CALIFORNIA
STARRING IN NEW TELEVISION SERIES STOP MODERN RADIO
RANCH STOP
YOURE WRITER STOP START IMMEDIATELY STOP
YOUR PARDAROO
KELLY ELLIOTT

It took us a moment or two to regain our collective balance after the dizziness
brought on by all the starting and stopping and the twenty-five-word-limit-
brevity of the telegraphic medium. Then the whole lot of us went wild. Giddy.
¡Golly-gosh-golly!

The aroma of Christmas dinner brought us back to some semblance of normalcy. There was the table to set up, places to set, dishes to fill. While the meats were cooling enough for proper carving, we made an impromptu decision that our mealtime prayer would be a long-distance-direct-dial telephone call to Kelly. We whooped-it-up and down Ma Bell's copper-wire-pipeline. Kelly added a few details about the television series. Send the first season, thirty episodes, he said, then I'll come out to L. A. to start shooting. Scrape out some space in the Flying Cloud, he added. Kerrie Mae and Bobbie Sue tried to give him a stern lecture about the Spud Gun, but no one was in the mood for it, especially the lecturers who laughed all the way through their ad-lib admonition about willful children and vegetable-hurling armaments. Ruth Etta showed him the ring by holding it up to the telephone handset. Tally had already finished reading one of his new books and was about to launch into a full-fledged literary critique when—thank goodness for fiscal responsibility, even by happenstance—Kelly had to sign-off so as to have time to get to the theatre.

Food and talk aplenty followed in the Berkeley 'Stream. A hopeful question over dinner: ¿Was Ruth Etta planning to move out to L. A.? No, she said, our residences may be apart but our lives are together. Besides, she added, we have to keep Surprise in the world. We'll all return when it's right to return. And I'll be there, ready and waiting for you. There were nods all around. Kerrie Mae began to tell about her graduate school work in hydroponics and aquaculture. We could do that in Surprise, we all chimed in. Bobbie Sue reported about her new friends studying mind expansion. We do that already in Surprise, we all observed. More nods. Tally had been quiet. Too quiet. He'd slipped away from the table, unrolled his pallet beneath it and was in the grip of what appeared to be a fine nap. A motion was made and accepted and unanimously approved to emulate the Littlest Surprise. And we all felt better.

We went into the Golden Gate City on Boxing Day to take in a movie, standing in a long line for 'To Kill a Mockingbird', which had just opened. Afterwards, we moseyed over to City Lights. Ruth Etta wanted guidance for a particular kind of book, which both Kerrie Mae and Bobbie Sue said could be had from a friend of theirs, Richard Alpert, a visiting prof at Berkeley but who spent lots of time at the informal bookstore salon. What are you interested in, he asked in scholarly tones but with an impish gleam in his eye. Ruth Etta linked her arm in mine, then told him, My husband and I started in lust, exploring love. Now we are in love, exploring lust. We want to keep that relationship all the rest of our lives. Magnificent, he said, quietly and solemnly, bringing his hands together as if in prayer, bowing to her. I can recommend the exact, right book, a new edition of an ancient work, 'The Kama Sutra of Vātsyāyana'. He turned to a shelf behind him, picked up a book with a passionate red dust jacket on which there was the image of an equally-passionate sculpture of two lovers, then presented it to us. I can't help but notice your necklaces, he said, his eyes softening, and I know the blessings they convey. The gift of this book is my blessing to you. He pressed it in our hands. ¿From where do you come? he inquired. From Surprise, we all said, as if in a responsive reading. ¡Of course you do! he said, smiling like the Buddha.

It felt like church ought to feel.

We dallied another day on the Brainy Bay, helping to reduce the leftovers to a manageable state, then headed back to L. A. This time we drove straight through so as to give us plenty of relaxing time before the Continental return flight. When we arrived in Burbank we had twenty-four hours, we had the Flying Cloud, we had the 'Kama Sutra'. Oh, tidings of comfort and joy, comfort and joy, Oh, tidings of comfort and joy.

16.

PARD-A-ROOS

Neither Ruth Etta nor I were morose on the trip to El Eh Ex to rendez-vous with the aero-bus back to Midland. The Everyman's Limousine was a pink-and-white melody moving along the main arterials feeding in to the Hub of World-Wide Travel, the traffic around it all in a constantly-moving counter-point. On the way we sang along with the radio, chatted and palavered, talked and touched, using silent moments as a great conductor would hang his baton in the air a split-second off the beat, as a Borscht-Belt-stand-up would drag out the 'ing' in the evening's final bah-dah-biiing. We were one now, and though we would be separated by the triviality of space there was no separation between us. In every consequential way, we were intimately connected.

A few days before, on the road trip up to the Republic of Berkeley, our talking had been all about the future, *our* future. When you're love-birds, the cooing's all about the two of you. As well it should be. But in the afterglow of the sweetness of having spent Christmas with our fellow ex-pat Surprises there was now more to add to our discourse. To start with, of course, the Big News, the page-one headline stuff. We were giddy and giggly over the prospects of the new television series, not in the least because the two life-long pard-a-roos and now brand-new-brothers-in-law would be working together. Not to mention that Ruth Etta's big bro had sent more good news from New-York-New-York during our long-distance telephone extravagance, reports of getting speaking roles, of getting good reviews, of making lots of pals in the industry, many of whom were headed out here, out West, to Tee-Vee City.

Then there were the page-two local-dateline stories about Kerrie Mae's progress in the Land of Matriculation, her rapid ascent through the degrees of scholarship, her impending attainment of the robes and hoods of academia, her doctoring of philosophy. We were proud, proud, proud, *proud*. There was also

Bobbie Sue, who needed no research to know which way the wind blows, who was born knowing when to come in out of the rain, who knew—furthermore—what was rain and what was not, what was in and what was out, and who, herself, was the solid foundation of any and every ivied-ivory-tower ever i-rected. We were even more proud, proud, proud, *and double-proud.*

And of course there was Tally, the toddling Taliesin, the Tiny Bard of Berkeley, the Littlest Bookmark, the Light of the City Lights Bookstore. Why, we said to each other, almost at the exact same time, he's so handsome he could be Kelly's son. A pregnant pause. A *faux pas* pause, if you can translate my mangled *français.* We looked at each other, Ruth Etta and I, the moment we'd said it. Mental calculations. Wheels whirling in the windmills of our minds. Then Ruth Etta said Kelly had said Tally could have been his boy had Tally been a year older. Hmmmmmmmm.... We both knew that mathematics was never the arena in which her older brother, my bosom buddy, would ever shine. When it was numbers, Kelly was klueless, number-numb, integer-insufficient. A longer, more-pregnant pause, if you'll permit pregnancy by degrees. It's Kerrie Mae's place to say, we both said, and said together. I kissed Ruth Etta's hand. She kissed mine in return. And that was that.

Surprise was an oasis in the space-time continuum, for as bookmark or yard-stick or mile-marker, time meant nothing in the Land of Handy Jones. Fads and fashions passed us by, what-was and what-will-be indistinguishable from the present moment, the what-is-now. But as process, time meant everything. That we lived in Art Deco aluminum-skinned tipis divorced us not a whit from the natural world. We kept in closer touch with the seasons than we would have had we lived in permanent houses insulated from nature by permanent fences and lawns and landscaping. We were quartered far from the lights of town and city, still able to see the sky, a sky regularly scrubbed-down and polished-up by the sand-storms of spring and the northers of winter, a sky in which the planets and the stars and the sun and the moon moved about with comforting and visible regularity.

And it was fittingly under that vast Cactus Cosmos that we absorbed much of the culture of the condensed and convoluted world back where the sky could be but little seen. We took it in through the flickering images of the films favored at the Flatlands Drive-Out Theatre, critically combing through the variety, the catholicism, the eclecticism, the wide range of the Reels on the Range that were most frequently on the marquee. We reveled in the artsy European film noir, we pondered the great works of the American masters, we offered-up dialog for the silent features, we thrilled to the shoot-'em-up cops-and-robbers of the B-grades. Yet of all that celluloid cornucopia the one we asked for again and again was Gene Autry's corny-sci-fi-horse-opera serial 'The Phantom Empire' and its companion feature film 'Radio Ranch'.

Why that was is hard to say. Maybe impossible to say—that is, to put into words—for our joy in the series and its full-length flick was more feeling than thinking. On the surface the reels were predictable. Beneath the surface neither stood up well to close inspection. Both were plagued with discontinuities—things like Gene's pistol falling to the ground during a fight but magically back in the holster when the fisticuffs ended, or like the bad guys arriving at the ranch on a 'cabin plane' that featured a living-room-sized cockpit in the interior shots but was no more than a little Piper Cub in exterior views, even becoming an open-cockpit biplane in a later scene.

Some of it was downright confusing. The futuristic realm of Maurania—what its occupants called their Phantom Empire—lay deep down in the earth below Radio Ranch, twenty-three-thousand feet as marked on the elevator that connected them to the surface, deep even to kids growing up in the oil patch. Aided by robot workers who wore tin stovetop-top-hats, its inhabitants went busily about mining their valuable stores of radium. Or sometimes the valuable stores were referred to as uranium. The value of either, or both, and the existence of either, or both, were kept hidden from The Surface People, meaning us Earth-lings, by a mounted cavalry called the Thunder Riders. If the robot trolls appeared to be the love-children of Abraham Lincoln and Dorothy's pal the Tin Man, the pointy helmets and capes of the Thunder Riders endowed them with the mien of a sci-fi Ku Klux Klan gone horseback. Yet when Gene's young side-kick Frankie Baxter—played by Frankie Darro—organized a pint-sized horse-back militia to counter the subterranean K-K-K, he named his fellow boy-scout-posse members the Junior Thunder Riders. Big bad guys, meet the little good guys, whom we'll call the Little Bad Guys. Dressed in capes and with tin buckets for helmets, they were more than just a tad reminiscent of their evil adult adversaries. But they had a motto—'To the rescue!'—which we took as our own, and, better still, we could actually join the National Thunder Riders Club and be Junior Thunder Riders ourselves. Just send in your name, it read in the credits, and we'll send your mother a pattern so she can make you a costume.

In spite of all that, there were obvious reasons to watch both—the serial and the feature—over and over. There was Gene—in his first celluloid starring role—with his regular-guy-good-looks and his regular-guy-good-voice and his snappy outfits, a grown-up hero who smiled as big and bright as a kid and did things that kids wanted to do. And Smiley Burnette singing along with The Beverly Hillbillies. And The Beverly Hillbillies singing Smiley Burnette's songs. And Betsy King Ross, who was cute as a bug and who could stick to the saddle like a tick to a hound, a bonafide tomboy but whose skirts a-flap in full gallop revealed the gams of a future vamp—a tantalizing glimpse that never failed to pump up the blood pressure of us pard-a-roos. And Darro, quick and tough and smart, a scrappy leader, big beyond his Peter Pan stature and a real, live movie star to whom we Surprises had an honest-to-goodness connection, his traveling circus acrobat parents having been pals of Sue Merriman's folks back in their Sioux City Sioux's Traveling Revue days.

Still, there was something more than all that that put me in yo-yo mode when it came to 'The Phantom Empire' and 'Radio Ranch'. Me more than the others, though they felt it too. It wasn't just Betsy King Ross's legs, though there was magic enough there. It wasn't just Frankie Darro's verve, his Little-Rascals-élan, though I fancied myself to be his distant kin. No, for me it was deeper, a thing more felt than reasoned, a hint of the shape of a world that had no shape, or had many, a world built of the layers of mystery and the mystery of layers, built of the layers of the earth above Maurania and the sky above the earth, of the layers of music tied to a ranch with a contract with a radio show, of the layers of how behind one thing there was always another, of how the evil in the world wore masks on top of masks. Then there were the layers of how the good guys could be mistaken for the bad guys, how the bad guys could be mistaken for the good guys, and how there were plenty of guys who weren't either good or bad but were just guys, stuck with their role and their fate and doing the best they could with the hand they'd been dealt. It was the same as sitting in the barber's chair with a big mirror on the wall behind you and a big mirror on the wall in front of you looking at the infinite reflections of your face and the back of your head, knowing where and with whom it starts but with no way of knowing where and with whom it stops. And all of that was in a movie, a thing of images and of the motions of light and sound.

So when Kelly's telegram described our new venture as a modern 'Radio Ranch', I was in it. We didn't know that Westerns were on their way out, and we wouldn't have cared. Cowboys-and-Indians still commanded plenty of ink in TV Guide and plenty of acreage on small-town movie marquees across the country. What we did know was that writing for television was getting better and more interesting. Tod and Buz—a couple of cool beatnik button-down proto-hippies—were in their third season traveling down 'Route 66', the Mother Road of American Angst. Rod Serling's 'The Twilight Zone' was in its fourth season, its slot about to expand to a full hour of weirdness. 'The Outer Limits' was to premiere later in the year. *Weltschmertz* was pervading the American *weltanschauung*.

Maybe the World-Wide *weltanschauung,* to be doubly-redundant. Nineteen Sixty-Three was fast becoming a big year for change all over the planet. You could feel it in the air, hear it on the radio, watch it on the news. Schmaltz was going passé. The seeds sown by the Beats were sprouting here and there and everywhere. The twentieth anniversary of the discovery of LSD was coming up in April, turning Eliot's cruelest month into Huxley's coolest month. Harvard was shedding itself of Tim Leary and Dick Alpert. Captain Trips had already brought his briefcase acid dispensary to the Realm of the Golden Gate where Owlsley Stanley was teaching himself how to synthesize it on his own and where—no surprise here, *n'est-ce pas?*—Bobbie Sue had become an early disciple.

It was a year oddly-bookended by music, starting out with 'Telstar' and songs about walking—we'll 'Walk Right In', sang the Rooftop Singers, though the 4 Seasons would 'Walk Like a Man' while Rufus Thomas was 'Walkin' the Dog'—the year then going out with 'Dominique', a French song about a Spanish red-headed saint who walked everywhere and also happened to be the patron saint of astronomers. Spoo-ky. In the midst of all that hoofing-it there were the Kingsmen sailing three days across the sea with 'Louie, Louie' while the Surfaris had a 'Wipe Out' as the Fireballs were laying down tracks to 'The Sugar Shack'. With Bob Dylan 'Blowin' in the Wind' in May and the Beatles declaring just after Christmas 'I Want to Hold Your Hand', the world would never be the same.

As if it could, come November, when the Populuxe Era was gunned-down by an insignificant wannabe-Commie and the Age of Belief in Government was gut-shot by a small-time strip-club operator. Then—on the personal front—there was last year's Ghost Writers On the Sly escapade and J. Emperor Hoover leering out of the television and all that business about the GPS and the carrier pigeon and the goons crashing the trailer-park Canasta Club. Mix in a little George Woodcock and I was off and running. It was the perfect time for Los Dos Pard-a-Roos to dish-up a dose of alkali anarchism. All I would need to do to get going was to write a treatment, a back-story to tell me—the writer—the back-drop for the big story.

Now, in the same way it was necessary for the writer to write, it's also necessary for the reader to read. ¿Why? you might ask, Dear Reader, thinking that I might be giving you the treatment with the Treatment. And you are right to ask, and right to think. Not only because it's always good practice to ask ¿why? and to think contrary thoughts, but also because the Treatment that follows may seem to be a digression, or a diversion, or a distraction, or all that and more. To which I agree—with a bit of unseemly pride, able to produce such a short work worthy of so many adjectives—though I validate my vainglory by quickly pointing out it's the more that's of gravest import, the more being that the typed treatise upon which you're about to embark—reproduced from the original, never-before-seen draft, replete with notes and corrections—this crude compendium of characters with its slightest sliver of plot is, in truth, a superficial parody of the subterranean parallels struck through Surprise and, therefore, the whole, round world. It is both chicken and egg and any one of the turtles going all the way down. Doppelgangers, twin-strangers, Santa-Clauses-and-clowns, all the look-a-likes lurking beneath the surface and behind the masks and make-up, these layers lay out the logic of all that is to come. *The thing that hath been, it is that which shall be;* sayeth Ecclesiastes, *and that which is done is that which shall be done: and there is no new thing under the sun.* And thus sayeth Thom Ed the writer: ¡persevere, and read on!

Bubble-Up
~~Hell's Gate~~
~~BUBBLE-UP~~
~~Hell's Gate~~
~~BUBBLE-UP~~

A post-modern television western
starring Kelly Elliott

by Thom Ed Jones
General delivery, Suprise, Texas

draft of February 25, 1963

It is somewhere in the indeterminate and indis-
criminate American West, a geography of sweeping
vistas and narrow, rocky canyons, a landscape of
~~barren and~~ buttes and hoodoos and mesas and remnant
plateaus, a desert land graced with the occasional
sparkling spring rising to the surface from nowhere
to form a stream running down to an uncharted river.
It is a land where capitalists and imperialists are
interchangeable, where bandit gangs and posses ride
the same horses, where the entrepreneur is both intrepid and insidious and where everyone is an entrepreneur, where the distinction between a black
hat and a white hat is an ethical proclamation, not
a fashion statement.

Well before Einstein, the Hopi understood that
place and time were intimate with one another, so
it is no mystery that this West belongs to an era
that is also indeterminate, existing in neither past
nor future, though perhaps it existed in a future
from a long-ago past, or perhaps it will exist in
a past from a far-away future. Nevertheless, in
this place and time there is never anything new,
only the old things being constantly re-born, where
old identities are buried and different ones dug up,
where old grudges are forgotten and different ones
set, where old dreams are nightmares but where
every nightmare is someone else's dream, where old
identities are stripped away and where -- if we are
hopeful -- people will be peeled back to their core
~~entirely~~ beings, back to their essences, and where --
if we are lucky -- those cores, those essences
will turn out to be good.

Surrounded by that painted cartoon landscape is
a narrow-mouthed box canyon -- in appearance more
Salvador Dali than Maynard Dixon -- from which flows
a small river whose source is a spring at the canyon's head. Gringo settlers came to call the waterway Hell's River for its lack of fish and aquatic
life and for its strong slufurous smell, naming its
source Boiling Springs for obvious reasons. The
canyon itself soon became Hell's Canyon and its
mouth Hell's Gate.

Its first permanent resident was June Bevier, a
former U. S. Army lieutenant who'd been drummed out
of the service for operating a house of ill-repute.
Not court-martialed, she had too many high-ranking
names on her off-duty roster for that, but sent
packing all the same. She'd been traveling west
after her forced retirement in search of somewhere
to start over when she chanced upon a nomadic party

of Native Americans of indeterminate tribal affiliation
who were headed east at an alarming rate of speed, wearing full regalia but mounted on a cavy of coughing
and snarling motorcycles. Though a bit non-plussed
by the band's machinery, June flagged them down so as
to inquire about the likelihood of potential locations for her personal reincarnation. They slid to a
stop almost as one, and when the dust settled a bit
she was relieved to see that -- at the least -- they
were riding bikes built by the Indian Motorcycle Man-
ufacturing Company, mostly Scout and Big Chief models,
every scooter painted bright red in color.

She spoke to them through an interpreter who seemed
to be part of their band and who first misunderstood
her question, thinking she was searching for the path
to spiritual enlightenment. Once the once-upon-a-time
mistress had cleared that up, they were pleased -- a
little too pleased, she thought later -- to tell her
of some land they wished to sell, adding that it had
great curb appeal and no property restrictions. For
how much? asked the comely former madam, perhaps a bit
eagerly. After a short parley, a very short parley,
the interpreter reported that the price was the same
as Manhattan's, twenty-four bucks plus all the beads
she could muster. As costume jewelry counted amongst
the implements of her trade, she countered with a flat
fifty dollars, sans the baubles. There was no quib-
bling from the No Name People, who smiled as they
swapped a painted deerskin map for five Hamiltons before quickly mounting-up and roaring off into the distance. June was ~~pleased~~ satisfied, though a little
surprised. There'd been no arguing the price, a thing
to which she wasn't accustomed, and none of the band
seemed the least bit remorseful ~~and~~ about removing themselves from their traditional home and hearth. On the
map the name of the place was written in the unfamiliar
language of its sellers, which ~~she~~ she, of course, couldn't
read, though she felt the longish word had a certain
graphic beauty, a thing that in another time and place
would have most closely resembled boxcar graffiti.
Our elders, he shouted over his shoulder as ~~kick~~ he
started his ride, called it Where-The-Creator-Forgot-
To-Bring-Her-Best-Things.

Madam Bevier was disquited but not discouraged. ~~On
the~~ She hastened to the nearest court-house to file on
her new holdings. The ~~xxx~~ clerk sniggered when presented with the map but managed to croak out a Thank-
You-Miss-Beaver as he presented her with the deed. It's
Bev-yea, she said matter-of-factly, by this stage in
her life well-accustomed to the routine mispronuncia-
tion of her family name, and to the crudities that
often followed. ~~Butbs~~ But what's amusing about the

land? she inquired, less matter-of-factly. Well, says
he in an exaggerated faux-old-timer's voice-over accent,
Hit taint very good water'n that air spring. She
shrugged, turned, and left the courthouse. It would not
be the first time that June Bevier had faced difficulty
-- and triumphed over it -- nor would it be the last.

     The clerk turned out to be partly right. But mostly
wrong. It was indeed the case that the spring seemed
unpalatable to critters of most every kind. Unlike any
other desert water hole, no tracks could be found a-
round it, no animal trails led to it, and even mi-
grating birds passed it by. Livestock could be in-
duced to drink the water, but only after it had coursed
several miles down the rocky sands of the Hell's River
channel. Even then, cattle that watered too often
at its banks quickly began to grow thin and bony, soon
becoming no more than mirages on the hoof. The few cowpunchers in the region who could remember early attempts to stock the canyon's ranges told of the cattle
being so thin they couldn't be seen well enough to
gather, but, luckily, they glowed and so could be
rounded up at night. Sometimes the cowhands laughed
when they told the tale, Most times they didn't.
     And it was equally true that people could only
ingest the smallest amounts of the water without dire
consequences to their digestive plumbing, giving them
a work-out at both ends, much the same effect as swal-
lowing a Roto-Rooter. But, still, the hot spring itself was not without benefits. First and foremost, it
was a mineral bath par excellence. A soak in Boiling
Springs would cure whatever was ailing the body at any
given time -- ague to asthma, pimples to pains,
dyspepsia to diptheria, headache to heartache -- even
if those taking the waters emerged smelling like the
Devil. But who cared about the rotten egg aroma emanating from the beaming bathers? The heavy,
leaden forms that had eased into the hot and steamy
churn fed by the sulfuric solution percolating up
from the primeval depths of the earth left the waters
of that munificient whirlpool a scant hour later with
limbs light and lithe, a spring in the step and the
next step the first step in the journey down the rest
of a pleasant day.
     June Bevier right away realized the resourse she'd
reaped, the powerful potential of her purchase. Instead of a bordello, she built a day spa over the spring
with a hotel connected to the spa and with a huge,
torch-lit sign atop her quaint outpost of civilized
living proclaiming in large, ornate letters "The
Bevier Lodge". In plainer, smaller letters just below
she added her motto, "Far Out In The Far West".

Amongst the cowpunchers and miners and border-busters
who came to frequent her offerings it was known as The
Beaver Lodge, though no one had the courage to use the
vulgar nick-name within the hearing of Madam June. As
if in counter to the unsaid but obvious insinuations,
she dressed her girls not in flimsy lingerie and impossible corsets and silly feathers but in mermaid outfits, each and every lovely lass thereby paying homage
to a healthy, natural world. More than that, each member of her entire school of pin-up fishes developed
expertise in one or another of several specialties --
some borrowed from the Orient, some borrowed from the
personal ads, some borrowed from ancient mystic tra-
ditions -- xxxx activities such as massage, numerology,
yoga, and the proper methodology for the application
of full-body cucumber cleansing. Those who wouldn't
pay for the added services would pay evenmore to watch,
and would pay most if it was one of their pards getting slathered down with pureéd cucumis sativus.

Instead of whiskey, she sold bottles of Bubble-
Up, which was nothing but fresh water drawn from a
pool high up on the canyon wall, Miss Bevier having
found the small reservoir by deciphering a note left
in small script reduced from the sellers' alien tongue,
a note that had been thoughtfully appended to her deerskin map. The pool was fed by a trickling but reliable
fount which permitted the enterprising madam to pipe
the agua fresca down to the canyon bottom. It was too
precious to employ for bathing or washing, instead
saved purely for slaking the thirst of her best guests.
Even so, this nog of necessity -- by whatever name it
was known -- was known to be scarce, so that bottled
drinks became the norm; indeed, the soda-dispensing
machine was pioneered and developed here.

Very soon, a bustling burg grew up around the Bevier
Lodge. The usual entrepreneurs found their way to the new
settlement, bringing with them xx the usual ideas for
the usual businesses and the usual services usually
found across the Western frontier, only to find a very
unusual community, one in which the usual usually
failed and the unusual usually survived. The oddness of
the place was a filter of sorts. The unusual newcomers
who stayed became the usual settlers, the usual newcomers who were capable of change became unusual, and
the dogmatically-usual left for the usual greener pasture
A few usual but useful illustrations follow.

Mayor Middleton drifted in from a failed family
plantation in the Deep South, exactly from where no one
ever recalled even though he often told them the name
of his hometown. Details about himx seemed to bear no
permanence,

even to include his appearance, which was so average
and innocuous that no one was able to describe him. His
mother had named his older brother President and his
younger brother Governor but, for reasons only a highly-
trained psychologist could ferret-out, chose Mayor for
her middle son. Believing that a name was the same as
destiny, Mayor Middleton moved from city-to-city, town-
to-~~town~~town, village-to-village, seeking mayoral employment in each new place. Sadly, such positions were
in short supply -- only one slot per jurisdiction -- and
came with complicated hiring processes. A discouraging
string of failures had led him like a trail of day-old-
bread-crumbs to the young, raw hamlet in Hell's Canyon.
     Maybe the wannabe mayor Mayor was right about des-
tiny. When he'd finished telling his story to the sympathetic ears of Miss Madam Bevier, she announced that
she'd appoint him to the post just as soon as the settlement became an official town. It was precisely the
encouragement that had so long eluded the dog-eared-
middle-son Middleton. Straight away he collected names
on a petition, set up ~~ballot~~ a voting booth in the lobby
of the Lodge, persuaded a couple of the Mermaids to
serve as clerks, then held an election. The ballot was
remarkable for its simplicity. There were three items
up for decision. The first read: Mark your preference
in organizing our community -- followed by two choices,
each preceded by a check box -- (a) a shining, bustling,
prosperous town or (b) a violent, vermin-infested,
unincorporated slum. The second read: for Mayor, with
another two choices and another two check boxes --
(a) Mayor Middleton or (b) Mayor Middleton. The final
item read: Write-in a name for our town, after which
the check-box was replaced by a long, open space. It
was as fair an election as was ever held in the American West -- maybe in the whole of The Land of the Free --
with incorporation passing handily, Mayor Middleton
winning in a landslide, and, as someone had unintentionally failed to extinguish the gas lamps illuminating the sign advertising The Bevier Lodge's special
bottled beverage, the new town was now officially
christened Bubble-Up, a fortunate name as it invoked
both optimism and whimsy all the while promoting a
~~local~~ major local product.
     More illustrations. Shortly after this historical
milestone, whilst stopping through for the night a
pair of itinerant evangelists -- Brother Bud Brothers
and his wife Sister Sissy Brothers -- finding no place
of worship instead found a new calling and founded a
church. Though they shouldn't have found it unusual --
being located in a place called Hell's Canyon -- what
they didn't find were the usual parishioners, nary even

a single congregant, for it turned out that Miss June's
Mermaids were far better fishers of men than were the
Brothers twain. In no time, having spent all their
saved-up years of love offerings on the new sanctuary
they'd built directly across from The Bevier Lodge, the
Brotherses had come down to their last spare dime -- but,
thankfully, as God works in mysterious ways -- at that
exact moment a revelation came to Brother Bud in a dream
in which an angel wearing a sequined jumpsuit said,
Build it, and they will come.

That very next day, Brother Bud converted their
little brown church in the arroyo into a chapel, suitable for both weddings and funerals and with an added
feature that virtually guaranteed foot traffic: a large,
well-stocked saloon. Before their conversions, the two
evangelists had met as young vaudeville performers, he
as a Toby character and she as a rag-time accordionist.
They put their old skills back to work and soon filled
the little chapel. Sister Sissy stood outside, squeeze
box balanced on her bounteous bosom, belting out the
best of Joplin while, through the swinging doors,
Brother Bud ran the bar. Here's the kink, and the brilliance of the clerices convenient vision: the drinks
came with a twist, and not lemon rind, as all libations
were free to any patron who'd first listen to Brother
Bud's Bible lesson. So it came to pass that the town's
drunks were soon able to quote the Good Book -- chap-
ter, verse, and line -- with the only downside being
that anyone conversant with the Gospel was automatic-
ally assumed to be an alcoholic.

Still providing illustrations, it should be mentioned that next door to Brother Brothers's Bar was a
small clinic run by Milford "Doc" Cassidy -- more Neal
than Hopalong -- and ex-pat from the medical profes-
sionwhose standard prescription was to offer his pa-
tients a small, pungent cigarette, hand-rolled in brown
paper, with the instruction, Take a couple of puffs
and look me up when you straighten up. ¶ Despite
persistent rumors of malpractice in all the major metropolitan areas, "Doc" was also an internationally-known
authority on butterflies. None of the locals spoke his
name without holding up both hands and using the
index and middle fingers of each to mime the quota-
tion marks around his nickname or, if their hands and
arms were otherwise in use -- say, carrying a patient
into the clinic -- they would invariably say Quote-
Doc-Unquote.

Speaking of mimes, two were employed at the bou-
tique apothecary-and-mercantile adjacent to Cassidy's
Clinic. Not long after the grand opening of The Bevier Lodge, one of the No Name Tribe had ridden back

to the spring to see how things were going with the new
owner, saw that there was no place to buy postcards or
souvenir spoons or rubber tomahawks, and, seeing that
as an oversight, sold his bike and began to build his
business. It should be pointed out that the No Name
Tribe each and all had names of their own, but they were
a multi-lineal people -- tracing their descent through
not only fathers and mothers, but also through friends
and neighbors and sometimes even passersby -- with the
result that a person's full name, like that of the Gypsy,
often took up a ream of paper. To simplify things,
tribal elders decreed that, while each No Name was entitled to entertain their complete moniker for legal
purposes, registered members were to be called simply
by their own choice of any two of their many given names.
Which is why our inquisitive native was known only
as Mark John, though after perusing his prices his customers began to call him Mark-Up John, and when the name
stuck, Mark John just shrugged before he added Up to
his sign out front.

Back to the mimes. A bachelor, Mark-Up doted on his
twins -- Nan, a niece, and Bert, a nephew -- whom he'd
sent to college back east. They were stellar students,
earning several graduate degrees -- including a post-doc
at the Greenwich Village School of Mimes -- but were
never able to secure a job, for the world at large still
considered Indians to be savages -- noble, perhaps,
picturesque, perhaps; educated, perhaps; but savages
all the same -- nothing more than unemployable cur-
iousities. Not to mention that having such long formal
names caused their application paperwork to be measured not in pages but in pounds, a distinct disadvan-
tage in an increasingly form-driven, standardized, one-
size-fits-all society. Therefore, like so many other
unemployed job-seekers, they headed West, eventually
winding up on Uncle Mark-Up's doorstep.

As a start-up, Uncle Mark-Up had little in
the way of permanent positions to offer up, yet was
anxious to have them put their degrees on his ther-
mometer. He offered room and board, came up with a
medical-care policy arranged through the clinic next
door -- where Quote-Doc-Unquote's standard prescription came to be highly-valued by the twins -- with the
icing on the cake being what was likely the very first
stock-option plan in the U. S. of A. The both of you
figure out something to do to help out, Uncle Mark-Up
told the two, who were too happy to oblige. We'll be
marketers, the duo said exactly at the same time with
the exact same phrasing and in the exact
same tone, exactly in that natural duet only available
to twins.

Excellent, echoed their uncle, who then introduced

them to June Bevier, who in turn introduced them to her
costume coordinator, who then armed the twins with the
necessities for their new enterprise. For Bert there
was a huge stock of magnificient feathers from which
he fashioned an equally-magnificient war bonnet, its bel-
licose beauty unblemished despite the bird-fronds having
come from peacocks. There was a single ostrich feather
in the swag which Nan added to her beaded headband, a
nice touch atop her skimpy chamois chemise which, even
in combination with her long braids, covered little of
her ample acreage. The rest of the pelt from the little goat-antelope was used to outfit Bert in a loin-
cloth, a garment, much akin to his sister's, that was
only a mere suggestion of clothing. Once fully rigged-
out, the twins each grabbed a handful of cigars and
posted themselves on either side of the doorway into
their uncle's retail emporium, a pair of flesh-and-
blood Cigar Store Wooden Indians. They even printed up
calling cards, though the savvy savages called them
business cards -- the first ever examples known to
marketing scholars -- calling their new enterprise
Irony, Inc., her cards reading "Nan and Bert", his reading "Bert and Nan", both ending with the phrase "Have
Pun Will Travel".
     The manikin-femikin simulacrumae had several rou-
tines. A few examples, for example. One was to aim
snarky comments at bystanders and passersby; the pigeon
pedestrians couldn't turn around fast enough to catch
the cigar-wielding mimes out of their pose. Another
was to switch those poses, sometimes so quickly the
switch occurred in the brief moment that an onlooker
would blink and sometimes so slowly it was hours before the switch was noticed. Or for the twins to secret
one of their business cards in the gawker's pocket without the mark's knowing it. Besides, the twins were
simply stunning in their get-ups, with the result that
a crowd of oglers was always gathered around. Business boomed, so much so that Uncle Mark-Up ran an ad
in the West Coast trades and hired a midget whom he
dressed as a Persian and had circulate through the crowd
collecting tips.

     In an indeterminate fashion -- which is not sur-
prising, really, given that actions are louder than
words -- the twin mimes Nan and Bert contributed to a
monumental change in the fortunes, and the history, of
Bubble-Up. It went like this. Whilst in one of their
graduate programs -- neither twin could remember which,
there'd been so many -- they'd befriended an odd but
brilliant lad known only by nickname, The Owl. They'd
lost touch over the semesters and the years of their

various degrees and varying institutions, but as the
news of the twins' venture spread xx through the
science-and-show-biz gossip network, The Owl sent them
a friendly letter of fond remembrances and, in passing, noted that he was looking for a summer work-study-
internship program. Did they know, he inquired, of anyone who'd employ an eager youngster pursuing a graduate degree in Eco-Chemistry. The twins didn't but
passed the missive along to Miss Bevier, who thought
it a splendid idea and cabled The Owl to present himself at the earliest opportunity. There were things
the Empress of Entrepreneurship wished to know about
her most valuable resource, the waters of Boiling Springs.

It took some time for The Owl to arrive. Though
he seldom stayed long in one place, he was not a good
traveler, having no licenses for operating mechanized
vehicles of any kind -- land, sea, or air -- and, not
being a particularly pleasant passenger, the Big-
Brained Bird Boy wasn't widely welcomed in the transportation industry, even as a paying fare. The train
was the only conveyance he could tolerate -- and could
tolerate him -- so, despite the Burg-In-the-Bad-Lands
not being situated on any railway, he managed to book
passage on a small feeder line that had an end-of-the-
tracks stop at an old, abandoned military outpost replete with round-house and turntable, a place where the
United States Camel Corps once took delivery of its
dromedarians before rotating the steam engines and
pointing its train of empties back towards civilization. Upon arrival, The Owl planned to rent a couple
of horses and pack the remaining distance into Bubble-
Up.

As his not-inconsiderable store of implements was
being taken off the baggage car, our young post-doc
research fellow pressed a fiver into a porter's
hand with the instruction to fetch a couple of suitable mounts from the livery yard. The pile steadily
building on the depot platform was almost complete --
a small mountain of boxes packed with test-tubes and
vials, flasks and beacons, alcohol-burners and pipettes,
Geiger Counters and mass-spectrometers -- just as the
stable-hand and two sturdy steeds hove into view.
And just as soon turned tail, so to speak, and high-
tailed it, to continue the metaphor, back to the
livery. The Owl showed no emotion whatsoever, as it
wasn't the first time he'd been denied service by
rent-a-horse purveyors.

For our budding scientist was a big man. Nothing
smaller than a Belgian or a Shire could hold him up.
He was over six-and-a-half-feet tall when his posture
was good but at all times barrel-chested, square-

shouldered, and topped with a large round head crowned
with an unpredictable shrubbery of jet-black hair. His
eyes, too, were big and dark, a pair of hockey pucks
set behind thick glasses, the whole of his ocular equipment over-shadowed by a set of prehensile, wing-shaped
eyebrows. As he was by nature a quiet man of modest
wardrobe -- naught but labcoats, differentiated one from
the other only by the remnant splashes of color from
various experiments -- and was fully moustashieoed and
bearded, his peepers were all that remained as his primary communicators. He blinked noticeably -- an important contributor, one would think, to his nickname--
and one could tell what was going on in the Turing Machine between his ears by the spacing and duration of
the blinks, much like the lights flashing off-and-on
in the whirring computers familiar to latter-day sci-fi
movie audiences. As he pondered a problem, the blinks
began slow and deliberate, their speed and frequency
gradually increasing in both measurements as the required logic was raveled and unraveled, assembled and
disassembled, tested and retested, until -- as the solution neared -- the growing frenzy accelerated into
a virtual orgasm of conclusion. It was a beautiful
sight, though not one for the faint of heart.
     On the platform that day, the porter -- a skinny,
wizened, old Irishman who painfully emulated a Southern
Negro drawl in hopes of getting better tips -- watched
in amazement as The Owl thought his predicament, mulled
the possibilities, assessed the alternatives, his large
lids opening and shutting slowly at first, then faster
and faster and faster until he remembered the history
of this particular dead-end depot and exclaimed a single
word: Camels! Instantly, the porter grasped the ele-
gance of The Owl's solution and pointed him toward
The Oasis, a bar across the dusty main street, over and
down a block. In moments our junior scientist had returned with an ancient veteran of the U.S. Army's failed
desert locomotion experiment, the decorated but be-
sotted non-com pensioner leading a pair of flea-bitten,
bedraggled Bactrians, which you'll recall as being the
two-humped models, perfect for the Big Boy of Brains and
his over-sized A. C. Gilbert Science set.
     Silhouetted against a Joseph Mallord William Turner
sky -- had Turner ever chanced to motor west to lay the
landscape groundwork for the likes of Catlin and Bier-
stadt, Remington and Russell, Moran and Dixon, Troup
and Cole -- the ponderous and fantastic cut-outs of
The Owl and his camelians made their slow-and-stately,
largely-uneventful trek down into the lower drainages
of the Hell's River waterway. Uneventful, that is,
until The Owl started nearing the narrows known as

Hell's Gate, where crystalline deposits began to appear
on rocks along the edge of the stream, a few at first,
then ever more common the farther upstream they coursed.
He collected samples, on a lark touching one especially
well-formed 3-D rhomboid crystal to his tongue. He'd
no sooner cameled-up than the world began to take on
bizarre and unusual shapes. He began to the hear the
wild colors of the canyon walls, see the songs the
snakes sang whilst slithering along the sage, feel the
thoughts of his companion Dromedaries, taste the sunlight as if it were lemonde squeezing through the air.
He learned the name of God, and promptly forgot it. He
saw himself from the inside out, then from far above,
floating over his own small scientific expedition. All
in all, it was the most enlightening and peaceful thing
he'd ever experienced.

He'd come down from his unexpected experiment by the time the camels knelt in supplication before the Bevier Lodge, sliding their scientific saddle-
fulls streetward. The Owl was a doer and a thinker,
not a reader, especially of fluff such as newspapers
and novels and poetry -- though he made exceptions for
the comics -- but went through the scientific literature fence-row-to-fence-row, and the more obscure, the
more he set stock in it. More tests would be needed,
for certain, but he'd bet money that he'd just discovered a naturally-occurring element interchangeable
with a hallucinogenic drug recently synthesized by the
Swiss scientist Albert Hoffmann and just as recently
reported in the Journal of Alpine Oddities.

As the camel-wrangler was dusting himself off,
Madame June stepped out to greet her odd, new guest,
but The Owl chirped before the Mistress could speak,
the first words out of his beak being, I need a place
to work. The second words being, And rename your bar
The Bicycle. As his arrival had all the earmarks of
genius, all the drama of a meteor-strike, and all the
urgency of an air-raid klaxon, Miss Bevier went to work.
Though Bubble-Up was, by-and-large, bare of bicycles,
one was scrounged-up nonetheless, and soon hung above
the re-christened bar, though not before several of
the Mermaids had tried-out the two-wheeler, failing
in fine fashion when their flipper-feet were found to
be futile pedal-pushers. The beautiful piscines wound
up riding balanced side-saddle on the rack on the back
of the bike, being pumped by the pedaler up front.
After a scant few weeks of furious investigations
and patient refinements, the Bicycle Bar in the Bevier
Lodge began to offer a new treat, Lolly-By-Golly-Pops,
laced with the newly-named Hoffmanium. And in scarcely

a few more weeks after that, Bubble-Up became the newest and bestest place to be. Anywhere. The motto on
the big billboard sign was quickly re-lettered to read
"Farthest Out In The Far West". And, now, how wrong
had been the county clerk's sniggering scribe. The
date of The Owl's arrival into Bubble-Up? April 19,
Bicycle Day.

     After The Owl's discovery of Hoffmanium and its con-
version to a consumer product the brash little burg of
Bubble-Up bloomed and boomed, bouncing bravely into its
boosters' bourgeois dreams. Already eclectic, it became ineluctably electric. The Bevier Lodge broke
ground for an expansion, Mark-Up John's Apothecary and
Mercantile did the same. Even Quote-Doc-Unquote Cassidy
took on a couple of resident interns. The only business
that didn't seem to feel the economic excitement was
Brother Brothers's Bar, where whiskey sales remained
flat, partly owing to purchasers plainly preferring
the Lolly-By-Golby-Pops and partly owing to the burg's
having developed yet another unusual enterprise, that
being the exportation of town drunks.
     We're fully familiar with the premise that each and
every Western town requires a basic roster of characters. To-wit: The good-hearted madam running a house
of ill-repute esconced in a frilly-roomed hotel above
a bare-knuckled saloon. The ineffective and unremark-
able mayor. The kindly doctor with a past. A general
store run by a tidy, tight-fisted propietor. A man of
the cloth. Saloon girls. And, most certainly, a town
drunk. Bubble-Up scored high on all, and in fact faced
a # surplus of the last group, the sots. So Mistress
Bevier began a service to help other small, needy Western towns by exporting -- for a small fee -- the community's overage of dipsomaniacs. Mormon towns were
especially lacking, were especially grateful, and always
paid in cash.
     Bubble-Up itself, however, had two glaring omissions
in its roll-call of roles. There was no bad man, and because there was no bad man, there was no sheriff. Though
maybe it was the other way around -- becasue there was
no law-man, there was no outlaw -- but, regardless, it was
an embarassment. For we, of course, are also at least
faintly familiar with the premise that the universe is
built on one -- or both -- of two principles. In the
East, it's yin and yang, the shady side and the sunny
side, each of the opposites complementing the other. In
the West, it's the Heraclitean notion that opposites are
merely the same thing in different states. Close, but
no cigar, yet in the end having the same practical effect.
What is a sheriff without a bad man, what is a government

without an enemy, what is a church without a devil? All
the while accepting that the sheriff and the bad man
are one in the same, that the government is the enemy,
that the church is the devil. The difference between
East and West -- you can put this in your hookah and
puff on it -- is that the duality moves slowly in the
East, but moves in the blink of an eye in the West.

     At first there were no restrictions of any kind ap-
plied to Lolly-By-Golly-Pops, neither in commerce nor
in use. After all, Bubble-Up was not built on either
the ideology of restrictions or the employment of such
restrictions. There was money to be made, and who
wished to restrict that? There was the pursuit of personal pleasure, and who wished to restrict that? Unrestricted commerce, unrestricted personal freedom --
those notions having purity and power.
     Trouble is, there is no purity in power, and little
power in purity. And more trouble is, the relationships amongst them all -- restrictions and money-
making and personal freedom and purity and power --
these relationships are very complicated. For purity
may be desirable in one's personal life, but will certainly be troublesome in one's commercial life. In
like manner, money is necessary to commerce, but mostly
troublesome in the personal realm. Not to mention the
other troubles, those occasioned by the power of power
in each, power being the most troublesome thing in
Creation, for no one wants to be subject to someone
else's purity, and no one wants to become someone
else's profit. Prophets and profits -- trouble-makers,
plain and simple.
     Yet the Bubble-Uppers were not philosophers, at least
not by profession. It was in their actions that their
philosophy evinced itself. Academics would call them
pragmatists. They would call themselves practical. Do
what works, they'd say. And, they'd continue, what hurts
the fewest people, and what helps the most people, saying as much not because they were soft-hearted -- though
many of them may very well have been true-blue, union-
card-carrying, left-leaning softies -- but because helping instead of hurting always works best. Being nice,
they concluded, was nothing more than easy-to-swallow-
practicality, a spoonful of sugar with the medicine and
that sort of thing. Stay out of the business of others,
they'd add, and keep others out of yours. Political-
ly, about half were conservative liberals, the other half
being liberal conservatives. But taken as a whole, the
Bubbly-Bunch were organic anarchists, people fashioning
civility on their own, people who'd seen that when ideology trumps practicality, civilization goes into full
retreat.

So what few restrictions there were arose as needed, gradually and informally. The first was that it was immediately obvious that Lolly-By-Golly-Pops couldn't be sold on credit or promissory note, for one of the finer attributes of the luscious lickables was that just a few touches to the tongue expanded the mind to the point that the pedestrian details of accounts payable were quickly —— and often permanently -- relegated to the dark back-waters of the subconscious. The upshot was that it became the norm for the pops to be pur-chased strictly with cash-on-the-barrelhead. The shops that sold the suckers became known as barrelhead-shops, soon shortened simply to head-shops.

The second observation was one seldom made by the bulk of the practitioners of free-enterprise capital-ism, but one that came naturally to the socially-oriented Saleswoman of Sin. Put straight, it's this: hoarding hurts the economy. Why? you might ask, filled as you likely are with admiration for the natural agil-ity of the free market to regulate itself. Let whom-ever pay whatever for whichever they want, you might answer, and the market will soon catch up, the price rising to meet the rising demand, or falling to meet the falling demand. The best cure for high prices is high prices. The best cure for low prices is low prices. But you would be wrong.

Long before she'd come to the environs surrounding Boiling Springs, Madame Bevier, Bubble-Up's a priori pur-veyor of pleasure, had seen first-hand the pitfalls pro-duced by the power purchasers of her minions' minis-trations. Her younger and less powerful clients -- she preferred the upscale and professional word "client" to her competitors' and censors' common vulgarities, pe-joratives such as Johns and tricks and curb-crawlers and so on -- her younger clients, those whom she affectionately dubbed her Bordello Boys, were ideal engines of economic energy. Nervous at the outset, they bought whiskey as they waited their turns. Whilst in the crib they never tarried, most often no longer than wham-bam-thank-you-ma'am, and as soon as they'd come, they'd gone, and afterwards most of the young cockerels believed they'd become cocks and consequently crowed considerably in the saloon, buying yet more whiskey.

While every mother knows that boys will be boys and will soon be forgiven for it, Miss June -- picking up where motherhood runs out of answers, where motherhood fails even to consider the questions -- our Mistress of Mysteries knew that boys will also become men, and be less-and-less forgiven for it. For as their whiskers wizened all the while their wham wound down and their bam boozled those once-grateful boys lost much of their thank-you-

ma'am, now having means -- meaning money -- to insist
on companionship -- meaning more of the lady-of-the-
night's night -- rather than settling for the pure and
natural raison d'etre of release. No longer feeling
themselves to be supplicants of the universe but rather commanders of their small realms, they took up
more and more resources and spent less and less in the
saloon. Social stratification status aside, these hoarders
of whoop-de-doo were a drag on the bordello bidness, leading our bawdy-house baroness to ban all behaviors that might be construed as cornering her
carnal capital.

So, having already earned her education in the economics of managed markets, the moment that Madam June
Bevier learned of a Lolly-By-Golly-Pop purchaser pro-
posing to pick up a passel of the puckerables at a volume discount, she pulled the plug. Now the law of the
land became cash-on-the-barrelhead and one-per-customer.

The party-pooper who popped the balloon was a dark-
visaged stranger who scurried out of town immediately
upon sacking-up a super-sized supply of the suckers.
That, alone, was telling, as one lick on the stick ordinarily sucked all the scurry out of even the most agi-
tated ambler. He was clearly up to something beyond
consciousness-expansion as the stranger straight-way
sold his samples to the notorious Derringer Duvalier,
high chieftain of the Acronymbos, a shadowy gangster
group so secret that their own name for themselves changed
daily, a new abbreviation being chosen from the letters
found in the first spoonful of Duvalier's regular lunch
of alphabet soup and graham crackers. It didn't take
the devious Derringer long to look at a horse-shoe,
much less a Lolly-By-Golly-Pop. Instantly, he concluded that while the condiment clearly couldn't put
the clip back in the clop of a crowbait cow horse,
there was nevertheless a powerful profit potential in
its ingredients. He sent one or two of the adult sweets
off to his laboratory for analysis. When the results
came back, he purchased the range on either side of
Hell's River, just down-stream from the narrows of Hell's
Gate, the latter serving as the name for his new spread.

Duvalier was born in Marfa, Texas to the hard-
scrabble, ne'er-do-well clan of the Bigginses but
raised in Roswell, New Mexico. Christened Bobby Dick,
he was the youngest of three boys, his older and much
larger brothers being Big 'Un and Barnhouse. Abandoned
by his parents, he was brought up by a single-mom-
grandmom who, suffering from a rare conjunction of dys-
lexia and malapropism, called him Dick Bobber. His

brothers called him Little Dick. You can imagine his
childhood. Or so you think.

In a cruel twist of the genetics handed down from
his grammy, Little Dick turned out to be a thlammer,
the term commonly applied to those unfortunate few with
an uncommon confluence of two disorders, lisping and
stammering. Though it was not a fatal condition --
oh, but how he often wished it were! -- he could only
speak in saliva-saturated gushes of parts of words
that squished and squashed, one upon the other, spraying a fine mist over all those around him who struggled to understand what he was saying all the while
leaving a permanent slime on his own mug that resulted in a perennial red, raw rash. He did what he
could, carrying a handkerchief to mop up the detritus
of his morphemes and phonemes, though he was never
able to keep a fresh supply of cloth ample enough or
dry enough to have much positive effect. As he ma-
tured from minority to majority, childhood to man-
hood, he replaced the hankies, first with ascots, then
later, when he removed himself to the untamed country
of Hell's Canyon, he began to sport large and gaudy
wild-rags of the type favored by the best-dressed of
the cowpunch tribe, these latter man-scarves also serving to cover the ever-present damp spot on the front
of his shirt.

His given name had been a vexation from the start.
Determined to be a Dick no longer than was necessary,
he became obsessed with securing the perfect, new bit
of personal nomenclature, spending hours and hours in
the local library, scouring volumes of ancient and forgotten lore, trying first this name, then that, never
satisfied, never ready to pull the trigger. Until one
fateful night when he took an uncharacteristic break
from his research. There was a secret military base
near Roswell, well-known to the locals, not because
of its impact on the town's economy, but rather for
the beautiful young WAC officer stationed there who
moonlighted by lightening the wallets of the Pecos
Valley boys who were pining for a push-ho with a real
woman. She made her assignations in the otherwise
underused women's powder room of the base Officer's
Club.

It was no surprise that Little Dick was well aware
of his shortcomings in the realm of romance, a knowing that put him in a paroxysm of nervous anticipation
as he awaited his turn in the ladies' loo. The very
moment he came up next in line he'd have bolted from
the batter's box but for the fact that he was stiff
from fear. Well, fear and that other, most powerful
of all of humankind's emotional equipment, the only

mechanism greater than reason, greater still than avarice, greater even than love, for which it is often mistaken, that being the emotion of human animal lust -- lust of the kind driven by the body's own collection of chemicals in its laboratory of lasciviousness, the kind that fuels the furnace of the mind's fantasy fabrication factory, the kind that can be explained in no terms other than those of its very own guttural vocabulary. He had no sense of his feet and legs propelling him forward, until, lo and behold, as if in a dream he had drawn himself to attention and presented his armament before the lovely louie, whose eyes danced -- kindly, it would have seemed to an impartial observer -- as she clapped her hands together and exclaimed, Oh, you've brought your derringer! an unfortunate turn of phrase which caused Bobby Dick to break ranks and fall into full retreat.

Not one to nurse either hurt or grudge, he had an almost immediate epiphany. He would be Derringer, small but dangerous. A Haitian correspondent's wire story in the Roswell Daily Record provided a suitable surname, one of refinement and mystery and more than just a touch of the sinister. Little Bobby Dick Biggins became Derringer Duvalier. It was fortune at its finest, his only twinge of sadness being that the trauma of the moment -- though both short-lived, moment and trauma -- the shock had erased certain details. He wished somehow to thank the comely commissioned coed officer for her accidental assistance, but her name, if he'd indeed ever known it, was no more than a blank spot in his recollections. Hints now and again would bob up in his brain, much like those coming to the window on the bottom of a later generation's Magic 8-Ball. Was she named for a state? No... Maybe a month? April, perhaps. No. Hmmmm... Not that it was important, really.

Meanwhile, back in town, the Proprietress of Pleasure had persuaded Mayor Middleton that their vibrating village in the valley needed a sheriff. Mayor Middleton, well aware of the gravity of his role in the community, spent the requisite time hemming and hawing on the issue, ultimately coming down squarely in the middle, uttering his usual position statement -- one which he would print up on placards during the next election -- which was: I can't say I'm for it, but I won't say I'm a-gin it. Taking that as a hearty endorsement, Miss Bevier telegraphed the only man in the country capable of corralling the crowds of the kind of consumers currently collecting in Bubble-Up. And, it might ought to be said that the

unflappable Madam's implacable heart fluttered ever so
slightly as the last STOP was affixed to the Western
Union missive by the sleeve-gartered-green-eye-shaded
telegrapher as with one, teeny-tiny key-stroke he
launched her correspondence of consequence on its electric journey of destiny.

A Texan by birth and a former U.S. Army Cavalry
officer by training, Oather ~~Kennedy~~ Kennedy Rodger cut
a remarkable figure. He was tall enough, but looked
taller. He was handsome enough, but looked handsomer.
Especially when he let slip one of his world-weary
smiles, a slight curl of the mouth that mimicked the
single ringlet of black hair that often emerged from
the sweat-band of ~~xhixxxix~~ his silver-belly Stetson, a
smile made more by the softening of his otherwise impartial and inquisitive eyes than by the gleam of a row
of perfect chompers. He was a bachelor, but had a
single child, a lovely, late-teen lass named Lisa. He
traveled with his deputy, Lance Reid, the nephew of
John Reid, Rodger's old Texas Ranger pal, known to
most of America's radio listeners as The Lone Ranger.
Lance, as you would expect, was sweet on Lisa, but,
true to his uncle's code of honor, never let his passion overcome his sense of propriety, oftentimes much
to Lisa's dismay and disgust. Star-crossed lovers,
they shared much in common. Each wore their hair long,
held back by a hand-built headband, hers a-glisten in
hundreds of star-and-moon-shaped sequins, his in understated Plains Indian beadwork. She wore neither
shoes nor bra while he wore custom snakeskin boots with
silver toe caps and stainless-steel heel taps, also
going bra-less, at least insofar as we could tell or
would wish to determine. She preferred long and loose
granny-dresses fashioned from gaily-printed cloth sal-
vaged from flour sacks. He gravitated to the kind of
blousy shirts favored by Errol Flynn under which the
young deputy gyrated in tight jeans several inches too
long that formed a puddle of blue denim over his rat-
tlers. The two youths were matched in skill and fear-
lessness when horseback, her having been taught by her
father, him by his uncle, she preferring bare-back with
naught but a halter-rope and he favoring a big double-
rigged Mexican with full tapaderos and more silver than
the U.S. Mint. Entire crowds would swoon when the two
rode by.
Growing up, the High Sheriff hadn't given much
thought to his given name. His boyhood pals called him
Ken, his grand-folks called him Oather, his mother called him Oather Kay with the opening O and the ending
Kay both long and drawn-out. His dad employed a vast

array of nicknames, the choice depending upon mood and
blood-alcohol level -- Daddy's, that is -- ranging from
the affectionate "booger" to the tougher "turd-head"
to the watch-out-I'm-coming-to-whip-your-burro "you-
little-sumbitch", so that by the time he was old enough
to enlist in the cavalry he was a cum laude graduate
of the University of Sticks-and-Stones-May-Break-My-
Bones-but-Words-Will-Never-Hurt-Me.

A grizzled old lifer relegated to the enlist-
ment detail reduced Rodger's almost-Biblical fore-
names to the initials O.K. It stuck. Which was OK with
O.K., especially when he ran for sheriff after his retirement from the horse troops as the initials-only
moniker was a marketing boon, advertising him as both
satisfactory and adequate, neither gung-ho nor pretentious, a perfect candidate to enforce those laws
that needed it but who would use good common sense in
dealing with those laws that just got in the way of a
robust local economy. The only drawback was that it was
the very dickens communicating amongst the law enforcement community, what with O.K. easily confused
with OK-without-the-periods-as-in-affirmative and Rodger
just as easily confused with Roger-without-the-"d"-
as-in-affirmative, all too often leading to Who's-On-
First exchanges such as: "You OK?" "Yes, I'm O.K.,
you know who I am." "Roger, I just want to know
if you're alright." "I'm O.K. and I'm OK, roger that?"
"Heard you OK, Sheriff Rodger." You can imagine the
rest. Later scholars in the study of police science
and criminal justice systems attribute the develop-
ment of the Ten Code to the law-enforcement communication travails of our very own High Sheriff. 10-4!

Along with Duvalier came his trusted lieutenant,
Boris "Blackie" Black, a man of unspecified age and eth-
nic origin who wore his ebony hair in a single, long
braid and spoke in what could only be described as how
a cowboy drawl might sound after its involvement in a
horse-wreck with a Russki accent. As dapper as his boss
was disheveled, Blackie was perennially decked-out in
suit and tie with a long, black cape over his shoulders
and a derby atop his cranium.

Duvalier's new personal assistant also made the relocation into the Hell's Gate Ranch. Muffin McWright
was not only the first woman MBA from a certain, well-
known private university back east, she was its first-
ever graduate bearing that pedigree. Her uniform was
a navy pin-stripe blazer, white blouse with red string
tie, a solid navy skirt, and black, low-heeled sensible shoes. She spoke with the precision of a Swiss
watch, the rest of her moving parts operating to the
same effect.

By mule train, Duvalier brought along scores of still-
crated World War I surplus army motorcycles, yet to be
assembled, painted olive-drab and still covered in Cos-
moline. Most were 18-horse PowerPlus Indian scooters,
the ones with front and rear suspension, a ~~useful~~ useful feature in the rocky and roadless desert country
of Hell's Canyon. There were also a few of the 15-
horse Harley-Davidson J-Model hard-tails, relegated to
serving as back-ups. His Troops, the term he applied
to the goons he'd hired as faux ranch-hands, didn't
know straight-up about a horse in the first place, and,
owing to the odd waters of the river drainage, horses
didn't fare ~~xxxxxxxx~~ well there, either, so the bikes
with the big twin-cylinder engines were a logical choice,
never mind that, when mounted, his henchmen were more
humorous than horrible, their costumes -- and costumes is the only word that fits -- consisting of shoulder capes, assorted varieties of hats, conchos affixed to every conceivable spot, and high-button shoes,
giving them the mein of a motorized mess of mutineer
minions matriculated to Treasure Island U.

The ranch itself was situated behind huge Gothic iron-
work gates, the gargoyles atop the posts on which they
were swung fashioned of leering skulls wearing cowboy
hats. Softening the Edgar-Allen-Poe-themed decor, Miss
Muffin -- who'd done some substitute teaching at the
elementary school level -- had ordered gay bandanas
tied jauntily around the necks of the grotesque sculp-
tural heads, the color and pattern of the snot-rags
changing based on seasonal themes. The headquarters
house was dark and foreboding, contemporary Boo
Radley in design, nevertheless light and airy in comparison with the Troops' bunkhouse, which was no more
than a large cave in the rocky canyon wall behind the
main house, a geological garage that housed both men
and motorcycles and smelled as if inhabited by trolls.
Between the two dwellings was a mysterious laboratory-
cum-carpentry shop, straight off the B-movie set of a
Frankenstein flick.

In the back of the ranch hacienda was Duvalier's
office, the war-room for his machinations to take over
Bubble-Up and gain control of Boiling Springs and its
secret spigot of Hoffmanium. In the adjacent study was
a bookshelf with a hidden mechanism that, when acti-
vated, rotated to allow passage into the thlammering
tyrant's secret sanctum-sanctorum, a space dimly illuminated by scores of sputtering votive candles
spread amongst three shrines, one to Woodrow Wilson,
one to Joseph Stalin, and one to Mao Tse Tung. In
their ghastly glimmer, one could just make out framed
photographs hung upon the walls, fondly signed by every

U.S, President and world leader since Coolidge. We
should note that Derringer would never fail to sneer
at the mention of Silent Cal, hissing through his teeth
in a fine spray that the hapless Harding's successor, once
he'd taken to wearing Western Stetsons and cowboy clothing, became the last incorruptible President.

     O.K. came to the same conclusion about bringing in
horses from the outside. By and large, they wouldn't
drink the water, making them useless mounts for his
deputies and any potential posse. A few of the imported Texian equines would give the river refreshment
a try but at once would become loopy and glassy-eyed,
thereafter refusing to stand complacently in their
stalls or, for that matter, obey any command issued by
any of the two-leggeds, the Hoffmanium-high horses
looking for all the world like hop-heads in an opium
den. A few people swore they heard snickering and snig-
gling coming from the stable once the nags had noshed
on the water, not nickering and neighing.
     But on his journies down into the declivity, O.K.
had seen distant bands of mustangs, seemingly unaf-
fected by the poisonous potion percolating up from the
planet's infernal interior. Taking Lance and Lisa
with him, they set out astride their last serviceable
steeds, scouring the sage, seeking out the wild, wild
horses. A curious thing happened. As curious as any
curiousity O.K. had ever entertained. As the patient
party neared the first band of renegades, the three
sensed that the mustangs could read their minds. It
was a clear -- and likely the only -- case of ESP,
equine-sensory-perception. O.K. first, then Lisa, then
Lance, each began to think calm and reassuring thoughts,
imagining themselves as honored partners with these magnificent magnificent mounts. The brave band of bronchos
slowed, stopped, then waited for O.K. and his young
riders to catch up with them. A mental telepathy
talk-fest ensued.
     What is your tribe? thought O.K., politely. We are
Pintos, instantly crossed the mind of their stallion
leader, followed by, And yours? In a rush, O.K.'s
whole history with horses flooded through his mind --
from the first beloved pony of his childhood greenest days
through the sturdy and reliable mounts of his cavalry
years and now as a lawman gone horseback to hunt down
bandits who rode motorcycles, his every inkling filled
with the love and admiration he'd always felt for these
ancient nobles of the animal kingdom -- the whole time --
which was, as your Timex ticks, only a twinkling of the
sweep-second-hand -- the whole of that brief moment
the band of Pintos were nodding and tossing their heads
in approval and agreement. We have sensed the evil

of the new humans in the canyon, agreed the mares, And
we, like you, see them as our enemies. Besides! snorted
the stallion, No riding machine can match us! The Pinto
colts -- with the inquisitive nature of youth -- observed that neither O.K. nor Lisa nor Lance wore spurs,
which pleased the ponies, and pleased them even more to
see that none of the trio of riders used curb bits. With
out a command being given, or even imagined, the band of
speckled speedsters struck off in a dog-trot toward town,
surrounding the riders as if they, too, were Pintos.

Bubble-Up was perfectly suited for the Pintos and
the Pintos were perfectly suited to Bubble-Up. Since
cattle had been long removed from the ranges surrounding the Suburb of the Sparkling Spring there was plenty
of good green grass for the small herd. And indeed,
Quote-Doc-Unquote Cassidy had been planting more grass
since ʒʏҳȸ Day One. Water was a little more of a challenge as even the Pintos could drink only so much of the
Hoffmanium-laced liquid, leading O.K. to quench their
thirst by supplementing the spring water with sodas.
All the ponies liked Cola Chica, a Mexican import, with
the good-old American standby CocaCola a strong second choice, even a few older horses actually preferring Royal Crown. None liked Pepsi or the citrus-
based sodas -- Seven-Up and Squirt and such -- or the
fancy formulae refreshments -- like Dr Pepper or Creme
Soda -- though, on weekends and holidays, more than one
of the band was seen with root-beer foam flecked on
their muzzles. No one thought it odd that O.K. and his
deputies began to call their mounts Cola Pintos, and,
before long, it was taken as the name of their breed.
O.K. headquartered in the lobby of the Bevier Lodge
as there was no need for the usual Sheriff's Office in
Bubble-Up as there was no jail. Not at all unusual,
given the lack of usuality in Our Town. And reasonable, as there was no jail because what little need
arose for incarcerating the occasional inebriated or
disturber-of-the-peace or minor miscreant was easily
handled by Bubble-Up's highly-progressive correctional
system - - surely the first of its kind in the land --
which consisted of taking unsalable Lolly-By-Golly-Pops
seconds and removing the sticks, thereby converting the
otherwise-wasted confection into service as a sup-
pository that would render the guilty party incapable
of harm to anyone or anything, it having been discovered -- and, from a sense of propriety, we'll ᵭᵭ not
go into those details -- that Hoffmanium, the active
ingredient of the crazy candies, was most fully and
most rapidly brought into the brain by being absorbed

in the nether regions of the human digestive apparatus. So, without passing Go or anything else, let us
go directly back to Jail. Whilst in this state of advanced inward direction and mental exploration, the
outmate -- what Bubble-Uppers preferred over the term
"Oinmate" -- was assigned to the Silly Stockade, a rustic but pleasant, well-manicured lawn surrounded by an
imaginary fence and reserved for anyone and everyone
convicted of A Big Case of the Sillies. The authorities' only concern was that, once in the Goffy Gaol,
many outmates refused to leave, and a fair number of in-
nocent folk either volunteered for punishment or sought
out small crimes to commit so as to be sentenced to
Silly. Fortunately, the flip side of their fretting
was that there have been no known cases of escape
from the Silly Stockade ever effected, enacted, or
even envisioned.

     Tipped back on his chair. his long legs casually
crossed at the ankle, his shiny custom boots balanced
atop the edge of the Sheriff's Table, his hat tilted
low over his eyes, O.K. could relax all the while he
kept a close ear and a keen eye on the heart-beat of
the hamlet. Surrounding him in the Lodge were the
sensuous sounds of the murmuring Mermaids ministering
to their clients, the soft and fat pulse of the bubbling spring a constant undercurrent in the background, punctuated by the periodic whoops and chuckles
of the Peanut Gallery watching their pards being pat-
ted down with whipped cucumber butter. At any hour of
the day or night, any day of the year, there was music,
most often bajan folk singers and mento and calypso
bands as the Head Mistress had spent a short assignment at Fort Wadsworth on Staten Island, just a short
ferry-ride from Manhattan where she'd often spend late
nights in the after-hour clubs listening to Lord Invader.
     Lifting the brim of his Stetson ever so slightly,
O.K. could see out through the large plate-glass
window into the Currier-and-Ives-meets-Mad-Magazine
street scene of the bustling Bubble-Up. The Cola
Pintos fit in to the little burg as if they'd always
been there, much like the sacred cows roaming the
streets of the villages and cities of India; everyone took them for granted, especially the Lolly-By-
Golby-Poo lickers, who, when under the influence,
apparently shared in the equine-sensory-perception and
could often be seen standing on the corner with one of
the painted ponies, the human gesticulating with both
hands, nodding in agreement, laughing xxxxxxxxxxxx

aloud as if in a silent movie, all the while the horse pawed the ground, shook and tossed its head, nickered and neighed, and nuzzled its conversationalist correspondent, for all the world the two of them clearly sharing a story and a good laugh.

It was the Cola Pintos to whom O.K. and the Bubble-Uppers owed the calm of their community, for the horses' natural nose for evil, coupled with their heightened sensitivity to all things, a knowing that was brought on by long exposure to the consciousness-expanding qualities of the waters of Hell's River, this uncanny combination permitted them to instantly sense who were the good guys and who were the bad guys -- an effect of the Hoffmanium that, sadly, humans never aquired -- so that very soon Duvalier and his agents of the Acronymbos found it impossible to infiltrate the Burg of the Babbling Brook. But if things were under control in Bubble-Up, only a bubble away things were about to boil over. For not being able to rely on the standard surreptitious systems of the spy trade forced the monstrous meanies to put all their rotten eggs in the equally-rotten basket of technology. It would be man-and-horse versus man-and-machine.

And therein lies our tale.

-get a new ribbon - maybe Bobbie Sue's pop can fine-tune my smith-c - the p and q and d keys especially

REMBER THIS! REMEMBER THIS!
 ① image and action first
 ② sound and music second
 ③ dialog last
 ④ let the actors work

Frankie DiCarlo
gave me this →

Keep for good luck

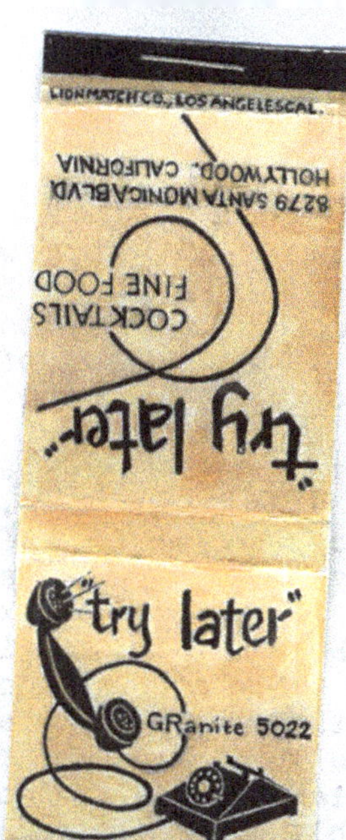

Frankie DiCarlo
gave me this →

Keep for good luck

17.

BUBBLE-UP

I began by writing a treatment, not for the suits or producers or directors, but written only for me. No one else was interested in reading it—only in the teleplays that came from it—though I sought out readers, a few of whom said yes, send it, but when it came down to putting eyes on the page they didn't have the time, most of the time not even having enough time to say they didn't have the time. But it's just as well. I had to tell myself the story in order to believe it. For writing is a lonely business, the kind of loneliness that must be embraced before it embraces you. There is the danger of being smothered. It's the kind of loneliness that's rich and thick and full of promise, the promise of the good things that can come from it and the bad things, too: the secret that must be kept, the knowing that no one else knows, the place in the wilderness only you have seen, the love you are forced to lock away inside your heart, shouldered-up against your fears and your desires. Too, there is the danger of being gob-smacked by it all, by the beauty of loneliness that you can only see when you surrender to the loneliness of beauty. And beauty is nothing more than the emotion of belief. And belief is nothing more than the product of the process of surrendering to the story. And the story is the only thing in this world that is true.

¡No!—I can hear you shouting, Dear Reader—¡It's facts! ¡Not stories! ¡Truth is in the facts!

Shout all you may, but you are wrong. Remember that I am ahead of you when it comes to the truth. Not because I'm the writer, for the writer learns the truth of the story no faster than does the reader. Indeed, if the story is good, the reader will learn more truth and learn it sooner than the writer ever will or ever can. We writers are merely word-wranglers, rounding up the wild and the green-broke before roping them out of the remuda and rigging them with bit and saddle, all the while you, the Reader-Rider, hold the reins, you with your butt in the seat and your boots in the stirrups, fanning their flanks with your cowboy chapeau, whooping and hollering.

I am ahead of you not only because I grew up in Surprise—hang with me here, grab some leather if you have to—but also because I took algebra. The pace of life in the Mesquite Metropolis encouraged us to be observers as well as participants, much the opposite of those pitiable brute-child-clones peopling the rat-race-world around us, those poorlings who were growing older but not up and growing wizened but not wise. Not to mention that everything we Surprises learned we learned from our non-teachers—from our parents and our friends' parents and from Handy Jones and Maya Gandhi, all of whom were merely older, more advanced students, and from one another, too—learning from them rather than from vomiting-down a dead curriculum chosen by some dull committee in the light of someone-else's current fad and fashion amidst their pandering to the politics *du jour*. We Surprises were free to know that the question was more important than the answer, that the only test that truly measured knowledge was the Test of Life. It may be safely said that we were imbued with the Tao of the Treeless Plains and the Gospel of Greasewood, a people who lived—as much as was ever possible—ism-less and ism-free.

Not to mention as we learned we were also led by our non-leaders, meaning we were led by example rather than by rule and regulation. And in learning and leading we came to understand that everything in the Universe is process, meaning by that a *way of proceeding,* a way of doing, and therefore that *truth is a process, not a product,* in turn therefore meaning that facts are the products of truth and not the other way around. So I was prepared for algebra when I came to my short stint in the College of Knowledge, my experience already informing me that truth wasn't the product of the equation, it was the equation, the answer being only the product of the truth and not the truth itself. And, you will recall, it was algebra what led me to fiction.

Also to the point: facts are mechanical, not spiritual. Facts are only the most recent guesses we have at any given time about the truth, truth itself not being bound by time. Facts exist only in the present and only for just that long, for there are no future facts and the facts of the past become little more than myth or dogma or curiosity or quarrel. Scientists—those lab-coated and bespectacled nerds—are constantly deflating old facts and pumping-up new ones. Historians—those note-keepers and recording-secretaries of the victors—are constantly changing their minds about what is a fact and what is not a fact, and about what difference it makes anyway. All the while the remainder of the fact-mongers—foremost among them the Plebiscite of Piety, in whose clan we count the philosophers and gurus and holy men and preachers and evangelists and politicians and leaders—all these have their own dark reasons for enshrining old facts and serving them by kneeling and prostration and by the giving of alms.

And so—because the facts are always in question—the truth is only found in fiction. For some it's the fiction of poetry, for some, the fiction of the short story or the novel, for others the stroke of the brush or the pencil. For me it was the screen of the Flatland Drive-Out Theatre, around and over it the southwestern night sky filled with stars and planets and the Milky Way and the occasional comet or meteor or moon-sliver and on the far horizons the dancing flames atop the flare stacks of the oil fields, the darkened landscape a blanket wrapped about me, in my ear the love-murmurs of the purring projector and the muffled voices from the speakers and the songs of the nightbirds and the howls of the coyotes and the rustling of smaller creatures in the ebb of the dialog from the film. Images. Images that moved. Sound. Sound that unrolled in words and in music. Stories. Stories shot by the Archer of Time into the obsidian-black night of the southwestern sage-and-scrub-brush desert.

Still, the facts intrude. It's what they do best. Let me illustrate. Maybe—now and again—there's a party going on inside your head, maybe inside your heart, maybe both. Maybe it's lively and gay, maybe it's quiet and collegiate, maybe it's relaxed and casual. No matter. Maybe you've invited over a few of your oldest and dearest friends—among them some closely-held beliefs, some well-worn ideas, some comfortable biases—maybe some recent acquaintances, too—in this new, second group a few notions, a few suggestions, one or two considerations, here-and-there an opinion. All-in-all it's an agreeable collective, prone to discourse but not to argument, more inclined toward gossip than toward discussion. It's a lovely evening and things are going swimmingly. The punch isn't anywhere near gone and there are plenty of cookies and cucumber sandwiches left on the trays and platters when there's a knock at the door. You ignore it, for the guest-list is complete. There's another knock. You ignore it, too. Then another. And another. If you make no acknowledgement the caller will go away, you think. But no. Instead, the raps grow in sharpness and in frequency, and, pretty soon, the knocking is so insistent you simply must do something. For your guests have stopped their chatter, now glancing anxiously toward their host, whispering amongst themselves. So you open the door—what else can you do—and there stands a Fact. And another Fact, or two Facts or three Facts right behind the first Fact, for Facts mostly travel in packs. They've heard the merriment, smelled the refreshments. They stand there with expectant expressions, their demeanor demanding. Thinking that you have a choice with Facts, you ask yourself, ¿do you let them in? or ¿do you send them on their way?

As you're by habit friendly and hospitable and constitutionally prone to practice politeness, you hold the door open as they enter. Things change immediately. Few of your dear, old friends get along with The Facts. Sides are chosen. Talk turns to debate, debate to argument, argument to shouting match. The Facts, of course, don't participate in the exchange. They're too smug for that, besides, they've only come with the intent of eating and running. During the ensuing cacophony of credibility—the operative notion seemingly being *the louder, the truer*—you happen to glance toward the buffet to see The Whole Facts and Nothing But The Facts, crumbs on their vests, punch dribbling down their chinny-chin-chins, the platters nearing empty and the serving-bowls, too.

An arbiter of truth you may be when all is quiet and a simple discussion is in order, but as the host you must spring into action. So you ring up the caterers, explaining as best you can the calamity that's clobbered your coffee-klatch. They assure you they've experience with such events, and with such eventualities, too, proving it on the spot by dispatching delivery-boys with more canapés, more cookies, more cucumber sandwiches, more coffee, more punch. The kindly caterers add that, in addition, they'll send along a couple of scientists and two or three historians to help straighten things up—ah, ¿remember how shabbily I treated that bunch a few paragraphs back? and how you nodded in agreement? but, ¡boy howdy! we're glad to see them now.

The caterers move in with resolve and purpose, re-stocking the plates and platters, refilling the bowls and urns, all the while reciting snatches of Auden's 'Funeral Blues'—an odd and disturbing choice, you think, until they begin to repeat, as a mantra, the line *Prevent the dog from barking with a juicy bone*—the scientists now alongside them with their crumb-brushes and whisk-brooms and dust-pans, the historians close behind, rearranging and relabeling it all, the whole lot of them chanting Auden as if they were Monks of the Anglican Order. As the tidying-up comes to a close, you are more than a little shocked and a tad-bit disappointed to notice—during all the fuss and feathers—that a number of your dear friends have gone home, leaving for the most part only your recent acquaintances to chummy-up to The Facts. Yet in a few moments the party continues as before. ¿Cucumber sandwiches, anyone? you ask, adding, We've plenty, thinking to yourself that every dog must have a juicy bone.

We sent The Facts on holiday for the 1950s, the 1940s having been so horrible that Facts of all kinds had fallen out of favor. So after the decline of Art Deco—its Armies of the Depression having formed in the bread lines only to march in the Diaspora of the Dust Bowl—after all that, Populuxe prevailed. As a nation we moved into Atomic Ranch bungalows, fitting them out with new appliances and Danish Modern furniture, putting ceramic-black-panther ivy planters atop our brand-spanking-new television consoles, painting our walls chartreuse, parking our new Fords or Chevrolets or Plymouths in attached garages. We fought a war in Korea but didn't call it a war. We blamed race riots on outside agitators, and did a pretty good job of convincing ourselves of it, drinking gin gimlets and basting burgers in backyard barbecues. We resurrected our old myths in new media— sing with me now, *Da-vy, Da-vy Crockett, King of the Wild Fron-tier*—hoping that the greatness of our founders could atone for turning the Indian into Tonto, the Negro into Amos and Andy, the Japanese into ashes. And to polish-off the Fifties, we silenced Kerouac and Ginsberg and Ferlinghetti by electing a Prince to be our president. Or so we thought. The Facts may be ignored for a time, but they never go away.

I have been saying *we* but I have been meaning *you*. Again, I invoke Surprise. In the Prickly Pear Purlieu there was no change in The Facts from decade to decade, or year to year, or, for that matter, moment to moment. By taking them as they came, Surprises found that Facts make good companions, among the best, really. The Facts are what they are, not in the least pretentious, and always reliable. They are helpful; indeed, no one was ever harmed by a Fact, only by ignorance of it. Because they are begat by the truth, Old Facts are the bedrock of knowledge and New Facts are opportunities. Because they are begat by the truth, no Fact ever minded being questioned or doubted. Because they are begat by the truth, no Fact ever required being believed for its existence. For ourselves, living always on the edge of easy—never in want but never in luxury—the very nature of Surprise demanded—and ensured—a comfortable relationship with The Facts. So when the earthen façade of the Damned-Up Fifties began to leak and then crumble ahead of the Factual Flood of the Sixties, as a native member of the Tribe of Surprise I was prepared and ready.

I'd begun the treatment by naming our hero Oather Blessing Kennedy in homage to the New Prince and by calling the little trickle of a rivulet Camelot Creek, but when the Tasmanian Devil of Dallas killed King Arthur and his bullet took our blessing, I accepted The Fact and made the necessary changes, Oather Blessing Kennedy becoming O.K. Rodger and Camelot Creek becoming Hell's River. Then the day after the Devil's dastardly deed the stock-market plunged to a new low, prompting our Suits to telephone with panic in their voices and with a new budget for the series in their contracts—Cut it by half, they said. So I did. I kept the same roles, but invoked Robert Graves's classic notion of *the weird*—the notion that everyone has an exact opposite in this life—then re-wrote the scripts to use the same actors to play at least two roles each, always the opposite of one another. Kelly, for instance, was both Sheriff O.K. Rodger and the lawman's evil nemesis, Derringer Duvalier, and so on and so on. I had to enlist help in doing this as oftentimes the two opposites would appear together in a scene, so I called up one of my old Canasta pals, Ray Harryhausen. He was the master-mind of the very best special effects Hollywood had ever produced, gems like 1953's 'The Beast From 20,000 Fathoms' and 1958's 'The Seventh Voyage of Sinbad', though, owing to his contractual commitments, he's only credited as Fred Holmes in our series. Another problem was that no one wanted to play Mayor Middleton—too middling, I suppose—so I simply added a costume element, a white pillowcase over his face and head, tucked into his vest on the bottom end and held down by his brown Fedora on the top end. When pressed, we could use anyone for the Mayor's part, as he rarely had anything to say anyway.

Other Facts were benign from the beginning. ¡Begin the benign! For one, I rapidly discovered—however comfortable I normally found the familiar confines of my 'Stream's aluminum cocoon—that the intensity of the writing process fairly quickly led me to the verge of *ex-'streamination,* a rare condition known to Surprises that can best be described as a kind of Airstream cabin-fever, rare only because we Surprises spent so much of our lives out-of-trailer. But when we were forced to remain en-canned for long stretches, say, a three-day blue-norther, the condition commenced, first amongst the more sensitive of our tribe but soon affecting even the strongest Surprise. Commonly-reported symptoms were *Josephation*—in which one imagined oneself in the belly of a monster metallic whale—leading to *constrication*—in which Wally Byam's walls seemingly began to grow smaller and smaller with the space they enclosed growing correspondingly tighter and tighter—until the afflicted 'Streamer was fully in the grip of an episode of *plumbing-crazy*—in which the victim was convinced that they were encased in galvanization, a flush of the toilet merely a handle-wiggle away. The only antidote, the only treatment, the only cure was to get out, to go somewhere.

Sunny So-Cal wasn't Surprise, so getting out of the 'Steam wasn't as simple as stepping out into the sage and scrub brush. It was more stepping outside so as to step back inside somewhere else, trading one container for a different one. Whilst hanging out with the Canasta Crew, Ray had mentioned a cozy-comfy little tavern called Try Later, named in a nod to the reply most often given actors and stunt-men and writers when calling the studios for work. He gave me an old matchbook with its phone number and address nicely printed on the cover showing the oasis to be in the fringes of Hollywood on Santa Monica Boulevard, which would be within easy motivating distance via the Ramblin' Rambler, a short cruise down Vineland or Hollywood Way from my berth in Burbank. Harryhausen said it was a place favored by the movie-lot blue-collar-crowd where for a dime—'to keep out the riff-raff'—you could join the Sunday Morning Club, your membership card thereafter entitling the bearer to a breakfast of ham and eggs, potatoes, toast, and a drink, all for a single simoleon. Even better—the special effects effector told me, to my astonishment and delight—the proprietor-owner-barkeep of the Try Later was none other than Frankie Darro, childhood movie star and scruffy-kid hero of 'The Phantom Empire'. ¡To the rescue!

A perfect place to start writing, I thought, so I beat-feet over to apply for my membership card, only to find the Try Later had lately become the Raincheck Room. Still a bar and grill, still with the same façade, and—I wagered—still with the same vibes. I inquired as to whether Frankie ever came by. The drink-meister nodded without putting down the glass he was polishing, pointing it instead to a corner booth where a short fellow was hunched over his high-ball. ¡There he was, in the flesh! I hope I didn't fawn and gush, but I most likely did. Whether or not, or in spite of, Frankie seemed genuinely pleased to meet a young fan who was familiar with his oeuvre, right up to his role as Robby the Robot in 'The Forbidden Planet'. Despite my not yet having become a regular imbiber, I nevertheless became a regular at the Raincheck Room—opening-up my Smith-Corona on the table-top of the same corner booth three or four times a week. Frankie would drop by to keep tabs on my progress, offering helpful bits about the business. In turn, I wrote him into the series, playing the dual roles of Head Wrangler of the Cola Pínto Posse and Main Motorman of Derringer Duvalier's Motorcycle Troops.

Having begun the benign, let us begin the beguine. A rumba at heart, its smoky Latin sensuality has been squeezed into a sheath of French ballroom pomposity and the whole of it slowed-down enough to permit its practice by the homiest of hoofers, a sort of middle-brow mambo. Cole Porter porter-ized it in the mid-Thirties—'Begin the Beguine'—and soon afterwards it became a staple in Surprise, a substitute samba of seductive simplicity, a shake-rattle-and-roll-of-the-hips slipped and slid into the Sagebrush City by none other than Rose Edna Eliot. Not the Porter original, but the Xavier Cugat rendition, Lois Hodnott trumped by Lina Romay. My mother-in-law, you will recall, has always been a Cugat fan of the first water, an avid advocate of his artistry, even a connoisseur of his cartoons. Not only did she name her son for the Chihuahua-carrying Cata-lonian, she danced the beguine so well and so often that she could do even the deep dips unassisted. As she often began the beguine in the buff, the first strains of the Cugat orchestra heard snaking out of the Eliot Airstream would draw a crowd of ardent admirers, all clustered around the crank-open windows, hoping for a undrawn blind or a louver left carelessly ajar.

The beguine never became part of 'Hell's Gate'—as dancers, the Mermaids did fine with dips but tripped all over themselves trying to tap, all Esther Williams and not the least bit Ginger Rogers—no, the beguine is merely metaphorical, the smooth-but-sanitized South American sashay so similar to the slang of the Surprises. The Hollywoodies weren't at all familiar with the way that Kelly and I spoke, our vocabulary in particular, but they were intrigued by it. We loved alliteration and interpretation. Our f-word was 'foockle', our s-word, 'schickle', our g-damn was 'dagnabbit', and so on. We cussed, but didn't curse, relying instead on cursing-non-cursing. While we entertained all the same sentiments and emotions as would anyone else, we simply expressed them differently. Bobbie Sue's golly-gosh-golly substituted for a wide range of exclamations, for example, all the way from your-hand-feels-so-good-when-I-hold-it-in-mine to slap-me-silly. A stranger happening on to our set would find themselves confused by our comradely constructions, befuddled by our boisterous banalities, victimized by our vocabulary, and dumb-founded by our definitions. Yet they all caught on, then quickly caught up. The habit reached out. The cast soon dubbed themselves 'casticles', the crew, 'crewsers'. Surprise-speak would have taken the country, had it not been for Richard Pryor, who—a few years later—made our way of talking seem quaint, quizzical, and a bit queer.

From time to time The Facts also appear in the disguise of practicality—Superman as Clark Kent, for instance, or every tough-guy-on-the-outside-but-softie-on-the-inside that Bogart ever played—simple and logical on the surface but complicated and illogical underneath. That was the case with color television. On the schedule there wasn't much of it in 1963 when we began pitching 'Hell's Gate'. 'The Flintstones' and 'The Jetsons' counted for all of ABC's color offerings, 'Bonanza' and 'Walt Disney's Wonderful World of Color' were the main plumage in NBC's peacock's tail. The Big Eye had nothing. And—wouldn't you know it—our deal was with CBS. Not that it mattered a lot, since very few folks could afford color television sets, and, even if they had, not many lived in markets where the local station had enough crayons to spit out color programming in the first place.

When it came to jumping on the color wheel, CBS was worst off, and they knew it. They also knew—even since the 1950s—that lots of television series were being filmed in color, even though they were being aired in black-and-white. 'The Walt Disney Show' was shot in color from the get-go, and others—among them 'The Lone Ranger', 'Superman', and 'The Cisco Kid'—went to color film well before their networks were ready to broadcast them. So we were lucky when we insisted on shooting color. They'd been planning to do it all along.

We insisted on using the best music in our television series, too, paving the way for the Smothers Brothers who followed a couple of years later. The suits weren't planning on our caviar musical tastes, though it was hard to argue otherwise because we were getting the newest and the hottest, the crème-de-la-crème of the pop culture. We got the bestest firstest, partly because we were cool, partly because no one else was doing what we were doing, and partly because of where we were. And where we were was the Capitol of the Angels, the Paradise of Palms, the First Nation of the Freeway, the Casual City. N-Y-C was once the home province of Art, but no longer. When the Brits began swamping the shores, the Beats beat it to El Eh, bourgeoisied-it to Burbank, hustled to Hollywood, the Mother Road having led the Art Nation to the West-Coast-Promised-Land, where the Beach Boys were tuning up, Grace Slick was about to leave the Great Society on an airplane, the Dead were coming alive, and the Byrds were fledging.

We had no Johnny Western singing our theme song. Instead, we invited a street musician who called himself L. A. Johnny West-Coast and carried a guitar which he never played. We dressed him in a rainbow-colored-sequined suit—which we assembled from various bits and pieces found in the trash cans behind Nudie's Rodeo Tailors over on Lankershim—then gave him a few tabs of Albert Hoffmann's best and let him yodel at will. No words, just yodels. Or maybe El Eh Johnny meant for them to be words, but they were—to coin a phrase that would later be popular in the ready-to-wear world—acid-washed to the point that they'd lost their word-ness. But what perfect theme music. It meant nothing, it meant anything, and it meant everything, all at once. Just as did 'Bubble-Up'.

Still—given our unusual story and the equally-unusual way in which we were telling it—we needed some kind of sung information to move the plots along, much as would have been done by the troubadours of an earlier age, so we prevailed on two of our favorite duos—the black gospel singers Joe & Eddie and the white folkies Bud & Travis—to take turns singing bits between acts in each episode. Though Bud & Travis had split-up in 1960, we coaxed them into helping us out and would like to think we were at least partly responsible for their getting back together in the midst of our first season. I've often wondered if the two groups—one ebony and the other ivory—inspired the employment of Nat King Cole and Stubby Kaye in 'Cat Ballou'. But no matter.

We also begged guest musical appearances from—among others—Jesse 'Lone-Cat' Fuller and his Fotdella, Ramblin' Jack Elliott, and Mother McCree's Uptown Jug Champions. It was a brilliant move. Brilliant, but problematical. And eventually fatal. Brilliant because our musical guests were themselves brilliant, brilliant because they were new to most of Tee Vee Land. Brilliant because our musical guests were unpredictable and thereby carriers of the germs of spontaneity, a delightful illness best illustrated on 'Hell's Gate' by what came to be known as the Kazootsuiters. Now, kazoos figured mightily in folk music at the time, a Fact which you may have forgotten. Perhaps on purpose. But wait, Dear Reader—before you hasten to decry this modest musical device, this toot-sweet miniature membranophone, this happy hummer of the hymns of the hoi polloi—know first that it was the principal instrument which facilitated the movement from the Great Folk Scare of the 1950s to the Folk-Rock-and-Roll of the 1970s. Think about it. It was the sincerity of post-war church-camp Kumbayahoos—when twisted and transformed by the irreverent and insistent impact of the rediscovered kazoo—that blossomed into the Burritos and the Dead and the Byrds and the Airplane. So we shouldn't have been surprised, looking back on it, to have had a hand in it, with the kazoos of Lone-Cat and Bobby Weir inspiring our cast and instigating impromptu hum-alongs. Eventually, everyone on the set carried one, some simply in self-defense.

The problematical part was that our musical guests, being guests, couldn't be counted upon for regular appearances. Indeed, their irregularity was their stock-in-trade. So I had to develop a stop-gap plan, which resulted in the creation of another character, Keith Lizard, the Guitar Wizard. A slightly more-temperate version of L. A. Johnny West-Coast, Keith could be relied upon only for his presence, but not for any other aspect of his performance. With his guitar slung low-down around his knees, his hair most resembling a tumbleweed, a cigarette of dubious origin stuck between the strings on the headstock, and every sound emanating from his general direction most like a growl with slight variations in pitch and dynamics, he became—to our utter surprise and slight dismay—a cult hero. His albums became best sellers amongst the hippest of the hip and his personal appearance became fashionable amongst the least fashion-conscious.

As to the fatal part, well, simply read on.

18.

FIZZLED OUT

Whilst I had been in the midst of my odd adventure with the Ghost Writers On the Sly, the brand-spanking-new chairman of the Federal Communications Commission—a pleasant and bright fellow with the odd name of Newton Minnow, a moniker that invoked a physicist-meeting-a-fish, or a fig-cookie-meeting-casting-bait, or a small-unit-of-force-meeting-a-small-fry—this newly-appointed political pinkeen swam up to the surface of the American Consciousness to denounce all of Tee Vee Territory as a Vast Wasteland. His scathing assessment was occasioned by the National Association of Broadcasters having convened their tribe in our nation's capital for their annual shindig, intent on little more, we may assume, than hobnobbing with the politicos, back-slapping one-another, and drinking and dining to their expense accounts' content when—much to their astonished amazement and cringing chagrin—the Big Small Fish waggled his tail at the whole of them, in one great gulp characterizing their industry— and I quote—as a "procession of game shows, violence, audience participation shows, formula comedies about totally unbelievable families, blood and thunder, mayhem, violence, sadism, murder, Western badmen, Western goodmen, private eyes, gangsters, more violence, and cartoons"—well, the nerve—before asking "is there one network president in this room who claims he can't do better?"

Now, a scant three years later, while re-reading his comments in the throes of my re-writes, I knew that I had risen to his challenge. Schickle, yes, I thought. 'Bubble-Up' is doing all of that in just one series. I was filled with patriotic fervor as I bent to the second year's episodes.

At that time the normal season for a television series was September through March, one episode each week, more-or-less, which required around thirty scripts, depending upon when the series premiered in the fall and whether or not the show got bumped for a holiday special. No bumps for sporting events in those days, as the World Series was still played out in the light of day and professional football wasn't yet important, if you can imagine. We filmed twenty-eight that first season then kept right on going until we had that many more in the can for the '65-'66 run.

Just as with any new show, where to put 'Bubble-Up' in the weekly schedule was problematic. We started out in a late-night Monday slot, 11:00 PM, just after another new series, 'Slattery's People', starring Richard Crenna and Ed Asner and Tol Avery, along with guest spots by a passel of marquee names, like Barbara Eden and Ricardo Montalban and Tommy Sands. It gave us a leg up as it was a serious show about state and local politics—something that hadn't been done before, maybe not since—drawing an audience perhaps constitutionally more inclined to delve into our own philosophical wackiness. Still, late Monday night wasn't a prime-time pigeon-hole, not during the buttoned-down half of the 60s. It was where an upstart Tee Vee series was apt to die, slowly and out of sight, fated to go—in the words of my in-laws' distant English kinsman, Thomas-of-the-Single-L-single-T-Eliots—not with a bang, but a whimper.

However—and you may have guessed it, Dear Reader—the machinations of the Vast Wasteland network suits hadn't factored-in the possibility of being surprised by Surprise. For that matter, neither had we. Nevertheless, it unfolded in this manner. Purt' near the only network affiliate of the Big Eye in our home environs was KOSA in Odessa, bearing the electronic guidon 'Your Eye on West Texas'. The station manager had become an aficionado of Maya Gandhi's Indian-Indian Tacos and was fond of bringing his communication colleagues out to her peripatetic roadside purveyance to indulge in the delectable delicacies. In particular, the program director at the station became particularly possessed by the caravanserai's comestibles, a fact duly noted by the mysterious meal-time mistress.

Kelly and I—button-busting proud of our project, down-right prissy-proud, proud even to the point of sinfulness, if sinfulness has a point—Kelly and I had sent a copy of the pilot to Threeb to offer-up at the Flatland Drive-Out Theatre. Let the folks back home know that the prodigal sons are making good out in the outer world, that sort of thing. After the first showing Maya Gandhi commandeered it, stashing the film away in the fabulous folds of her serape, saving it until KOSA's hungry program director made his next Indian-Indian Taco trek. The conversation—carried out in the shade of her equally-fabulous sombrero—was short but effective. Three good outcomes: customer got some special attention, KOSA got a better rating, we got a better slot.

First. Maya Gandhi never talked to customers. Only smiled. And not always that. And now Mr. Program Director has been seen—by his own people, amongst others—carrying on a conversation with the inscrutable Indian-Indian. A conversation in which she apparently sought a favor. His personal ratings soared.

Second. Local affiliates weren't compelled to take anything-and-everything that National sent their way. Local PDs knew—or at least thought they knew—what would play well in their territory and what wouldn't, so they'd pick and choose. That fall, the Big Eye had a mostly fine line-up on Wednesday evenings: an hour-long network news program at 7:30 followed by 'The Beverly Hillbillies' and then 'The Dick Van Dyke Show'. The next-in-line 9:30 slot should have been a gimme, too, since they were only up against NBC's 'Wednesday Night at the Movies' and 'Burke's Law' on ABC. The problem for the local affiliates was that CBS had pegged that spot for a new sitcom, 'The Cara Williams Show'. Right. Me, neither. No one else, apparently. The KOSA program director replaced it with 'Bubble-Up' which was soon the beneficiary of a wave of what we now call social media but what was then simply called gossip or talk or rumor, coming as it did in barber shops and beauty salons and at feed & seed stores and Ser-Sta-Gros all around the Permian Basin. KOSA's ratings soared.

Third. We were quickly a local hit, a regional hit not long after, then all across the western half of the Lone Star State and into the eastern half of the Land of Enchantment. Suits in Los Angeles and New York took notice, even though more than one of the Brooks-Brothers-Brigade had to be reminded that New Mexico was, indeed, part of the good-ole-U-S-of-A. The upshot was, in the early promo listings for the next season, 'Bubble-Up' had 9:30 Wednesday evenings all to itself and 'The Cara Williams Show' was nowhere to be found. Our ratings soared.

Plain and simple, nineteen-hundred-and-sixty-four was a big year for us. As it was for most everybody. It was the year of the Beatles. It was the year of the Ford Mustang. And the Civil Rights Act. And the Vietnam War, and marches against the war and sit-ins against the war and burning draft cards against the war. It was the year of the last episode of 'Looney Tunes'. It was the year that Ken Kesey and the Merry Pranksters set out in their bus, the year that Leary and Alpert published 'The Psychedelic Experience'. On a higher note, it was the year Martin Luther King took the Nobel Peace Prize; on a lower note, the year Nikita K. took a boot in the keister, and on a sad note, the year Sam Cooke took a bullet in the Hacienda Motel.

Surprise, on the other hand, was having a small year. The price of a barrel of West Texas Intermediate Crude was under three bucks and stagnating. Cattle prices had taken a dive a couple of years before and were still weak, the only hope for their recovery being a good, wet year to cut feed prices. Instead, it was a bad, dry year, only half the annual precipitation. So it was fortunate that we Californio Ex-Pats were riding high. We were able to bring our dear hearts and gentle people—a few at a time—to come see how the television sausage was made. I managed to bring Ruth Etta out on a more generous schedule, seeing as how there weren't so many bookings at the Shifting Sands Mobile Motel, given the Permian Basin's economic eddy, and because she was a good hand on the set, having a keen eye and a fine ear. Not to mention that I worked best when we were together. Only three Surprises stayed put in the Cactus Kingdom without making the trek Westward-Ho. Threeb—who loved movies and television as much or more than any human being—said he was afraid that seeing the shows-in-the-making would ruin the whole experience for him, sort of a spoiler-alert on a grand and philosophical scale. ¿Seeing? we laughed, ¡But you can't see! You'd be surprised by what I see, replied Threeb, with only the hint of a smile. Handy Jones said, firmly, he'd already found his Paradise and ain't no man needed no more 'n one Paradise. Maya Gandhi, when invited, only kicked-away one of the many unnamed cur puppies that happened to be snarling and snapping at her skirt-hems at the moment, then looked up without so much as a grin, which we took as saying that she preferred to stay home and tend to her taco trade.

It was all fun and games, this work, even though up to now we only knew about the fun. And no one was having more fun than me. The characters were almost writing themselves. I felt like a reporter when it came to what was going on in Bubble-Up; things simply happened on their own and I just did my dead-level best to get them written down. The music was a special treat. Behind the villains it was all elevator-Muzak stuff—Percy Faith's cut of 'A Summer Place' got lots of play, followed closely by Liberace, the most frequent choices being 'Easter Parade' and 'Moonlight Sonata'—and for the good guys it was The Fireballs, both 'Torquay' and 'Bulldog', Jørgen Ingmann's recording of 'Apache', and two versions of 'Walk Don't Run', the original jazz cut from Johnny Smith and the

rock-and-roll version from The Ventures. For old times' sake we also threw in
the occasional Surprise childhood nostalgia number, favorites amongst the pile
being Henry Hall's Orchestra's rendition of 'The Teddy Bears' Picnic' along with
'El Cumbanchero' and 'Begin the Beguine' from Xavier Cougat, the latter two in
a tip of the hat to the Siren of Surprise, Rose Edna Eliot. During chase scenes it
was B. Bumble and the Stingers giving the old one-two on 'Bumble Boogie'. In
the few fight scenes—which we always filmed in slow-mo—it was Cole Porter
singing his own 'Anything Goes'. The opening credits for every episode featured
Paul Horn and the Chico Hamilton Quintet's version of the Fred Katz tune
'Pluck It'—we were huge fans of Katz, most especially the score he'd written for
Roger Corman's 'Bucket of Blood' and on which Paul Horn also blew a very blue,
very cool sax—then over the closing it was Liberace again with his signature song
'I'll Be Seeing You'. And—of course—there was all that new, great rock-and-roll
and folk and folk-rock and country-and-western stuff hitting the air-waves, some
of which began coming to us ahead of its official release.

Soon after the characters asserted control over their own beings, the plot
followed suit. Which was much needed. As you can see in the treatment—with
which, I trust, you have made yourself familiar—it's clear that I only possessed
the vaguest, simplest, plainest notion of what would actually happen on the show.
I'd had too fookling much fun writing the back story and birthing the various
and sundry roles to have spent much time on what these fictional folks would be
doing. Part of it, too, was my naiveté—I had confused meanness with evil all the
while I had underestimated the ordinariness of the former and the complexity of
the latter. Growing up in Surprise I'd only learned of either by experiencing their
opposites—kindliness and morality—and realizing, mostly in the abstract, that
for every light there was a darkness.

My stint with the Ghost Writers on the Sly had at least given me an inkling
of the other side, the shadow side. It was left to Bobbie Sue to accelerate my
education. The Doyenne of DIY became part of the Current Events sweeping the
planet, first helping out in her own Berkeley neighborhood—like any well-raised
Surprise would do—only to be slapped-down by the authorities often enough
to realize that when you can't work within the system you have to work against
the system, or, put into Surprise phraseology, sometimes the pot needed to be
stirred. So she took her big spoon to San Francisco in early May to march with
students against the war in Vietnam, joined the Berkeley Free Speech movement
in October, and was one of the eight-hundred-or-so of her fellow Free-Speechers

arrested during their December sit-in at Sproul Hall on the campus. Bobbie's activism was a close and personal reminder that important things were happening in the good-vs-evil arena, and as a writer crafting a part of the message of the masses, I was perfectly poised to say something about it all.

Or, rather, the characters in 'Bubble-Up' were ready to let 'em have it. I was only there with a loose rein, giving slightly-ever-so-much guidance, mainly to keep-'em-out-of-the-wire, as my father-in-law Shad Eliot was fond of instructing young cow-hands. And, of course—and to stick with the cow-punch metaphor—I had to drive them to a new pasture, to fresh grass, as there was already a lot of over-grazing on our ranges. For half a decade, Rod Serling had been busy addressing the notion that all bad people have some good in them and all good people likewise have some bad and that we don't always know who is whom and which is what, and all of that always with an eerie twist. On the other side of the planet—literally and figuratively—Ian Fleming had already taken the simple evil of greed and bollixed it up with the greater evil of technology, though, confusingly, it was also always the clever technology in the hands of the rugged, independent, individualist hero that saved the day. The best so far in dealing with the same issues that confronted the denizens of 'Bubble-Up' were the philosopher-troubadours Tod and Buzz—by then, Tod and Linc—cruising their Corvette down the Mother Road from week-to-week as they delved into the zeitgeist of the American hoi-polloi. But their four-season journey had ended in March, so, in a small, unplanned happenstance in the big, orderly machinations of the Universe, here we were, ready to take up the slack.

The first character to step up and help out was The Owl. It was his discovery, after all, of the naturally-occurring LSD in the waters of Boiling Springs that had set off the chain of events that would force the hand of good and evil alike. He was a person, but not of people, his only temptations being test-tubes and his only companions being the *apparati* of the laboratory. He thought no further of his work than beyond the conclusion of the conclusive experiment, having neither interest in nor regard for the use of his labors or the employments of his outcomes. In the grand melody of life he was a walking-talking leading-tone, as happy going down the scale as going up it, the symphony of shadow and the symphony of sunlight equally pleasing to his ears. No mad-scientist, he was as rational as a UNIVAC perched atop a dowdy lab-coat, as cool as a stainless-steel lab-table, as cuddly as a centrifuge, at heart nothing more than a FORTRAN-fueled fidgeter with the work-ethic of an army ant. Amoral in the purest sense, he was easily bought by whomever boss or whichever side had the most interesting experiments to be run and the most challenging problems to be solved, and—it should go without saying—also had the most money to fund his fantastic forays.

If the Owl was—I came to understand—the perfect personification of *technology*, then his exact opposite in the drama was the cavy of the Cola Píntos. If he was naturally unnatural, they were unnaturally natural. Being horses, they were Mother Nature's offspring from the git-go, beings predicated on intuition rather than reason, wired by genetics rather than operating by artifice. Beyond being born to be what they were, generations of co-existence with the consciousness-expanding currents of Hell's River had allowed the Cola Píntos to acquire, through Darwinian-selection of the fittest and fastest and far-out-est, a psychedelic psyche that gave them remarkable powers to instantly apprehend the thoughts and feelings of all things—man or beast, animate or inanimate, natural or unnatural—meaning that Derringer Duvalier and his evil Acronymbos found it impossible to infiltrate the intimate intersection of idyllic pleasure and cozy commerce that was the little burg of Bubble-Up. The moment the bad guys neared the Hamlet of Hip the ears of the empathetic equines would prick up, Sheriff O. K. would pick up his guard, and the pricks would be picked up in short order.

So it shouldn't have surprised me, although it did, that, without my even having considered the value of the plot device, at some point in the series I realized the dastardly Duvalier had surreptitiously and successfully communicated his quandary to the BRAINIAC boy—perhaps with the use of Carrier Pigeons, or maybe Mexican Message Bats, or perhaps a Ouija Board—the communiqué in whichever medium causing the Owl to decamp from Madame Bevier's Lodge and remove himself to the Doctor Moreau Memorial Research Lab at Hell's Gate Ranch Headquarters, where he immediately set about a series of experiments. He first explored the most obvious solution, which was simply to make the Acronymbo spies less obvious; no, let me rephrase that, make them *much* less obvious, *much much* less obvious, meaning invisible. To that end the Strygiformes Scientist developed a powerful anti-matter spray. Which was a wildly-successful failure. The instant the spray settled on an object—or a person—the target became invisible. Success. But the second instant after the spray settled on an object—or a person—the target disappeared, as in *ceased to exist*. Failure. Though it was a complete success for yours truly, the writer, as it led to several *very* funny episodes, such as The Owl eliminating the motorbikes of one or two of the Goons—the few who'd dared mistreat him—by re-labeling the anti-matter spray to mimic a can of STP, or the time that the anti-matter caused the bottle in which it was contained to disappear, thereby disgorging its contents onto the ground and leaving an invisible spot that immediately turned into a hole all the way through to the other side of the Earth, which almost immediately filled with magma from the Earth's core, resulting in a thirty- or forty-foot tower of lava rock protruding from the hole, perfectly smooth and with the exact diameter of the original container, a bewildered Chinaman perched on its tip. Still, regardless of anti-matter spray's usefulness to me, it was, all in all, not what Derringer Duvalier had in mind, seeing as it was much less Claude Rains in the 1933 horror classic 'The Invisible Man' and much more 1951's 'Abbott & Costello Meet the Invisible Man'.

Stealth by disguise was the Owl's next approach. Since his boss and his boss's boys were already operating incognito in their everyday lives—fraught with their daily phantasmic fripperies, little more than frontier Fauntleroys with their fedoras and capes all encrusted with rustic Western bling—our avian techno-geek went to work developing what he called 'spynicks', surreptitious surveillance robots that could pass over, under, or through the senses of the psychic steeds. The eye of the spynick was a small camera with a big roll of film, motorized to take snap-shots at intervals of ever so many seconds. The film had to be retrieved and developed to be useful, requiring that the spynick be able to both sally-forth and sally-back. The Owl began with birds, his spiritual kin, first employing pigeons, then falcons, neither of which performed satisfactorily, the weight of the camera equipment wearing out the one and the other too easily distracted even by what little natural prey would be encountered on the round-trip flight to and from the Smelly Spring. Other kinds of animals were tested, but with no better outcome. The camera box was too obvious when mounted on the head of a cow or coyote, not to mention that stray cattle and stray prairie wolves always attracted attention and were either captured or killed. Snakes wouldn't hold still for the machines to be attached, were likely to bite the hands of their handlers, and never grasped the concept of fetch-and-return. And so on.

Which led to the Owl's abandonment of the strategy of disguise, replaced straight-way by the logical next steps, *difficult* and its cousin *impervious*. In doing this the Owl had clearly anticipated the methodology that would be employed decades later during the Cold War in which each side knows full-well that the other side is spying on them with satellites and high-altitude airplanes and etcetera, but is forced to realize that such technologies are difficult to detect and mostly impervious to interference or destruction. He began building small aircraft carrying little more than the camera and a crude steering mechanism which caused the vehicle to behave much like a boomerang: aim it at the target and equip it with a mechanical system to turn it around once its film was fully exposed and then point it back toward its launching place.

As the Owl's experimental machines grew in complexity and efficiency— simple kites at first, then miniature hot-air balloons, and on to various small model airplanes—O. K. and the Bubble-Up Posse closely followed the various follies foisted on them by the far-away foe and responded with newer and better ways to thwart them. The first waves of animal-borne spy-boxes had been easily captured, but the air-borne spy craft were more troublesome. There weren't enough good marksmen—certainly no Davy Crocketts with their trusty Betsies—in the Happy Hollow of Hoffmanium to keep up with the sheer number of spynicks launched by the Acronymbos. By the end of the first season O. K. had even resorted to importing South American Goliath Bird-Eating Spiders, which worked well-enough for a time but—as they couldn't dine on the mechanical aircraft they captured—the Titanic Tarantulas soon began preying on almost anything and everything that poked its hapless head up above ground-level, necessitating, in order to preserve the familiar fauna, that the Bubbly-Burg's badge-bearer would be forced to violate several international laws aimed at preserving the angry arachnids.

Every success is a big, ripe fruit filled with the seeds of its own destruction, of which some kernels of collapse are universal to all and some only partic- ular to a given achievement. On the grand scheme score, it should go without saying that admiration for success only comes from a distance. Those nearest to it—but not of it—revel principally in envy, making a show of public applause all the while demeaning and dismissing in private with double-doses of *harrumph-I-could-have-done-that* and *of-course-it's-all-in-who-you-know* along with triple-whammies of *so-what* and *who-cares* and *what-luck*. And in any case, all successes are fast forgotten, a fate—sadly—not shared by failures.

Being new to success, we were taken aback by the sniping that began at the first rise in our ratings. Soon our shock gave-way to taking cover, dodging as best we could the pot-shots aimed at the particular positives of our program. We were so wet-behind-the-ears that we didn't even see the wall, much less the writing on it. First it was complaints from the network green-eye-shades about the costs of the synchronization licenses for all the kick-fanny music we were using. Then it was niggling over costume and set design expenditures that soon turned to out-and-out wrestling matches over using location shots. By the last part of the season the network wonks were working religiously on rescheduling our slot, pitting it against heavier and heavier competition from the other networks.

What had happened was a little bit of this. And a little bit of that. One little bit of this was Leary and Alpert's book, which only required reading no more than the reviews to cause even the stuffiest of the stuffed-shirt corporate cats to finally figure out what Hoffmanium was, and moreover—at least in our little corner of the Vast Wasteland, if you please, Mister Minnow—it was something that belonged to the Good Guys in our plot, not to the Bad Guys. Indeed, the Good Guys of Bubble-Up bore more than a fair-to-middlin' resemblance to the un-washed contemporary sorts peopling the nightly news who were marching in marches and sitting in sit-ins and loving in love-ins and being in be-ins and all of whom were assumed to be smoking funny cigarettes and licking hits of acid. Our Bad Guys resembled, on the other hand, the cops and the politicians who weren't marching or sitting or loving or being or dabbling in anything more than brutality. Another little bit of this was that our ratings weren't just going up, they were going up with the wrong demographic—those self-same unwashed intellectuals—meaning we were popular with the very sorts of folk who were unpopular with the network noodle-nicks.

Still, given our ratings, we could have weathered the little bits of this. A little bit of that, however, was more than we could absorb. And the last little bit was my fault, all my own fault, because I'd been thinking. I'd been thinking about the dramatic curve of the series, thinking about what made the real conflict in the show—thinking too much, now that I think about it—thinking about the inherent amorality of technology and the corresponding inherent amorality of technology's sponsors and enablers, those being the State and the Corporation, thinking whether or not that made those of mankind who were living outside the State and the Corporation inherently moral. Thinking, ¿was it that simple, was it that complicated? And wondering how I would answer these big questions in my small television series. And then thinking and wondering also, ¿what about meanness, what about evil? ¿were they merely clumsy technologies for the achievement of power and riches, were they things all their own?

While I was pondering, preoccupied with my precocious perusals, the characters in 'Bubble-Up' were going on with the series in spite of my inattention. The dinky-but-dastardly Derringer Duvalier even deigned to deploy a newly-added assistant, a spy-without-portfolio who called himself Kirby J. Eager and whose cover consisted of costuming himself as a convivial conveyor of consumer comforts. Dressed-up in Betty Crocker drag, he'd position himself in a roadside stand on the outskirts of the anarchic Eden, just on the other side of the city limits—not that Bubble-Up had official limits marking where the little town began, rather, there were signs delimiting where everything else commenced, marked on the inward side 'Leaving Bubble-Up. Crossing into the Outside World. Beware.' There—just out of the legal reach of the long limb of Sheriff O. K.—the round-faced fop sold faux carpet sweepers, little machines affixed to a mop handle, looking for all the world like crumb-catchers on steroids, hiding as they did the Acronymbos' spynick *apparati*. K. J. Eager was, I quickly realized, the anti-Maya Gandhi. Just as quickly, the suits back in Corporate Tee Vee Wasteland H.Q. realized the unmistakable similarities with our nation's chief law-enforcement officer, none other than the Head Fed, the Giant G-Man, the cross-dressing criminal catcher, the hovering Hoover himself.

Not long after Christmas of '64, the trades announced—in what was an offensively-small story-let, no more than a paragraph, really—that the show's producers had let costs for music synchronization licenses get out of hand and, as a consequence, 'Bubble-Up' would be dropped at the conclusion of the season.

I didn't know what to say to Ruth Etta, so I telephoned. We traded sighs. And silences. Now you've got some spare time—she almost giggled—¿how 'bout you write some letters to me? I wasn't quite yet capable of chuckles, but I felt a whole lot better.

<h1 style="text-align:center">19.</h1>

<h2 style="text-align:center">THE MOVING FINGER WRITES</h2>

I yam what I Khayyám
And I Khayyám no more.—from the song-cycle 'Popeye, the Sufi Sailor-Man'

The hardest part of our series's cancellation should have been delivering the bad news to the cast and crew. In person. *Should* have been. But the way Holly-weird and Los-Angle-ease work precluded our being able to honor that duty. Which is because anyone who reads the trades finds the news out just as quickly as anyone who should be in the know in advance before the knowledge is public knowledge. It's a first-come-first-served information dissemination system out there, only one step removed from the whispers and rumors of the grape vine, and in the entertainment culture—where hope always rises to the level of belief and jealousy always sinks to the level of hatred—such a way of spreading the word is especially disruptive.

Having thus been denied the gentlemanly propriety to let our people know before we had to let our people go, we did the next best thing. We threw a Surprise party for the cast and crew. Not a surprise party, but a Surprise party. We called back to the Mesquite Bean Metroplex and asked Maya Gandhi to ship out a huge pack of her Indian-Indian Tacos, which came by means of the Greyhound Bus Line, fitting on so many levels. Handy Jones composed a speech to be read at the festivities which Threeb took down in dictation on his Braille typewriter, a nice gesture but one that sent us scurrying for someone who could read the missive at our gala. Rose Edna offered to bake a cake out of which she could jump, which would have been a great hit had Kelly and Ruth Etta not intervened. I suppose every family needs to have at least one or two secrets that remain secretive, with the exact anatomy of the Beguine Bombshell evidently being the younger Eliots' choice. Not to worry, however, as the ever-resourceful

Bob Merriman crafted life-sized piñatas that were perfect images of several of the most-despised of The Big-Eye's Tee Vee Network Suits—one of whom, oddly, was the perfect likeness of the Ghost Writers On the Sly executive who'd been shadowing J. Emperor Hoover in television news conferences—the papier-mâché personalities then being filled to bursting with various adult candies, which, for various reasons including various statutes-of-limitation of various criminal codes, such varieties will receive no further description here. We even sent a personal invitation to Secretary Newton Minnow to come join our cast and crew, but got not even a polite pre-printed refusal.

As best as anyone remembers, it was several days before the bon-voyage blow-out had blown-out—the last Indian-Indian Taco having been wolfed-down and the piñata pieces having been pawed-through for the remaining confections—an unwinding that wound up with the Casticles and Crewsers of 'Bubble-Up' using-up most of their hang-dog-moping-time so as to be ready to hit the bricks with their best feet forward in search of the next role and the next job.

Kelly and I were a lot more invested in Bubble-Up than the bulk of our buddies. While the Surprise party had its moments, we knew we'd need to get out of Burbank before we could bounce back, so we set off for Berkeley and what we knew would be a warm welcome from Bobbie Sue and Kerrie Mae and little Tally. On the way out of town I had a cancellation of my own to consider. We stopped-in at Hollywood Rambler Land, 'way out west on Hollywood Boulevard, where I'd been banking on buying something snappy to supplant my staid station-wagon. The slick-'em-quick-'em salesman had set aside a nice, barely-used Studebaker Avanti, a snow-white '63 model with a red leather interior, a stunning machine, absolutely gorgeous, what Sophia Loren would be if she were an automobile. When I slunk into the showroom to give him the sad news, he simply glanced up from his newspaper, said he'd already heard, and went back to the Lah-Times. My brief burst at being a big-shot was already a bust. Walking back out into the parking lot and the So-Cal sunlight, the old pink-and-white rambling wagon was—to my surprise and delight—a welcome sight. I was never cut out to be a swell.

It was spring, so we took the inland road, US 101, up past King City, leaving the windows down, swapping the salt-spray scent of our usual coastal highway route in trade for the massive waves of perfume rolling off field-after-field of Salinas Valley wildflowers—fiddleheads and delphiniums and California Poppies and lupine—followed in short order by the sensuous scents of the blooms blossoming in the orchards of almond and cherry and apple and apricot as we neared San Jose. It was a feast for the senses—aroma therapy, before aroma therapy was hip—so that by the time we bounced over the bridge and into the Brainy Burg of Berkeley we'd lost most of the sour sadness stemming from the suspension of the series. Good thing we'd been brought 'round to a good mood. We were going to need it.

We parked by the Merriman mini-bus—its once-merry montage having melded into a moribund and somewhat morbid spate of scenes from the past year's protests—then halloo-ed the camp as we fairly hopped up the steps of the northern-outpost Airstream. Opening the door, we found the Surprise ex-pats standing just inside, waiting, their suitcases packed, their faces long and dark. Kerrie Mae was clutching a couple of letters, Bobbie Sue was fingering a freshly-opened telegram, and Tally was tapping his toes, impatient to get going.

Kerrie Mae handed over the letters, the first to me and the other to Kelly, while Bobbie Sue began reading the wire. ¡Sent by the Double-Joneses from the Odessa Western Union station!—Bobbie Sue fairly barked—TODAY HANDY JONES TRADED PARADISES STOP WILL HOLD WAKE WHEN YOU ARRIVE STOP ADVISE PLANS STOP. We've already sent a reply, added Kerrie Mae in a quiet but steady voice. We're packed and ready, chimed in Tally.

Before either of us grown-up guys could make so much as a peep, Bobbie Sue fixed a sad, sweet gaze, first on Kelly and then on me. That was the sad news, she said, now for the bad news, nodding at the letters. We looked down, almost in unison. They were from the Selective Service System office in Andrews, several months old, having been forwarded around much of West Texas. Seems the last information the Draft Board had was that Kelly and I were still in Lubbock, but not still in college. Report to the Selective Service Board in Odessa for your induction physical—they commanded—this coming January. Meaning, of course, *last* January, more than three months back. We've called the Board, too, said Bobbie Sue, told 'em you'd come up after Handy's funeral. Without another word we all wriggled and wrestled into the wagon and pointed it toward Surprise.

It was the first time there was no magic in the landscape rolling past the Cross Country Nash-Rambler, only a numbing night-into-day-into-night-into-day-into-night in a series of filling stations and cheap roadside diners separated by too many miles of macadam. Someone stayed awake with whomever was driving while the other three napped or slept, so, though it seemed forever, we made the run in a record ramble. Tally proved to be an especially good roadie, his already well-known brilliance now graced by a maturity that belied his not-quite-six years, always ready with small-talk to keep the driver wide-eyed and—had we asked him—confident enough to have taken the wheel.

We found the whole town waiting to greet our arrival in the Sagebrush Suburb. Threeb had been scouting for sign from his perch in the cupola atop the Old School House. When he espied the Rambler American's sealed-beams slashing through the shinnery, he straight-way alerted the entire body politic, though, when I think about it even these many years later, how Blind Billy Bob had seen us coming remains a major mystery. Given the gloomy goings-on, we had anticipated a scene befitting the strains of 'The Song of the Volga Boatmen'—and not Glenn Miller's version—but, instead, cruised right into 'Happy Talk', all the Surprises welcoming us and asking about SoCal and Berkeley and filling-us-in, all at once. I, of course, was nigh-on to ecstatic for the touch, the scent, the eyes of Ruth Etta.

The comfortable chaos continued for a bit, a merry mix of hugging and squeezing and kissing and back-slapping and crying and laughing, until, almost on cue, a quiet fell on the Surprise Town Square—meaning the little clearing in front of the south-east veranda of the Old School House—as the de-facto town council surrounded us travelers. We have been making plans since your telegram arrived, offered Bob Merriman, affirmed by nods from the Eliots and the Double-Joneses. Some things couldn't wait, added Sue, with nods all around again. Let's get some sleep now, threw in Shad Eliot, as we'll begin at sunrise tomorrow, ten of seven. Rose Edna yawned in agreement. When Ruth Etta stepped forward with fresh towels and linens to fit out a couple of the unoccupied 'Streams in the Shifting Sands Mobile Motel so's Kerrie Mae and Tally and Bobbie Sue and Kelly could have their own quarters, I felt more a part of something than I'd ever felt in my life—I had a home, a home with Ruth Etta, and I'd come back to it.

The world's best alarm-clock—coffee in the percolator, bread in the toaster, ham and eggs in the skillet—the aroma of breakfast had the whole village out-and-about well-ahead of sun-up. We Texian-Work-Release returnees were particularly affected, a real breakfast being a real luxury to a couple of guys who'd been really batching-it, not to mention to a little college family forced to economize with convenience foods, old-timey Grape Nuts and Wheaties and new-fangled Pop-Tarts and the like. As plates were cleared and washed and dried and cast-iron skillets run full of water to soak for a later scrub, as coffee pots were filled anew, as sweaters and jean jackets were thrown-on over tee-shirts and work-shirts, the Surprises began to filter out of their 'Streams, gathering quietly in the Square, cradling steaming splatter-ware-coffee-cups against the late-March early-morning chill.

A low bank of clouds on the eastern horizon slowed the sunrise just enough to still the small talk and stop the few scattered, quiet conversations so all of Surprise was silent by the time the first full rays lit up the front of the Old School House, precisely at which time my parents—the Double-Joneses, Gene D. and Mary Ellen—stepped up onto the veranda and began the Funeral of Handy Jones with a simple recounting of the long and remarkable life of the man himself, concluding with their own tale of how he'd brought them to Surprise. They didn't leave the porch, instead making room first for the Eliots, next then the Merrimans, each adding their own chapters to the story, each couple remaining on the school-house steps at the conclusion of their piece.

When the three Foundling Families had finished, my dad stepped forward—evidently having received the short straw in some earlier drawing—saying, I have several important announcements. Handy Jones died today, or maybe yesterday, I can't be sure, he began, broadly smiling at his own joke—before continuing—Immediately after which our non-governing ad-hoc town council met, or, rather, held a communal visit, in order to make several crucial decisions, none of which, of course, any of you need obey, as Handy Jones would wish, of course, instead relying upon your individual intelligences and good hearts over and above your obedience.

Daddy Double-Jones's first announcement of the non-council was followed by a second of the crucial decisions, the proposal that the Old School House be given—insomuch as anything that was never owned by anybody could be given to somebody so, maybe better said, bequeathed—to Handy's closest and dearest companions, William Roberts—a name which took us a moment to recognize, having called him Threeb for so many years—and Maya Gandhi. ¡Proposed anonymously and passed unanimously! the others on the veranda shouted. Threeb and Maya Gandhi, standing to the side, both beamed.

The second crucial decision was to entomb Handy Jones beneath the Old School House. My father reported that there had been some debate—or, rather, discussion, he described it, parenthetically—over this topic, as it was well-known that Handy had often informed anyone-and-everyone who would listen that he preferred to be hung on a barbed-wire fence like a coyote rather than be sent to a funeral home to be embalmed and painted-up with cosmetics and decked-out in a new suit and a pair of cardboard shoes. There was no sentiment for the latter course of action amongst the conferees, but no conviction for the first, until Threeb and Bob Merriman offered a solution, which they'd deliver momentarily.

The last crucial decision was pure Surprise. Seeing as how Handy Jones had most recently been studying Camus, it was widely felt that quotes from the philosophical Frenchman should be placed all about our community. Hence my dad's humorous reference at the beginning of his report. The quotes, painted on boards affixed at eye-level to steel posts, would serve as intellectual street signs, an especially nice touch given that Surprise had no streets of the ordinary civil-engineering variety. A secondary suggestion that they be replaced annually at the Vernal Equinox with quotes from a different source—one to be selected simply by an inventory of the most popular reading matter found in the burg's various water-closets—was accepted as well. Mother Mary Ellen Jones held up the first, ready for installation: *The only way to deal with an unfree world is to become so absolutely free that your very existence is an act of rebellion.* A lusty cheer of approval was raised by the crowd, out of which quickly flew several comments and an additional suggestion, which carried immediately: don't ever take down the old signs, just add new ones every spring. ¡Hip-hip-hoorah!

The hoop-la subsided as spontaneously as it had erupted, after which Bob Merriman and William Roberts took center stage. The younger man began by recounting the Last Days of Handy Jones, which they'd spent closely together, hard at work collecting Handy's parables—sunrise to sunset, every day for a month or more—the old man reciting as the young man captured the philosophical bon-mots on his Braille typewriter. With every parable, Threeb reported that Handy grew a bit more wizened and wrinkled, his eyes still a-sparkle but his skin more and more leather-like, as if a spoken parable was a liquid life-essence that could be inhaled back into the body, but once committed to paper was no longer free to return, the body drier and dustier with each written word. It had been tiring for both. Threeb confessed his secret relief when Handy offered up the last of the life-sayings early on Saturday afternoon. It was a doozy, too, the essence of the man and the man's history as well as the spiritual guide for the community that had grown up around him. Threeb was careful in his rendering, stopping Handy several times to confirm the wording. On the final pass, Handy exclaimed ¡Perfect, perfect! Then quietly died. Threeb reached for his hand, then touched his face. Handy Jones was smiling, his skin and bones the texture and construction of an old coyote hide. The written lines, Threeb concluded, were the strands of barbed-wire Handy had strung for the only fence he ever sought.

We cheered again, this time through our tears, our hearts as happy as they were sad. We carried on for several minutes and would have for several more if Bob Merriman hadn't held out his arms and hushed us. Handy had handed his fiddle to Threeb many years ago, so there it will remain—said Bob, followed by— We sought to give his favorite rocking chair to Maya Gandhi, but she protested, reminding us that she wore too many skirts for any such seating apparatus and suggesting, instead, that a sarcophagus be fashioned from the slats taken from his bed and a few of his chairs. Which we have done. We have also—the Merry Master continued—dug a tunnel under the Old School House, northwest to southeast, and run through it a rope plaited by the Eliots using old inventory from the One Sock Shop, then run the sox cable clear through to the other side where it has been attached to the casket. As Bob Merriman related the details, he pointed to a woolen-argyle-cotton-crew cloth chain, virtually at our feet, leading to a small hole that disappeared under the veranda. Each of us will take a turn— he instructed—at pulling Handy along to his final resting place, stopping the moment a brightly-colored ribbon appears. Maya Gandhi, Bob asked, reverently, ¿Would you start?

The inscrutable Indian-Indian nodded in affirmation, bowed, said a prayer, hoisted the rope over her shoulder, took a long step forward, then stopped and offered the hand-made hawser to the next person. And so it went, citi-zen-by-citizen, step-by-step, only a few feet at a time, but with prayers and holy signs of various kinds and sometimes a very short story from each celebrant, the whole of Surprise become a string of human prayer beads. The bright ribbon had yet to be seen by the time that each Surprise had taken their turn, so it fell to Bob and Threeb to take the rope together and pull it the last few feet to the appearance of the marker.

Once again, a great shout went up, then came back down as a whisper. When the quiet had made itself known throughout the crowd, Threeb produced a page

filled with the embossed bumps from his Braille writer, then in clear voice read
The Last Parable of Handy Jones:

*You are not the system. You are either its victim or its enemy. If you are its enemy,
you are either a person of principle or you are not. If you are an unprincipled enemy,
you seek only to overthrow the old system in order to replace it with a new system of
your own devising. If you are a principled enemy, you seek only to overthrow the old
system in order to replace it with nothing. All principled enemies of the system are
anarchists; all anarchists are principled enemies of the system. ¡Long live Nothing!*

By then it was nigh onto noon, necessitating that a short break be taken
before we all reconvened on the Square to partake of a funeral feast of such
fundamental proportions that both Methodist and Baptist seminarians have
since studied its accounts as essential to their matriculation. There were covered
dishes and uncovered dishes, biscuits in baking pans and on baking sheets, home-
baked cakes and pies and breads and rolls, iced tea by the gallon, coffee by the
urn, cornbread and cornpone, and from root cellars far and wide Mason Jar upon
Mason Jar yielding their stores of last year's black-eyed peas and green beans and
squashes and tomatoes and corn and jalapeños and habañeros and cabbage and
pickles and pickled okra and nopales and prickly-pear jam and mesquite bean
jelly. There were hams and Spams, pot roasts and pot-lucks, one-dish-dinners
and casseroles, slices of olive-loaf and meatloaf, along with crackers of all kinds
accompanied by canned meats of a variety that would amaze the most worldly
cowpuncher on the widest of ranges, sardines and oysters and anchovies and
kippers and mackerel and tuna and salmon and all of them in any sauce to be
had anywhere, be it mustard or tomato or cottonseed oil or water or just plain
smoked. After we'd all eaten our fill—and perhaps the fill of a whole host of other
folks—Threeb and Maya Gandhi played The Song of Surprise, he on the Handy
Jones Fiddle and her on the open-backed hand-drum she called, variously, the
bodhisattva bodhran or the Tomasina-Tomasina.

As the last notes were drifting off, Ruth Etta and Kerrie Mae and Bobbie
Sue were sacking up left-overs for Kelly and me, doggie-bags-for-future-dog-
tags, loading up take-out for take-cover, providing something to sustain us on
the long journey ahead. The Double-Joneses added a copy of Camus's 'The
Stranger' to my sack, the Eliots completing Kelly's with their Cousin Tom's

'The Four Quartets'. Then, just as soon as possible after Threeb drew the last pull on his bow, the six of us Foundling Surprises plus little Tally, the one New Surprise, all loaded up in the Creepy-Crawley for the long, slow drive to the Federal Building in Odessa in order that we Dos Draftees wouldn't wind-up unintentional dos-draft-dodgers. We sang all the way, just as we had done with the Ukuladies not so many years back, and, once again, just as we had always done, made the gig just in time. The Greyhound out front was boarding. Our two seats were open. And it was just as well.

20.

THE EMPEROR'S NEW CLOTHES

After a short ride and an induction physical of roughly the same duration, Kelly and I were sworn-in to the U. S. Army, immediately upon the conclusion of which brief ceremony a series of various conveyances were employed to transport us to Basic Combat Training, a trip more than long enough for 'The Stranger' though not quite up to 'The Four Quartets'. As we traded our books back and forth—apathy and absurdity exchanged for hope and divinity—we began to understand that the Double-Joneses and the Eliots had, even if only inadvertently, chosen the exact, right readings to prepare us for war and for our preparations for war. Not that we said as much, for we were yet young men in the company of other young men and therefore approached Camus and Cousin Tom with the proper horror and reverence only in our secret minds whilst merely with nonchalance and cynical humor in our public persons.

In one of those odd, inexplicable and infrequent gestures of government generosity—or just plain, dumb luck, and with all that we know of the world suggesting the latter as the more likely of the two—Kelly and I were both assigned to Fort Ord for basic training. Karma, I suppose, as that particular military base had strong connections with our home town of Surprise, the first being that it was named for Edward O. C. Ord, a mathematical genius—which endeared him to me—and the second being that one of the thirteen of his surviving children—the awkward-ly-named Jules Garesche 'Garry' Ord, but then, golly-gosh, with a total of fifteen offspring to enumerate, when all the births were included, such a task required a thorough mining of any and all available monikers, the awkward amongst them— this young Garry Ord had been the valiant man who initiated the charge up San Juan Hill only to be killed just as he reached the top, losing not only his life but also losing his share of the glory to Big Teddy Bear. And it was Handy Jones, you'll recall, who was also at San Juan Hill, armed only with his hélicon and his bullet-proof smile. The third and last connection was that the fort named for the Ords, *père* and *fils,* was but a-hop-and-a-skip from the Brainy Bay of Berkeley, allowing we two new soldiers the potential prospect of a warm, comforting, nearby destination should we be granted leave during our indoctrination.

Which—indoctrination or induction, you figure out the difference—began with the process of equalization, at which the Army is excellent, meaning that each of us former civilians was outfitted equally miserably, our pompadours perfunctorily peeled off, our feet fitted with boots and shoes that were but approximations of the proper shape and length and width of our tire treads, our torsos and trunks draped in fatigues and uniforms of the same order of tailoring as the boots, until lined-up—and we were always lined-up ¡nuts-to-butts! for something or somebody—we had begun to look like true government-issue grunts. Yet equalization was only superficially about appearances. Or maybe it was fundamentally about appearances. Look alike, think alike. Think alike, act alike. That was the large theory. Soon enough in such a scheme, orders would become little more than routinized permissions, and doing what one's told to do would become the ultimate liberation. Lean, mean, fighting machines we would be, each and every one of us.

Still, despite our regimented coiffures and identical draping, we new recruits as yet remained nothing more than small, individual hypotheses of that big concept, hypotheses which needed to be put into practice under the eight-week regimen of The Fort Ord Boogie. *Standing tall and looking good / All I see is Hollywood.* Nine days of five miles from the barracks to the firing range with a ten-pound M14—not a gun, a weapon—running the whole way, running everywhere else, too, with push-ups for our recreation, ham-and-slimas our cuisine, our only entertainment the mad dash to the phone booths any time we got the chance. By the end of May of '65 we'd been rode-hard-and-put-up-wet, chewed-out, chewed-up, and spit-out, finally ready for AIT—Advanced Individual Training—for our MOS—Military Occupational Specialty.

Curiously, all the while we were being equalized and regularized and normalized we were given questionnaires to fill out after which the whole lot of us was interviewed individually to see how each of us still-mostly-square-pegs could be fitted to the proper round hole. They learned straight away that Kelly was an actor, so, not having any other idea about how to use such talents and skills as those of the thespian, instantly assigned him to the Infantry. Crazy, you might say, but—as Howard Hawks and Stanley Kubrick knew and as Gary Cooper and Kirk Douglas proved—the drama's all with the foot-soldier.

So Kelly was given orders for Fort Polk, smack-dab in the middle of Louisiana, hot and humid and home to all four species of North America's poisonous snakes. It was also home to Tigerland—a jungle-operations training site, the nearest thing in the U. S. of A. to the terrain of South-East Asia—making an assignment to Polk nothing but a way-station on a sure-as-shootin' trip to Saigon. Kelly didn't seem the least bit worried, though Surprises of all ages smiled only through gritted teeth at the prospect, save Tally, the newest Surprise, who reworked his G.I. Joe action figure into a right-smart likeness of his and his mother's hero. On the one hand, boys from Andrews County, much less those from the Sand Dune Suburbs of Surprise, were a physically hardy lot, making Kelly, despite his professional calling, as tough as nails and as sharp as a cactus needle. On the other hand, unlike his geographical brothers, he possessed another, even more-helpful trait: being an actor, he could, at will, switch off the innate repugnance for authority that comes as part-and-parcel to those of us from the Realm of the Oil-Patch Kingdom. The resultant mix produced what looked to the Infantry to be a top-notch ground-pounder. By the end of summer, he was in-country, assigned to Tan Son Nhut Air Base.

They had no trouble at all with my assignment. Seems an all-draftee military had never been in the plans of the generals and strategists who'd been running the various outfits ever since the Second War to End All Wars. No, the elite alumni of the various service academies had counted on calling up the reserves when the next war rolled around, thereby being able to dip into a ready pool of men and women who'd have had training in one useful thing or another and would be ready to dive right into the swim of all those things. Instead, the politicos baffled the braid-and-brass bunch by announcing that the personnel sent to enforce the Gulf of Tonkin Resolution—newspeak for the War in South-East Asia—would be called up by the Selective Service System for hitches limited to two years, with only one annum to be spent in Vietnam. It was a revolving-door way of waging a war. Having to train a bunch of conscripts—and train 'em while the war was underway—wasn't a happy thought. So when they came across a draftee who came fully-equipped with an employable skill there was no delay or debate. The Signal Corps needed writers, and I was that.

I was to report to Fort Gordon, Georgia, where they were kicking keisters 24/7 training radio operators to bounce microwaves off the troposphere. We'd been given ten days' leave between Basic and AIT, which I divided up between the Republic of Berkeley and the Outpost of Surprise. I needed the time and was loathe to leave, most especially my Ruth Etta—we had correspondence to catch-up on, basic having had basically no time for letter-writing. But leave I did, arriving in Augusta near mid-June, too early for new-crop peanuts but just before the peaches had all been picked. Not that I was able to enjoy either goobers or Freestones as new orders had preceded me. My AIT was now OJT. Someone up the chain was a fan of 'Bubble-Up' and had finagled me a spot with the Army Pictorial Service as a script-writer for 'The Big Picture' television series. My duty station was to be the famous Astoria Stage in the Queens Borough of the Big Apple, where the Marx Brothers had shot their first two films—'Cocoanuts' and 'Animal Crackers'—and where the first Sherlock Holmes talkie was made, and where, many years later, 'Sesame Street' would be videotaped. It was, clearly, the perfect place to fashion military propaganda films for the American masses.

Kelly's luck was just as good as mine, if a little slower in coming. He'd hardly been on base a month before he earned an attaboy R&R stint at Vung Tau, the self-proclaimed Pleasure Capital of the World, a town that smelled oddly but pleasantly of fish and salt water and cheap beer and cheaper perfume—all of it together a rich *eau de cologne* that came from the collision of capitalism and communism—a community in the truest sense that was but a couple of hours and an eternity away from the fields of combat. No sooner than he'd hit town he ran into several of his Broadway pals who were part of a USO troupe working the Vung Tau R & R Center. They invited him on stage that evening. Kelly did his Kelly-thing, very likely including his imitation of LBJ, which—coming from a fellow Texan—was spot-on and also which—coming from a Surprise—was mercilessly-honest, the resulting combination therefore being very, very funny. The Aussies in the Peanut Gallery—and there were big mobs of them—quickly cottoned-up to Kelly's accent, a twangy, musical way of talking as outrageous and as charming as their own. The base big shot—most likely a Republican—was also in the audience. After the show the whole lot wound up at the Spring Flowers

Bar singing 'Waltzing Matilda', the Aussies favoring the Broadway-show-tune-sounding-sonority of the Peter Dawson version, the Americans imitating Burl Ives, and Kelly throwing in verses from the Bill Haley & His Comets rendition of 'Rockin' Matilda', replete with the whistling introduction. Then Kelly, a fair dinkum singer in his own right, led the Aussies in several Lefty Frizzell tunes, most memorably 'The Long Black Veil' and 'Mom and Dad's Waltz', a pair of tear-jerkers that tapped-in to the evening's zeitgeist, with even the U.S. Army HQ-honcho swinging his scrambled-egg-ball-cap as he swayed and sobbed with the impromptu choir. Over drinks sometime between 2300 hours and sunrise a heretofore unknown position had been created for the Boy from Surprise as the brand-spanking new U.S. Army/USO liaison specialist for Vung Tau.

Despite his cushy assignment as an REMF—Rear-Echelon Mother …, well, I'll just leave that there—Kelly was still oh-so-close to the brush. Vung Tau was, after all, home to military units from the Aussies to the Kiwis to the Yanks. There were ammo depots, secretive Signal Corps installations, the 36th Evacuation Hospital. The battle lines were but miles away, not scores of miles away. It was known that even the VC drifted in to do their own R&R along the sands of Cap Saint Jacques. No matter the beautiful beaches nestled between the blue South China Sea and the soft, green hills. It was the mouth of the Saigon River and there was a war going on.

I was near a river, too, the East River, living in the Steinway neighborhood—yep, that Steinway—as the nearest Army bases, Forts Totten and Hamilton, had no place for me to bunk. ¡Yee-haw! There was nothing but the Queensboro Bridge between me and Mid-Town. I wore pressed khakis while I studied my trade, the U. S. Army paying my tuition and room and board, my business not war but the glory of war. Nevertheless. Yes, nevertheless. Not that I wanted to be slogging through rice paddies, dodging AK-47 rounds instead of yellow cabs, but I felt left out. I was part of the war, but I wasn't in the war, both too close and too far away.

My disquiet was eased indirectly by Ike—yep, that Ike—and directly by Lank Spangler. Our 34th president—one of our nation's best and one of my own, personal favorites—was born in Texas near where the Katy crosses the Red River, after which he was raised in the First Cowtown in the West, what we Texians call *that other Abilene* so as not to confuse it with our own Abilene, The Key City.

Throughout his life he enjoyed the works of Zane Grey, played a mean game of poker and a fair round of golf, and showed promise as an oil painter. You may think that his place in history owes to his having whupped the Nazis before leading the nation into the Populuxe Era, but you'd only be superficially correct. Those were outcomes, mere products of the man's greatness. I offer, for your deliberation, how much grander the Grand Old Party would be, and how much more united the United States would be, if every President slavishly imitated Ike, spending most of their time on the golf course—a better place than the halls of governance in which to improve one's lie—and concentrating their intellectual skills whilst playing five-card draw or seven-card stud or Texas hold'em—instead of gambling with the Nation's future—and relaxing with paint-brush and palette—instead of with their fat-cat donors. Harrumph.

How Ike helped me out was he established the United States Information Agency, an outfit whose mission was to tell the American story, but not like it was being told by Hollywood or by the Trotskyites, most members of Congress at that time making no distinction 'twixt the two. Besides establishing the Voice of America, the USIA opened Information Resource Centers—which were nothing more than propaganda libraries—all around the world, including one in Huế, just up the coast from Da Nang, near the northern border. Early in March of '66, the Buddhists in both towns took a detour from walking the path to Nirvana in favor of marching down the boulevards of the two cities in an effort to oust the South Vietnamese government and the armies of the U. S. of A. Pacifist monks demonstrating in the streets and burning buildings, a few even immolating themselves in front of news cameras, all this was bad mocus for the PR juggernaut of the Free World. When the ah-ohmmmmm-meisters torched the USIA library in Huế, the higher-ups in Washington decided that what was needed was someone from our side who'd put boots on the ground and write up the real story. The real story, that is, as perceived by the Big Bird Brass. When volunteers were sought, I figured I was their man, being a fiction writer and all, so I answered up. I cabled Kelly that I'd be in-country by mid-June. He wheedled a pass to Vung Tau for me, promising his bosses that I'd do a puff-piece about how well they were running their outpost in the Las Vegas of the East. Besides—Kelly could be heard cackling over the return telegram—he'd scheduled a performance by Lank Spangler, who was then traveling with a USO tour of South-East Asia.

Tommy Turnbough—Lank's real name, which is how we knew him before he got famous—grew up in a place very much like Surprise, two counties up, a tiny burg called Short Pump, sited a bit north of the slightly-larger town of Meadow and a bit west and south of the barely-larger community of Ropesville. Five years older than Kelly, he was playing music well ahead of us, hitchhiking through the Oil Patch, busking anywhere he could draw a crowd. Surprise was tailor-made for his sort of artistic entrepreneurship, making him a regular the first time he dropped into Handy Jones Hollow. Even in those early days his repertoire included what were to become two of his signature songs—'This River Don't Burn' and 'Jim Beam Homicide'—along with a few covers of the hottest up-to-the-minute radio hits and a big dose of titles that were purt-near unknown to white folk in general and perfectly unknown to the white folk of West Texas in particular. In the category of little-known music he did an especially fine version of Screamin' Jay Hawkins's 'I Put a Spell on You', at the conclusion of which the girls couldn't be pried off with a crowbar. It was a sinful song, primal at a level for which there are no words, and so to redeem himself—he was, after all, a product of his mother's church, the First Tabernacle of the Divine—he'd always follow that number with a medley of railroad songs, kicking off with Elizabeth Cotten's finger-picking standard 'Freight Train', segueing into Robert Johnson's 'Love in Vain' and from there building in intensity with 'Mystery Train'—Junior Parker's version, not Elvis's—and on into Howlin' Wolf's 'Smokestack Lightning', finishing with the rocking-rhythm-and-blues-gospel-come-to-Jesus-revival-hymn 'This Train', that last tune one Tommy had learned directly from Sister Rosetta Thorpe.

He'd picked it up during camp meetings at the aforementioned church, mesmerized by the powerful black woman who dressed in her Sunday-go-to-meeting best while packing a white, triple-humbucker Gibson SG Custom all the while unleashing a voice that could be easily and quickly cranked up to eleven. But Thorpe wasn't the only itinerate figure of strength to bring the message to the First Tabernacle Church of the Devine. Mae Turnbough, Tommy's mother, was ecumenical to the Nth degree. She welcomed any and all who had the passion—especially if the message came with music—right down from the scientists of Mary Baker Eddy's laboratories to Blind Willie Johnson—who may have made his only trip west just to preach in the famed tent—to gurus from the Indian Subcontinent to Eastern mystics to holy men from the western Native American tribes to calypso's Lord Invader.

Just as she'd roped-out the best messengers, she threw a big community-loop for souls. At any and every meeting the congregation would be made up of people of all colors—brown and black and red and yellow mixed and mingled among the white—and all ages and all walks of life. Should the question be raised or even hinted at, Mother Mae would fairly shout in defiance, ¡Souls have no color! The prissy and prejudiced wouldn't cross her, but that didn't mean that her speckled flock went unnoticed. Senator Joe McCarthy and his clones in the House Un-American Activities Committee got wind of the First Tabernacle Church of the Divine and straight-way sent J. Emperor Hoover's minions on a mission to Terry County to serve papers on the whole lot. Nothing so American as the dual practice of egalitarianism and religious freedom could be tolerated when the practicers were colored and talked funny. Let 'em integrate one church, and, by golly, the PTA would be next and after that the movie theaters and in short order the chain of dominos would fall right into the country clubs and voting booths. Problem was, the First Tabernacle of the Divine was a true taber-nacle—it was transportable, a tent, an ephemeral structure risen only around the spirits inside—so, having no permanent address, the Fee-Bees were forced to track the place down whilst it was in action on its home turf, as opposed to assaulting it through its bank accounts and corporate offices. Truth be told, there wasn't hardly a meeting that didn't involve a lot of hand-waving and rolling on the floor amidst the folding chairs, the physicality of all of that being celebrated in the speaking of unknown tongues and, hovering in the air, the prospect of a diamondback or two being handled by the hardest of the Holiness-hard-core. Part way through the first service the Government Guys took leave, never to return, their subpoenas un-served, the hair still standing up on their backs.

Of all that, young Turnbough took what he saw as useful, not useful as in the theatrics of a career in the performing arts, but useful as in the delivery of his own message, his own music. He took on a new name better suited to this new persona: 'Lank'—in a self-deprecating nod to his own gangly frame and in rhyming tribute to the predominance of the Christian name Hank in the country music universe—and 'Spangler'—a surname that invoked the vivacious visual vibrations sparked by his rhinestone-sequined jackets. The remade man was a walking Zen parable, a honky-tonker with a gospel upbringing, a para-doxical prestidigitator who was incapable of passing up either cabaret or church camp meeting, a white boy who sang like a black man—and sometimes like a black woman—a country hick who was a voracious consumer of philosophy, a red-neck Rastafarian who never sullied his body with booze but who never turned down a hit of the Mexican Weed or a tab of Sandoz Laboratories' best. He was behind the line but out front of the curve, a throwback to the past who was ahead of the times, a permanent resident on the cusp of change. Perfect—in short—for the present moment.

It was a short time but a grand time in Vung Tau. On my ride to Saigon I cobbled-together a glowing report, an alliterative appraisal of Kelly's commander's competency in creating such a fine R&R retreat as a respite from the ravages of the war raging all-around-all-around. I squeezed in some subtle strokes on Kelly's role in the shin-dig, spicing-up the story with scads of shiny stuff on Lank. Read and re-read throughout the subcontinent, it was a feature-piece so full of itself that it has never been equalled, a paragon of puffery that set the standard for spin, rumored ever since as a core component in the clandestine courses crafted by propaganda purveyors of political parties of every extreme that populate governments—both recognized and otherwise—the wide world over.

I did not fare so well with the belligerent Buddhists. To begin with, there was no bit of bull-schickle in their story. It goes without saying that protesters who purposely set themselves on fire are either lunatics or heroes. The Buddhists weren't lunatics. The South Vietnamese government leadership—corrupt to the point of clownishness, bad to the point of buffoonery, inept to the infinite—they weren't heroes. We—the U. S. of A.—were neither, just wedged-into a middle-muddle of our own making, the middle being the no-man's-land that the bosses never want to hear about. In the Vung Tau story I didn't so much stretch the truth as enlarge it. In the Huế story I was being called upon to subdue the truth, which wasn't in me, so I focused instead on telling the personal, the human-interest angle. Big mistake. I should have known better, should have known from my upbringing in Surprise and should have known from my stint as a writer in The City of the Angels that the more personal a story is, the wider the swath it cuts across the universe.

Saint Woody Guthrie once wrote on his guitar This Machine Kills Fascists. He was onto something. Likewise, the personal story—in the hands of those of us who write and paint and sculpt and dance and sing and play—comes with the unwritten slogan This Art Kills Ideology. Which is why art so terrifies governments of every kind and every time and every place, ideology being the defining force of organizations of every stripe—the church and its prophets, the corporation and its profits, the government and its taking of prophets and profits—these organizations shielding their fundamental motive of greed—for power, for money, for privilege—in the rhetoric of that same ideology.

The only saving grace of the South Vietnamese government was that they weren't communists, and, really, it's still too early to evaluate whether or not that was a grace of any kind. For communists and capitalists, Buddhists and Baptists— no matter—are also sons and daughters, brothers and sisters, husbands and wives, mothers and fathers, friends and neighbors, good and bad and smart and dumb and handsome and ugly. People. No more, no less. But not the message to be issued under the imprimatur of the United States Information Agency. No attaboy for me.

Kelly didn't re-up, but he volunteered to stay in-country for the full term of his service. He had it good and knew it, doing work he was good at for folks who appreciated it. As for me, the brass didn't want to send anyone back to do any more personal interest writing, so I finished up at Astoria Stage, spending most of my time learning the technical side of the moving picture trade. Coming out the other end, though wiser and more in the know, neither Kelly nor I could tell Country Joe what we were fighting for. By late spring of '67 we were both free men, just in time for the Summer of Love. We needed it. And it was just as well.

21.

I, LOVE, ROCK-AND-ROLL

'd gone into the army toting a Ticket to Ride, marched through basic training on The Eve of Destruction, shipped out as the Universal Soldier, got no, no Satisfaction listening to The Ballad of the Green Berets which was Kind of a Drag and made me want to plead Help! before shouting I Ain't Marching Anymore even though That's Life and The Beat Goes On. No matter that I'm a Believer diggin' those Good Vibrations, I could only Paint It Black, being a Nowhere Man who wasn't Homeward Bound and could only Daydream about Kicks and some Good Lovin'. Oh, and Wouldn't it Be Nice? if we could all be Happy Together—For What It's Worth, I'm just saying—'cause I'm a Man and I've got Somebody to Love and I know She'd Rather Be with Me. There was nothing to stop The Sounds of Silence of My G-G-Generation for The Last Time except to scream over and over and over again We Gotta Get Out of This Place.

I emerged just in time for Scott McKenzie and some gentle people.

Kerrie Mae had matriculated in biochemistry, earning her Bachelor's and Master's degrees before switching to the College of Agriculture for her doctorate. Weary of focusing on the small stuff—even with the prospect of getting to peer through the biology bunch's brand-spanking new Stereoscan electron microscope—Big Sis was driven by big ideas for the big stuff. She could see with her own two unaided eyes that the two biggest threats to humankind—short of the politicians having their way and turning the Cold War into a Hot War—those two biggest problems were water and energy. Such views made her a pariah amongst the test-tube-tiara-ed bio-chem crowd who figured that every problem could be solved in a laboratory, whereas over in Ag the gimme-cap-farm-and-ranch-get-dirt-under-your-fingernails set were already deeply concerned with the same issues that motivated my sis. And rather than aiming for a research career of journal articles and conferences and committees and all the footnoted-blah-blah-blah of academia, she was instead a scholar of the practical who planned to come back to Surprise and build wind generators for the electricity needed to pump the brackish water up out of the salty Santa Rosa aquifer and push it through reverse-osmosis desalination filters so as to be able to operate acres and acres and acres of aquaponic farms. ¡Far out!

Not quite fully discharged, Kelly and I missed her hooding. But soon's we could ditch our G.I. garb we both beat feet back to Berkeley to revel in the aftermath of her coronation. It worked out OK, even better than OK, as Ruth Etta met us there, driving the Pink-and-White Road-Rally Rambler up from the Republic of Surprise. And speaking of surprise—*¡bah-dah-boom!*—there was very little surprise in Kerrie Mae's Philosophy-hoo-Doo achievement, though we were all more than a little miffed that she'd not yet won the Nobel. No, the big surprise was in the beaming Bobbie Sue, now only three months away from delivering the Second Newest Surprise.

Whilst Kerri Mae clucked over her like a born-again mother hen, Tally gave us the scoop. Just having turned 8—not yet hormonal but within view of the impending change and so now beginning to develop an interest in all things connected with the reproductive cycle—the brash young Brainy-Boy, who'd long known that he himself was a love-child, had quickly done the calculations to establish the *amore*-begets-*bambino* scenario for the baby in Bobbie Sue's basket. His logic was impressive. As the threesome were almost always together, and as when it was a twosome it was almost always Bobbie Sue and Tally giving his mom some study time, the not-so-longer-tiny Tiny Turing Engine marked the moment as sometime on Saturday night, January 14th past. That day Bobbie Sue invited the 'Stream-hold occupants to accompany her to the Human Be-In planned for Golden Gate Park, but Kerrie Mae was working on her dissertation defense and any be-in, much less one billed as a gathering of the tribes of the whole hominid race, promised to run much too late for the philosophy-doctor-in-waiting and her young 'un, leaving the merriest Merriman to make her own way.

On the night of the event, Tally's report continued, there was much music—The Grateful Dead, the Jefferson Airplane, Big Brother and the Holding Company, Quicksilver Messenger Service—and there was plenty poetry—Richard Alpert and Allen Ginsberg and Lawrence Ferlinghetti and Gary Snyder—plus there was the singular, first-ever West Coast appearance of Timothy Leary.

There were rumors that The Owl would be distributing free acid—altered consciousness having been illegal only a few months—and that the Merry Pranksters' bus 'Further' would be available for oohing and aahing. It was a hippies' home-show, a fan-fair for freaks, a convention for the unconventional. Tally was bummed-out big-time that he was barred from be-bopping along behind Bobbie Sue, for most of the worthies on the playbill that night were his pals from the City Lights Bookstore and the rest were his heroes, especially the musicians. The next morning he paid particular attention to Bobbie Sue's babbling summary of the goings-on from the night before, noting especially her glowing generalizations of the cool conversation she recounted between herself and the Prince of Psychedelia, that bright-eyed leprechaun of LSD, Doc Leary himself. We listened respectfully to Tally's analysis, nodding gravely and supportively, but that fall, when Bobbie Sue named her newborn Starlight—the baby girl smiling impishly even before her first swaddling, her eyes dark and intense and sparkling—we recalled his conclusion, again nodding gravely, but this time in admiration of the smack-on sentience and the powerful mind of the First New Surprise. Thence ever after, Tally was consulted on any and every matter of importance.

There was a second surprise, one both figurative and literal and one more subtle than the first. Threeb had ridden out with Ruth Etta for his first trip West, perhaps for his first trip anywhere that wasn't effected on the Creepy-Crawley. No question that there was no one more deserving, no one better suited than was the original Third-Eye Surprise to sample the upcoming Summer of Love and its mind-expansion explosion. Bobbie Sue fitted him out in a pair of oversized Ray-Ban Aviators, shod him in double-hemp-tire-tread huaraches, wrapped him in a tie-dyed kaftan, found him a white cane painted in a scroll of pop-art flowers, then carted him all over, to City Lights—where they had a reasonable selection of avant-garde titles in Braille editions—and then on several strolls around Haight-Ashbury, her arm locked in his as she deftly dodged the street-clowns and petty-larceny-panhandlers juggling for space with the spaced-out. Showing him the sights, so to speak, or, more accurately, showing him to them. In his new garb, his ancient vibe radiating in a veritable hippie halo, he was an other-worldly stand-out in a world of other-worldlies, a groovy Gandalf come riding in from the country to save the San Franciscan Shire. He was also—we all realized, all of the same moment—the Handsomest Surprise.

The quorum of the other five-and-three-quarters Surprises was glad to see the two of him: the good-ole Threeb and the newly-arrayed Third-Eye Threeb. Though it must be said—here and now—that my own feelings were ruffled with a few wrinkles. The first and foremost furrow was the practical impracticality of a Threeb-some. ¿Where would Ruth Etta and I lodge the newly-coined King of Kamp? We had our own work to do. A lot had happened since we'd married ourselves, and most of it had happened whilst we were separated by time and space. The demise of 'Bubble-Up'. The war. The death of Handy Jones. The war. The draft. The war. Living in New York, New York. The war. We had to get to know one another again. That was bad, as we'd done that once already. Still, we had to get to know one another again. But that was also good, for the first go-round was marvelous, wonderful, a grand and glorious adventure. ¿Wouldn't the second be better? All we needed was some time together in the same space, that being the only confluence of circumstances sufficient to repair the excesses of too long, too far away.

For—and perhaps owing to those forces of Einstein's space-time continuum—up to now Ruth Etta and I had been inhabiting a constant honeymoon, lath-ered-up in lust fueled by lack of physical contact and by our own skill in letterotica. We assumed, as one does when one is young—in that time when IQ trumps OJT, when smarts are smug and experience is ignored, when wise-arse whips wise-dom—that what-was was what would always be, especially in the realm of romance. I, at least, didn't yet know that love is immutable only in its need, its fundamental rapaciousness, its sine-qua-non-ness, but otherwise and in every other way constantly and everlastingly changing its shape, its appearance, its description. Which makes it a constant discovery, or a constant rediscovery. Love is the river of Heraclitus—first those waters, now these—the river which you cannot discover but which can only discover you.

Kelly is not, has never been, and never will be an insensitive person. The plain fact is this: just being Kelly is a full-time job, and he's very good at his work. Still, he's capable of a surprising gesture now-and-again, one of those fabled exceptions that prove the rule. So, outwardly appearing to be unconscious of the soap-opera cranking-up inside my head, he offered to rent a student flat in Oakland for the summer, one big enough—he said with a wink aimed at his little sister and me—for himself and Threeb. Ah, all was good.

The summer. We'd made no firm plans about it. We mostly wanted to see one another in a setting that allowed for enough empty calendar for a good visit. Never mind that Kelly and I needed to find work. Already we each had several leads—both from our new Army pals and our old show-bidness buddies, him for some television work in New York and me for re-writes in El Eh—which took some pressure off. On the other hand, Ruth Etta couldn't leave the Shifting Sands Motel in her mother's care forever, and when the weather cooled in the fall Threeb would need to be back at the helm of the Flatland Drive-Out Theatre. Only Kerrie Mae and Bobbie Sue were set for the coming year, the former as self-appointed midwife and post-doc student at the Big U of CA, the latter in her new role as mother-in-process and in her continuing position as a free-agent gurvi on the Council for the Summer of Love.

When left alone, things have their own way of working out—in any case, life is right, said Saint Rainer Maria Rilke. Kerrie Mae needed help with Tally, Bobbie Sue needed help with New Baby and needed even more assistance with the squillion flowers-in-their-hair-hippies-to-be who were in the midst of following their ears and their gentle hearts to the City by the Bay. The rest of us could feel the sea-change happening and—it so happened—happened to have just enough of the King's Coin amongst us to last through autumn with enough change remaining so as to still be able to contribute to The Free Store—mindful as we were of The Diggers's admonition that today was the first day of the rest of our lives—and so as to still be able to do our own thing in trekking from venue to venue to experience the newest, best-est, greatest music of all time. In short, we managed to have time to hang out and help out.

And when time came time, we wasted little of it. Or wasted all of it, if you choose to take the point of view of those who favor future possibilities over present realities. The summer's first big whoop-de-doo—the Fantasy Fair and Magic Mountain Music Festival—was to be held the second weekend of June on Mount Tamalpais in Marin County, just over the Richmond-San Rafael Bridge. Originally set for the weekend before but postponed by rain, the line-up was a work-in-progress right up to the first count-off. No matter, it was a killer slate with all the usual suspects and a few mainstream acts thrown in for good measure. The one disappointment turned out well, too, as we'd seen Sparrow listed on the playbill only to learn it wasn't the famous Calypsonian singer The Mighty Sparrow at all but was, instead, a new local group—The Sparrows—but who would shortly be known as Steppenwolf. ¡Get your motor runnin'! Yet it was a gentle weekend; no fights, no hassle, people even picking up their trash and leaving the grounds better than they found them.

The following weekend—just before the midweek Summer Solstice and Ruth Etta's birthday—we all trucked down to Monterey—or, more accurately, we rambled and bused—to soak up the first-ever Pop Festival at the County Fairgrounds where big post-modern pyramid roofs shielded old-timey stands on either side of a vast field filled fence-row-to-fence-row by a multicolored sea of the human tribe, the Be-In in its true Be-ing. We didn't get in a hurry driving down as the Friday line-up was a little lame—come on, The Association and Johnny Rivers, for criminy's sake, and the once-edgy Eric Burdon & the Animals, the first hard-arse rock-and-rollers to succumb to pretension, oh, wait, ¿wouldn't that be The Moody Blues? never mind—but Saturday and Sunday were smack-on. It was our first exposure to Moby Grape—country rock long before the Flying Burrito Brothers—who led off Saturday evening, and whom we followed up and down the coast ever after, from The Ark in Sausalito and the Avalon Ballroom in San Fran down to The Bank in Torrance. Most folks only know Moby Grape from their posters—and so what, they're the best of the whole lot—but we dug their music, three guitars that wove in and out like the strands in a fine rawhide quirt overlain with vocal harmonies that were all-at-the-same-time sweet and raw and delicate and powerful. Through them we found our bragging rights, too, as at subsequent gigs they were often on the bill with cutting-edge bands from our native nation of Texas, those being the electric ensembles The Conqueroo, The 13th Floor Elevators, and Shiva's Headband. They may think they invented country-folk-rock and psychedelia on the West Coast, but we citizens of the Realm of the Armadillo can offer-up a mighty convincing history in refutation.

Bobbie Sue, ordinarily the most adventurous Surprise, took seriously her new role as infant incubator, touching nary a drop of alcohol or whiff of smoke or drop of acid for the term of her gestation. That did not keep her from love, no, not at all, for it was—let us not forget—the Summer of Love, but in her new regimen she only practiced love on the grand scale, now extending the love she'd always had for her fellow Surprises to the whole world. Or at least the wholeness of the world in which she found herself. When she wasn't serving free stew and coffee-can-whole-wheat-bread at The Free Frame of Reference she was tending bad-trip cases and minor maladies at The Free Clinic or handing out rations and supplies at The Free Store. All that and yet never too busy to boogie along with our gang from one concert to another, all the long summer long, having—quite clearly—fully fleshed-out the free in freedom.

Kerrie Mae came when she could. And we all understood. As her frequent stand-in, Tally was our constant trouper, helpful, well-mannered, unfailingly cheery, but always able and willing to offer-up a shrewd analysis of the music, the politics, or the social science, most often all in the same quip. In between music outings, he guided Kelly and Threeb around San Francisco and environs, going to the beach on sunny days—Phelan Park for the view of the bridge, Bolinas for an all-day excursion—and visiting various city attractions when the weather wasn't attractive. During those same intersessions, Ruth Etta and I motored down to Angel Town to do a little work—the Flying Cloud had been rented-out during my military expedition and required some spit and polish, plus there were re-write possibilities to explore—but mostly just to have a little alone-time.

Tally was born to the practice of making pals, any and every time there were potential pals to be made. Already the darling of The City Lights Bookstore, he was outfitted with the best qualities for enlarging his already large world of acquaintances and friends, by nature being both unassuming and unafraid, self-confident without being self-indulgent, and always, always, always more interested in you than you were in him. And you were always interested in him.

Amongst the many buddies he added to his Etch A Sketch Rolodex during the Monterey Pop Festival were several Gestalt groupies from the Esalen Institute. Young Tally was taken with their beaming smiles and the great, billowing aura of calmness that enveloped them, the two phenomena so strong that any person in their presence couldn't help themselves but smile in surrender to the peaceful power of awareness. As soon as he'd absorbed a healthy dose of their good, good vibrations, the young pre-teen philosopher straightway fetched Threeb to make introductions. Which was unnecessary, as when the Gestalters and the New Sage of Surprise—Handy Jones's hand-picked successor, and, ¡oh, that Handy were here!— when this cosmic crowd were within halo-distance of one another the connection was instantaneously made, the whole of them embracing in a group-hug of perfect oneness as if they were old friends merely long-separated. They spent the remainder of the festival digging the music and the moment together, intense conversations carried out with looks and gestures and bodies all tuned in to the same tempo and turned on to the same spirit. Long before the last fat chord had rung out, an invitation had been extended, accepted, and modest arrangements made.

Within a few weeks Ruth Etta and I were again due to haul ourselves to The Mayberry of the Valley on another foray of reclamation work on the 'Stream and so we offered to tote Threeb down to Gestalt HQ and deposit him there. It's a beautiful drive, as I've already reported, but on this trip made all the more beautiful by the currency of current events, i.e., having survived the Army, having begun the Summer of Love, and, first and foremost, having Ruth Etta near again. Just out of Big Sur, Esalen was hung on the steep, sharp cliff between Highway One and the Pacific Ocean, a few hours south down the coast from the Brainy Bay and about twice that north of our destination in Burbank. On arriving, we pulled our modest Cross-Country Rambler off the macadam into their equally-modest parking area, stepped out, and even before we could un-jumble our road-jitters we were silly-slapped by the sea breeze and the salty smell of the ocean and the sound of the surf surging onto the rocky shore below us. It sounds corny to say we drank it in, but drink we did, very nearly to inebriation.

Once we could get our get-alongs going we got around to Reception, the only check-in desk in the known universe—I might point out—where the receptionists not only smile like they mean it but in point of fact really do mean it. Threeb was expected, and though Ruth Etta and I weren't, the Esalen crew took us in as if we were. Walk about the grounds, they suggested, and, please, take a soak in the waters. *Clothing optional,* they added. After we'd meandered around the Institute for a bit, we found ourselves at the Bath House, just above the hot-spring pools which were in turn just above the cold Pacific. *Clothing unlikely,* that should have been the proviso, as amongst the dozen or so seekers of enlightenment smiling up at us from the rock tubs there was nary sight of covering of any kind. Nudity had no impact on Threeb, as one might expect, and Ruth Etta, being her mother's daughter, was constitutionally predisposed to the blissful state of *déshabillé au naturel.* As for me, it was the Summer of Love, I was free from the Army, and I was not about to be the only schmuck sporting a fig leaf in the Garden of Esalen, so within a time so short it was marked only by the speed of snaps and zippers and buttons the three of us were in full and open communion with the universe, our portable facades in a pile on a large rock behind the pool.

Au naturel is natural for good reason. After the soak, we walked up the cliff to the bath house, past its out-door massage tables where Gestalt was being rubbed-in along with the fragrant oils, then once up top were invited to listen in as Fritz Perls moderated an ongoing discussion of the primacy of process—that is, what's happening—over content—that is, what's being talked about. There was mention of the empty chair, a fuzzy concept that was confusing to me but was received with nods of understanding and approval by the assembled seminarians. Back at reception, Threeb got his room assignment, told them that he'd be interested in exploring the possibility of becoming a massage therapist—to which they smiled and nodded in affirmation as if they expected it—after which we made our *adieux*. Just as we were about to reach the parking lot Ruth Etta and I realized with a start that we'd never dressed. We'd simply been carrying our clothes along as if they were *accoutrements* required only for the unenlightened. Which was true. But as the highway was dominated by a fundamental lack of enlightenment, we quickly garbed ourselves, girding up for the the rest of the journey.

Just before I pulled out of the parking lot and onto Highway One, Ruth Etta looked back to see Threeb, his nakedness outlined spectacularly against the ocean horizon, waving his arms in a big, slow farewell. Knowing it was pointless— logically, at least—to return the wave, she did so nevertheless, then turned back as we were finding our way into traffic to say, matter-of-factly and to no-one in particular, that Threeb had a natural gift for massage. Though I've never quite gotten a grip on gestalt, I'm certain it was the empty chair that guided the Rambler back to the City of the Angels and on into the burbs of Burbank.

22.

EXODUS

Ruth Etta needed wheels to bring back to Surprise. Gallantly, I offered to part with my beloved Nash wagon, that venerable vehicle of middle-class vagabondage. No, said she, I've been using it for the past two years and it just can't do what a pickup can do. Too much stuff to haul around the Shifting Sands Motel, she added in further detail and firmer tone. No problem, said I, frankly relieved at not having to give up the classic Cross-Country. Soon's I could I made my way over to Hollywood Rambler Land to call on the fellow who—during my short-lived heyday as a big-shot tee-vee writer—had found me a clean, slightly-used Avanti. The least I could do was give him first crack at supplying me with a small truck. His eyes lit up as I unrolled the roll-call of my requirements, me at first thinking that he was actually glad to see me despite the fact I'd backed-out on the stud-Studebaker scoot-ass car, only a bit later realizing he had something himself that he needed to unload and here I was, the perfect patsy purchaser.

He led me out onto the lot and over and around to the back corner, pointing out a shiny, white-over-turquoise pickup truck of the oddest mien. Square and clunky, it had a grill as if it were an Edsel on steroids or a Mack road-tractor sucking a lemon. Or as if it were a Studebaker Lark, but bigger, the progeny of a liaison between said Bird-Mobile and an International Harvester Travelall. Which proved to be the case. Sort of. The homely little lorry was a Champ, the South Bend, Indiana automaker's rebuttal to Detroit's Ford Ranchero and Chevrolet El Camino. Unlike those last two, which were mid-sized cars dressed-up in pickup beds, the Champ was a sturdy truck chassis topped-off with a car cab. This particular beauty was a showroom demo and so therefore came fully-loaded— air-conditioning, a Flight-O-Matic automatic transmission, its drive-train driven by a mild version of the same 289 V-8 that came in its glamorous Italian-designed sports-car cousin, its cushy-car interior topped-off with, wonder-of-wonders, a

202

new-fangled 8-track cassette player. Whoa—back-up, did I just say *beauty?*—
that quality, as you know, is in the eyes of the beholder, and there weren't many
beholders in SoCal who beheld the comely Champ with the affection that I
instantly felt for it. Since salesmen sense these things before we buyers know
them, sensible Mister Slick-'Em-Quick soon signed me up for the good bargain
that only his manager could approve. Right. Who else in the Golden State was
meant for this little work-mule but me?

I parked the Everyman's Estate Wagon on a side street and drove the Champ back
to Burbank, honking the horn smartly as I pulled up alongside the Flying Cloud.
Ruth Etta stuck her head out of the cabin door, wide-eyed at first but almost immediately squinching-up into full beetle-brow. I coaxed her out and walked her around
her new ride, rattling off specs and features as she pursed her lips and pondered it
from various angles and in various postures of her own. Racing my mental motor
but with my persuasiveness paused in park, I was getting nowhere at full-speed.
Thankfully, turquoise is known to have powers and maybe this particular paint
was more than just pigment—who knows, the Studebaker people were always 'way
ahead of the curve, so far out in front of the masses of mediocre American motorists
that these prescient automotive pioneers went bankrupt shortly after our Champ
chugged off the assembly line, their financing failing before the consumer wave
could catch up with them—but all that aside, for whatever reason I began to have
an out-of-body experience, looking down from above, seeing myself babbling along
in a circle as I spewed out content, content, content when Ruth Etta was all process,
process, process. ¡Gestalt! a couple of days ago I was guileless of that whole way
of thinking and now I was its object lesson. With no small effort I floated myself
back into my being, finally able to shut my flapper by holding the keys out to her.
We jumped in. Without another bit of content I turned the air-conditioner down
to meat-locker and the 8-track up to Patent Pending, seeing as how Mr. Rambler
Raconteur had inadvertently left the player loaded with a hot-off-the-press demo
cassette of 'Sgt. Pepper's Lonely Hearts Club Band'. It's wonderful to be here, it's
certainly a thrill… all the way over to Hollywood Rambler where I hopped out to
retrieve the Little Man's Limousine.

In the wee hours of the night, Ruth Etta woke me with a flurry of kisses. As
I reached to embrace her she pushed me away with one hand, dangling the new
keys in the other. Not here, she said, let's do it in the turquoise truck. The mere

suggestion of her inspiration shook the dangles out of my own dangler before we could fully fall out of the Flying Cloud and into the soft Southern California summer night. A few fumbles with the key in the door, no more, and we plunged completely into the moment of the coital christening of the Champ, champagne neither called-for nor needed. It's getting better all the time, I thought in a flash, then in the same flash knew that I knew the answer to ¿What do you see when you turn out the lights? because not only do I know it's mine and I can tell you if I would, but, why-why-why-why-why-why-why-why—oh-my, I was getting by without any help from my friends, blowing my mind out not in a car but in a Champ and if I could only stop my mind from wandering I'd love to turn you O-oh-O-on, O-oh-O-on, O-oh-O-on, O-oh-O-on-O-oh-O-on…

I came out of my rutting reverie to lights coming on all over the trailer park, from Shastas and Kenskills to Avions and Airstreams, sleepy voices trying to sing along with the sergeant and his band, lonely hearts beginning to beat all as one. Ruth Etta is a moaner but not normally a screamer yet the thought still rushed through my head that the Prettiest Surprise had surprised our canned-ham camping community with such enthusiasm in her endeavors that she woke them one and all until, until—a little content creeping into the process—I noticed that the keys were in the ignition—¡of course, of course! a naked woman has no pockets for keys or fobs—realizing all of a moment that in our rocking and rolling a misdirected toe or foot or who-dares-think-whatever-other appendage had nudged the switch over to accessory, bringing all eight tracks to life. ¡Sit back and let the evening go!

Next morning, over tea and marshmallow pies, we were talking about the space between us all, a space grown larger by a number of things that weren't important yesterday, specifically that the summer was nearing autumn and with the change in the seasons there'd be a change back to the most important of those things, that being me being a re-write tradesman in Hollywood and Ruth Etta being the proprietress of the Shifting Sands Mobile Motel a thousand miles away. The obvious question hung in the air. More content. Ruth Etta, sensing it, I suppose, began to hum 'Fixing a Hole'. Process. At the bridge I joined in singing, she instantly adding a harmony part, over and over until the dishes were done and our bags packed for a trip up the coast in the Champ to join The Brainy Bunch for another weekend of music. By the time we stopped marching and settled into the air-conditioned cab I knew better than to ask her again to move out west.

Merging onto the freeway I casually remarked that I was familiar with a great motel right on Pismo Beach. Looking over her sunglasses at me, Ruth Etta smiled and wondered out loud if it had truck parking, then popped our one-and-only lonely cassette back in the player. By the time we checked into our favorite overnight in the Clam Capital of the World we knew all the same melodies and all the same lyrics as did Billy Shear and the act you've know for all these years.

Many miles and many music weekends later the calendar was nearing mid-September, Bobbie Sue was nearing her due-date, and Threeb was nearing his anointing as a Gestalt massage therapist. This next trip was to be a big one, so Ruth Etta and I drove the poor, neglected Pink-and-White Pride of American Motors up Highway 1 so as to bring Threeb along for the upcoming birthday-zero of the Next Surprise. There was a slight delay in Big Sur as we had to talk Blind Billy Bob back into his bourgeois baggies as he'd been basking buck-naked long enough that he'd rather grown to like it. No matter. Turned out we weren't in much of a time-crunch after all as the as-yet-to-be-bouncing-baby Merriman—for the time being still in charge of her own schedule—took a few extra days to arrive, not appearing until the 23rd of September, right smack on the Autumnal Equinox. Saturday's child she was, full of grace, twinkling in the manner of her given name, replete with all her digits and a comely head-full of hair.

We participated to the Nth in the oohing and aahing and cooing and clucking, doing what else we could to assist with mother and child. Which wasn't much. Truth be told, Mother Nature has more hand in helping new mothers than has anyone else. We will nevertheless and unabashedly give ourselves a pat on the back for realizing—in rather short order—that the best contribution we could make was to give the Berkeley Bunch some elbow-room. Kelly was due in Gotham by month's end for some work in the soaps but Tally was in fine fettle, relishing his new status as no longer being the Youngest Surprise and—in view of his step up the ladder of seniority—ready, willing, and excited to help out around the 'Stream. Without worries or qualms we left the new foursome in their own capable hands.

On the way back south we stopped at Esalen for Threeb to collect his belongings and his copy of the official communication attesting to the accomplishment of his apprenticeship. Once again the friendlies up front suggested that we relax a moment or two in the hot-spring spa and, oh, ¿wouldn't the new graduate give us each a massage? show off his chops, so to speak. I shouldn't have been surprised, but I was. Maybe even nonplussed. I didn't know what to think, or even how to think. My mind went into full muddle. I'm a guy, ¿right? and he's a guy, ¿right? and I'll be naked, ¿right? Here I stood in the Palace of the Present Moment, poised in the portal of the process center of existence as we know it, and I was all content. But not Ruth Etta. All process, she didn't need to think about it at all. She took my hand, then Threeb's, and no longer than it required to walk down to the Bath House we Tres Surprises were bobbing about in our birth-day suits, the waters warmed by the earth below us washing away *what was* with *what is,* leaving *what will be* to fend for itself.

Despite the noonish hour, the morning fog hadn't lifted, which turned our eyes and ears inward because the heavy air not only brought the horizon to within arm's length but also spread the sound of the surf so that it came at us from every direction. It was calming, especially for me, this focused idyll of the senses. We talked very little. I remember only one conversation, about how very different was the effect of the natural hot spring from that of water out of the hot side of the faucet. ¿The minerals? No, Ruth Etta offered, for the water in our Cactus Capitol is hard enough to cut with a cross-cut saw. ¿The temperature? Don't think so, I added, since Ed Ruud's invention can be set to whatever caloric degree we desire. ¡Wait, that's it! said Threeb with emphasis, adding, We've no control over the hot spring, either temperature or hardness or supply. We can only surrender to the natural. Surrender, he concluded, being the first step of process. Of course, we all agreed, without another word spoken.

A moment later we arose in unison as if in an Esther Williams number, toweling off as we mounted the few steps up to a pair of tables already prepared for our alfresco massage. Ladies first. Though I've never tired of seeing Ruth Etta in the nude, I was relieved this time that Threeb draped us each in a soft cloth. Not a very big cloth, just large enough for strategic placement. He started with her shoulders and back, next her arms and hands, then down the big muscles of her legs. Even through the haze the sun was warm and I had almost dozed off when he asked her to roll over on her back. I couldn't not watch. Her back arched slightly as he tucked the drape in between her legs. It was a reaction I knew so I was lucky to be lying on my stomach. Her feet, then her legs, her back arching again when he reached the insides of her thighs, then his hands on her stomach, moving upwards in big, strong circles, her hands ever-so-slightly gripping the sides of the massage table. When he reached her breasts she trembled, turned her head to me, her eyes dreamy, and slowly and deliberately mouthed I love you. I don't think I'd ever seen anything so beautiful.

I tensed up when it came my turn. But if Threeb took notice I couldn't tell, instead putting his hands straightway on my shoulders and in a few minutes, maybe less, I felt my whole body giving in. Surrender. The first step in process. He followed the same order with me, and by the time he had me turned face-up he could have touched me anywhere, any way, and it would have seemed natural and right and—let us not deny—delicious. Ruth Etta was right, he had an innate gift, capital-I-less—totally involved with the other, perhaps from a life of being biologically-eye-less—and carrying with him and pouring out of his hands and fingers the spirit of Surprise.

After showering and dressing, Ruth Etta and I had a bit of a wait in the Nash-mobile as Third-Eye made his goodbyes amongst the staff. The sun was coming out, the windows were down—no refrigerated air in the Wonder Wagon—and we were relaxed and recharged and rewound. Ruth Etta, who'd had been looking towards the Pacific horizon, turned, put her left hand coquettishly in my lap, then after a stroke or two said with an impish smile that I'd certainly enjoyed my first massage. I should have been embarrassed by the content of the remark, but I was learning process.

They would leave on the morrow, and I would be sad to see them go. Sadder still that they'd be taking with them the Summer of Love.

I'd have been insufferably gloomy except that it's impossible to feel down in autumn, the most glorious of seasons. Yes, Dear Reader, I risk offending you or contradicting your opinion with such a grand and sweeping avowal, but a right-thinking person—as my father often put it, the right-thinking person curiously always in agreement with Pater Jones, as you soon will be with me, too, you being a right-thinking person and all—after an examination of the evidence the right-thinking person will surely stand side-by-side with these incontrovertible obser-vations, which I hereby offer. Winter is the night, time for sleep and rest, the hibernation of the senses and the soul, all grays and white. Spring is the morning, full of hope and promise but also fraught with mistakes and dicey thunder-stormy weather and dreams that begin over-blown and are soon little more than mists in a soon-to-be-forgotten consciousness, the whole of it too green, green being amongst the most difficult and obstreperous of colors. Summer is the afternoon, the languid nap after dinner, indolent, lethargic, incredibly selfish, all warm blues and cool violets. But autumn—oh, ¡autumn!—'tis the evening, the reward, the harvest, the perfection in the balance of night and day with crisp mornings and warm afternoons, the satisfaction of achievement, the laying-back of stores for the coming darkness, Orion preparing his return, everything bright in oranges and yellows and reds and the rich siennas.

Apart from the fall pick-me-up, I was also availing myself of one of the best antidotes for depression, one of the best antitoxins for angst, one of the best cures for curmudgeon-hood, one of the best medicines for mopery—that being busy-ness in general and, that most excellent elixir, busy-ness at one's work. As to the *-ness* of busy-ness, lots of that was going on in the IQ Ghetto. There was Starlight to goo-goo over, Tally with whom to engage in ever-more-esoteric discourse, Kerrie Mae with a discovery-a-day in the aquaponics arena, and thoroughly-modern-matron Bobbie Sue back in full form at work with the Haight-Ashbury Neighborhood Coalition and The Diggers, New Baby along 'side the way and a fierce maternal fire-for-a-better-future ablaze in her mama's countenance. All that despite the inexorable erosion of the free in freedom—the Free Clinic and the Free Store founded by the community anarchists falling to the government-green-eye-shaded bureaucracy of capitalist-social-services, the Mimes soon replaced by the world's first Clown College and its mirth-for-money mantra, all of all of that as evidence that the hippies who'd spawned the yippies who'd morphed into zippies were being replaced by *clippies.*

I was getting plenty of re-write work, too. Enough television for my daily bread and enough film for the butter. But as these are jobs that frequently appear out of the blue and always come with a deadline of I-need-this-yesterday I could only venture north during the dry spells, which seriously cut into my music-appreciation-time. Nevertheless, I *made* time for the big events. I answered Bobbie Sue's beck-and-call to attend the Hippie Funeral—devoted son of Mass Media, as he was described by his undertakers—held in October on the first anniversary of the outlawing of LSD. I had to get back to El Eh so missed the following weekend's Sit-In To End the Draft in Oakland, where Joan Baez was arrested, sentenced, and did ten days in the slammer. There was darkness growing, even in autumn.

The Summer of Love was over. The 60s were winding down. Whilst Kerrie Mae was keeping court with the post-docs and Bobbie Sue was behind the scenes building community, Tally was pre-teening as Starlight ruled the realm of the rug-rat. In spite of all that, or perhaps inspired by all that, The Ukuladies underwent a resurrection. Instruments were coaxed out from the backs of closets and storage spaces, old numbers dusted off, new numbers added to the set-list, and the two Youngest Surprises fit into the arrangements, Tally on the soprano ukulele along with taking charge of repertoire, Starlight for the boogie-and-babble parts. Judiciously, I was only invited for moral support and baby-dandling.

We took Christmas in Surprise, catching up with the old folks—who were, no surprise, getting older, an altogether good thing—and getting the low-down on how the general goings-on were going. Maya Gandhi's peripatetic hush-puppy proprietorship was setting new sales records, which was no surprise, Punto Rojo remained in fine fettle, which was some surprise—¿how long do horses live, anyway?—and our favorite Indian-Indian could still beat the bongos with the best of them.

In the only negative note on the numerical financial front the drive-out movie business was in serious decline, partly due to the increasing number of TV antennae accumulating in the Gotham of Greasewood but mostly as a consequence of a corresponding decline of darkness in the night skies, which in turn correlated with more and more mercury-vapor lamps dotting a horizon that was itself more and more comprised of drilling rigs and rework rigs and gas-flare towers. At Ruth Etta's suggestion that he put his training and innate gifts to use in order to bolster his declining drive-out theater income, Surprise's resident Third-Eye opened a massage salon in an oil-patch-office-trailer refurbished by master-mechanic Merriman, the new-old-movable moved to a prime spot on the Shifting Sands Motel grounds, an attractive design painted on the roof available for birds and pilots to see with a smaller version affixed above the door for viewing by the rest of us, the images in both places consisting of a mystical face with its two biological eyes closed but in its forehead a wide-open and penetrating third eye, the whole surrounded by the letters S-I-G-T at the four cardinal points. It was intended to be an initials-only name, as you can certainly understand why Threeb would have missed both the pretty obvious pronunciation to rhyme with *light* and the ironic humor produced by such pronunciation—with neither missed by Bob Merriman, who soon spread the vocalization far-and-wee, if not the joke—in spite of or because of all that, the ensuing business was so brisk that Maya Gandhi brought her burgeoning brisket brasserie into the confines of the Shifting Sands, ensconcing her operation under a semi-permanent tent-fly erected to the side of the rub-down wagon. Also concomitant with the establishment of the newly-formed Surprise Institute for Gestalt Therapy, the normally-florid correspondence between Ruth Etta and I slowed down both in temperature and in the number of letters per week. Too much of that busy-ness on both our parts, I assured myself, never mind that the content cyclotron in my consciousness required some conscious cooling-down. Process. Breathe. Process. Breathe. Process. Breathe.

1968 wasn't exactly Dickens's the-best-of-times-the-worst-of-times, but it was likely the most curious of times. The music remained good, despite several popular bands disbanding—Buffalo Springfield in the spring, The Yardbirds in the summer, Cream in the fall, then at the beginning of winter Janis leaving Big Brother and the Holding Company, Eric Burdon leaving The Animals, Peter Tork leaving The Monkees, and Brian Jones playing his last gig with the Stones. The music was still good because there was new talent with fresh new stuff—Canned Heat; Creedence Clearwater Revival; Crosby, Stills, and Nash; Iron Butterfly: Led Zepplin; Steppenwolf—and because the old standbys were bringing out their own new stuff—The Beatles all in white, The Byrds hanging out with the Sweetheart of the Rodeo, Johnny Cash in Folsom Prison, Dylan coming back to life at Carnegie Hall, Van Morrison in a garden all wet with rain, the Rolling Stones at a Beggar's Banquet.

But while it may have been the dawning of the Age of Aquarius, the non-music universe was running head-long into the barrow-ditch. Lank Spangler plunged off the Caprock in February; in April, Martin Luther King was gunned down in Memphis, Bobby Hutton in Oakland two days later, then Bobby Kennedy in June; and in December the Zodiac Killer set about his work. The Chicago Police rioted at the Democratic National Convention, students rioted in New York, over a million marched in France, thousands of football fans stampeded in Buenos Aires, the Rooskis invaded Czechoslovakia, the Troubles began in Ireland with the police beatings in Derry, and three U. S. astronauts saw the dark side of the Moon five years before Pink Floyd got there. As if a final shot was needed, 'Hair' opened on Broadway ensuring that Hippie, Devoted Son of Mass Media, was indeed dead.

There was the Decade of the 60s. Then there was the Era of the 60s. Altogether two very different things. Any school-child can tell you that the Decade began the first moment of the morning of Friday, January 1st, 1960, ending straight-up midnight on Wednesday, December 31st, 1969. Any flower-child can tell you that the Era began Sunday evening, February 9th, 1964, with 'All My Loving' on The Ed Sullivan Show, only to end with 'Sympathy For the Devil' at Altamont Speedway, just after sundown on Saturday, December 6th, 1969.

I drove up to Berkeley the following Monday, the 8th. Kerrie Mae's post-doc grant was to expire with the end of the fall semester. Bobbie Sue knew that it was time to bring the revolution home. We spent a few days bustling about, putting things ready, making sentimental sorties to the City Lights Bookstore and our favorite haunts in The Haight, but no later than mid-week we had the 31-foot Liner hitched up to the Nash-Mover, the Merriman Mini-Bus serviced and packed, the expedition set to set-off cross-country. Tally and I took the lead, Kerrie Mae and Bobbie Sue and Starlight herding the VW Wagon on the back-door—¡ten-four, good buddy!—making our wandering way back to Surprise. We weren't fast, but we weren't in a hurry. Bobbie Sue had booked an Ukuladies tour of dates that led like bread crumbs back to a Christmas Eve gig at The Old School House in Surprise. And it was just as well.

23.

THE DARK AGES

If all they have is a hammer,
You and me are the nails. —Lank Spangler, "If They Had a Hammer", unreleased

Someone slipped us a mickey that was so fine, oh, so fine, just before they Rick-rolled us into the Dark Ages. All we could remember was a bland voice—don't worry, be happy—singing out of different faces that all looked the same, causing the synthesized chorus that we thought was us to mumble Wake me up before you go, go where you want to go, do what you want to do, even if it's better than the best that we can do, yes, oooh we want to take you where we built this city. But by the 90s we finally, finally figured it out—the groove of the 60s had worn into the rut of the 80s. The revolution had failed—well you know, we all wanted to change the world—and even though the joker said to the thief there must be some way out of here we knew better 'cause we could hear the sound of marching, charging feet, boy, knowing always, always, always we'll be fighting in the streets, the shotguns singing the song, for who cares if we got down on our knees and prayed we don't get fooled again? the change it had to come. And it was us. And we were it.

Not that it happened all at once. No, not at all. Oodles and oodles of warning. Brian Jones bobbing in his swimming pool, Jimi crashing-out in London, Janis cashing-out in Hollyweird, Mama attacked by her own marvelous heart, the King gone to grace in Grace Land, and then to end it all John Lennon caught comin' thro' the rye on the steps of the toniest of the tony addresses in NY-squared. ¿Was that not enough? how about MTV the first crack in the facade, FOX TV the full split. ¿Was that not enough? I'll see your Kent State and raise you a Munich and a Watergate and if you're still stayin' alive and that's still not enough, then ¿how about a Jonestown?

We should have seen it coming. And maybe we did. Or maybe you did. Me, I watched the whole baker's dozen of the Get-And-Grab-Years from the sidelines, being got but not getting, grasping but not grabbing. Me, the last Surprise still situated on the Smog Shores, still scruffling about for scraps of script-work, still sending fingerotica from the envy-green keys of my Smith-Corona in letter-after-letter-after-letter-after-letter to Ruth Etta, she still as constant as the Morning Star, still just as bright, still just as far, still the heart of Surprise.

Young Taliesin was educated in the City Lights Bookstore by writers and readers of poetry and he was educated at his mother's knee as she studied biochemistry and agriculture and the confluence of the two in aquaponics and he was further educated in the care of Bobbie Sue in Golden Gate Park and in the streets and avenues of Haight-Ashbury and in the doors of the Free Store and the Free Clinic. He educated himself, too, as a free-roamer of quiet museums and libraries and of hectic thoroughfares filled with street-buskers and soap-box speakers. In all these ways he grew in the full complement of the arts and the sciences and the cultures and their counter-cultures.

As poesy was his first language Tally never considered himself a poet, since speaking in that way seemed, to him, to be the original, natural human language, all other languages which had been reduced to writing being unnatural or self-made and self-conscious. The tribes of indigenous peoples who lacked scribes and the children of any tribe or nation before they grew old enough to learn their alphabets, these were all poets, he often pointed out, adding that the objective of written language—and, hence, the schools that teach it—is to drive the poetry out of the child, as the Authorities of governments and corporations and churches, all and each, are always in constant fear of any and all poets, as it's common knowledge that all rhymers are known to be professional upset-ters-of-applecarts. For all these reasons he turned to the visual arts and soon became an important contributor to the financial health of the Jones-Merriman household through the sales of his various works.

Before his age had struck the double-digits he'd announced that he'd outgrown post-modernism, and in his 'tweens began formulating his own *ism*. A proponent of process over product, a believer in being, an advocate of action, an empiricist without ego, a phenomenalist sans smuggery, Tally was comfortable in beginning with an idea—which he took to be nothing more than an expressible inspiration—

which he explored methodically all the while without setting parameters on the product. Trust the process, he would admonish his elders, and the product will take care of itself. At first he called himself a *methodist* and his manner *methodism* until his mother and Aunt Bobbie Sue broke the bad tidings that the followers of the brothers Wesley—¡o, for a thousand tongues to sing!—had pre-empted his nomenclature. Soon afterwards he propitiously came onto a copy of Robert Graves's 'Oxford Addresses on Poetry' with its excellent essay on *bâraka* and—after a careful reading had instilled in him the notion that spirit suffused the inanimate as well as the animate—settled on *art-mechanic* and *art-mechanism* as describing himself and his way of working and thinking. ¡Roll up your sleeves!

Wind is endemic to the Wastelands of West Texas, as constant as the three-hundred-and-sixty-degree horizon. There is never the question of wind, but only inquiries as to what substances may be lifted in its tide and carried along in its current or as to from what direction it will come and so foretell the wanderings of weather systems and the likelihood or unlikelihood of the moisture that is always needed. It is so ingrained in the life of Surprise that only one of its extremes is cause for concern, that being when there is no wind, as air that is perfectly still—*dead air*—has an ominous weight and a frightful presence.

Several of Bobbie Sue's maternal aunts and uncles and cousins of various removes had worked at the Wincharger plant in Sioux City in the 1930s—not to mention that more than one or two of the little 6-volt radio charger models were in early use in Surprise—so the concept of wind-generated electricity was already firmly in the fiber of the returning Prickly Pear Purview Ex-Pats. As was their solid footing in the knowledge that under foot, deep under foot, sat the Santa Rosa Aquifer, too salty for man or beast or plant in its natural state, nestled snuggly in its sandstone and shale repository, but not so saturated with sodium that it could not be made sweet and useful when pumped up and filtered down. The land of Surprise—the dirt itself, not the realm—wasn't so promising, mostly alkaline aridisols which weren't so hot for agriculture. For mesquite, yes—cactus, yes—shinnery, yes—juniper, yes—and a prime producer of scorpions and tarantulas and rattlesnakes. But not row-crops. Sunlight, on the other hand, was in plentiful supply, only bested in the Lone Star State by El Paso—which, by some reckoning, is only marginally situated within the governance of the former Republic—with Surprise enjoying each year complete solar saturation three-out-of-every-four days.

Straightway Kerrie Mae and Bobbie Sue formed Los Tres Círculos, which they called an 'uncorporation', the three circles representing sun and wind and water and their uncorporate logo the three-circle-heart tattoo that had long graced each of the proprietresses. Pater Merriman, the original Bobster, was beside himself with joy. Not only had the prodigals returned, but with them came new things to make and to build and to maintain. He set to work, first erecting tanks and greenhouses and then experimenting with how to scale the Wincharger up to agri-industrial proportions. In the meantime—until the wind machines would become satisfactory in size and service and dependability and which, it turned out, wouldn't happen for another decade or so—he and Shad Eliot built a series of shed roofs for rainwater harvesting. The Double-Joneses pitched in to help with the flora—lettuce and watercress and cucumbers and basil and tomatoes and various kinds of squashes—and Sue Merriman—with her proclivity for fauna—became the fish-whisperer. Rose Extroverted Edna stepped in to handle marketing, Ruth Etta providing the distribution, Threeb dropping down and holding fast the spiritual anchor. It was, in short, a predictable Surprise enterprise, one-for-all-and-all-for-one-and-none-for-nothing.

Soon after the repatriation of the Fabulous Foursome and well before their only XY-chromosome-carrier began body-surfing the tide of pubescence, Tally sought out quarters of his own. The two-and-a-half ladies needed more space for their added frills and fluffles while he needed plain and spartan space in which to work. Not to mention how important such a move would be for any boy barging into bro-hood whilst completely engulfed by the girly gender. Uncle Bob and Granddad Shad found him a nice, vintage Airstream Bambi which they set up alongside an old oil field trailer that was perfectly suited to serve as an art studio. Tally commenced a frenetic work schedule, creating small *objets d'art* in his workshop, marketing them throughout the Golden State through his contacts at City Lights and shipping them out by means of parcel post, the local route-man being a daily customer at Maya Gandhi's Indian-Indian Taco Tent.

Whenever there was a lull in the mail-order-art business Tally took to painting huge, realistic landscapes on discarded billboards and highway signs, placing them in such a way that, from a moving vehicle, it seemed as if the viewer was in the Old West of John Ford movies or on the surface of the Moon or in some sci-fi-fantasy-land, illusions so realistic that even the most whimsical themes misled travelers. One thing leading to another, he soon experimented with other canvases, turning first to galvanized metal or, when he could get it, stainless steel, creating the skies in these faux landscapes by applying his own specially-developed patina, a coating that caused the bare metal to reflect the real sky as it appeared at the very moment the piece was being viewed, an effect that seemingly rendered invisible whatever might be on the other side of the giant canvas.

Bamboozling bewildered bystanders and by-passers would be sufficient end in itself for most young *artistes,* but not for Tally. He could see the pertinent potential of his new process, a system which he soon shrewdly shrouded in secretive formulae and esoteric equations, for the Shire of Surprise was suddenly coming under scrutiny from the Authorities—which was Tally's term for the personnel of the Corporament, which in turn was Tally's descriptive definition of the nebulous but powerful amalgam of international and national *incs* and governments and organizations and religious orders that owned all the hammers and—in his estimation—swung them in such a way as to make us all nails. Women running a company that wasn't a chartered corporation and was motivated mainly by doing good as opposed to doing whatever was necessary for profits and prophets was bound to appear, sooner rather than later, in one or more sets of Corporament cross-hairs. There was plenty of evidence that mail was being opened and phone lines were being tapped, both sets of skullduggery accompanied by a sharp increase in unidentified and unexplained scurryings in the dark hours. Tally quickly realized if he built one of these land-sky-scapes in a large circle that anything within it would be effectively invisible. Such as an Airstream, for instance. Or maybe a whole village.

Getting in and out of the circular enclosure, especially with the trailer, proved to be a formidable challenge as gates are by nature cumbersome and ugly and prone to malfunction and—most importantly—highly visible. So, instead, he built walls with a foot-print in the shape of a large @ sign with the Airstream occupying the place of the *a* and the opening just large enough to pull the 'Stream through. He called the structures 'p@tios', though others sometimes simply called them 'invisibles'. A fortunate by-product of the design was that in the same way that the exteriors blend in with the landscape, the interiors could be painted to suit the occupants so as to allow them to look out on pretty much any scenery they fancied. Surprise—which from its founding had never stood out from its scrub-brush surroundings—began to actually disappear, one 'Stream at a time.

Living in his own digs whilst digging into his art works and erecting p@tio after p@tio, keeping the kind of schedule that suits the self-motivated but confounds the world around them, Tally became such an infrequent visitor to his maternal manse that he missed a very, very important event. On some indiscernible but indispensable and immutable night, Starlight retired a girl but arose as Star, a young woman. The impish cutie-pie emerged from the cocoon of childhood a beautiful butterfly bearing the vim and vigor and visible *accoutrements* of her mother, the smarts of her aunt, and an other-worldly spirit that sprang up from her roots as a love-child. She's one of those girls who seems to come in the spring, hummed Tally, one look in her eyes and you'll forget everything—he continued in a low whistle—you had ready to say—the song tormenting and delighting him at the same time, which is—as those of us with romantic experience are well aware—the exact way one feels whilst falling in love. Strangers in every way except in their household history, they found each other anew, began dating on her 18th birthday and married on her 20th. A child was born two years later—the post-penultimate annum of the 80s—whom they named Merriwoman Eliot Jones in honor of the nuclear families of Surprise but whom they called—mercifully—Merri Elli.

A little back-tracking. After the two had taken their betrothal to its logical conclusion—love and marriage, love and marriage, go together like a…well, you know the rest—Tally had wasted no time in spiriting away the spirited Star to blissful cohabitation in their cozy Bambi. But even before the rice had all been shaken from the guests' wedding finery and even before the tin cans tied to the bumper of the newlyweds' getaway truck had stopped bumping and bangle-bouncing behind, and fully aeons before the icing on the cake had gotten all stale and crusty, our brand-spanking-new empty-nesters Kerrie Mae and Bobbie Sue set about redecorating their Liner, first painting it inside-and-out with murals reminiscent of the original Merriman Mini-bus, then Michelangelo-ing the ceiling with stars and planets and comets and the moon in all her phases, lastly delivering the *coup de grâce* to their old-but-homey habitat by converting the smaller of the two sleeping quarters into a library, leaving only the one, big bed for the both of them. Gossips a century before would have retreated behind their folding fans to cluck and whisper over the outright obviousness of this Boston marriage—as likely in envy as in approbation—but there having always been a chronic shortage of rumor-mongers in Surprise no one took notice, not even so much as arching an eyebrow when the two gorgeous grandmothers-to-be thenceforward refused to refrain from casual and natural but plainly-public handholding—right there in front of Gawd and everybody—and were never ever after known to kiss one-another in any manner except squarely on the mouth.

Besides the Return of the Natives, some new folks had come to Surprise, the first permanent settlers since the arrival of the Foundling Families. Followers of Zarathustra, they hailed from Karachi. A big bunch of their ilk had come to the U. S. of A. in the late 60s, not for the Summer of Love, but for the Endless Season of Work. They were good at it, too, as industrious as they were polite, their physical beauty as breathtaking as the spice in their lentils. The family of Khan—Ali, the father, Fatima, the mother, daughters Saba and Yasmin, sons Mustaq and Shahzad—had lit first in Houston, then worked their way north and west until they found territory more familiar in climate and geography, settling in the old Ser-Sta-Gro which they renamed the Paki-Store and from which they began to sell gasoline and groceries and convenience items.

And from which they reinvigorated—in an interesting twist—the by-then-somewhat-moribund One Sock Shop. Anticipating by several decades today's social networking marketing model, Ali Khan began repurposing the oddest of the odd remnants into caps, dying and decorating them along common styles such as the fez and topi and karakul, but also the more ornate Sindhi. His first customers were a few scattered but serious Zarathustrian Elvis impersonators—who already knew Ali from his having picked up a few look-a-like gigs at openings of Pakistani restaurants in Sugar Land, billing himself as The King Khan—his satisfied chapeau clients spreading the word by mouth and example until Khan's Kreations dominated the Eastern Elvis trade.

As one might expect in the Haunts of Handy Jones, the newbies were welcomed as if they'd not been immigrants at all but instead as if they'd been nothing but the dearest friends-and-neighbors merely returned from a long absence. The two boys—Mustaq, whom the regional rednecks called Moustache, and Shahzad, whom the same bunch of bozos called Shazam—had trained as pilots, adding to the family industry by operating the Flying Carpet Aviation Service to provide short-haul air-freighting and occasional aerial spraying. Father Ali and Mother Fatima almost returned to the swamps of the Pirate Coast when they first met Maya Gandhi, given her name-sake connection to the India of the East, though the children—who were each and every one as American as apple pie—weren't in the least concerned. Not to worry, for the Skirted Sultan soon assuaged the Khan parental units when she created a heretofore-unknown delectable dish fashioned from *cabrito,* or mutton when goats were in short supply, the tender flesh spiced-up to after-burner level with loads of turmeric and cumin, ensconced in a pita-bread-burrito-wrap, the whole of which she called a Paki-Taki, this new multi-national food item to be marketed exclusively through the Paki-Store.

Joe Pyne had been taking nickels while airing provocative talk on the radio waves since the 50s. Edgy talk, stimulating talk, rabble-rousing talk, but not talk that was—at its core—hateful or demeaning. Since his day—which, coincidentally, died with the 60s' dying-out of the dawning of the Age of Aquarius—a new crop of babble-heads had begun broadcasting, much like the border-blasters of old, but instead of selling goat-glands and lineament cure-alls their product was hate, that inexhaustible ego-elixir for which there seems to be a correspondingly unquenchable thirst. Tally and Uncle Threeb—the two of whom having conspired together to share the mantle of philosopher handed down by Handy Jones—the two called these venom vendors The Vocal Idiocracy, further elaborating that the Corporament Authorities employed these talking-pimple-heads to manipulate the other two divisions of the pot-shot plebiscite, those being The Silent Majority and The Muted Minority.

From somewhere out in the haze of the kHz kozmos an especially virulent voice was fast becoming the standard-bearer of sleaze. Red Nekkid was his handle, hurling hate his hot-button, the *hoi polloi* his unwitting homies. His followers gleefully called themselves 'Red Nekkid's Lug-Nuts', blissfully unaware of their unintentional self-deprecating humor. Professing to be political, his targets were either the undefinable—mainly those symbiotic Siamese siblings otherwise known as The Government and The Enemy—or they were the undefended—mainly The Poor, The Immigrants, and Anyone Who Wasn't White and Wealthy. With an accent thicker than his skull, he railed relentlessly from his secret studio across the border, naming names when he knew them, making up names when he didn't, offering outrageous charges with invented facts and—here's the best part—relieving his follower stooges of substantial amounts of their savings through the sales of his books and pamphlets and the solicitation of contributions to his confusing charities.

Someone—perhaps a scorned suitor of one of the stunningly-sexy but excruciatingly-shy-and-modest Khan clan cuties, or perhaps a loud-mouth lunch-mouth sent lurching off by Maya Gandhi, or perhaps nothing more than some mean-spirited scum who'd lost their direction and stumbled by surprise into Surprise—regardless, some slime-ball had alerted Red Nekkid to the existence of the fur'ners running the Paki-Store. He quickly drew a bead on the honest and hard-working Pakistani proletariats, accusing them of various and sundry offenses against the body politic, demanding investigations and insulting their customers, making a compendium of crudities his constant commentary. Before long his laundry lampoon-list included Los Tres Círculos—clearly because the liberal-leaning-environmentally-friendly-non-extractive industry was upside-downing the natural Gawd-given-Amurican-way of pillage and plunder and, worse, because it was run by uppity women rumored to be switch-hitters—the role-call soon naming the Surprise Institute for Gestalt Therapy as well—clearly because the Lug Nuts and their Big Wrench couldn't fathom a massage session without the wink-wink-happy-ending, and they were durn sure that a wink-wink-happy-ending administered by a guy, even a blind guy, would sho'nuff put them into the twink-twink category, though in fairness it must be added that there were more than a few of those in the blue-collar bourgeoisie who reasoned that such attention from an eyeless feller might constitute a free hall-pass in the gender-bender junior-high of Lug Nut lust, nights on drilling rigs being what they are…

XITE's signal was so strong it knocked fillings from teeth across a four-state region, strong enough that on clear summer nights I could pull it in all the way out in the 'Burbs of Burbank, even though I mostly avoided it like the plague that it was. I figured ¿Why depress yourself on purpose? Still and all, when I was lonesome, even bad news about home was better than no news. Summer Solstice of 1990 fell on a Friday, which was also Ruth Etta's birthday, giving me plenty of reason to feel sorry for myself, so I bought a bottle of hootch and holed up in my Flying Cloud with a sizable stack of 'Hey, Big

Boy!' magazines—including several of their all-color issues—along with two boxes of cheese crackers and a carton of garlic-onion dip. Out of boredom more than out of despondency I flicked on my trusty 6-transistor Sony just in time to catch Mister Gnarly Nekkid bally-hooing over a new registrant on his roster of ridicule, that being the Shifting Sands Mobile Motel—he boomed—lambasting the little hostelry-on-wheels as a veritable den of iniquity, calling it a rendezvous for rough-neck-roust-about romantic assignations and a way-station for illegals and drug-mules, the whole shebang run by the little town flirt. ¡That was it! I Popeyed, shouting ¡That's all I can stand and I can't stands no more! as I jumped from the 'Stream's folding lounge to the phone with one leaping lunge, cheese nibbles and fold-outs ricocheting all across the cabin, my fingers flying over the touch-tone pad. Ruth Etta answered right away, and, right away, I could hear a huskiness in her voice, the kind that comes from crying. You weren't listening to the… I began, but she interrupted before the question was fully posed, Yes, I was, she answered. Quietness on both ends of the line. I'm coming home, I said. The sooner the better, she sniffed. For good, I added. More crying, but now happy tears. More quietness. I knew you'd know when to return, she sighed. Then it was my turn to cry.

The pink-and-white Wandering Wagon needed some repairs before it could survive a summer sojourn 'cross the desert. While it was on the lift at Rambler Land I arranged to have an after-market air-conditioner slapped under the dashboard, a nice chrome-clad unit from the J. C. Whitney catalog that when turned-up on low-setting would give goose-bumps to a polar bear and when dialed-down to deep-freeze would keep your popsicle from pooping. Before month's end I was on the road, the Flying Cloud fastened-on behind, finally reaching Surprise just after sundown as the entire night sky began lighting up with Independence Day fireworks from shows all around the compass, Andrews to Odessa to Goldsmith and even back to Eunice. I was home, and it was just as well.

24.

¡HAPPY DAYS ARE WEIRD AGAIN!

The skies above weren't clear again, we sang no songs of cheer again, and we no longer lived a life of ease. We didn't live in a yellow submarine, either. But we'd made it through the 80s. And I was back in Surprise. Now to get Surprise back in me.

I'd arrived in time for the ceremony that formally announced baby Merri Elli as a human being. Andrews County church folks—at least the few of those preachers of the parables of polyester willing and able to motivate over the hill to the Greasewood Gotham—those congregants called it a Christening, while the Surprises simply dubbed it a Dubbing. We hereby dub thee Merri Elli, you know, that sort of thing. A complete course of cooing and chin-chucking after the prayers, followed by punch and cookies whilst the Ordinaries tarried, then later an evening of good cheer and hail-person-well-met.

What with the Fourth of July having fallen mid-week and preparations for the Dubbing occupying the balance of its seven days we'd none of us had time for a proper visit. So, once the outsiders were off to the boudoirs of their brick-and-mortar burgs, the Extended Foundling Families—which included those of us progeny present-and-accounted-for, along with Maya Gandhi, of course, and now also numbering the Khan crew—the group of us sat down for a feast. A homemade barbecue pit had been fashioned earlier in the day by artfully layering well-cured mesquite wood into a hole freshly-dug from the earth in the clearing southeast of the Old School House, a grate of expanded metal placed over the top for a cooking surface, and ¡presto! an instant and newly-made contraption of ancient provenance with immediate import, recognizable to hominids and humans of all eras and cultures and continents. We put it to work, then unloaded the larders of our Wally Byams. There was chili, both *verde* and *con carne,* accompanied by hamburgers and ham sandwiches, potato chips and potato salad, Indian-Indian tacos and Pakistani curries, hot dogs and hot tamales, barbecue brisket and baked beans, coleslaw and corn salad, the whole washed-down with gallons and gallons of iced tea, both sweet and mint, and loads of lemonade, the *coup de grâce* conferred with pies and cakes and brownies and halva and phirni.

Bob Merriman, despite his recent advancement into the ranks of the octogenarian order—having joined the club which already numbered all the first members of the Foundling Families, save his bride Sue, who was herself only one annum shy of her own entry—the Bobster had prepared a special shaved-ice summer drink based on his legendary Sinfandel, a concoction that was essentially a wine smoothie and which he called a Woozy-Woothie. Fearing that the Pakistanis' religious persuasions would preclude their partaking of potent potables of such persuasion or of such nomination the Master Merriman made inquiries of their patriarch, Ali Khan, who reminded him that the family were followers of Zarathustra and were therefore free to make their own choices in life, once, added Ali, the individual had reflected and meditated with a clear and logical mind subsequent to having carefully attuned said thinking-noggin to the best and highest order. Bob assured Khan-senior that his Woothies were the best and highest of any order, but, sensing that they perhaps had another take on both levels of ordination, did some research of his own, soon learning, in turn, that Zoroastrians possessed a long-standing tradition of enhancing the qualities of the mind through the use of Haoma, called Hom by some, which, in turn, was produced from the herb ephedra, which, in turn, grew abundantly in the Rattlesnake Realm, but which, in turn, was known hereabouts by the common name Comanche Tea. In honor of the Eastern Surprises, the Merriest of Merry Men brewed up a batch of the insightful beverage, which he renamed Liquid Leapin' Lizards and which soon became a fine alternative to Sinfandel and Woozy-Woothies, even for followers of the Western Ways. ¡Take me hom, country roads!

As the merriment of the day mellowed into a reflective respite—brought on, to one degree or another, by the meditative ministrations of the various Merriman mishmashes—stories were told and facts and figures exchanged with an eye toward my ear. Catching me up on events, as it were, vignette by vignette. The smoke from our hillbilly hibachi drifting slowly up into the darkening skies set a proper mood.

For strange clouds had been building in the cosmos all that year, though no one noticed it much until the Great Broccoli Brouhaha of the first month of spring. You'll recall, Dear Reader, that the then-sitting President of These United States—after summarily rejecting a serving of the cruciferous vegetable—had—in a fit of petulance and poor nutritional preference—banned the green flower clusters from Air Force One. Snickers were heard around the nation only to be supplanted by the seething fury of the Broccoli Lobby, amongst whose sympathizers could be found the proprietresses of Los Tres Círculos, their uncorporation having developed into a major supplier of broccoli in general and the only purveyor of its production by means of aquaponics. The industry Broccolistas arose in arms, angrily waving stalks of the crisp culinary crowns as if the blossomy boughs were the pitchforks and torches of the agrarian revolutions of olden days, shouting vows to deliver 10 tons of their best to the very doorstep of the White House. Not to be left out, Kerrie Mae and Bobbie Sue overnighted their own broccoli bounty of several selected heads which they'd shaped through the practice of bonsai so as to resemble small shrubs, an impertinence that landed them squarely on the special Vegeterrorism Watch List, a roster of vine-ripened revolutionaries secretively maintained by the Fee-Bees but shared with the Spy Gooks of the CIA in what is still thought to be the only known example of inter-agency cooperation amongst our Nation's spooks. Counter-operative rumors were started and innuendos intoned, all suggesting that the maid-mavens of Los Tres Círculos were genetically-modifying God's own gourd family into zucchini zip-guns and cucumber cudgels, armament that would self-compost after its heinous usage—if not eaten first—thereby leaving no trace of a murder weapon suitable for evidentiary purposes.

Tally chimed in with his own unsettling snippet. He'd been hacked. Several times. Not the variety of intrusion into one's cyberspace that would become only too prevalent a couple of decades later, but the old-timey technique of hacksaws and crowbars employed in attempts to gain entry into the filing cabinets and fire-safes in which he kept the hand-written journals containing the formulae for the different layers of the coatings used on his p@tios. Even though he'd written them in Greek—something he'd picked up as a child whilst reading the epigraphs favored by Uncle T. S. as lead-ins to his most important works—since the bungled-burgles Tally had taken the precaution to distribute the bound notebooks around several different locations. Of equal importance as to their security, the Boy Wonder added, no single journal was sufficient to bring about the coating, requiring—and this last bit also a technique he'd picked up at City

Lights Bookstore whilst ingesting all of Tolkien, to include *The Silmarillion*—yes, necessitating the use of a master journal to integrate the various volumes. One journal to rule them all, Tally quipped with a grin, unable to resist the opportunity for a little literary showboating. And the key journal, the Nabob of the Notebooks, he kept with him always. Then turning serious again, he added that, although the rapscallions' efforts had to-date been bereft of success, a pattern had emerged, a thing in itself perhaps as dark and dastardly as their intended crime.

Shad Eliot—prowling the prairies horseback as he was prone to do—had had an encounter with a group of home-guard-volunteers who called themselves the Stranger Wranglers, dressed in faux-military camo, and piloted almost-identical pickups, each rig marked with a garish rear-window decal bearing the image of what looked to be a clown on meth, sort of a rip-off of Big Daddy Ed Roth's Rat Fink cross-bred with The Joker. ¡Helping out strangers while patrolling the borders! they proclaimed upon accosting Shad for the first time, a bit high-handedly at the outset, their arrogance quickly tempered by the metallic ringing of a shotgun shell being chambered into the breech of the old cowpuncher's Model 12 Winchester. Shad rested it across his saddle horn, holding both the presence and the attention of the pair of black-hatted wannabe-vigilantes while he recited the whole of Cousin Tom's 'Sweeney Among the Nightingales', beginning, as anyone who knew the elder cow man would expect, by translating the poem's Greek epigraph: *Alas, I am struck deep with a mortal blow!* Delivered with a hiss through his clenched dentures, the poem sent the Agamemnonites high-tailing, their black 4X4s flattening the flora and frightening the fauna whilst scattering rocks and sand in their getaway. Afterwards Shad made himself ready should he ever encounter their lot again—said he to our circle, the light in his eyes partly a-twinkle and partly a-flame—by loading up the tubular magazine of his Perfect Repeater with double-ought buckshot and brushing up his own mental magazine on the entirety of 'The Waste Land'. The Stranger Wranglers thereafter kept a discrete distance between themselves and Real Wrangler Eliot, but Shad remarked that the attempts on Tally's laboratory were always coincident with sightings of the black pickups.

All around the convivial circle heads bobbed and nodded in agreement. At the Shifting Sands Mobile Motel, Ruth Etta reported that she'd quit taking renters without references. Likewise at SIGT, where Threeb now only took referrals from reliable clients. True, there'd been a boom in oil prices, a thing that always brings in new people—a few of the usual unsavory souls usually amongst them—but everyone in these parts had been through so many boom-and-bust cycles that the mechanics and characteristics of the ups and the downs were so firmly ensconced in the local *weltanschauung* so as to be second-nature. Yet this latest raft of riff-raff was different. These weren't oilies. These weren't even oil-field trash. These were, well, not just weird, but marked by a weirdness touched with malevolence.

There are no coincidences in this world, offered Pater Double-Jones, quietly but firmly, his pronouncement followed by a dark crack in the conversation, an enormous emptiness of words that hung over us in a pall, a quietness that was not simply the absence of sound but more so a hiatus so heavy that no sound could pierce it. It was a crushing burden, one that could only be lightened by a question, inquiry being both feint-and-parry to the broadsword of oppression. The move fell, quite naturally, to Mater Mary Ellen Jones-Jones. What shall we do about Kelly Elliott Daze, she said, with merely a smidgen of a suggestion of a query.

More bobbing and nodding from the conversants. Excepting me, whose face must have reflexively screwed itself into a facsimile of the upside-down-treble-clef-mark of punctuation that in proper English substitutes for up-talk. Mother Double-Jones—natural teacher that she was—consequently aimed the balance of her remark at me. That's with a *z*, said she, amplifying her comment with a question directed squarely to her prodigal son, ¿What's a Look-a-Like, anyway?

The eyes and ears of Surprise now turned to me for satisfaction. I cleared my throat, perhaps a bit theatrically. I assume, I began in a stentorian tone—assumptions being fine jumping-off places for voices of authority—that spelling *days* with the last letter of the alphabet indicates a celebration of some sort, probably the work of a Chamber-Pot of Commercialization. Yes, yes, everyone agreed. Likely because this year—I noted—is the 25th anniversary of 'Bubble-Up'. Looks of awareness all around. Our short-lived series—I continued—lives on in the minds and hearts of a following of fans who call themselves Bubble-Uppers, though—I added, sadly—their detractors call them Look-a-Likes as these devotees go to great lengths and considerable expense to look like the various characters in the series, embracing even the most obscure as well as those who may have appeared in but a single episode. Not only that—sotto voce, now—those who reenact the dual-role characters are at all times ready, willing, and able to assume the weird of their chosen part, each Sheriff O.K. Rodger look-a-like trained and equipped to quickly metamorphose into Derringer Duvalier, Lance Reid into Blackie Black,

Lisa into Muffin McWright, and so on. You may be most familiar—I added as a bit of informative trivia—with the most common genre of Look-a-Likes, the Elvis impersonators.

Having the floor, I was no more ready to relinquish it than would be an itinerant preacher after being asked by his unsuspecting hosts to say a few words of grace over supper. I therefore launched immediately into a yarn worthy of The Brothers Grimm, a titanic tale built of the smallest details, a story drenched in gravitas though leavened by ironic humor, a recounting replete with the intimation of a moral message. Without stopping and with hardly a breath, I told it all. Of how the series had fallen from public consciousness during the Police Action in South-East Asia. Of how an anonymous but intrepid soul had later spirited-away the original films from the clutches of the network ninnies, only to find that the reels had been stripped of their sound tracks, inadvertently or spitefully, no-one knowing which. Of how the now-silent series episodes began to appear in late-night surreptitious screenings at underground movie houses where the air was thick with smoke from various Mexican herbs and where the concession stands sold Twinkies and Little Cathy Cosmic Cupcakes along with tabs of The Owl's best as well as buttons of the finest peyote, some reporting—I added parenthetically and with calculated emphasis—the natural psychedelics to have been imported from a sage-seeress in a teensy-tiny town in Texas, my comment causing all eyes to turn to Maya Gandhi, who said nothing but smiled like a searchlight. I continued as she beamed, telling of how the audience would read the actors' lips, straining to translate the dialog, gleefully clapping and shouting as first one line, then the next was unraveled. Of how, first during the showings and later at conventions and conferences, the Bubble-Uppers would make suggestions followed by discussions which were followed by arguments and, now-and-again, followed by fisticuffs, all spurred by suppositions over what songs comprised the musical score for each episode.

Eventually I was forced to take a breath. In the impromptu interregnum, first one Surprise, then another and another and yet another intervened to insert more information about the upcoming celebration. Sue Merriman still worked a few horses for her best clients, who were among the upper crust of the social pie in the Permian Basin—the clients, not the horses, though a sentient person would plainly prefer the company of the latter to that of the former—and each of whom sat on the various community committees and townie task forces that were generally responsible for the kind of contrived culture in which any event with a cutesy name was corralled. Her sources pegged Kelly Elliott Daze for the first Saturday evening in August, the 4th, all events to be held at KOSA TV, with nothing planned aforehand, especially not on Friday, as a date even that early in the Month of the Perseids was within striking distance of the beginning of the high-school football season, a holiness not to be trifled with in these parts.

Nothing *officially* planned until the dinner and ceremony—interjected Star, with emphasis on the adverb—who herself had a friend from Mothers' Day Out in Andrews whose husband was co-owner and principal driver for The Glitter Bus Travel Lines—you may have seen their coaches, Dear Reader, vintage Scenicruisers custom-painted candy-apple-red-with-pearl-dust-flakes and emblazoned with their motto, 'We put the sparkle back on the bus'— and whose complete roster of equipment, meaning both motorcoaches, had been booked on Saturday morning for what the owner-operator had been told would be a parade from the airport to Surprise.

Bob Merriman nodded vigorously. If his esposa Sue was a horse-whisperer, Bob was a machine-whisperer, and, like her, retained a few long-time clients in the Twin Cities. Amongst them were the members of the 1OOMPG, which seemed at first glance to mean one-hundred-miles-per-gallon, but didn't, standing instead for *One-Original-Owner-MoPed-Gang*. Though the confusion was indeed a clever coincidence. The club—no more gang than 'Our Gang'—was comprised of now very-matured elite East Coast teens from the 1950s who'd had the where-withal for European travel. Adventurous debutantes and beaus, they'd spent wonderful summers careering about the Old Countries on small smoke-belching two-banger mopeds, falling in love with one another and with our nation's quaint mother-lands and—this is not to be trivialized—also with their rattling rides. Many kept their wheels, if not their *amis et amies*, bringing the brash motorized bicycles back stateside and then—when many of their wealthy families relocated to the scrub-brush 'burbs overlying the Spraberry Trend in order to avail them-selves of its cache of West Texas Light-Intermediate Crude and all the bidness that bubbled-up with it—the silver-spoon-pedal-pushers carried their bikes into the southern-most reaches of the Llano Estacado. ¡Southwestward ho!

Those once-lovely ingenues and once-limber mangenues had long since succumbed to the pull of gravity and the piling-on of pounds, the pert and perky girlish breasts now stretched and sagging, the flat-bellied boyish abs grown paunchy and portly, to such point that there were barely enough cubic centimeters in the rasping two-stroke motors of their beloved mopeds to readily transport the fullness of their riders. To eliminate as many unnecessary ounces of weight as possible the senior cyclists took to moped-ing in the almost-altogether, wearing little more than thongs and flip-flops, the more modest of the ladies adding a tube-top, which—when properly placed to cover the, er, strategic points—in its resting place on the torso more nearly resembled the cummerbund from a spandex tuxedo. As for wearing traditional motorcycle club colors, well, they ingeniously tattooed the club insignia on their bare backs. Hard-core to a person, they disdained Vespa owners as power-mad elitists, the Moped Gangsters preferring their French VéloSoleX or their Czech Babetta or their Austrian Puch, and having absolutely no truck with purchasers of later, smoother models, such as J. C. Penney's Swinger from the 1970s. When fully-dressed and afoot they trended to black turtlenecks, well-worn berets, pleated trousers for the men and flouncy knit skirts for the women. They drank nothing but Pommac, which had to be smuggled-in by operatives of the shadowy Sparkling Fruit Juice Underground, and—though not as a result of imbibing the sweet-but-tangy apple sodas—were in constant trouble with the Highway Control, mostly for driving too slow or for violating the no-motorized-bicycles prohibition on Interstate 20. The Moped Mamas—if the truth be laid bare—looked forward to the traffic stops, always insisting on being frisked, though, after hundreds of such law enforcement actions, none was ever known to having been so much as subjected to even a rudimentary pat-down. They were an eccentric lot, to be sure, but knew a great mechanic when they saw one, keeping Bob Merriman busy, who kept their rides buzzing and bangling. During the most-recent group tune-up, they'd off-handedly mentioned to him their plans to crash the unofficial Kelly Elliott Daze Parade.

Rose Edna Eliot checked in with a comment. An outfit calling itself The Capital Clown Caravan had made inquiries about rates for renting the entire inventory of rooms at the Shifting Sands, but their having no address beyond a post-office box on the shabby side of the District of Columbia caused them to be permanently placed on the don't-call-us-we'll-call-you waiting list. Odder still, a group of Elvis impersonators had also set their sights on joining the procession. Before anyone could ask how Mistress Eliot might be aware of such a thing, the former Chautauqua chick-a-dee casually conceded that she still kept up with doings in the entertainment world and had read their press release in last month's 'This Land Is My Land, Not Your Land' touring newsletter. ¿Elvises? incredulous looks ricocheted around the barbecue pit bunch for several moments, stopping only when Kerrie Mae and Bobbie Sue stretched and yawned, then stood up with the muffled exclamation ¡Too much! ¡Time for bed! ¡We've got a whole month to worry about this! And they were right.

As most of the Surprises began filtering back to their 'Streams I stuck around to help tidy-up the camp, checking for stray embers, putting the dirt back in the hole that had been our DIY barbecue pit, then chasing down the odd scrap of napkin or dropped item of silverware. Our people being inveterate neat-niks the task was easy-peasy. When I'd completed my self-appointed chores, Ruth Etta was waiting for me in the Flying Cloud, holding a couple of bath towels. Before I could make the purring-growling sounds that were bubbling up in my throat she held up a hand, much like a cop directing traffic, then asked ¿When was your last massage? Hmmmmm. Esalen, 1967, I stammered. She scowled in a caring way, observing that she feared as much. Overdue. 'Way overdue. So I've a treat for you, she added, grinning as she took my hand and led me out into the night.

The lights were on in the SIGT rub-down wagon but dialed-down to soft. The door was unlocked. Threeb was busy putting fresh sheets on the massage table, cool jazz playing on a boombox, the smell of sage rampant. At least not Enya, I thought with relief. Though I wouldn't have minded a little of the primal perfume of patchouli—sorry, it's a 60s thing. Ruth Etta set the towels on the table, latched the door, then set about undressing me. Slowly. Despite knowing full well that Threeb couldn't see so much as a road-side fusee in a dark room I was, nevertheless, more than a bit embarrassed—pardon, Dear Reader, the Freudian slip masquerading as an embedded-word pun—though Ruth Etta's hands and fingers soon transformed stifling embarrassment into stirring excitement. Lie down— she whispered—on your stomach. Now I couldn't see anything, either, yet, still, I could hear, and what I heard were her snaps and zippers and the rustle of her garments. There were other sounds, too. ¿Threeb's clothing? Even if I could I wouldn't dare to look now.

Esalen came back to me in a flood of memory that carried along the flotsam and jetsam of sense and sensation. Surrender, the first step. I stumbled at first, but immediately upon being touched strode fully into the process. Four hands— it turns out—are light-years more than two-hands-plus-two-hands, an arrangement not arithmetic but geometric. The Gestalt parlor began to smell of sea breeze and salt, the jazz began to riff with the pulse and crash of the surf. Then a curious thing happened, curious but curiously natural: now-and-again there were only two hands on me, and when it was only two hands I could feel them trembling, as if the absent hands were still at work but on a body other than mine. I began to hear murmurs that could be mistaken for moans, pauses in the waves of breathing that could be mistaken for gasps—fully a third measure of both belonging to me—an aural massage all its own, weaving in and out of the music, each sound becoming part of a larger rhythm. For a brief moment, content elbowed its way through process. ¡A massage à trois! But process is powerful—I am proud to report—and soon repelled the interloper, picking up the steps where they'd been left off, relaxation leading to anticipation, anticipation to excitement, excitement to ecstasy, then ecstasy to the final step in process, which is liberation in the opening of the inner eye.

Not once did I open my outer eyes. And it was just as well.

25.

LANDING IN ODDLAND

Parades weren't common in Surprise. In point of fact, so uncommon as to hardly figure at all in the cultural chronicle of the clever community, though that was about to change. Partly, it was an historic lack of demand. The Big Six-Pack of holidays—Memorial Day, July 4th, Labor Day, Thanksgiving, Christmas, New Year's—all these were celebrated with family and friends, meaning, of course, all of Surprise, but with neither need for nor expectation of outsiders. Once or twice there had been an iota of impetus to hold an event to which Ordinaries could be invited into town, but no such notion ever met with success. For one example, a proposed Groundhog Day extravaganza was tabled when no agreement could be reached as to whether or not prairie dogs could be considered either suitable stand-ins or passable pop-ups in lieu of the rodents regularly associated with the folklore fable, nor did it advance matters that the coordinating committee had chosen to call the anticipated annual affair Doo-Dah Day out of genuine though misplaced affection for Stevie C. Foster. For another example, a rather similar proposal for April Fools' Day was shelved owing to popular opinion that there were far too many fools in the world to relegate them to a single day, besides which no-one wished to sully what is arguably the most hopeful of months, Uncle T. S. E.'s puzzling pronouncement notwithstanding.

In addition to there being nothing beyond a desultory demand for parades, there was also the ultimate drawback of impracticality. Simply put ¿where would a Surprise parade be staged? There were no streets or avenues or boulevards in the City of Curiosity. There still aren't. Pathways, yes, both spiritual and physical; trails, yes, both intuitive and visible; walks, to be sure, both figurative and literal; but no other common thoroughfares. The single, itinerant four-way Stop! sign hardly constituted a street system. Indeed, parades are so impossible along the Alkali Alameda that I can recollect only two, the first in commemoration of the surprise Surprise victory in the Shafter Lake Skipping Stone Spectacular and the second to celebrate the Denver Bongos having forty-fived every opposing team in the Great Post-War Permian Basin Six-Man Football Season-to-Remember.

In consequence an entirely new way of parading had developed, organically and spontaneously, a manner marching to the beat of a different drum. This *nueva marcha* was made of many small adjustments to the normal John Philip Sousa shtick but the big, fundamental changes boiled down to but four. The first of the quartet is that the marchpast became a march-around, that is, instead of the parade-marshal and the honorees and the bands being situated afoot in formation or on horses or atop floats or in snappy convertible cars marching and riding and driving past the throngs gathered along the way, in Surprise the looked-on dignitaries gather on the veranda of the Old School House whilst the onlookers tramp in a circle around the building, giving everyone equal opportunity to view and be viewed. The second change, bluntly beholden to the Bongos Bash, was that finger-snapping replaced both the beauty-queen wave usually employed by the paraders and the shouts of huzzah usually offered by the crowd, a refinement that added a cool, jazzy feel all the while it encouraged and abetted pleasant and thoughtful conversation amongst all the participants, spectators and spectacles alike. Third, every parade in Surprise ended in The Howdying—which has no counterpart elsewhere but which is the part of the event most treasured by the Surprise stead-fasts—a quaint custom in which the dignitaries step down from their aerie on the porch and mingle with the onlookers, continuing until everyone has howdied everyone else, constituting a warm meet-all-greet-all as fine as anything ever found in a country Baptist Church service—but without the burden of first having to endure the sermon—a happy sort of pandemonium, an uproar of back-slapping and hugging and baby-kissing and hand-shaking all carried out amidst the kindest of words and the biggest of smiles. The fourth and final alteration, one that should be emulated world-wide, was that no invitations were extended to, nor the presence permitted of, politicians of any ilk—past, present, or hopeful—and never a permit issued for displays of any armaments, military or otherwise. All parades in Surprise have ever been and will ever be peace-marches of the purest order and of the most orderly purity.

Before it was the Midland International Air and Space Port it was the Midland International Airport and before that the Midland Airport and before that the Midland Army Airfield and before that, at the very beginning in 1927,

Sloan Field. It was never Oddland Air Terminal, but that's what we Surprises called it. Not out of spite, but out of habit, a habit we got into sometime in the late 1950s or thereabouts, a brief moment in which a coterie of far-thinking citizens in each of the Twin Cities slipped back and forth across their borders in a conspiracy to form one great, unified *la ciudad de las cosmopolitas.* It was a tall order as two towns more different but more closely-linked can be found nowhere else on the planet. They were and remain a terrestrial dwarf star binary system, the two forever circling about their common center of petroleum, one in suits and ties and the other in chambray and jeans, one in glitter and the other in grease, one in boardrooms and the other in barrooms, one giving the orders and the other carrying them out. For what will seem to be the obvious reasons, the enterprise of melding the two into a Mega-Mesquite-Metropolis never achieved much momentum. One intractable sticking point was—no surprise—what to call the new Big Burg. Those on the east side opted for Midessa, those on the west preferring Odland. Those of us observers in the Peanut Gallery in between were drawn irresistibly to the second, especially when we realized that it must, perforce, be pronounced *odd-land.*

It was still the custom in those days to get to the aeropuerto a bit ahead of the expected arrival of the person or persons whom you were there to meet and greet and thence pick up for delivery elsewhere on *terra firma.* Time for a cup of coffee, a shoe-shine, or—better yet—time to engage in people-watching, that most primal of human pastimes, which is truly an idyll, and which I myself enjoy as much as anyone. Maybe more, as I count it as field-work in the work of writing, our craft being first and foremost driven by observation, followed by a right smart parcel of thinking—which is the most difficult labor of the whole process—and, only lastly, by the selection and assembly of words into sentences, sentences into paragraphs, and paragraphs into the whole of everything. Just as with writing— in which there are no hard-and-fast rules but rather a host of conventions and customs masquerading as dicta—proper people-watching is furthered by a few simple considerations. First: dress to watch, not to be watched. Chinos, brown sensible shoes, a plain shirt and—if the weather requires—a nondescript jacket. Second: behave to watch, not to be watched, for which one should be armed with a newspaper or magazine or book to use as one would employ a duck-blind or deer-stand within which one might lurk, invisible to the passing prey but still able to keep one's peepers in preparedness. Third: so as to remember but not be remembered, never write *per se* but instead take the notes from which you will later write and to that end have handy at all times a writing-stick and a small journal ready to record the instant details, those which disappear from the mind also instantly, for while fleeting observations are almost always the most transitory they are also almost always the most powerful—here now begging Billy Blake's indulgence of my slight paraphrase—constituting as they do the universe in a speck of dust and eternity in the present moment.

I had driven over in the Champ as we were smack-dab in the depths of the dog days of summer, the happy little Studebaker being fully one-half of the Surprise motor pool that was equipped with anything beyond a 4-70 air-conditioner, that latter appliance being perfectly useless because when the outside temperature is in the 90s having all four windows down in an automobile traveling 70 miles-an-hour—or, in our case, a pickup with both side windows lowered and the breezeway window slid open—such approach merely funnels the super-heated atmosphere through the cabin at a higher rate of speed, cooling the passenger compartment not a whit but instead creating a Venturi effect similar in impact to that of a blast furnace. I parked in the lot and trudged into the terminal, ambled to the arrival area, bought a couple of newspapers—both the Odessa American and the Midland Reporter-Telegram—then quickly took up residency in one of the torture devices that substitute for chairs in every known airport in the world.

I began with the gossip rags, gleaning what I could about the heights to which the latest local molehills had risen, those micromountains being the kinds of goings-on that get front-page ink in small cities and in their orthogenesis push the national and international happenings to the back of the front section. The Reporter-Telegram was mostly bidness, reporting the potential of a rosy near-term jump in the price of crude oil owing to turmoil in the Middle East, that sort of thing. Still, the clowns coming to town for National Clown Day merited several inches of lead on Page One, announcing that an evening soiree was to be held in the Odessa Room of the Hilton in downtown Midland and highlighting at which particular shopping malls the professional pierrots planned to perform during the afternoon. There was even a sidebar bullet-point-history of the official commemorative calendar consideration crafted for the Bozo Brigade, the outline noting that Tricky Dick, at that time in history our nation's Clown-in-Chief, had signed the bill that enabled the first week of August annually thereafter to belong to the painted pundits, specifically the month's first Saturday to be theirs and theirs alone. So very fitting, as the Comedian Commander was only ever happy in the most awkward ways, similar to the clowns themselves only different, him being a Reverse-Smokey-Robinson, the tears false but the sinister smile all too real. The Odessa American covered the petroleum prospects, too, only ignoring the clowns, instead laying out the events planned for Kelly Elliott Daze, mostly detailing the dressy dinner to-do slotted for the Midland Room in the Odessa Hilton on East University. No sidebar for 'Bubble-Up', I noted with chagrin, though with great relief I found no mention in either pulp about any parade. I thence turned to my magazine, from behind which covers I studied the people-zoo passing by.

West Texas, generally speaking, is the Noah's Ark of fashion, featuring specimens of every species, often in pairs, and this afternoon was exemplary. Midland oil-and-gas executives in shiny suits with white spread collars and yellow-polka-dot silk ties; old cowmen in starched white snap shirts under silver-belly Stetsons with pressed jeans haphazardly-shoveled over custom boots; here-and-there a townie in navy blazer and club tie paired with pleated khakis and a pair of faux-Gucci loafers; one or two older insurance-agent-types in plaid pants and Members Only jackets; a considerable number of working stiffs from Odessa sporting oil-field mullets cascading over muscle shirts tucked-in to tight Wranglers; even a few yeomen clodhoppers in feed-store gimme caps and khaki-short-sleeves and well-worn Redwing work boots. Not many hipsters or skaters this early in the decade, but lots of young guys in tees under unbuttoned flannels squeezed into skinny jeans and scuffling along in partially-laced Converse All-Stars. The women ran a similar gamut: matrons in flouncy denim skirts with matching-denim blouses featuring hand-appliquéd red-bandana yokes all bedazzled with rhinestones; business women in dark jackets and straight skirts and white blouses with black string ties; college girls in baby-doll dresses and sneakers with slouch-socks over tights or in peasant blouses and pleated dresses and cowboy boots; teeny-boppers in drainpipe jeans or bike shorts and tees; all of the feminine gender coiffed in curls of every variety, layered or bobbed or up or down or teased or spiked or pressed or fluffed—curls, curls, curls, every last head curly—leaving me sorely smitten with nostalgia for the long-long hair and short-short skirts of the 60s.

Friday afternoon and evening the region had been replete with thunderstorms wreaking their usual havoc on summer airline schedules, the cancellations and delays having carried over into Saturn's Day, so I got in some bonus people-watching, the big pay-off coming with the landing of an old, government-gray DC-3 that could have been a decommissioned C-47 in its appointments, its only civilian distinction being a large logo on the aft-end of the fuselage, which image consisting solely of a monotone likeness of The King, his eyes closed seemingly in prayer, his mouth open in song, microphone in his right hand, the enormous Bill Belew collar framing the slightly-pudgy cheeks associated with the Later Las Vegas Era. The grizzled gooney-bird taxied almost up to the terminal, stopping a short distance from the jetway snorkels before opening the passenger door at Elvis's right shoulder so the ground crew could roll a stairway up alongside. First one Elvis emerged, then another, and another and another and so on until about a dozen Kings were strung out in ragged file across the apron, gyrating into the terminal. It was a curious sight, monumental in some ways, silly in others, but in every way compelling. There were Elvises of various persuasions, including— amongst the usual double-XL middle-aged honkies—two Bros in 'fros, a Chicano in pork-chops, two matronly Soul Sisters in dreadlocks, at least one Oriental of indeterminate gender, a bearded-and-turbaned Sikh, and, bringing up the rear, a squarish-woman who most resembled J. Emperor Hoover in drag. I mentally tipped my imaginary hat to my mother-in-law's intelligence report. Smack-on.

¡Your attention, plea! ¡Your attention, plea! ¡Flight bwabed durthy ecket fum jarb-ulonga kaga sutra anding at haight blurbble! ¡Passengers maimer luggage et camel sale bumble skreetch!

I put away my notebook and newspapers and magazine—sorry, I forgot to mention that I'd chosen The Christian Science Monitor to keep the bored and the chatty and the curious from sitting beside me and striking up a conversation— then stood up and slowly shook the creases out of my chinos before moseying toward the jetway door, musing as I meandered, mulling over the magnificence of such a marvel of acoustic engineering, wondering whether the same scientists who had pioneered putting the faraway sound into long-distance phone calls had been employed to craft airport public-address systems, those conveyances of important information which are to the ears what the lobby seats are to the arse. ¿What universities did they attend? ¿Massachewsit Indoctrination of Technofal-lacy? ¿Cal Tetched? ¿What degrees did they take? ¿Disingenuous Engineering? ¿Were they Mush-Mouth Mechanics majors, minoring in General Gibberish? My noggin was noodling at full throttle, my mind on a roll and out of control as I strolled up to *haight blurbble* for what had to be Kelly's flight as it was the only arrival estimated for this hour and also as anyone could count the gates at Oddland Air Terminal on one hand with fingers left over and see them all with only a slight turn of the head even whilst wearing an eye-patch.

Just as I took a position on the outer limits of the departure lounge the jetway door burst open, a clutch of clowns caroming out, a boodle of Bubble-Uppers gaining on their giant shoe-heels. Instant pandemonium in the gate area. Clowns honking squeeze-horns, soaking bystanders with squirt-flowers, pinching pretty girls, mugging the hired-help, sneering at the children. Bubble-Uppers staying aloof from the slap-stick, looking like refugees from a costume clearance sale. The crowd of crazies almost as quickly heaving and hoofing haphazardly toward luggage *camel sale bumble skreetch*, leaving the dazed and discombobulated in their wake.

In the ensuing moment of quietude Kelly strolled off the plane, stopping to pose for the bank of paparazzi that had been staying clear of the clown-chaos. But the photogs paid no attention to Kelly, either. They were, instead, expecting several politicos reportedly on the same flight. Sure 'nuff, the white-shirt-red-tie-American-flag-lapel-pin-navy-suit-squad finally made their way from the ramp and into the lounge, surrounded by a cloud of minions and apparatchiks, the whole pack with their noses in the air sniffing about for the scent of sound-bites. Kelly—who was never nonplused—switched instantly from minor celebrity to major observer, the two of us taking in the talking points, waiting for the madness at baggage claim to calm down before we made our way over to pick up his stuff.

We didn't twiddle our thumbs quite long enough, however. Kelly's bags hadn't yet come out. Worse, the clowns' had. More and larger squeeze-horns. Rubber chickens. Rubber fishes. Flag-bang guns. A clown being yanked around by a dog leash attached to an empty harness. One riding a unicycle. A couple of radio-controlled miniature model cars, zipping around and up and over the luggage carousels, turning flips, cutting U-ies, bumping into one-another and into any and every other object in the baggage claim, running over feet, smashing into shins, chasing small children. Shrieking and squealing and shouting. Little laughter, except from the clowns themselves. Then no laughter at all: the demolition-derby R/C clown cars collided head-on at full-speed.

The impact instantly immersed us into an 'Elvira Madigan' moment, clowns and clown-victims alike, everything now drug down into slo-mo. The terminal

Muzak dropped to dirge-tempo—y o u ' v e g o t a f r i e n d i t ' s t o o l a t e b a b y y e a h i t ' s h o w c a n y o u m e n d a b r o k e n h e a r t m i s t e r b i g s t u f f—making musical molasses for the score playing behind the aerial ballet of little wheels and fenders and bits of plastic body parts slowly tumbling upwards, the clowns moving dreamily toward the wreckage, their painted smiles upside-downing into angry frowns, a long-and-drawn-out *¡Ohhhh....foooo....kullll!* the curse low and slow and rumbling, a thunderclap moving at glacial speed, unleashing a mud-flow of profanity of such venom and vigor and inventiveness so as to be shocking even in the Roughneck Realm. It seemed like hours of flotsam and jetsam floating and jetting and fragments fragmenting and rubble rattling and all of it bouncing and clattering and twitching and shaking—seeming even as long as days, maybe, the physics of spinning being what they are, that it takes longer to spin-down than it takes to spin-up—though, in truth, it was but mere moments before the last of the debris came to rest and a measure of stillness was returned, mere moments before the clock came back to normal, mere moments before we spectators returned to consciousness to see the clowns clustered around the newly-decommissioned remote-controlled annoyances, deep in electrome-chanical triage, shouting inquiries about the nearest hobby shops. It was several moments more before one of the stunned citizens pointed them to the telephone directories tethered to the pay-phones strung out along the walls.

Several buses were parked along the passenger pick-up curb. First in queue were the two flagships of the Glitter Bus Line, next a dented and rusted old school bus with a carrying-rack, the whole contraption having been painted government gray, likely with the kind of cheap bristle brush used by house painters, and following what would prove to be the Kings' un-kingly coach were several idling limousines. Our informant had intimated early-on that the dazzlingly-red Scenicruisers had been reserved for the Bubble-Uppers. The clown crew—perhaps not having such good information, or perhaps not caring about any kind of information, even were it available—began pushing and shoving and squirting and honking to effect their entry to and occupation of the first of the Glitter Bus buggies. The Bubble-Uppers—who were only Look-a-Likes, after all, and neither impersonators, like the Elvises, nor masqueraders, like the clowns, and so had real lives apart from Kelly Elliott Daze, making them simple but resourceful citizens—our Bubble-Up re-enactors huddled up, took a parley, and, after counting their heads and the clowns' noses, realized that they themselves needed only one of the 40-passenger conveyances. A spokesperson was picked who forthwith ceded the excess space to the Ersatz Emmett Kelly Klan, though—and ¿are we surprised?—when the handshake deal was closed the clown's clasp contained a joy buzzer.

The Elvis Entourage had already begun to fill the Great Gray Bus, some climbing up on top where they promptly plunked-down several karaoke-boom-boxes and began to wiggle away to the strains of several of The King's most-requested numbers, several times on several different requests at the same time. While the political candidates were jockeying for position at the limo line, a careful observer—no, wait, even a reckless, deaf-and-blind observer—could see and hear the Mo-Ped gangsters collecting in the parking lot, shedding their unnecessaries, greasing down with sun-tan lotion, and topping off the tiny tanks on their motorized pedal-pushers with precise mixtures of motor oil and gasoline. I sought out the Bubble-Upper who'd just had his hand buzzed by the head Bozo so as to let the Look-a-Likes know how to get to Surprise and to tell them that Threeb would meet their bus at the highway so as to lead them the rest of the way into our village and that even though he was blind he was a careful driver and, anyway, he'd be in the Creepy-Crawley which was not only very slow but also would be easy to spot. And, by-the-way, that Kelly and I would go ahead of them to let the locals know that the festivities were forthcoming. The Lead Look-a-Like had—as you would not be surprised to suspect—several questions, most of them framed more as incredulous comments than as pure-dee inquiries, such as ¿Blind? ¿Creepy-whatty? ¿What does it look like? No worries, I said, you'll grok the Creepy-Crawley the instant you see it, and, trust me—I added, putting a hand squarely and confidently on his shoulder—Threeb has never had so much as a traffic warning. No mention—I thought it fair enough under the circum-stances—no mention did I make of the fair number of Maya Gandhi's pups that went missing during the period of young Blind Billy Bob's driver-training.

Whilst I was giving the Bubble-Uppers the where-for and what-how we were joined by several of the Elvises, who listened carefully, rendering their assent and comprehension with a constant stream of *thank-yew-thank-yew-thank-yew-vurry-much* mumbled over and over and over, laid to rest only by their own leader, who turned out to be the fellow impersonating Gladys, Gladys having been Elvis's mom. She/he first turned to her/his charges—Boys. ¡Boys! Listen-up. Mama sez yew mind yer manners.—then back to me, saying nothing, only smiling and nodding as I continued. When my welcome-wagon spiel had been fully delivered to the Look-a-Likes, I turned to Gladys. There's word on the street about some clown trouble, she/he offered. While I stood there trying to think of of something to say, we had a small moment, looking one-another eye-to-eye, perfectly aware that we each knew the other from a time in the long-ago past and equally aware that we each also knew that the other didn't know from where or from when. I was about to make a corny comment, like ¿Haven't we met before? but was saved from staleness by the clowns' bus shooting away from the curb, squealing as much rubber as a Scenicruiser ever squealed, the limousines right behind buried in the black cloud of the bus's diesel exhaust. The remainder of us turned to our own transportation.

Cranking my neck around as I backed the Champ out of its parking spot I espied a pair of rotating red lights atop the roof of a mid-70s Plymouth Volaré, all button hubcaps and black-wall tires and several whoop antennae, clearly an old-and-worse-for-wear-and-tear police unit, its original insignia unceremoniously stripped-away, the shadow of its bygone badge partly-covered-over by the gloriously-misspelled office of its current commander, *CONSTABEL.* Check this out, I nodded to Kelly, who cranked his head around, too, in time to see a half-dozen or so black four-wheel-drive pickups—each one jacked-up over a set of big, dumb, silly tires—slowly jerking and lurching along behind the satrap's sedan. *Cantare, oh-oh-oh-oh.*

On the way to Surprise, Kelly and I traded bits and pieces of information, mainly about why the only two people from the original cast and crew to attend Kelly Elliott Daze were Kelly and your humble dazed describer. Here's the scoop. Hembre Hawser—who played both Lance Reid and Blackie Black—had had a chip on his shoulder from the first day of filming as everyone on the set took to calling him Hem Haws owing to the fact that he was never ready with his lines yet was too vain to call for them from the script-girl. Not to mention he never liked playing a supporting role, which was a pity as he's never yet been cast in the lead in anything beyond an antacid commercial, and that only once. He was last known to be sulking in his room at the Hollywood Y, though he still shows up to auditions from time-to-time.

Linda Lewis—filling the parts of both Lisa Rodger and Muffin McWright— may have been the best actor of the lot, for she was clueless. I mean completely *clueless*, the human incarnation of Gertrude Stein's Oakland, where there's no there there. Being without personality whatsoever she only existed when she was playing a part, and when she was playing a part she had no other mode of existence to interfere with the role *du jour*. We tried penetrating her impenetrable persona with humor, for example calling her Patty as a take-off on one of the world's greatest-ever rock-and-roll songs—Fort Worth's own Ray Sharpe's 1959 hit—but she never got it. Jokes, innuendo, irony, teasing of any kind, it was all simply wasted on Linda. Off the set she was so absent from her own being that she was eventually misdiagnosed with dementia and committed to a nursing home whilst still in her 30s. She's been there so long—Kelly noted, sadly—that she's grown to love the part, steadfastly refusing to leave the Hallucination Hotel notwithstanding the diagnosis having been rescinded many, many years back.

L. A. Johnny West Coast was truly crazy at the beginning and remained true to form. Years later he took to claiming he was the Archangel of American Folk Music, his copyright claims for 'Blowin' In the Wind' and 'The Gates of Eden' landing him first in the legal system which then deposited him in one funny-farm after another. In a curious twist, the Archangel of American Folk Music later claimed that he his-own-self was L. A. Johnny West Coast. Half the musicologists believed one and half believed the other, with no-one believing both and no-one believing neither, either.

Others of our bunch had just up and died. Frankie Darrow on Christmas Day of '76. Joe of Joe & Eddie in early August '66 in a car wreck. Anaïs Archambault—our Madame Bevier—went naturally and peacefully, by all accounts, in '84 at Plum Village in the south of France, where she'd gone to study with Thích Nhāt Hānh. Bud of Bud & Travis just last year. And the remainder of those absent-but-living were all doing fine but simply doing other things: Ray Harryhausen living in London; the complete cavy of Cola Píntos employed elsewhere, some on the rodeo circuit but most in circuses and children's pony rides and traveling carnivals; and probably still middling along was the fellow who played Mayor Middleton, though no-one seems to be able to remember his name.

All was right-about-ready in the Suburb-Sans-Streets when we rolled in. Banners had been hung around the Old School House. SURPRISE—HOME TOWN OF KELLY ELLIOTT AND THOM ED JONES proudly read the largest, WELCOME BUBBLE-UPPERS said one almost as big with all the warmth that tempera paint could deliver, while a third and smaller sign proclaimed, more philosophically, IT'S ALL A SURPRISE IN SURPRISE. So as to leave plenty of space for the crowd to easily circle 'round the Shinnery Seat of Non-Governance, folding tables had been set on the edge of the clearing under the little bits of shade offered by the larger of the mesquites and catclaws, the cardboard sideboards spread with checkered cloths and stocked with plates and napkins and silver service and outfitted with big crocks of iced tea and lemonade and water.

Knowing that the Ukuladies would be much too involved in the festivities to offer a performance, Rose Edna had sent out a few feelers to former contacts in the entertainment biz, locating a couple of up-and-coming combos to provide some oom-pah-pah. One was an afro-appointed albino triplet set of sisters who called themselves The Folk Ewes, the newest big thing in the newish nook of the industry known as folk-punk, the trio drawing raves for songs like 'Michael, Row Your Boat Somewhere Else', and 'Good Riddance, Irene', not to forget their show-stopper, 'Motherless Children Don't Get Told to Clean Up Their Rooms'. For a change of pace, The Chill Billies—five back-woods beatniks who happened, each and everyone, to be a William or a Willie or a Bill, no Sam—these hep-cats from the hollers were slated to play every other set. The boys in berets and bib-overhauls, the world's one-and-only smooth-grass-fusion band, were itchin' to pick their banjos, strum their gee-tars, bow their fiddles, and thump their washtub on relaxed instrumental numbers that included 'Blue Rondo a la Turkey In the Straw', 'How High the Moonshine', and the all-time sentimental favorite, 'April in Paducah'.

Bobbie Sue's mom's big-top upbringing made her the hands-down favorite to fill the role of de-facto Surprise Parade Marshall. Wearing a t-shirt that read ¡*Carpe Diem, Dadgummit!*—which, an impartial observer would be quick to note, still fit her nicely—Mother Sue had been bustling about the pretend parade grounds all morning, moving sticks and rocks and the occasional cow-patty away from the path of the moveable grandstands, ordering the proper placement for the picnic tables, pointing the pickers to their respective stages—one on either end of the building—and most importantly providing the air of command essential to all such events. The moment we pulled in, Madame Merriman barked orders to have someone drive the Champ over to the Shifting Sands Mobile Motel whilst Kelly and I were led to our places on the veranda. Visiting would have to wait.

26.

BAD SCHICKLE

Schickle happens.—from The Zonker Zen Parables

Dree-e-ye-e-yeam, dream, dream, dream. I entered a dream state as we took our places on the reviewing veranda. It was that kind of day, custom-made for a daydreamin' boy who wonders what can it mean to a daydream believer who's always dreaming the impossible dree-e-ye-e-yeam, dream, dream, dream. The Oddland Airport Terminal people-parade melding into the Elvis-imperson-ator-boogie-woogie melting into the candy colored clown they call the sandman morphing into the sleep-walk slow-motion moment of madness in baggage claim. Dree-e-ye-e-yeam, dream, dream, dream, ¿who am I to disagree? Sweet dreams are made of life could be a dream, hey-nonnie-ding-dong a lang a lang a lang, No, wait, life is but a dream, sh boom sh boom, but dreams can tell a lie, even once upon a time in your wi-i-i-ild-est dree-e-ye-e-yeams, dream, dream, dream. I'm always dreamin', 'cause I've got a dream, I've got to share it, ¿will you take part in my life? that is my dream, it's what you make it, doo wah, doo wah. Dree-e-ye-e-yeam, dream, dream, dream, all the while in the far distance thunderclouds are threatening, in the middle distance the tentacle-antennae of the Creepy-Crawly are kicking-up a slowly-rising column of dust that is settling just as slowly over the caravan of buses and pickups inching along in its wake, the flashing red emergency lights of the constable's cruiser causing the cruddy coffee-cream-colored haze to pulse slowly in synchronization with the throbbing anvil-heads towering all around us, nearer and nearer. Dree-e-ye-e-yeam, dream, dream, dream, you tell me your dream, and I will tell you mine but not till you tell me ¿how long must I dream?

Right away the Bubble-Uppers hopped up onto the parade veranda, crowding around Kelly and I, their costumes and studied mannerisms sparking one déjà vu after another, wave upon wave of flashes of auditions and rehearsals and sound-stages and the wrap-party finale. Look-a-Likes are a sub-set of the universe of geeks, but the most jocular of the lot, happy as clams to dress-up in the skins of fictional characters, all smiles and enthusiasm and the best vibes this side of a fresh-rolled fatty. We made room on the wooden-deck dais for the Elvises, too, aliens arrived from another of the geek outposts but as a class not so happy as the Look-a-Likes because bearing the weight of impersonating a real person—especially a hero, double-especially a flawed hero—now, that's some heavy schickle. Still and all, their mood rings rarely ran to black and there was always about them the need to be loved and the aspiration to return that love—both need and aspiration inversely proportional to how convincing were their impersonations—in other words, just the same as each and every one of all of the rest of us, different only in how far they were willing to go to show it. Don't be cruel to a heart that's true. Or to a heart that dreams.

By all rights there should have been at least a few Cola Píntos on the veranda to round-out the dignitaries, for what's more dignified in a parade than a high-stepping, high-spirited horse. But no such luck, for none of the original cast of prancing ponies had perambulated to Surprise and, even if they had, the spacious veranda was not nearly spacious enough for both man and beast, so to serve as substitutes Shad Eliot had collected a cavy drawn from mounts loaned by his day-working-waddie buddies and was at that moment ground-tying the borrowed broomtails around the perimeter of the rough clearing that sufficed as the Surprise town square, a square that was more circular than rectangular but equally irregular as to either of those two geometric figures.

Whilst the old wrangler was arraying his remuda, Parade Marshal Mama Merriman was doing her best to bunch-up the bystanders so as to be able to give them the go-ahead to get going on the go-'round. But she wasn't having much luck. The festive crowd was too busy being festive and by force of nature too feisty to pay attention to the mental suggestions sent forth from the mind of the life-long animal-whisperer, so, for a second, Sue-Sue was stumped. But only for a second. About as long as it took for the watch's tiniest hand to take its next tic, she popped into her 'Stream, dug out her hope-chest—which in Wally Byam World was simply a large coffee can—rummaging through it 'til she found a pea-whistle from her days with The Sioux City Sioux's Super Revue, thence emerging with the chrome-plated aerophone clenched tightly between her dentures, a series of sharp, shrill blasts soon commanding the consideration of the crowd. In moments, the Kelly Elliott Daze Parade was in full promenade.

Heading up the gangly group was Blind Billy Bob, balancing—as if it were a drum-major's baton—the flower-scrolled white cane Bobbie Sue had bought him in the Haight, stepping high himself and keeping right good time with the brass band playing in his head. Next came Marshal Merriman, and alongside her Pater Jones. Since Surprise was such a small village the honorees on the veranda almost always outnumbered the crowd marching before them in review, so it became customary to base the number of circuits taken around the Old School House on a simple mathematical formula, that being setting the trips past the veranda equal to the number of honorees divided by the size of the crowd. To illustrate, if there were 30 dignitaries on the veranda and 10 Surprises in the crowd, there'd be 3 passes. My dad's job was to manage the math so that Sue could manage the mob. Whilst the two of them were calculating and controlling, the remainder of the community straggled by and strolled along, in one sense—that of the particular—having no set order, but in another sense—that of the general—having the definite form and shape of any group of onlookers anywhere. In other words, the crowd was simply a crowd, in spite of its small size and in spite of its doing the parading whilst what would be the parade body on any other Main Street was fixed in location on the low-brow-lanai of the Old School House.

Self-conscious of their slight numbers, some in the march-around took delight in behaving as if they were the honorees—giving the beauty-queen wave and throwing penny candies at the dignitaries—which seemed to give the crowdlet greater presence—all the while snapping their fingers as well as shouting out bits and pieces of phrases and sentences as parts of conversations that might or might not get completed in the requisite number of turns around the grounds. Most of the dissected discussion parts were directed at Kelly, as no one had had time to even so much as say hello before he was whisked away to the reviewee-riser. Though it should be said, here and now, the startling appearance of the Bubble-Uppers and the Elvises spurred a fair share of comments—all polite and positive, this being Surprise—and questions—all probing and prescient, this being Surprise. Those of us on the porch-dais had comments and questions of our own which we hurled down on the tramping horde, mostly of the you-haven't-changed-a-bit and what's-for-dinner variety. Kerrie Mae and Bobbie Sue were clearly flirtatious in their exchanges with Kelly, Ruth Etta and I doing our part to keep up by blowing kisses back and forth, Tally and Star holding up little Merri Elli whilst they pointed out to the baby who was whom and what was what amongst the odd bunch cooing and mugging for her, and—linked arm-in-arm and moving in unison like a small float—Mother Mary Ellen and Mother-in-Law Rose Edna and the Bobster. The Khan clan—our latest Surprises—took to our parade paradigm like proverbial ducks to water. Father Ali and Mother Fatima, dressed in traditional Pakistani outfits, pranced primly in the procession as if boot-scooting the schottische to the reedy rhythm of the zurna. The girls—Saba and Yasmin—wore the more modern garb popular in Karachi whilst be-bopping behind Star, sashaying up to dandle the baby at every opportunity, much to the delight of all three. Sadly, brothers Mustaq and Shahzad were relegated to simply cheering the event from the Paki-Store's gas pump as they looked on from their assignment to mind the mini-mall. Only Shad Eliot stayed aloof from the marching merriment, for he—as did Gene D. and Sue—had a parade function, that being to stay mounted for crowd control, on its face a silly provision as in size there was not much crowd to control and as in composition there was no crowd that needed controlling, but the elder statesman of the cowboy nation—bow-legged and bumfuzzled afoot but lithe and graceful a-horse-back—whenever possible preferred to do his work from the hurricane deck of a pony.

Dree-e-ye-e-yeam, dream, dream, dream. Distant lightning triggered the low growl of near-by thunder triggering the return of the dream state. Dree-e-ye-e-yeam, dream, dream, dream. Across the town-square-circle the cracker constable and a half-dozen Stranger Wranglers dismounted from their rigs just the other side of the pony cordon marking the city limits. The Khan boys stopped them behind the Paki-Store. An argument. A scuffle. Gun shots. Horses bolting. Dree-e-ye-e-yeam, dream, dream, dream. The Mesquite Mayberry meeting the Twilight Zone—'The Fishin' Hole' spiraling into a black hole.

The Howdying had already begun when the brouhaha began. Kelly and I were first out of the chute, the Bubble-Uppers and the Elvises coming pell-mell behind us, both costume crews doing their best to help one another down the steps. Ahead of me I could see Shad lean forward into the saddle as he dug in with his spurs. In a couple of lopes he'd leaped into the midst of the ruckus. Maya Gandhi—neither fond of marching nor of parades—had staked herself all morning at a corner of the Khan Kingdom of Commerce to help the boys sell Paki-Takis during the event. Without rising from her characteristic criss-cross-applesauce seat she whistled for Punto Rojo, who immediately set about gathering the scattered ponies. Threeb's drum-major duties had caused him to end up on the south-east side of the clearing at the last circuit of the march-around, so he was almost on-scene when things got western. No matter the tumult going on all about him, he stood for a brief moment—cool as a cucumber wearing sun-shades, cocking his head from side to side, getting a bearing on the auditory landscape, opening his Third Eye to the vibes—before advancing straight into the fray, his Summer of Love white cane held out before him like a bayonet.

Kelly and I moved almost as one, the crowd parting before us as the Red Sea before Moses. We were at the Paki-Store in a thrice. Though we could have sauntered over. We rounded the corner of the tiny shopping center to see the high-strung constable's hands held high over his head, his eyes as big as the muzzle end of the Senior Eliot's shotgun barrel and, beside him, the Stranger Wranglers all wrangled into a tight bunch, roped—evidently—by a large community loop thrown by Threeb, who was holding his end of the riata, a Ray Charles smile painting his countenance. Behind Shad, Mustaq and Shahzad were dusting themselves off, straightening their tee-shirts and blue jeans, checking to see if their kushtis needed re-tying.

Without taking his eyes off the littlest lawman, Shad filled us in. These yahoos—he slowly swung the stock of his Model 12 along in a lazy arc to point out the crestfallen captives—these boneheads were jumpin' on the Khan kids there—jerking his head toward the two young Pakistanis behind him—shoutin' about 'em bein' un-American and hollerin' go-home-immigrants and calling 'em rag-heads when anyone can plainly see they're wearin' gimme-caps and, tell truth—Shad said, truthfully—I'd stood all I could stand and I couldn't stand no more, so myself and Threeb—he continued, now with an unmistakable touch of pride—who's been takin' roping lessons from me—adding, parenthetically—a blind roper, now, fellers, I figure that'll eat into these hoodlums' high-sidin' in the hoosegow, ¿won't it?—before concluding—and 'twixt the two of us we put the ki-bosh on their deal. Though three or four—interjected Blind Billy Bob— weren't in the big bunch and slipped off in their pickups, hot-rodding it out of here. Next time I should employ a bigger loop—he noted. ¿The shots? I asked.

Barnaby Fife there—Shad pointed to the cringing constable—aerated his brogans tryin' to get his pistol unpacked from his holster.

I turned to Kelly, who'd turned back to eye-ball the parade participants who'd in turn beat feet over to see what was going on and to see whether or not it was still on-going. Kelly—his Tiger Land post-boot-camp training kicking in—was taking a head-count. Scowling after the first noggin-numbering, he took a second survey at the conclusion of which he growled—We're missing Star and the baby. At that Tally struck out on the run to check his 'Stream for mother and child.

Just as he disappeared over a dune and into the catclaws on the other side of the clearing we heard a distant snarling sound, faint and high over head but growing louder and nearer. ¿Any of you Bubble-Uppers have binoculars? I queried, and had no sooner spoken than a Look-a-Like looking like The Owl stepped forward, volunteering that he had a set of vintage field glasses, which he promptly pulled from under his lab coat, nestling the binoculars under his huge eyebrows, then straightway began scanning the skies, not an easy job as the distant thunderheads had advanced in our direction and the heavens were part-ly-clabbered. Presently he called out, identifying the unidentified flying object as a radio-controlled helicopter, a Du-Bro Shark, to be precise. Who besides a look-a-like would know such a thing, I thought to myself. Odd model—he continued, aiming his mechanical opticals at an object that had just dropped down from the clouds—its pontoon skids are big yellow shoes and there's a clown-frown painted on the cabin nose—then, almost in an aside—those models usually have shark's teeth decals, but—now reflective—really, what's the difference in a shark's smile and a clown's frown. I now knew more than I wanted to know about the toy chopper but still didn't know what I needed to know. ¿What's it doing? I implored ¿where'd it come from? The substitute Strigiforme, his telescopic peepers still fastened on the large model aircraft, proceeded to pipe-out a play-by-play—Can't read a compass direction… but it's slowing to a hover… over the clearing… it just dropped something—we watched as best we could using only our naked eyes as the snarling grew louder and nearer, trusting the look-a-like Owl to keep his course and his commentary—OK, banking… banking… taking off. By now the improbable aero-machine had drawn close enough that we could all watch the clown 'copter trundle off in a westerly tack.

As if in a ballet the radio-controlled egg-beater evaporated into the lowering clouds just as Tally burst from the brushy bower. We met him in the midst of the clearing at the drop-site of the just-now jettisoned jetsam. He bent down, picked it up, studied it, looked around, then said, almost absent-mindedly—They're not in the 'Stream. But I know what's happened to them.—holding out the airmail missive for all to see. Tied to a caliche-rock was a small scrap of paper on which had been drawn a crude head-and-shoulder figure of a white-face Auguste, the clown's gloved hands thrust forward in the sketch, gripping, in one mitt, the torso of a stick-figure woman, in the other, the leg of a stick-figure little girl.

The Khan girls wriggled their way into the inner circle of the neck-craning crowd, took one look at the crazy correspondence, clapped their hands over their mouths, their eyes growing to the size of Moon Pies, then with a shriek struck out for the west city limits. No one seemed to notice the girls go as all peepers were pointed at the piece of paper and its portent of peril. Shocked murmurs began to ripple around the remaining onlookers, burbling into a rolling boil, someone soon blurting out ¡A posse! the suggestion becoming a clamor ¡Form a posse! ¡Form a posse! immediately others countering ¡No! we need a search party, quickly followed by a hubbub of comments, pro and con, a noisy and chaotic bantering that could have been the beginning of a discussion had the storm not struck, the skies crackling, the thunderhead making good on its threat, the wind instantly rising-up, first in a cloud of dust, then fat, hard rain drops, the rain turning to hail, forcing our whole bunch to beat a hasty retreat for the Old School House. On the way several grabbed the victuals from the sideboards. Others glommed onto the folding chairs that hadn't yet flown off. Shad and Threeb and the Khan boys tarried long enough to throw a tarp over the prisoners. Soggy and shaken, the Surprises and their Surprise guests were soon assembled in the community assembly hall.

Dree-e-ye-e-yeam, dream, dream, dream. All I have to do is dree-e-ye-e-yeam, dream, dream, dream, oo-ooh dre-e-e-e-e-am-weaver, I had too much to dream last night, I had too much to dree-e-ye-e-yeam, dream, dream, dream, the summer storm slamming into Surprise, slinging slivers and shards of a sorry dree-e-ye-e-yeam, dream, dream, dream, ¡wake-up! ¡wake-up! ¡get out of bed! welcome to my nightmare, I think you're gonna like it when the red, red robin goes somewhere over the rainbow, off to see the wizard, because of the wonderful things some day you'll wish the clouds are far behind you. If only there was a yellow brick road.

27.

THE CASTING

A riot of responsibility ensued inside, a flurry of functions instinctively assumed by each citizen, a scene superficially straight out of the Keystone Kops but which was in fact—underneath the outwardly-chaotic comedic commotion—a tightly-orchestrated operation conducted with the cool calm of Mission Control, carried out with the urgency of a big-city news room, and stoked with the steely seriousness of the Command Center at NORAD. While there was no hiatus in the hubbub of comments about sheriff's posses and search parties, each and every Surprise took up one or more tasks all the while they talked and opined. The guest Ordinaries threw in, too. Some started coffee percolating whilst others rinsed thermoses and metal cups. Some cleared tables so as to lay-out the pot-luck dishes saved from the squall, some scratched around for paper-plates and plastic-ware, some began assembling sandwiches, still others unfolded the collapsible chairs. The Folk Ewes arrayed their gear in one corner, the Chill Billies in the corner opposite, the Elvi set about assessing their boom-boxes for storm damage, the Bubble-Uppers stood about smoothing-down one-another's get-ups.

Yet, while such spontaneous self-organization is satisfying and even subtly sublime—in a wonky way, of course—the liberation of the captives and the capture of the libertines required a plan. I looked around, expecting one of the elders from the Foundling Families to take charge. But no. They were all in their eighties. They were looking to their children for leadership. It crossed my mind, maybe for the first time in my own time, that we—my g-g-g-generation—that we were now the g-g-g-grown-ups. I looked around again, this time to the Six Surprises. My sis and Bobbie Sue were hand-wringing over Star and Merri Elli, Ruth Etta had her hands full providing consolation to the two of them, Threeb was third-eyeballing the goings-on, and Kelly—well, Kelly is an actor, ready to lead provided the role calls for it. I am a writer, I thought, the one who invents the leaders and the followers, the one who plans the plots. So it would have to be up to me.

With as much authority as a gargle can muster, I cleared my throat loudly enough to claim the attention of the room. After a few guttural sputters all eyes were turned my way, all ears bent to my voice. The storm has slowed us down—I began with the obvious—but it's also impeded our enemies—I enunciated enemies with the emphasis of a curse before confirming more of the obvious—the storm's also given us time to plan… time to prepare—I waited for a longish moment before concluding with a command phrased as an invitation—¿Shall we council?—followed by an invitation couched as a command—¡Let us have some volunteers!—the command and the invitation immediately eliciting nods of assent all around. Good—I confirmed in gratitude—turning to Eliot the Senior to ask for an opening prayer. The cowboy cleric closed his eyes, lifted up his face, then offered a recitation.

Westron wynde, when wilt thou blow,
The small raine down can raine?
Cryst, if my love were in my armes
And I in my bedde again!

The ancient plea had just been launched Heavenward and the council had yet to come fully underway when the first volunteer spoke up, an offer made in a strange voice, a man's voice issuing forth from a woman's face, yet a clear voice, a voice that bespoke authority. It was Gladys. We can help—she/he said. ¿Are you kidding? someone demanded. ¡You're Elvis impersonators!—added another, emphatically, as yet a third chimed in—And you—pointing at her/him—you're only a copy-cat King in drag. Gladys stood for a moment, waiting for the tumult to subside, then spoke, now directly to me. We knew we knew one another the moment we met this morning—she/he began—though at first I couldn't remember exactly from where or from when. Till now. She/he paused—an overly dramatic touch, it seemed to me—I was your contact at Ghost Writers On the Sly—she/he said, with what I detected as a sense of accomplishment—before I got this gig—she/he waved her/his hand toward the motley crew of ersatz Elvises—in which I am charged with running the Government's witness protection program. She/He then beckoned the troupe to come forward, one by one, for introductions.

It took a few moments for the weird roll-call: Elvises who'd been mob informants, Elvises who'd been cat-burglars, Elvises who'd been foreign agents, Elvises who'd been numbers runners, on and on and on, each of whom had turned state's evidence and each of whom were now on the hit-lists of various Mafia families and crime syndicates and shady government organizations and major corporations. We'd like to help—Gladys said at last, then added, warmly—the King always had a soft-spot for little kids, and, besides—she/he concluded, practically—it'll go a long ways on our community service credits. The Elvises all nodded in agreement—underscoring their assent with a muttered cacophony of *thank-yew-thank-yew-thank-yew-vurry-much*—each impersonator then rattling off a litany of advice, the particulars arising from their respective areas of expertise. It's too obvious—several older Elvises pointed out—a note dropped by a toy helicopter. They want all of you to try to track down the hostages—clarified the Oriental Elvis—while they are elsewhere perpetrating some other meanness—added an Italian Elvis, with a following footnote—which is why this situation calls for a couple of posses, one to rescue the bambina and the other to bag the bad guys. And a third detachment to person the base camp—concluded a Soul-Sister Elvis.

A lingering lacuna. We were a bit dumbfounded. ¿Are all Elvises in the witness protection program? we wondered. ¿Are all clowns bad guys? our wondering continued, though the latter was a much easier concept to consider. Whilst we mulled over this muddle in our individual minds the general consensus of the worthies gathered in the room soon became apparent. Each and every person stepped forward, all of the Ordinaries, all of the Surprises. Now it was time for me to step in and step up.

Kelly and Tally, you take the Bubble-Uppers—I began—you'll need to go horseback, so Shad will join you. Head west since that's the direction in which the R/C chopper left. ¿Horseback? shrieked the Bubble-Uppers—¡we're Look-a-Likes, not stunt doubles! Shad quickly assured them that his mounts were the real thing, honest-to-goodness Cola Píntos—a slight prevarication but one necessary to the greater good, a white lie that at the very least brightened up the Look-a-Likes a little. I continued giving instructions—Threeb and Bob Merriman and I will take the Creepy-Crawly and the Stranger-Wranglers' pickups accompanied by those of the Elvises who wish to join us. ¡Perfect!—Gladys answered for them—Elvis was a man of action in all his movies, and I'll stay here to help coordinate—she/he said, firmly, adding—coordinating's what I do best. Then you meet up with Rose Edna and the Joneses—I replied to my former employer—and your bunch will hold down headquarters here in the Old School House. Sis and Bobbie Sue and Ruth Etta, you'll need to stay mobile—I suggested—so that you'll be ready to spring into action once Star and Merri Elli are located. When I took a breath, Mustaq and Shahzad spoke up, asking if a light aeroplane would be of use. ¡Of course!— we all cheered—their offer not only welcome but also causing me to realize we'd have to have some communications gear for all these moving parts—so I asked the impromptu assembly if anyone knew if our burg retained any old Civil Defense walkie-talkies from the Cold War Scare. Yes—said my dad, who'd been in charge of that sort of thing during his school-master days—we've got at least a dozen, so far as I know still plugged-in to the chargers. Fine—I replied—distribute one to each posse and one to Ruth Etta and one to headquarters and one to the Khan Kids and see how many remain that remain charged-up. The thugs'll be listening—interjected the Sikh Elvis—¿any of you know how to converse in code? Better than that—Ruth Etta offered—we are all fluent in the slanguage of Surprise. Plus— Kelly elaborated—we have our own names for the pastures and draws and sand-blow-outs and mesquite mottes and any and every other feature of this place. The Elvises seemed impressed. As did the Bubble-Uppers.

I thought I was done. But not so. For some time Tally had been trying to get a word in edgewise, or any other wise. Here was his chance, and he took it—It's important that I go with Thom Ed and the Elvises—said the first New Surprise, further explaining—I know what they're seeking—a ripple of silence spread out from his words until a hush hung over the whole room—I should have suspected something—he said, almost sorrowfully—those bizarre bungled burglary attempts these past few months, the corn-ball constable, the sinister Stranger-Wranglers… someone, somewhere, is after the formulae for the p@tio coatings…and those are in my journals…and that explains the kidnapping and the otherwise unconnected ransacking…a diversion to draw us away from their real purpose—we were processing this as fast as we could, but idea light-bulbs were rapidly beginning to blink-on over the assembled heads—then Tally continued his logic to its conclusion—and the journals are my obligation and I'm the only one who knows what needs to be known to keep them from falling into the wrong hands. But…but… but…—Kelly exclaimed by way of stuttering—¿shouldn't you be leading the search for your daughter? No—Tally's voice softened—my father will do just fine.

Looks of surprise and confusion rocketed around the Surprise gathering, but in the midst of it the two of them—Kelly and Tally—stood transfixed, looking at one another, one in wonderment, one in admiration, each in the profound acknowledgement that comes of blood recognizing blood. They embraced, the lost now found, the uncertain now certain, the four of us closest to the two of them now unburdened of a four-decades'-old secret. The group hug that followed was joyous, if solemn, broken only by the big front door of the Old School House blowing open in a blast of wind.

Seemingly borne by the turbo-charged zephyr, Saba Khan burst into the Courthouse of Cleverness, mud thickly-caked on her Steve Maddens and splattered all over her powder-blue stonewashed mom jeans, several brightly-colored over-sized stuffed buttons in one hand, a frilly cuff and a frillier collar in the other, the young beauty talking excitedly in a patois of Urdu and Sindhi and Valspeak. Sister Yasmin, close behind and equally muddy, clutched Merri Elli, who, in turn, clutched a baby-fist-full of squirt-flower petals. Star soon brought up the rear, muttering as she kept tripping on a large, odd ribbon dragging alongside her.

¡We sent up huzzah upon huzzah as we rejoiced and were rejoiced! Once everyone had hugged the rescued and the rescuers and—for good measure—had hugged each and every one-another, a happy curiosity prevailed. ¡Oh, a moment to remember, a double-group-hug-day! We soon caught our collective breath— ¿What happened? we asked, each of us at the same time, and before allowing time for an answer, followed in like manner with ¿how'd you find them? It was only fair—the questions coming all at once—that the answers should come all the same way, detail-upon-detail spilling forth in excited relief. The dialog that ensued was a thing of beauty, which I shall organize and summarize as best I can.

Star started the tale. In the first moments of The Howdying a pair of punchinellos appeared on the edge of the parade crowd, generally mugging and miming the bystanders—Yes, several noted, we recall them—before the slap-stickers began schlepping their schtick toward little Merri Elli, chucking her chin and making silly faces, notwithstanding that the baby was hardly amused, screwing up her small face in the pout that every parent knows to be prelude to a full-fledged howl. But before a peep could be produced, bedlam broke-out across the town-square-circle immediately upon which moment the lead jester jerked the infant from her mother's custody, his prankster partner purloining the baby's parent by pinning her arms behind her back, the abductees thusly packed and pushed and prodded to one of the trailers in the Shifting Sands Mobile Motel. ¿The Toolpusher Suite? interjected Ruth Etta, adding, It's just recently been rented to Crackers Mud Logging Service. Probably, as it's plastered with Rigid Tool calendars—replied Star, before wrapping up—where they put Merri Elli in an empty drawer and tied me down as best they could before bolting out the door— then with a sneering comment—Only a couple of clowns would use a Möbius band for a rope, as any Bozo should know that more than one dimension is necessary to make a good knot. She finished her part of the saga with an observation couched almost as an afterthought—Those wisecracks ransacked the trailer, muttering all the while about journals, journals, journals. And even through the storm we could see that several other 'Streams had been trashed. They didn't seem to be after us, after all—Star stated evenly, then directly to Tally—they were only interested in your notebooks.

Now Saba and Yasmin jumped into the ring with their own tag-team talk, telling of the rescue in sentences and phrases started by one and completed by the other. Upon hearing Kelly's alarum the two girls—who had seen the pierrots plaguing poor Merri Elli—rushed to the area where said Augustes had last been beheld. From there the pair of Pakistani Penny Parkers picked up a trail of very large footprints, the track augmented by multi-colored pieces of cloth that had been ripped-off by and impaled upon various mesquite thorns and cactus needles, the giant tread-marks and costume bits soon leading them to the Shifting Sands Mobile Motel and the afore-mentioned Toolpusher Suite. They arrived too late to spot the perps but just in time to seek shelter from the storm where the four of them waited in the 'Stream for a lull.

Immediately upon conclusion of the brief recounting there was a jumble of general discussion amongst our tactical teams, the essence being that, Hey, now we can pool all our forces into one company to pursue the evil-doers, who—since the storm was in the midst of moving out—who soon would likely be light-foot-ing-it on the lam, perhaps with the just-now-nabbed notebooks. Best not do that—said several of the Elvi, Let's stick to our original plan—addressing our arched eyebrows by explaining that the clown corps needed to remain convinced that the captives were still captive and therefore that all our resources and all our resolution would be focused on liberating mother and daughter rather than being directed toward the defense of the journals. Cartoon light-bulbs blinked-on in the thought-balloons tethered above each of our noggins as we rapidly recognized that the King Krew were correct. Regardless, modifications are in order—Threeb quickly added—pointing out that the constable and his Stranger-Wranglers surely heard our cheers and, even though they were near to negative numbers on the Stanford-Binet scale, still had to be dealt with to ensure their inability to tip-off the technology thieves. We've got folks who can handle that—offered Shad Eliot in his slow, cowpuncher drawl, nodding to Mustaq and Shazad—it'll be a while before it's not too gusty for your powered kite so let's put them strays in the bus so's the driver can take 'em 'way, 'way out in Lea County afore he lets 'em out somewhere along the Pluto Parkway where they won't be a burden to nobody. Then he can come back for another load. In the meantimes, you two take a walkie-talkie and get that flying-carpet-crate ready to go airborne. The Karachi Kids grinned big-time.

Their sisters Khan, flush with their successful liberation of the abductees, were fairly jumping up-and-down in excitement to enlist for additional assistance, so Ruth Etta took a walkie-talkie and whisked Saba off to the Tool Pushers' Suite to help the inn-keep return things to appear as if the captives had not been sprung. Then—mindful of the mutual-admirational-society that had formed between Yasmin and Merri Elli, Kerrie Mae and Bobbie Sue invited her to help keep baby and baby's momma safe and comfortable and—importantly—ensconced out of sight in the Old School House. For which Gladys would add her/his services, she/he offered again, all the while she/he would be keeping up chatter from the base-camp walkie-talkie that would leave eavesdroppers convinced that mother and daughter remained the sole objectives of the hunt. The Pakistani parental units pitched in, too, pledging to fuel-up the Creepy-Crawley and the Stranger Wranglers' over-grown-pickups, noting that in the Paki-Store they had on-hand plenty of batteries for flashlights and rolls of duct tape and heavy twine for the posses' eventual prisoners.

The Bubble-Uppers had quietly huddled-up in their own hinky-dinky-parlez-vous, mulling things over amongst themselves, but had quickly reached some kind of consensus. They had no Mademoiselle from Armentieres but instead bravely sent forth one of their own Madame Beviers to weigh-in on the greater general impromptu planning conference—We're only Look-a-Likes—she began with her eyes down-cast—we're not good at any of the things a posse does—then lifting up her orbs with fulsome pride and a glint of steel, before continuing—but our characters are good at those things, and we're good at our characters, so we've all decided to look only like the good-guy-roles for the rest of this episode. Except for me—hooted the fellow costumed as The Owl—since my character goes both ways. Same for me—mumbled the Mayor Middleton Look-a-Like—since I only flip-flop. Also for us—chorused the Bud & Sissy Brotherses and the Mark-Up Johns and the Doc Cassidys and the pairs of Nans and Berts—since we're never anything else but ourselves. A shout of acclaim issued forth from the remaining Look-a-Likes, who found an empty room in the Old School House to change, the Derringer Duvaliers fishing-out their O. K. Rodger rags, the Blackie Blacks swapping their long braids for Lance's hippie hair and beaded headband, the Muffin McWrights shucking their foundation garments and trading their navy blazers for Lisa's prairie dresses, the Troops shedding their goon-gear for gen-u-ine cowboy costumes.

During the brief time-out occasioned by the Bubble-Uppers' re-tooling, my pop and the Bobster—the former being the community theoretician and the latter being the community practician—posed a joint query which had, heretofore, not been addressed, fervor and emotion having so far prevailed over finesse and elucidation. ¿Exactly what will these two posses do? they inquired, with the quick addendum ¿And how will they do it? Funny, but we hadn't thought that far ahead. Hmmmmmm…we replied in concert, sounding pretty much like a Bubba-aum meditation group—*hmmmmmm bubba-aum mau mau,* The Rivingtons on a doo-wop sand dune reservation, *hmmmmmm bubba-aum mau mau*—our pre-vocal pontification humming along for a rather longish time before Shad—the community peripatetician—shouted the answer ¡Will James!—our group responding ¿Will James? before Tally—his bulb the brightest of the bunch, him being the one-hundred-and-twenty-watt Taliesin—chortled gleefully, Yes, yes, Will James, 'Cowboys North and South'—¡a wild-horse trap!

Grand-père and petit-fils launched into a tête-à-tête, pretty much to our exclusion as we struggled to recall details from the first volume of the Canadian cowpunch writer's compendia of cow-country customs—You've got an unfinished p@tio due north toward the Big Rig Highway—said Shad—Yessir, outer wall up and coated—Tally began to answer, interrupted by his granddad—Meaning the meanies can't see it—With the inner wall coated but not yet painted—added Tally in assent—Meaning once inside they won't be able to find their way out—Shad continued the logic, his every deduction excitedly agreed-to by the young architect of illusion, each ratification acknowledged with the exclamatory allusion ¡A wild horse trap!—Exactly—smiled the elder Eliot in conclusion.

The rest of us had been catching on, phrase by phrase, catching excitement with each exchange. Two pincer movements—I offered in a general statement to all—then followed with assignments. Kelly, you were the real O. K. Rodger, or at least as real as O. K. Rodger ever was, so it's up to you to lead the Look-a-Likes. Your dad should go with you as he's the best horseman in these or any other parts. You and your Bubble-Upper unit take the west route, the one that the clowns would expect us to follow in search of the captives. Nods of agreement. I once worked for Gladys—I volunteered—so my place is with the Kings. We'll come around from the east. I'll need Threeb and the Creepy-Crawly, too, and Bob Merriman as well, as we'll need at least one of the Stranger-Wranglers' big-dumb-arse-silly pickups. My dad and mom will be best employed to stay here and help Gladys and the Khans. Sis, you and Bobbie Sue probably ought to amble over to Los Tres Círculos in case any clowns choose to converge on the uncorpora-tion. Ruth Etta's already personing the Shifting Sands to report any sightings of boomerang Bozos revisiting the scene of the incarceration. Rose Edna is the natural to handle outside communications, as someone should let the Kelly Elliott Daze committee know that the home-town tee-vee star is in the midst of a real adventure—then she can make an anonymous call to the Red Nekkid Rant Line to gloat over the kidnapping. My guess is that the clowns stay tuned-in to hate radio—I added as an afterthought.

Threeb was already starting towards the door—¡Elvi, Ho!—hollering with such enthusiasm and conviction that the impersonators tarried nary a wink to so much as even blink at the prospects of striking out across the sand dunes with a driver who could only see with his third eye. Taking their cue from the Jumpsuit Junta, the Bubble-Uppers—who'd just emerged from their impromptu Green Room, each and every one arrayed in their good-guy gear—likewise fell in behind the Impersonator Platoon, making a bee-line for their waiting mounts. Sensing that we were about to be the cowboy who hopped on his horse and rode off in all directions, I hurriedly intervened—Whoa, now, everyone—I said, as coolly as I could—let's stop long enough to draw up a map and lay-out some language before setting the white gloves on our Mickey Mice to point to all the same Minnies.

Gathering everyone together, I started in by pointing out the obvious—the ability and willingness to point out the obvious being a thing that I was coming to understand as being a fundamental quality of leadership—We need some maps to label, one to give each column and one to give Gladys and one to the Surprise Air Squadron. The Parents Khan nodded, braving the remnants of the thunderstorm to beat feet over to the Paki-Store, returning in moments with a handful of 1954 Col-Tex Star-Compass Road Atlases—solely issued by Ohlenbusch Oil Co. up in Lubbock and so being one of the few gimme-maps that bothered to show the Permian Basin and the Trans-Pecos. Those are rare—I informed them, economically—to which Father Khan merely smiled before noting that he had at least a case of the collectibles remaining.

Eliot the Senior grabbed a couple and the Bobster took the third, the two men unfolding the three charts on a table so that all could gather 'round for a good look-see. Pater Jones asked one of the Elvi to look over his shoulder, then handed pencils to Gladys and the Madame Bevier Look-a-Like as he applied labels in Surprise slanguage to the map in the middle. This is Andrews—he began—which we call Kirby West, on account of the vacuum cleaner factory. The highway that runs from there to Eunice we call Big Rig Road, and we don't call Eunice Eunice, we call it Nina Simone because Eunice is her first name. North of Big Rig is called Johnny Horton—my dad singing a snatch of 'North to Alaska' before returning to his *recitavio*—There's a highway between Kirby West and Kermit—we call the smaller town Toad Hall, ¿you get that, don't you?—and we call that road The Dan'l Webster Raceway—Mark Twain, he added, seeing the puzzlement widely-shared by the Bubble-Uppers and the Elvis Attachment—before continuing—In addition to that through-way, there's the paved road from the Dan'l Webster to Jal, this connecting road is the Hard-Tail Highway—Jal, he added, is on Muleshoe Draw, so the name for the whole micro-region is the Jenny-Slipper-Slide. Eyes were glazing amongst the non-Surprises, so my dad took a moment for Gladys and the faux June Bevier to catch up their cartography notes.

But hardly more than a moment. Here's Frankel City—pointing out a tiny spot on the map where there was no spot at all—which we call Fullerton because that's its original name—which is just west of what's now known as Shafter Lake but which we call Big Salt in honor of Handy Jones—Gene D. added both parenthetically and reverently—then just south-west of Fullerton and barely south of Big Rig Road is another salt playa we've dubbed West Salt, for the obvious reason. Now—the Welsh patriarch yet had more to add—there's another road that connects the Big Rig with the Dan'l Webster and runs down south past it through Coyote Corner—¿What's the Surprise name of that place? someone in the crowd asked—Just Coyote Corner, as not even a Surprise can better that, he barely breathed in reply—but we term the road itself The Steel Square as it makes a right-angle with a Farm-to-Market that goes back to Kirby West. Over here— Gene D. swung to the far side of the map—is the New Mexico state line, or as it's known in Surprise, Outer Space, and just beyond that is Monument Draw, better known in these parts as The Cemetery, then on beyond that is the highway between Jenny-Slipper-Slide and Nina Simone, a road we've always called Pluto Parkway—and not owing to the Disney character—and even on beyond that last feature of our solar system is San Simon Swale, for which we have no slanguage name since so very few of us have ever gone that far into the sunset. Some additional important landmarks—my dad Gene D. was fully back in his role as a teacher—would include Los Tres Círculos, which we call the Big Venn which comes from the geometric diagram, and which is situated in the general vicinity where Cemetery leaves Outer Space along Rattlesnake Ridge and which is also where the Ogallala Aquifer gives way to the Pecos Valley Aquifer. Though you really can't see that from above-ground—a breath—There are other things that can't be seen, either. They are the p@tios, around which Tally and Shad will guide their respective columns. Which leads me to the unfinished p@tio, which is there—as he drew the @ sign—just north of us and just east of Tarantula Draw. And we—he made his last mark, a large, dark exclamation point—we are right here—in the midst of Shinnery Motte.

Whilst Gladys and June were finishing their fill-in-the-blank charts, Shad Eliot suggested to Bob Merriman that maybe he ought to carry along his fowling piece. ¿Shotgun? squeaked a Bubble-Upper. ¿Why a shotgun? Calm down, we don't shoot living things in Surprise—said Shad, evenly—but we can't let flying clown-craft report back on us—a pause for emphasis—If it flies, it dies—growled the head Eliot, gutturally-echoed by the Bobster, who took that opportunity to take the impromptu podium to suggest that—should either of them find it necessary to shoot down a radio-controlled 'copter—the walkie-talkie talk should be buzz and bark about city-slicker-hunters bumbling-about on the opening day of snipe season. But there's no such thing as... began the Italian Elvis, who stopped, then smiled broadly. And speaking of bark—continued Bob Merriman—I can, if it please everyone amongst our tacticians and strategists, call on my coyote pals to drift down from the red-dirt draws of Gaines County into Johnny Horton so's they can keep the clown caravan from escaping to the Gold Rush. Assent quickly given all around, as the Bobster just as quickly darted off out the door and into the unwinding weather to retrieve his twelve-gauge.

One of the Lance Reids piped up to ask where the notebooks were secreted. Tally deftly dodged a direct reply by reiterating that the job at hand was to make the clownsters think that the notes were hidden in the unfinished p@tio so as to lure them into the trap. We need plenty of walkie-talkie talk about keeping them away from the construction site—said the Architect of Surprise—but which answer neither muted the murmurs nor quelled the questions, as inquiring minds want to know, so the look-a-like Owl parried with an inquiry as to why any of the notebooks were of any importance anyway. Because—said Pater Jones, jumping into the discussion—transparency is the most powerful weapon there is against despots and tyrants and oligarchs—with Tally adding—And my process allows layers to masquerade as transparency—with Gene D. finishing off the civics-cum-science lesson—And since they already have a virtual monopoly of layers through which we cannot see, we need to have layers of our own, if only to provide shelter for our homes, our homes being the physical extension of our minds and souls and, hence, of our very freedom. A heavy silence, eventually broken by another Bubble-Upper who asked, partly in consternation but mostly in confusion, ¿But who are *they*? The corporament, the Surprises said, almost in unison, and immediately one Elvis after another filled out the roster of meanness of the corporament club—the big corporations—said the large, over-stuffed Elvis—the mob—said the Italian Elvis—the big churches—said one of the Elvis soul-sisters—the government—finished Gladys, with finality.

Will you not at least tell us more about the journals, implored one of the Mark-Up Johns, more in interest and curiosity than in nosiness. Tally opened his choppers to speak but Shad beat him to it. My grandson—he said, fondly—is Scots on my side and Welsh on his mother's. Tally is his nick-name, Taliesin his full name, which is also the name of the chief bard of the Celts. Like his namesake, Tally is both poet and philosopher, songster and scientist, keeper of the hearth-fire and seeker of the spark. I have seen his journals—Shad the Eliot now speaking in the tones of a preacher of the Southern Baptist persuasion— and they are named The Dog and The Lapwing and The Roebuck, their master journal named Gwydion, the same Gwydion born of trees who is magician and trickster but whose powers and work are done for the benefit of good, just as is told in *Câd Goddeu* which is also called 'The Battle of the Trees'—or the same Gwydion of 'The Chronicles of Prydain'—which Tally read as a child—and the same Gwydion who is brother to Coyote in the stories of the Plains Indians and brother to Rabbit in the stories of the Cherokee, the same Cherokee from whom came—directing his gaze toward the Elvi—the lineage of the King of Rock-and-Roll. A reverent hush now held the hip-shake horde. Gene D. waited an appropriate beat, then spoke to Shad—I trust that you will recite from 'The Battle of the Trees' as our pursuit develops today. Use the walkie-talkie. Tally will hear it on his trek, I will hear it here at home, in all likelihood the Clowns of Arwan will hear it, too, and though they understand it not the power of the poetry will not be the lease diminished. ¡It was a teaching moment of the first order!

One more question—queried the only heretofore quiet Elvis—¿How do we drive them into something that can't be seen? ¡The third pincer! exclaimed Tally. It's a construction site, with equipment and supplies and whatnot stacked and stored and parked and piled on its north side, nearest Big Rig Road, from whence the deliveries are made. Once the two land columns are within striking distance we'll call in air-support from Johnny Horton to reconnoiter the road and augment the coyote defense line and, if necessary, drive the Bozos back south toward the trap. The Pakistani patrol pilots, who'd heretofore been preoccupied with their flight-plan note-taking, looked up from their pencils and knee-board journals with a question of their own—¿What's our signal? As you'll be on the Magic Carpet—smiled Tally—your walkie-talkie code name will be Steppenwolf, so when you hear me start singing, start making low passes along the highway. Besides which you are followers of Rumi ¿are you not?—Mustaq and Shazad nodded vigorously in the affirmative—in which case you'll understand the meanings of the verses from *Câd Goddeu* as this epic poem of the Celts flows from the same springs of wisdom as does the poetry of your people.

This is dry country. Average annual rainfall is not much over a foot-and-a-quarter, perfect for cacti and mesquite and shinnery, suitable for reptiles and tarantulas, barely sustainable for goats and sheep, certainly short of what's needed for dry-land row crops or good grass or tame cattle. More to the point, it's country in which there's no such thing as *average*—excepting in the minds of statisticians and in the opinions of optimists—and, beside the point, what moisture does come comes in increments and intervals that aggravate agriculturists, bedevil bankers, and salt-season all sunny dispositions. Old timers in these parts—*old* measured in experience, not age—those who stick are wont to describe precipitation in the Prickly-Pear Purview as *fifteen inches a year, and you oughta be here the*

day we get it. A slow, soft, steady rain is a rarity, and today was not the exception that would test the rule. The storm that had been building since late morning whipped-in, whipped-up, and whipped-out before trundling off toward Eunice. The lids of the thermoses had just been screwed tight when the clouds began to break. We emptied-out into the clearing.

All was now ready. But just before we mounted up to set out, Kelly proffered the notion that each column needed a guidon. ¡Capital idea! went up the general cry. ¿What'll the Bubble-Uppers fly? followed Kelly. A Muffin McWright blazer, offered a Lisa Look-a-Like, who'd just doffed hers. A sparkly-gold lamé jump suit for us, suggested the Elvis of the East, preempting Kelly's follow-up question. Mama Khan motioned to hold everything a minute, allowing her to fetch a couple of dilapidated brooms from the unsold inventory of the small Surprise Shopping Center. Mice and silverfish had long since gnawed the broomcorn bristles away, leaving only the handles handily available as guidon flagstaffs. No sooner had the pin-stripe hacking-jacket been tied onto the broomstick than Maya Gandhi seized it and took her seat side-saddle atop Punto Rojo. The Oriental Elvis hoisted up the jump suit guidon and hopped-up into a forward position on the Creepy-Crawly.

The Elvi were about to punch the play buttons on their boom-boxes when someone noted that the Bubble-Uppers held cassette recordings of the lost music from 'Bubble-Up' but had neither stereos nor monos. No problem. The Kings had a spare, and—before anyone could say otherwise—the twin posses were off on The Great Andrews County Clown Hunt, the rock-a-billy strains of 'Mystery Train' rockin' from the east with 'It's All Over Now' rollin' from the west.

And it was just as well.

28.

¡TALLY HO!

On a sparse land small things loom large, large things enormous. In the clarity after rain the undulating sand-dune-dry-swale prairie perfectly dripped in dazzling detail. Prickly pear wore purple-ripe tunas nestled between blossoms of white and yellow and red. Everywhere were stands of neglected sunflowers—*Helianthus neglectus*—startling now in front-and-center focus, spindly stalks tall and rangy in crayon-box greens set-off with heads of neon-yellow-gold, drawing dramatic dot-and-dash outlines around the dunes. Dark emerald greasewood and middle-range-green juniper were scattered about above the dusky olive-drab smudge of shin-oak. Atop and over the sand-hills bunch-grasses spread out, some vibrating, some motionless as the warm-wet breeze stirred or slackened—blue-grama's eye-lashes a-flutter, switchgrass standing stoic, needle-and-thread's spirals a-tremble. And anywhere that the masses of white sand gave way to patches of red dirt there sparkled a chrome-yellow-and-lime dusting of broom-weed. Trees, too, even in this tree-less land, catclaw acacia and honey mesquite alight in chartreuse and shamrock-green and sage-earth-tone, here-and-there the quaking tops of a few lonely Rio Grande cottonwoods poking up from the washes. Around all this the endless horizon, above all this the infinite sky, all taken together a boundless geometric whole that opened The One Window to the Universe, its panes of cerulean separated by sashes and stiles of distant anvil-head thunderclouds.

The Clown Hunt had begun. Our unlikely posse caravan crept and crawled over the rising and falling sand dune prairie, the Stranger-Wranglers' re-purposed pickups poking along behind the Creepy-Crawly, Elvis impersonators populating each, our traveling tempo the rocksteady recording of The Charms's ska song—hill and gully riders, were we, hill and gully, up and over the hillocks, bottoming in

"

the draws, bending down low now, hill and gully—eyes searching for clown clues—
being careful how we went now, hill and gully—ears straining for any sound of R/C
'copters—we danced right 'round every hill and gully—carving an arc designed to
drive the Auguste gang into the wild clown trap—hill and gully riding, hill and gully.

Surprise was hardly out of sight when the walkie-talkie crackled, Shad Eliot
reciting the opening of *Câd Goddeu* to let us know that the Look-a-Like Legion
was also underway. *I have been in many shapes Before I attained a congenial form.*
spffftz *I have been a narrow blade of a sword. I will believe it when it appears. I have
been a drop in the air.* skrrrcht *I have been a shining star. I have been a word in a
book. I have been a book originally. I have been a light in a lantern.* kaaack… *Over
and out…*zzzt-paapp. Keying the mic, Tally responded from a following stanza. *I
have been the string of a harp, Enchanted for a year In the foam of water. I have been
a brand in the fire. I have been a tree in a covert. There is nothing in which I have
not been… Over.* Click.

We pressed on. Roadrunners darting before us. Red-tailed hawks and harriers
hunting overhead. Vultures high aloft, soaring in slow and languid circles, save
one renegade bird flying in from the north-east in a straight line. Threeb heard
it just as Tally and I recognized the herky-jerky flight of a DuBro Shark. We
stretched out our arms to pin-point it for Bob Merriman, who was already cham-
bering a shell into his 870 Remington. He took a bead on the Bozo egg-beater,
and, just as it flared-up to bank before turning back, dropped it with a single blast
of triple-ought buck-shot. Tally waited a beat or two, clicked the walkie-talkie,
then announced to anyone listening that we'd come across some city-slickers
hunting on the first day of snipe season. The Elvi had a good laugh. When the
hoo-rahs died down, Tally got back on the field phone and added that we didn't
want anyone to go north. Silence on the other end. *¿Copy?*—squawked Tally. A
nervous moment before Shad radioed back *Roger that. We'll keep 'em from heading
toward the highway. Over.* Tally smiled, saying to no one in particular—That
should point the clowns in the general direction of the p@tio.

We continued to hew to our course but followed our noses. In the same way
the rain had sharpened our sight the ozone had opened-up our olfactory organs,
the fleeting atomic-threesome scrubbing-away the dust whilst shaking-loose the
myriad scents from thousands and thousands of tiny wild-flowers and rain-wet
leaves and rain-soaked stems and stalks all in an olio of the odors of garden-spade-
fresh earth, the grand mixture producing a perfume known only to the desert, a
cologne seldom sensed, ephemeral but as mighty as the musk of sex and, like that

most primal of scents, most seductive in the most secret reaches of the languid landscapes of lovers. And, I should add, very practical just now. For Surprise—whilst in the midst of the oil patch—was in its immediate environs oil-less, so the moment that our noses detected the first pungent whiff of petroleum penetrating the aromatic air we would know we'd traveled far enough to the east, a clear and simple sign to turn north to complete our pincer movement.

Today's sage-brush sachet was having a particularly strong effect on me, suffusing my very soul, stepping smack-dab into the middle of my mind, shouldering-aside the task at hand, reminding me that I'd seen hardly anything of my dear Ruth Etta all the live-long day. So I borrowed the two-way from Tally—besides, I reasoned, it was time for some diversionary chatter—*¿Got your ears on, Holiday Out? Over.* Click. *Ten-four, Four-Eyes.* bzzzat *Over.*—which I took as a clever reference to the Creepy-Crawly—*¿Any guests checked in? Over.* Click.—which I hoped the pranksters would take as an inquiry as to whether or not the captives had been found. *Negatory, Four-Eyes.* pfffst *Holiday Out, over.* I swore I head her wink. But back to work. *¿How 'bout you people out west, Big Venn? Over.* Click. *Big Venn's got nothin' either, Four-Eyes.* skrccch It was Bobbie Sue. Her, I swore I heard giggle. Before I could add my ten-four the air came alive again, this time with Shad's electronic drawl. *The Mounties keepin' our peepers peeled. Over.* pfffft *Ten-four that.* Click. I handed the walkie-talkie back to Tally.

We held our easterly track for another half-hour or so, which didn't carry us more than about five miles—the Creepy-Crawly having come by its name honestly—but even at that distance still having traversed a good bit to the Fullerton side of the p@tio wild clown trap. I was mulling over whether we'd gone too far when my schnozzola sniffed a slight snort of hydrocarbon. ¡Perfect! I exclaimed proudly to myself, then gave Tally the sign to pull-up and parley. We're splitting up here—I announced to all—Tally and Threeb and I will turn north, followed by one pickup load of Kings. Bob, you go with the other pickup units. Keep headed east to serve as a decoy contingent—turn your boomboxes up to Patent-Pending and spin your tires every now and again so's to make your presence known—then turn north when you come to the first paved road—Mister Merriman will know it, I said to the Aron Approximators—which will be just south of Fullerton, then take the jog up to Big Rig Road and then turn back west and keep on going 'til you see a pack of coyotes sitting on the north side of the highway. Mister Merriman can check

in with the canines, but they'll likely be whining and looking to the south—here
the Bobster nodded in agreement—stop there and strike-out cross-country in the
direction they're pointing. You'll come to the p@tio trap in two, three miles. We
should arrive from the south about the same time. And speaking of time, now is the
time—I nodded to Tally—to call in air support. Clearing his throat, he keyed the
mic, holding his free hand out as if he were an arena-rock show emcee, announcing
And now music maniacs, put your hands together for ¡Steppenwolf!… then, shifting his
stance, holding the radiophone as if it were a microphone *Well, you don't know what
we can find, why don't you come with me…on a magic carpet ride. Over.* Click. No
radio traffic in response from the Karachi Kite, but the sound of the little airship's
engine changing in pitch affirmed that the message had been both received and
acted upon.

The wooden-duck Elvises about to split off on the decoy drive—good-hearted
to a fault—sent up a cheer, fired-up a couple of ghetto-blasters, then kicked up
a rooster-tail of dirt as they high-tailed it in the general direction of Kirby West.
Tally took the field phone back up and began another stanza from *Câd Goddeu. I
have fought, though small, In the Battle of Goddeu Brig, Before the Ruler of Britain,
Abounding in fleets… Over and out.* Click. My grandfather—Tally said to me,
confidently—will understand this passage to mean that our column has divided,
the smaller part turning now toward the wild clown trap and the air-force alerted.
The young poet-inventor had scarcely finished his explanation when the public
kilohertz began to reverberate with the elder cowboy's resonant recitation. *Indif-
ferent bards pretend, They pretend a monstrous beast, With a hundred heads, And a
grievous combat At the root of the tongue.* zzzzt *And another fight there is At the back
of the head. A toad having on his thighs A hundred claws, … Over and out.* bzzzack.
Tally interpreted again—He's decided to split his bunch also, one part staying
west while Granddad Shad turns north, just as we're doing. And while the toad
reference is a bit up in the air, even for me—Tally briefly furrowed his brow—I'm
pretty sure he means that the main body of the Look-a-Likes is staying on the
original path. Ten-four, Tally—I thought to myself.

Morning light in the desert is invigorating, clear and crisp—even in the dog
days of summer—bright, transparent yellow tending toward blue. Its afternoon
light, in contrast, is calming, a scumbling of pastel warmed by a day's worth of
living, rich gold with lemon highlights leaning to red. Idling along on the Creepy-

Crawly, a blind mystic behind the wheel, a Brythonic bard riding shotgun, a payload of Elvis impersonators hanging helter-skelter off the deck—that's the sort of procession that permits communion with the very light itself, photon by photon, most especially the long, slow wave-lengths and lustrous polish of the post meridian. The universal constant slowed to a lolly-gag.

A familiar snarl broke my reverie. Tally and I immediately began to scan the skies in search for another home-spun drone. But no luck. Threeb granted us time for a second look—humoring us, I suppose, as Blind Billy Bob's sonar is seldom wrong—before offering that the remote-control hobby-motor hubbub came from ground-level. Sure enough, a bread-box-sized motorized model Volks-Wagen Beetle bounded out of the brush ahead of us, cutting across our bow, stuffed with stuffed-clown-dolls protruding from every window, caroming crazily about the greasewood. Threeb brought our bewhiskered sand-dune gondola down from flank-speed—which was hardly any speed at all—to full-stop, permitting Tally and I to jump overboard and retrieve the troublesome toy. As the Bobster's blast-gun had gone with him, we resorted to simply snapping-off its wee whoop-antenna before turning the R/C Beetle over on its back to decommission it, the little drive wheels still spinning, the front axle vainly wiggling from side-to-side, helpless as a toppled-over terrapin. But we knew it meant the clowns were close at hand, given that the signal transmitter intended to control the pesky radio-controlled cootie had much less range at ground level.

Tally held his hands up to call for quiet, then took the walkie-talkie. *I was in the sand fortress, Thither were hastening grasses and trees. Wayfarers perceive them, Warriors are astonished At a renewal of the conflicts Such as Gwydion made…Over.* Click. Instantly the air waves sparked to life with Shad's response. *Through charms and magic skill, Assume the forms of the principal trees,* pzzzzzzt… *With you in array Restrain the people Inexperienced in battle… Over.* crrtch I wasn't understanding the two bards, my puzzlement evident to the younger. I told the others—Tally interpreted in a low voice—that we were within striking distance of the pierrots to which your father-in-law answered that they, too, were closing in on the clowns and that it's important to keep the Bubble-Uppers and the Elvises from getting over-anxious and tipping our hand. Hearing the translation the contingent of Elvi crowded around the two of us looked a bit hurt. Tally—always a sensitive soul—immediately picked-up on the Kings' feelings. Choose your battle music and ready your boom-boxes—said the Bard of Surprise to the sideburns-and-pompadour pack—Granddad Shad's admonition wasn't a reflection on your experience, with which you are each greatly endowed, but was, rather, a note of caution about the perils of excessive exuberance at this sensitive moment, and no-one—Tally said, fondly—can understate the effervescence of the Elvis Impersonator Nation. The Kopy Kings, smiling broadly, broke into silent shoulder-shakes and hip-thrusts in both assent and appreciation.

To Threeb and me Tally gave the final instructions—Each time I quote another set of lines from *Câd Goddeu* we will bear slightly more to the north-north-west in step-wise fashion with the Bubble-Upper bunch, who'll be mimicking our movements but to the north-north-east. ¡Let us have good fortune! said the Poet of the Plains before keying the field phone. *When the trees were enchanted There was hope for the trees, That they should frustrate the intention of the surrounding fires... Over.* Click.

Shad riposted right away—*Better are three in unison, And enjoying themselves in a circle And one of them relating The story of the deluge...* pfffazt ¿*Come back, Kings?* Over. Tally smiled, then said quietly—I'll let him know that I know that he knows the plan—*I know the star-knowledge Of stars before the earth was made, whence I was born, How many worlds there are... Over.* Click. We traveled a few minutes on our new course before Shad let us know that his column was adjusting again—zzzzt *The black cherry-tree was pursuing. The shin-oak swiftly moving ... Over.* Having gotten the hang of the ancient banter, Threeb changed course on his own, Tally communicating the same to the Bubble-Upper posse by completing the stanza—*Before him tremble heaven and earth, Stout doorkeeper against the foe Is his name in all lands... Over.* Click. By now we were nearing the unfinished p@tio, which should be visible—as much as an invisible wall can be visible—and in plain sight the moment we would top the next dune. As we reached the last bottom a voice very near to excitement crackled over the citizens' radio-waves, the pitch rising with each successive line—*I have been a spotted snake upon a hill; I have been a viper in a lake; I have been an evil star formerly. I have been a weight in a mill...* gcccht Then a line that even I could identify as an ad-lib—¡*Yee-haw and over!* I needn't tell you—Tally smiled—that the enemy is within sight, then turned to our pilot, saying—let us make our charge, insofar as the Creepy-Crawly can effect such a maneuver. *My cassock is red all over. I prophesy no evil. Four score puffs of smoke To everyone who will carry them away; And a million of angels, On the point of my knife.* ¡*Over!* ... Click.

Threeb brought the venerable vehicle's throttle up to full-creep, propelling us at warp-crawl to the top of the rise. From that lofty elevation we beheld an epic sight, *The Battle of the Trees* come to life as The Battle of the Clowns. In the center of the scene, directly ahead, there was a blur in the landscape—what must be the p@tio—into which was disappearing the tail-end of a clown-car. Coming behind from the north and east were the Stranger-Wrangler pickups that had separated earlier from our column, gold-lamé-jump-suit-guidon flapping in the wind, boom-boxes a-blare sounding Elvis's show-stopper 'I Did It My Way'. High over head a small aeroplane circled the fray, a white crescent moon and star painted brightly on its dark-green vertical stabilizer. From the south and west the Bubble-Uppers had spurred their stand-in Cola Píntos to full gallop, Shad Eliot leading the charge, Kelly close behind, Maya Gandhi in the thick of the pack flying the Muffin-McWright-blazer-pennant, the strains of 'Jumpin' Jack Flash' barely audible above the pounding hooves. Though we were giving it our best-The-Little-Engine-that-Could-effort it was certain we'd be last to the fray. But not to worry, for when we arrived at the battle-ground there was not so much as a skirmish underway. The Bubble-Uppers were circling the p@tio clockwise, the Elvi counter-clockwise, the harlequins pinned inside.

Shad had already dismounted and was standing before the opening of the trap, finishing-up a transmission on his walkie-talkie. Just called the bus driver to bring the stagecoach around to the highway so's we can haul these hombres to the hoosegow—Shad informed us—now let's stick our noses in the trap and get a count on our captured-clown cavy. We stepped inside the p@tio to find a passel of punchinellos poking aimlessly around, mugging their own reflections in the shiny walls, pointing and laughing at one-another, shooting water from squirt-flowers, one white clown sneaking up behind a hobo clown to try to pull the endless chain of hankies from his pocket, a tramp offering a trio of white Augustes a buzzer hidden in a handshake but getting no takers. Shad made a quick pasture count—Eleven—he stated, flatly—a baker's dozen—the cowpunch pierrot-wrangler adding, when we looked over in disbelief—the Glitter Bus picked up a couple 'way out on the Hard Tail Highway, probably our kidnappers. Before we could express agreement with his tally, Tally pointed out that there was only one clown-mobile, a red-and-white Nash-Kelvinator Metropolitan, the convertible model. We shouldn't have been surprised.

The heat of battle had re-awakened Shad's trail-boss training. Tally, you take my pony and you and your dad lead the Bubble-Uppers on the return ride to

Surprise—he began his orders—it'll be sunset soon enough and we don't want dudes horseback in the dark—continuing with a nod to the p@tio—and I'll stay with these grease-paint gunsels 'til we can load 'em up in the Glitter Bus. Bob and the Elvises in the pickups can hold-up here with me to help keep 'em corralled, then escort us back. Thom Ed and Threeb, you start back now on that contraption with however many of the Kings it'll hold—Shad sighed—'cause it'll take you an hour or so to make the run. And—he smiled broadly—in the meantime I'm going to recite the rest of the poem to the Merry-Andrews so's to give 'em some culture. As he strode back into the enclosure his raspy recitation began to unroll—*Handsome is the yellow horse, But a hundred times better Is my cream-colored one, Swift as the sea-mew, Which cannot pass me Between the sea and the shore*—his voice started to trail away—*Am I not pre-eminent in the field of blood? I have a hundred shares of the spoil. My wreath is of red jewels, Of gold is the border of my shield.*—the tramp and hobo clowns already tearing-up, sniffles building into soft muffled sobs—*There has not been born one so good as I, Or ever known, Except Goronwy, From the dales of Edrywy.*—and with that we re-boarded the Creepy-Crawly and headed home.

In every way imaginable the big celebration that had been planned for the parade and abandoned during the crisis was bigger when it was taken back up after the day's extraordinary events had come to their exemplary conclusion. The Surprises, of course, were there. Plus the Bubble-Uppers. Plus the Elvises. Plus the Chill Billies and the Folk Ewes. And plus the 1OOMPG riders, who began straggling in to the Catclaw City around dusk, so caked with dust and road grime that we had to hose them down in order to marvel over their thongs and tube tops and tattoos. The poor souls had been pedaling and pushing and now and again riding—though only in spurts and spates—their Babettas and Puchs and VéloSolexes ever since we'd all left Oddland Air Terminal that morning, some ten or more hours earlier.

All us clown-hunters showered and spruced-up whilst the headquarters crew hauled out the left-overs, arraying a feast of formidable portions. There were plenty of Paki-Takis and a variety of other dishes—both covered and curried— even peanut-butter-and-banana-and-bacon sandwiches. There was a spectrum of beverages—infant, youth, adult, and tee-totaler—though it should be noted that no grown-ups tee-totaled that night as tension-relief was in order. After the meal the musicianers set to their work in an impromptu concert, trading out sets with the Elvi karaoke crowd, taking requests from the Bubble-Uppers, and sparking—yes, it must be admitted—more than one or two Kum Bah Ya moments, none more nostalgic than when the Ukuladies re-formed for a couple of numbers. Along about midnight we all began to repair to our dwellings. Ruth Etta opened the Shifting Sands Mobile Motel to our guests, the overflow camping out in the Old School House. Kelly threw his gear in the Liner with Bobbie Sue and Kerri Mae in what looked like—to the gossip corner, at least—as the beginning of a permanent residency. Threeb gave up his penthouse to Gladys, so Ruth Etta offered to make room for the Sightless Sage at our place.

By bedtime only the small clouds remained, the major line of thunderstorms having moved far west into New Mexico, though a few continued to fire-up to the north and north-east, their towering cores flashing with pulses of hot-white and bright-yellow-orange and hail-stone-green, the distant display ringing three-quarters of the horizon. The waxing moon—two days from full—had risen an hour before sunset, the partly-opened sky so bright that we'd be able to see no more than the stars of the Summer Triangle high overhead, so bright that even if the clouds all cleared away we'd not even be able to enjoy the Perseid meteor shower—my dear Ruth Etta's favorite celestial event—only days away from its peak. No matter. Our sky is always beautiful, always worth watching. I drug a couple of nylon-webbed lounging chairs a short walk away from our 'Stream. She and I slouched back in our Wally World recliners, listening to a constant carol of crickets punctuated every-now-and-then by a hooting owl or a howling coyote, wishing we were seeing the whole sky-show but hoping to catch glimpse of at least one shooting-star, all the while lazily holding hands across the awkward aluminum arms, trading bits and pieces of talk about the goings-on, about how things are seldom what they seem—except when they're exactly what they seem—about how the layers of things obscure the real nature of things—except when the layers are themselves the thing—about who employed whom to do what to whom, and why they did it—and about whether or not we'd ever know any of this stuff, or any other stuff. We circled around the truth in that way for a glorious hour or so, until—at last—a brilliant blaze of green crossed low in the eastern sky. We took the meteor as a sign, folded up our collapsible Adiron-dacks, and headed back to the Flying Cloud.

Ruth Etta and I kissed, then kept kissing, undressing one another in the dark, slowly and carefully at first, soon impatiently and carelessly, dropping, then tripping over jean-shorts and jeans and panties and briefs and shirt and top and bra, making our way to the bed garment-by-garment, our long kiss broken only when she turned to open the blinds, flooding our cabin with a soft summer breeze that smelled of rain-wet wildflowers and glistened with the blue glow of the almost-full moon, both scent and light suddenly illuminating—patiently waiting there for us—the nude form of the Most Handsome Surprise. Ruth Etta cooed as she slid in beside him, pulling me down with her.

I awoke sometime between moonset and sunrise. I couldn't go back to sleep, and I didn't want to disturb my roomies, so—quietly, without even dressing—I let myself out into the small hours, into the darkest black just before day-break. I unfolded one of the camp chairs and faced it east. The clouds were gone now, all of them. I'd no sooner taken my seat 'til straightway I saw a brilliant flash low in the north-east—a short, white dash—right after that a longer red-orange streak trailing behind a pin-point of light, then another, and another, and another, more dashes, more tails, some thin and slight and brief, some fat and tapering and stretching far-across, different colors, the sky alive with stars falling and shooting, one after the other, so many so quickly you'd no sooner catch sight of one than the next would grab your eye, such that you couldn't possibly watch all of them or concentrate on any single one, the heavens now as vibrant as they'd been dormant the night before. It was a wondrous thing.

Still—even in the midst of it—all I could think about was how I wished they'd been there for Ruth Etta last night, for the two of us… Then a curious thing happened. No sooner had the idea fully formed than it, too, burned out, for as the sky lightened the comet-bits themselves began to fade away in lock-step with the growing dawn, the cinder of the spent mind-meteor now a revelation in and of itself—the Perseids had been there *all along*…of course…of course, all of the night, first hidden by the dark clouds, then obscured by the bright moon, in perfect analogy to the truth we'd talked about only a few hours ago, the truth—I now saw, I now knew, I now understood—the truth to be a thing as difficult to find in the darkness as to recognize in the light.

EPILOG: AN INFINITE ONION

The universe is an infinite onion—layer after layer after layer—from which you may peel away as many layers as you wish—one after another after another after another—yet no matter how many layers you remove, it is onion all the way, for the onion is not hidden within the layers, the onion is the layers. — The Penultimate Parable of Handy Jones

A great deal has happened in the quarter-century since the first-and-last-one-and-only Kelly Elliott Daze Parade. A great deal hasn't happened, either. And in the way of all things, there is a balance 'twixt the two.

The Foundling Families are gone, all peaceably, all with grace, all into their nineties, all into the bosom of their descendants. Maya Gandhi is gone, too, Maya Gandhi who—having no descendants in the biological sense—one day walked out into the dunes, taking her cross-legged throne before taking her last breath, by the time we found her already having become a Hindu-Mayan-mum-mified-multi-colored-serape-draped-Parvati-Ixtab. Punto Rojo followed along behind her, though his remains have yet to be found, and—as we are all quite sure that his genetic structure is more closely related to that of the King Clone creosote than to that of his equine kin—we will not be surprised should one day we find him back in Surprise.

In a matter of days after the Daze, Tally and Star changed their common surname to Jones-Eliot-Merriman thence becoming known to all—familiarly and familial-ly—as The Jems. The following year they produced a second child, a son, whom they named Robert Xavier Eugene Shadrach in tribute to fathers grand and great-grand. The new baby was called Bobby-X into childhood but now, a young man, answers to Bob-X. The Khan Kids all returned to Surprise after their various university degrees, each taking positions with Los Tres Círculos, the two girls in research, the two boys in production, all as equity partners. With the four young Khans having now begun their own beautiful Surprise families a trailer-housing boom is currently underway in the Sand-Dune Shangri-La.

Though the casual visitor would never know it. We found the remote-controlled DuBro Sharks to be especially chilling, even more frightening than the clown crew, the crude drones being the precursors to a more dangerous planet, our prescience patently proved soon since. Occasioned by these ominous airbornes, Tally immediately modified the p@tio design, topping the original spiral with a roof of moveable panels, individual slats that could be angled and the whole rotated so as to allow the sun to shine-in and the wind to blow-through and the rain to rain-in but so as to offer drones and satellites and spy-planes no more information than their own reflection. This new structure—which we came to call N@ilus for its resemblance to the marine mollusk—now houses all our 'Streams. Even the Old School House and the Paki-Store have been painted over in coats of pigments based on versions of Tally's formulae so that there is now naught of the Community of Kindness that can be easily seen, little more, actually, than an artificial motte made up of the burg's inventory of intellectual street signs clustered about amongst the acacia and greasewood in an amorphous circle, the center of which is occupied by a single-pole-four-way-*Stop!*-sign. Surprise has become almost impossible to find.

The clowns never went to trial, which is too bad, for it would have been a spectacle worth watching, if only for the amusement of discerning—between those in the docket and those in the legal system—which clowns were which. In plea-bargaining deals the whole bunch of Bozos owned up to various lesser charges, the tramps and hobos getting off with the lighter sentences—owing, I suspect, to their sad silhouettes—the Augustes, both red and white, with the longer sentences—owing, I'm still suspecting, to their garish grins. Though none served so much as an hour in the hoosegow, being sent instead to various karmic-rehab retreats, rounded out with community-service stints at clown-themed kiddie fast-food joints. Without a trial, we've yet to learn who hired the clowns or to what perverted use the formulae were intended had they been obtained. Though we'd not likely have discerned those facts during the adversarial process—the presentation of evidence and the arguments for and against— as the drama of the courtroom would be just more onion. So we did what we could with our own paring-knife in the form of a plea of our own to Gladys, who, for several months, made discreet inquiries on our behalf, but not even with all her/his shady connections and dark resources—and, yes, perhaps some figurative arm-twisting, and, double-yes, some literal arm-twisting, not that we wished to know anything about *that*—never could she/he penetrate more than a few layers into the skullduggery. Suffice it to say that the conspiracy which fostered the incident is in all probability deep and wide. Not that we—by nature—are paranoiacs or conspiracists, believing as we do that human beings are more good than bad and more likely to talk than to keep quiet, and not that we doubt there are, indeed, conspiracies, and not that we doubt there are, indeed, evil people. It's just that we Surprises are certain that most folk who work in league with others to do foul deeds are mostly unwitting and often unwilling. We're quite sure that avarice, sloth, and the lack of curiosity remain the principal threats to civil life.

As to Gladys herself, well, we've lost touch. The day after the Daze she/he sought to re-hire me, this go-round for a new organization she/he had just founded, the Pharmaceutical Follies, the business of which was to craft brand names for the burgeoning bevy of prescription drugs being produced by the medical corporament, which companies she/he predicted would one day advertise to the masses much in the same manner as any other creator of comestible commodities, but—while I was both flattered and touched by the kindness of her/his offer—I found the prospect of participation to be humorous but the process to be humorless and so therefore declined, as politely as possible. All that I recall of my Gladys-sightings since then is that—somewhere, sometime—I saw she'd/he'd written a tell-all memoir of her/his government service, 'Cross-Dressing Confessions', or something on that order.

As Elvis impersonators are eternal and Look-a-Likes limitless, both groups continue to this day, with only their rosters being updated from time-to-time as some sign-out and others sign-in. Their members make the occasional pilgrimage to Surprise, the older ones to maintain their ties, the newer ones to establish them, all wishing to keep alive the extraordinary story of the time when each impersonator and each Look-a-Like was called-upon to step-up and be what they pretended to be, and by doing so—¡golly, gosh, golly!—helped save the day. As for us, we are always happy to see them for we see them for what they are, good souls with grand—if goofy—sensibilities.

¿And as for us? Having lasted this long in the acting game Kelly gets as much work as he wants, for the most part in the parts he wants, while his all-time favorite roles have become husband and father and grandfather and getting off-book in preparation for the possibility of being cast as great-grandfather. Bobbie Sue and my sis still love their work, they still love each other, they still love Kelly, and—it should go without saying, but I'll say it anyway—still love their families and their Surprise. Those, both biological family—Tally, who remains in firm control of both sides of his brain, and Star and Merri Elli and Bob X—and adoptive family—Mustaq and Shazad and Saba and Yasmin—all continue to prosper and in so doing continue to light the way with hope for the future. In the present moment, Threeb's third eye sees as well as ever it has, his powers having moved him—gracefully—into service as the Sage of Surprise, pleasing the spirits of both Handy Jones and Maya Gandhi. Ruth Etta—ah, my Ruth Etta—she remains the most beautiful creature in all Creation, each passing year adding its little ornaments in wrinkles and pounds and gray hairs and blemishes, the sum of which only makes her the more stunning, the more desirable, the more delicate, the more powerful, the more precious. Me, I remain a writer, who has more to say the older I get and the older I get knowing the better how to say it.

And as for this place, my unpainted desert, it is eternal, its subtle soil-siennas balanced by the alabaster blanc of its dunes, their gentle rise-and-swell off-set by prickly-pear pastels and malachite-green mesquite mottes and grasses of gold and gamboge, the whole stretched-out starkly beneath skies of cobalt and cerulean in which float the sun and the moon and the million-million stars and the clouds sketched by the brushstrokes of the endless wind. In its center—*in the center of all things*—is Surprise, still so small in all the things that can be numbered that you'll miss it if you're not a seeker, still so huge in all the things that can't be numbered that you'll miss it if you're not prepared to find that which you seek. We are few, but there are no limits to our curiosity, to our kindness, to our love. We are not rich, but we are productive. We are not pretty, but we are pleasing. We are—in short—a model for the world, which should be both as big as us and as small, made up entirely of little, unexpected, pleasant surprises.

And it would be just as well.

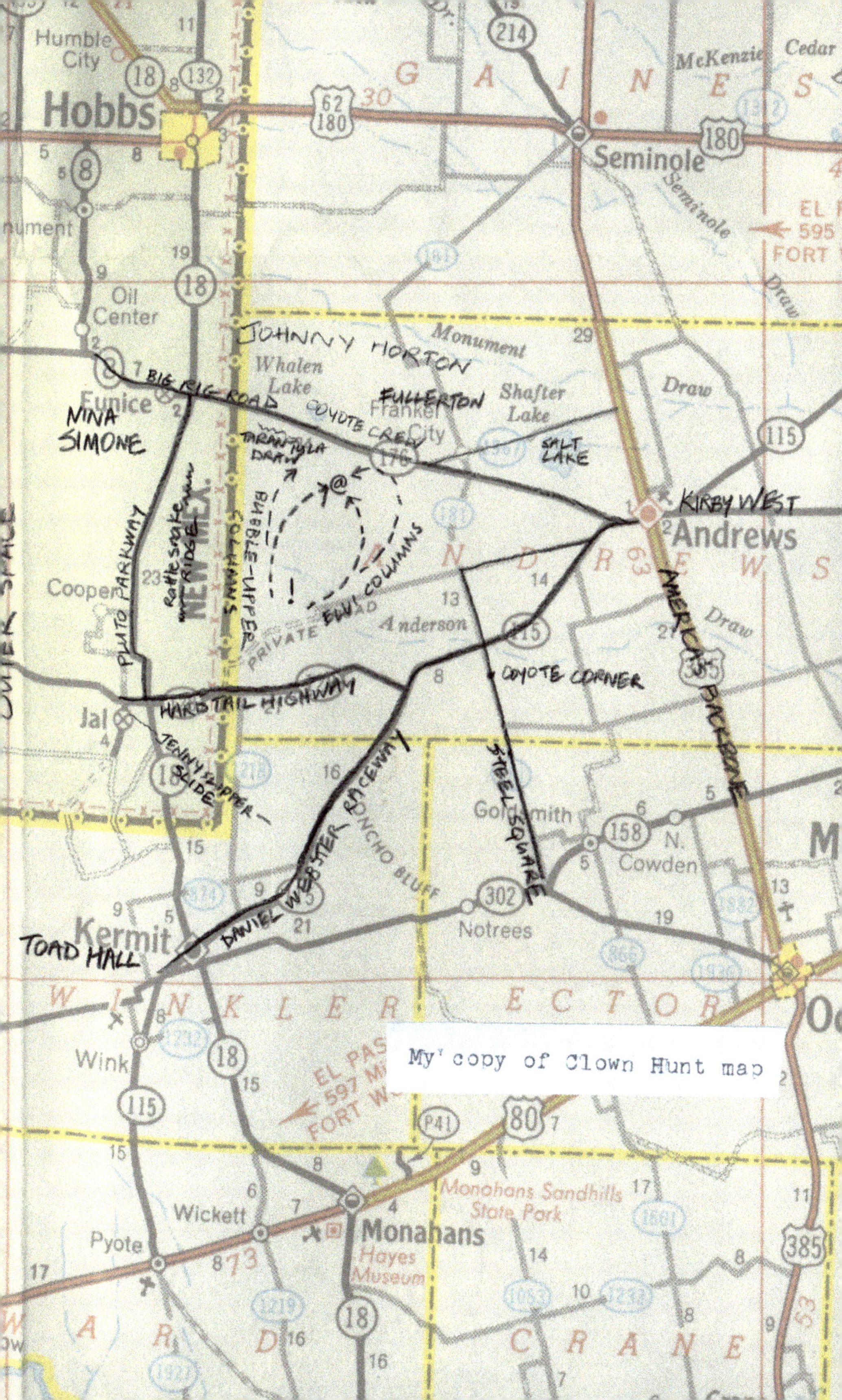
Humble City
Hobbs
18
132
8
2
62 180
30
GAINES
214
McKenzie
Cedar
180
Seminole
1312
5
8
nument
Oil Center
19
18
2
JOHNNY HORTON
Monument
29
Whalen Lake
FULLERTON
Shafter Lake
Draw
Seminole
EL 595 FORT
7 BIG RIG ROAD
Eunice
NINA SIMONE
2
COYOTE CREEK
Franken City
176
SALT LAKE
115
TARANTULA DRAW
@
KIRBY WEST
1
Andrews
63
OUTER SPACE
RATTLESNAKE RIDGE
NEW MEX.
BUBBLE-UPPER
COYOTE CHAIN
PRIVATE ELVIS COLUMNS
Cooper
23
14
Anderson
13
AMERICA PACKAGE
385
Draw
27
PLUTO PARKWAY
115
COYOTE CORNER
HARDTAIL HIGHWAY
8
Jal
4
TENNYHOPPER SLIDE
18
215
16
STEEL SQUARE
Goldsmith
6
5
N. Cowden
158
1932
974
9
DANIEL WEBSTER RACEWAY
RONCHO BLUFF
21
302
Notrees
19
13
TOAD HALL
Kermit
9
5
WINKLER
ECTOR
Oc
866
1936
My copy of Clown Hunt map
Wink
212
18
EL PAS 597 MI FORT WO
115
P41
80 7
15
9
Monahans Sandhills State Park
17
1881
Wickett
7
4
14
385
Pyote
873
Monahans
Hayes Museum
1063
10
1233
53
1219
18
1927
16
16
CRANE
RD
A
WARD

ABOUT THE AUTHOR

My own country is not far removed from Surprise. This is my first novel, but I've written three other books, six plays, and the songs on a dozen record albums, besides having contributed prose and poetry to a number of various other publications. I teach songwriting and creative process at Texas Tech University, where I'm also Artist in Residence at the Southwest Collection / Special Collections Library.

THE AUTHOR'S ACKNOWLEDGEMENTS

Andy and Alissa Hedges were there when I first encountered the Look-a-Likes who generated the question that became the gist of Surprise. Along the way, I've received welcomed encouragement and valuable criticism from friends and family, each of whom read draft after draft: Terry and Jo Harvey Allen, Trisha Alley, Amy Auker, Cari Babitzke, Justin Burrus (who also took the cover photograph), Kent Calder, Barry Corbin, Max Evans, Terri Hendrix, Michael Horse, Bob Horton (Lank Spangler's creator), Judith Keeling, Deb Carpenter-Nolting, Marsha Pfluger, Emily Wilkinson, Ian Wilkinson, and Luther Wilson. Mark Hartsfield's outfit—notably Cari Caldwell and Amanda Sneed—put shape to the book itself. Bonnie Wilkinson contributed a well-crafted matchbook cover. Katelin Dixon was brave enough to serve as copy editor. My wife, Mary Ann—as always—never let her puzzlement over what I do and how I do it overcome her enthusiasm and support for me and my work. These folks are—each and every one—Surprises of the first order.

My thanks and appreciation to all.

Andy Wilkinson
Lubbock, Texas 2017